BORN BY BONDS & BLOOD

BETWEEN SHADOWS AND LIGHT
BOOK TWO

First printed in the United States of America in December 2025.

Cover Design by Via Veritas Vita Press
Copy Editor: Enchanted Inc. Publishing

ISBN 978-1-953139-21-4 (Paperback)
ISBN 978-1-953139-30-6 (Ebook)

Published by Via Veritas Vita Press
Website: www.rachelhetrickwrites.com

First Edition
10 9 8 7 6 5 4 3 2 1

BORN BY BONDS & BLOOD

BETWEEN SHADOWS AND LIGHT
BOOK TWO

RACHEL HETRICK

VIA VERITAS VITA PRESS
COPYRIGHT © 2025 BY RACHEL HETRICK

TO THE SILENT SEEKERS,

*To those who find solace in the
quiet corners of the world,
in tranquil coffee shops
and charming libraries with
only words to keep them company.*

ALSO BY RACHEL HETRICK

The Infiniti Trilogy

Curse of Infiniti
Defying Infiniti
Infinit

The Fallen Heir Series

The Heir's Descent
The Heir's Betrayal

Between Shadows & Light Series

Forged By Flames & Fury
Born By Bonds & Blood
Divided By Darkness & Devotion

SIGN UP FOR RACHEL'S AUTHOR NEWSLETTER

Enjoy interactive maps, short stories, and other exclusives from this series and others by subscribing to Rachel's newsletter and visiting her website at:

www.rachelhetrickwrites.com

CONTENT WARNING:

This book contains themes and specific scenes that some readers may find distressing. Please read with care and take breaks if necessary. Your well-being is important!

Trigger warnings for: alcohol consumption, violence, death (specifically a warning for the death of a toddler), loss in pregnancy, verbal and emotional abuse, manipulation from a family member, mention of physical abuse, panic attacks, and passionate kissing.

NOTABLE PLACES IN
BORN BY BONDS & BLOOD

COUNTRIES
- PHILDETERRE
- JERR PINN
- LUANDI

REGIONS
- THE ALBANISTIC DESERT
- THE BLACK FOREST
- THE CYRO COVES
- THE ELEMENTAL MOUNTAINS
- THE GLASS FIELDS
- THE LEVEL PLAINS

LUANDI

TOWNS & CITIES
- AJORR
- BOWHOO
- CANDIJEEAN
- CYANTHIA
- SHONGBAY

OTHER PLACES
- THE TINY HOUSE
- THE PORTAL TO THE DARK
- THE BOULDER FIELD
- CHATEAU LAVFOR

CYRO
SEA

ELEMENTAL
MOUNTAINS

CYRO
COVES

ALBANISTIC DESERT

SHONGBAY

BOWHOO

GLASS FIELDS

PORTAL TO
THE DARK

AJORR

CHATEAU
LAVFOR

CANDLIBAN

CYANTHIA

THE BOULDER
FIELD

BLACK FOREST

TINY HOUSE

PHILDETERRE

LEVEL PLAINS

JERR PINN

Prologue

LENORA

L enora couldn't stop the gale of laughter that erupted from within her chest as she sprinted through the gardens. Her dark raven hair flew out in waves behind her as she darted around a large hydrangea plant. The scent of the flowers lifted her spirits, urging her farther into the maze of her father's garden.

"Where are you running, Nora?" a young man called from behind her. Light footsteps ate up the distance between them.

With her heart pounding, both with adrenaline and with excitement, Lenora turned around a corner and hid behind a tree.

"You can't hide from me," Leo teased, his voice soft and filled with a warmth that melted Lenora from the inside out.

Lenora peeked around the tree, her pulse still racing as she met his gaze. The sunlight filtered through the leaves above, casting patterns around his face. Time seemed to slow.

With a mischievous sparkle in his silver eyes, Leo lunged for her, but Lenora darted away, her laughter trailing behind her. Strands of her ebony hair blew about her, flying through the air as she ran away from Leo.

He pursued. Though she had once been the same height as him, if not taller, he'd vastly outgrown her in the last year, and his long strides eclipsed hers as she reached the fountain in the center of the garden. With a strong arm wrapped around her waist, he pulled her to a stop, spinning her to face him. Leo moved a strand of Lenora's hair from where it'd gotten caught in her mouth, his calloused fingers brushing gently over her skin.

"I believe that's the third time I've caught you, my sweet bloom."

"Is it?" she asked, a smile on her lips as she tilted her head to the side. She'd never grow tired of staring into his bright eyes, especially as they stared back at her like she was the only thing he could see.

Lenora jolted awake as the carriage hit a large bump. In less than a second, Leo and the garden vanished.

"Are you all right, my lady?" Kaylene, her handmaid, asked from where she sat across from Lenora in the cramped space. Her long auburn hair was looped up in a perfectly braided crown around her head, and the light streaming in from the small window exaggerated the freckles sprinkled across her pale skin.

It'd been so real.

For a moment, she'd been happy.

For a moment, she'd been back with the man she loved more than the breath in her lungs instead of traveling to marry a man she'd never met.

A man she could never—would never—love.

Never again.

LENORA STIFLED A sob by covering her mouth with her gloved hand. She couldn't let them hear her. Couldn't. They couldn't see her like this, in this state of utter distress. They couldn't.

She couldn't.

Couldn't breathe.

Her chest heaved, and she whimpered into her damp glove again. The linen closet in which she hid smelled strongly of lavender and soap, a scent powerful enough to slither through her glove and fill her nostrils as she failed to prevent another gasping sob.

It would start soon.

Her wedding.

The king would wonder where she was.

Everyone would.

And she'd be here, hiding in the linen closet, hoping no one would hear her as she mourned the start of her new life. And more importantly, the death of all that she knew. The death of any chance she had at happiness. At freedom. At the man she had once loved.

Before he'd shattered her heart into pieces.

Lenora released her mouth, pressing her lips shut as she tilted her chin up, leaning her head against the wall. A pin Kaylene had placed in her hair pinched the back of her skull, and she ripped it out with shaking fingers. Then she pulled another and another until her hair dropped down her back and clung to her wet cheeks.

But somehow the action released some of the panic, and she took a trembling breath.

She was in the middle of another uneven inhale when a determined set of footsteps clicked down the hall in her direction. She stopped breathing again, clutching her hands to her chest, one still gripping a few of the hairpins.

To her dismay, the steps stopped outside the linen closet.

Lenora squinted up into the sudden light that entered the room when the door opened a crack.

"Oh, my lady." The woman with dark hair in tight ringlets sighed, kneeling down just outside the threshold. By the wrinkles around her eyes and the emphasized crease in her forehead, Lenora guessed she was at least ten years older than she was. "I thought I might find you here." The woman, Merla, had been assigned to her the moment Lenora had arrived at the castle in Cyanthia. She was to be her new handmaid, joining Kaylene.

Merla reached out her calloused hands, taking one of Lenora's shaking ones between them. "You poor thing," she said, and while there was sadness in her eyes, it wasn't the kind of pity Lenora was ready to reject. Instead, her gaze carried an air of understanding, as if she could sense the fear and trepidation weighing the future queen down. "You're so brave, my lady. So, so brave to be here." Merla stroked Lenora's gloved hand.

The rays from a nearby window in the hallway cast a golden glow over Merla's lovely dark skin, illuminating and bathing her in a warm welcoming light. Whether it was due to the warmth from the window or simply Merla's reassuring presence, Lenora's quivering breaths slowly became more even, and her spinning head and racing heart calmed down as well.

Like a budding leaf, Lenora relaxed her muscles and unfurled the fist that held the hairpins. A few of them clattered to the floor.

"Take your time," Merla said, her voice soft. But her attention flicked to the hallway at the same time Lenora's did.

More footsteps.

Hurried, and by the sound of the voices, irritated.

"Hush now," Merla whispered, dropping Lenora's hand and jumping to her feet. She closed the door without a single creak, and her footsteps clicked down the corridor toward the new ones.

"Have you seen the future queen?" a male voice asked, his voice deep and commanding. "It's almost time for the wedding to begin, and no one has seen her in over an hour."

"I'm searching for her as well," Merla said, her voice lacking every ounce of the gentleness it'd held a few seconds earlier. "Might I suggest the gardens? I hear she's quite fond of them. And let me know if you find her, will you, gentlemen?"

There was a moment of silence before the heavier footsteps, likely those of the king's royal guards, faded away.

When the door opened again, Merla held out a hand. "Come," she said, beckoning Lenora to stand. "Let's get you a glass of water and something to eat. Then we can discuss what you'd like to do next."

A WHIRLWIND. THAT was what the day had been. She couldn't even remember the vows she'd spoken that bound her to the man walking beside her. Before she'd known it, he was offering her his arm and leading her out of the throne room and the sea of unfamiliar faces.

Unfamiliar, that was, except for her father, Kaylene, and Merla.

The latter two she'd been grateful for.

Her father . . . Well, she would've preferred he'd stayed in his estate in the Black Forest. The smug sneer on his face when she'd walked past him, newly appointed as queen of Phildeterre, sent a large enough shiver through her that her new husband gave her a startled look.

The throne room echoed with the residual cheers of well-wishers, and the weight of the tiara on Lenora's head seemed to hang heavier with each step.

Outside the throne room, servants and courtiers bustled around them, eager to assist in any way possible.

"Thank you, but your presence is not needed," Butch said, waving them all away. "We require a moment alone." His voice carried through the hallway.

Alone.

With a stranger.

One she'd had no choice but to marry thanks to the arrangement between their fathers. A contract that, through their marriage, completed the unification of the five kingdoms under one throne. Her husband's throne. Her father and his territory—Haysinlin, no longer a kingdom—would receive a representative—her—in unified Cyanthia.

A bargaining chip.

A hostage.

And King Valryn, her husband's father, had gotten what he wanted: a single throne upon which to sit and rule all of Phildeterre. Only, he'd died not long after the marriage was announced.

And Butch . . . She glanced at her husband's profile. He'd received a woman he didn't love. A stranger. A wife to bear his heir and the spares.

Lenora's stomach tightened with a growing sense of dread twisting into knots. Her heart raced as Butch led her to the grand staircase. Despite the week she'd been there, she'd hardly left her chambers, and the unfamiliarity of her surroundings felt as if a hand were grasping her around the throat. If she didn't sit down soon, she might faint. Why did Merla have to tighten the corset so much? There was hardly any room for her lungs.

"Are you all right?" Butch asked on the landing of the second floor.

Lenora's tongue felt as though ivy had wrapped around it, taking it captive. The most she could do was nod.

Butch gave her a hesitant look a second longer before he led her to the third floor, where the royal rooms were.

Lenora struggled for breath.

Married.

To a stranger.

And he was likely expecting . . .

"I thought we might walk through here, though it's longer. But if you're not feeling well, we—"

"I'm fine." Anything to prolong what he inevitably expected of her.

Her duties, as her father had referred to them.

The room he led her to was filled with portraits, and the more she studied them, the more she recognized the faces from her history lessons. The rulers of the kingdom of Cyanthia. She corrected herself inwardly. Up until King Valryn, Butch's father, the people in the portraits had only ruled Cyanthia. But King Valryn and Butch, they ruled the entire country of Phildeterre.

"I must apologize for not being present the past few days. My father's burial demanded my attention," Butch said, his deep voice vibrating through her. Despite his words, there was a distinct lack of sorrow lingering within them. He'd stated his father's death as if it were a change in the weather.

"I understand," Lenora said in a voice softer than she'd intended. But it was as if his mere presence stole the precious air from her lungs.

A stranger.

Not Leo.

She was alone with a stranger. How she longed for freedom—to rip her arm from his and run out of the portrait hall, the castle, and Cyanthia.

Butch cleared his throat when Lenora said nothing else. "I understand this is not, I suppose, an ideal beginning," he continued, his tone tentative. Lenora remained silent, and that seemed to make him speak more, as if trying to fill the silence. "I'm sure this has all been very difficult for you. And I know we barely know a thing about each other, but . . ." He turned to face her, taking her cold hands in his large warm ones. "I hope, in time, we can remedy that." His chestnut eyes swept over her in a faltering gaze. It didn't escape her notice when he lingered longer on her lips. He tilted his head down, bending until there was hardly space to breathe.

A stranger.

A complete stranger.

Lenora turned her head away, tearing her hands from his as if he'd set her on fire. She stumbled backward several steps. Not a second later, she realized her mistake.

She'd just rejected the king.

He'd be angry. Livid. She was his wife—his to do with as he pleased. Her father had given her one rule to live by in her new home, and she'd failed it already.

All she had to do was give her new husband whatever he wished.

And she'd already failed.

"I'm sorry," she whispered, tilting her chin down until she was staring at the polished floor. "I'm so, so sorry."

"Hey," Butch said, his voice surprising her with how soft it was. "Hey, look at me."

His boots appeared in her line of sight as he stepped in front of her again. As her gaze slowly trailed up his wrinkle-free trousers, she noticed his hands tucked into his pockets. By the time his ornate jacket came into view, her eyes were blurry with unexpected tears. Not a single blond hair was out of place on his head, and the crown that rested atop it glowed in the light from the few curtained windows.

"I'm sorry," she said again, forcing herself to stare no higher than his lips. She couldn't bring herself to meet his eyes.

"I said look at me," he repeated, and he took a step forward.

Lenora waited for some sort of strike as he pulled a hand from his pocket, and she flinched, closing her eyes. But a second later, his finger hooked the bottom of her chin and gently lifted it up.

He only spoke when she opened her eyes, his hand lingering for a second more before it dropped back to his side. "You have *nothing* to apologize for, do you understand?" His jaw clenched as he took a deep breath, his brows knitting together. "Nothing."

"But I—"

He held up his hand, and once again, she flinched. Butch winced, quickly lowering it. "I shouldn't have been so forward. We're strangers. I shouldn't have assumed . . . I apologize, Lenora." It looked like he struggled to swallow, and he glanced over her head at the door on the other end of the portrait hall. "I'm sure you're exhausted. I certainly am. If you'll allow me, I'd like to walk you to your room."

Lenora's eyes widened. Her room. A stranger in her room. In her bed.

As if he read the panic spreading through her like a fungus, he cleared his throat again.

"I'll drop you off at the door and see to it that Merla and your other handmaid come attend to you. I didn't mean—I wasn't implying—" His words died off, and he opened and closed his mouth twice before he spoke again. "We *are* married, but I would *never* push you to do something you aren't wanting. It'll always be your choice, Lenora. Always. I promise you that." Butch held out his arm, his face drawn as he waited.

Though her heart still pounded in her chest, Lenora gave a small nod and took his arm.

And when he dropped her off at her door and bid her good night, she drew up enough courage to speak.

"Thank you, Butch."

PART ONE

Chapter 1

EVANGELINE

FOUR YEARS LATER

Evangeline Lia Shry glared at a map of the world with Phildeterre at the center. It rested on the wall across the room from her, and by staring at it, she continued to avoid all eye contact with the fair-haired man sitting in front of it. Her hands, which were chained together with two metal cuffs, clenched and unclenched the fabric of her tunic—a tunic that had once been a light yellow and now was several shades darker and ripped in a few places.

She ran her fingers over the fraying hem, using it to ground herself in her stubborn silence. The loose threads were a reminder—staying silent kept Emmalee safe.

Her gaze darted to a half-eaten tray of food resting on the table near her. The mere sight of it made her stomach gurgle, and heat rushed into her cheeks.

The man in front of her didn't seem to notice. "Where is Estrada?"

It was a ridiculous question, and every time he asked it, Evangeline fought the urge to point out how stupid it was. How was she supposed to know where her best friend—now an escaped criminal—was? She'd been locked in the king's dungeon for at least three months if she'd counted correctly, though it could've been longer. It was hard to tell down in her cell, especially when the days tended to run together.

King Butch shifted in her periphery, narrowing his gaze at her. But she had returned her attention to the map, dragging it away from the tray of food that kept whispering to her.

To the right of the king, standing at attention, was a man in a royal guard uniform with a deep blue collar—a marshal. He watched her with a frown etched upon his forehead.

When she noticed her gaze drifting toward Marshal Thorne, she heard the words he'd whispered into her ear right before he'd arrested her.

"Keep your mouth shut." Four simple words to which she'd clung during hours upon hours of being asked the same set of questions over and over again.

Standing next to the king, Thorne also served as a reminder to stay quiet, whether that was his intention in giving her the warning or not. Still, she repeated the mantra she'd created during her time sitting in front of Butch— staying silent kept Emmalee safe.

With that thought in mind, she clamped her jaw tighter, ignoring the pain throbbing deep beneath her molars.

Her determination must've been written over her face because a vein in the king's forehead swelled as he slammed his hands down on his desk.

Butch's sandy-blond hair, which typically held a crown, was in disarray from the number of times he'd run his fingers through it with a sheer look of hatred in his chestnut brown eyes. Loathing directed at her. He'd taken off his jacket and rolled up the sleeves of his tunic, likely because his anger was causing him to overheat, if his red face was any indication. Evangeline smirked. He'd even undone the first several buttons of the tunic. And if his appearance wasn't enough to show how close he clearly was to losing his last grasp of control over his fury, his voice was.

"Answer. The. Question." The words came out as a low growl. He stood up, glaring at her.

Evangeline lifted her chin, finally meeting his glare with one of her own. As dangerous as it was to bait the king, she found it quite entertaining to frustrate him. It filled her with some sort of satisfaction to waste his time simply by keeping her mouth closed.

In fact, she had yet to speak a single word to the king.

Thorne, on the other hand, was a different story—one she couldn't think about while having a staring contest with Butch.

"Speak!" he barked, his nose scrunching. Butch had yet to raise a hand against her, which had surprised her after the first time her silence turned his face the color of a beet. She'd been struck on the cheek for less by men far inferior to the one sitting across from her, yet the king kept his hands to himself.

Knowing it would infuriate Butch that much more, Evangeline broke eye contact and went back to staring at the map. It worked.

With an exasperated sigh, the king waved to Thorne. "Return her."

It was the moment she'd been waiting for, and she kept an eye on Thorne as he passed behind her to summon the lower-ranked guard who'd take her back to the dungeon.

As if it knew what she was about to do, Evangeline's stomach growled once more—and she pinched her lips together.

It had to be believable. Evangeline preemptively rose to her feet as Thorne and another guard entered the room. Unfortunately, she hated that guard as much as the other two men in the king's office. Had hated him ever since he'd dragged one of her acquaintances away right in front of her. She'd taken to calling him "the Mongoose" even though she knew his real name.

She took a step around the seat they'd placed her in when they'd brought her to the interrogation; however, she stuck her foot underneath the edge of the chair leg so it caught, and she tripped. On the way down, she bumped the table, knocking the tray and its contents to the floor.

The tray clattered and the food went everywhere. Evangeline winced as she hit the floor on her knees, but the pain was worth it. Next to where she'd landed, a half-eaten roll sat, waiting to be grabbed and hidden in her eager hands.

Using her body as a shield to hide what she was doing, Evangeline snatched the roll and smushed it in her left fist. It wouldn't be fluffy, but at least it wouldn't be molding and as hard as a rock like the ones they gave the prisoners. Her stomach leapt at the thought of eating it when she got back to her cell.

"On your feet," the Mongoose said, yanking her by the upper arm only a second after she'd hidden the roll.

Steeling her expression, she tried the think of how she would've reacted had it not been part of her plan—if she really had just tripped in front of the men holding her prisoner.

It probably would've been humiliating. She avoided eye contact with any of them, hoping that would be enough to convince them that she was embarrassed when, in fact, she was quite proud of herself for succeeding.

"Send a servant to clean up this mess." Butch gave the order to no one in particular as the Mongoose pulled Evangeline out of the room. The door closed behind them.

"Worthless," the Mongoose muttered, shaking his head as he pinched Evangeline's arm in his tight grasp.

She winced when he stopped in the middle of an empty hall, forcing her to halt too. The roll in her hand seemed obvious, as if the Mongoose could look down at any minute and notice it.

But he didn't. Instead, he sneered at her. She'd remembered him the first time he'd looked at her that way—the fear he'd instilled as she'd trembled in the alleyway. It had been over a year since he'd grabbed her wrist outside the shop she'd once worked in and threatened her after arresting the woman who now occupied the cell next to her own. She'd noticed the small crescent moon scar over his left eye and the way he'd ogled her like she was something to be possessed. Something to be used. Then disposed of.

Kendrick Stoll, as she'd found out later, was older than her, but not by much—at least from what she could tell. She'd given him the nickname because the expression she'd seen him wear the most was similar to the only mongoose she'd witnessed, which had hissed at her in a forest and scurried away. Rodent-like, to be sure. The guard had large, beady amber eyes that, when he was upset, seemed to bulge in an unnatural way. His nose was small and pointed and often wrinkled, at least when he was around Evangeline, though that was far better than when his eyes darkened with something else. He was mean—meaner than any of the other guards she'd come into contact with.

The nickname fit perfectly.

"It'd be a wise idea to start answering the king's questions, unless you want to spend the rest of your life in the dungeon," he said, his glare bearing down on her.

Though she wanted to ask how he knew she wasn't speaking—it was only ever Butch, Thorne, and her in the king's office during the interrogations—she thought better of it. Besides, it wasn't as if the king's office was soundproof. If the Mongoose was standing guard outside the door, it was probably all too easy to eavesdrop and realize that she hadn't spoken at all.

"You think you're smart? That you're somehow protecting that monster?" His voice came out as a growl when he leaned forward, forcing Evangeline to bend away. She bristled at the guard's mention of Emmalee.

Everything in her wanted to fight back and defend her friend, saying Emmalee wasn't a monster, just a mother and wife still in immense pain from the loss of her family. But if the taunts and insults hadn't worked coming from the king—and they hadn't—then they weren't going to elicit a response when uttered by the Mongoose.

"If it were up to me, you'd be missing your head just for helping her get away." He shook her once, hard enough that the chains around her wrists rattled. "She's a murderer, and if you hadn't stepped in"—he let go of her upper arm and reached down, grabbing her left forearm only inches from where the smushed roll hid in her hand—"she'd be in chains. Or better yet, you'd both be dead."

The Mongoose's grip on her forearm tightened when his eyes traveled toward her closed fist. His head tilted as he straightened, a smirk spreading across his lips.

"What's this?" he asked, moving his grasp farther down until he held her wrist by the metallic cuff.

Evangeline tried to pull away, but he pinched her fist until her bones ground together, and she released the bread with a yelp. The roll—now shaped like the inside of her hand—fell to the floor, where the Mongoose stared at it.

With a dark laugh, he smashed it into the stone brick with the toe of his boot, raising Evangeline's wrist higher so she had to stand on tiptoe.

"Stealing from the king?" he asked, his words laced with a poisonous sweetness. "Not the brightest wick, are you?"

He returned his grip to her upper arm, dragging her down the hall at a quicker pace—one that forced her to do a mixture of an uneven walk and jog.

Down they went, farther and farther into the depths of the castle until they ended at the bottom of a winding staircase that led to a black pit. The dungeon reeked of urine and decaying rat. Maybe more than one.

The Mongoose dragged her past a row of cells on both sides of the hallway, all lined in iron bars. It was hard to tell which cells were empty and which were occupied since her eyes hadn't yet adjusted to the darkness and the light of the torch by the bottom of the stairs only reached so far.

Evangeline braced for the impact of the stone floor as the Mongoose shoved her into the cell she'd been held in for the past three months. She caught herself somewhat awkwardly, trying to work around her cuffed wrists. Her right shoulder and hip took the brunt of the impact. Evangeline winced. The stone scraped against the bare skin on her arm as she sat up and glared at the royal guard.

"No dinner. And next time you try something like that, I won't be so kind," the Mongoose spat, slamming the iron bars shut. He marched toward the winding stairs that led out of the musty dungeon, slamming his fist against the iron door of a cell nearby, making the prisoner within skitter to the back.

Sighing, Evangeline grimaced as she stood, rubbing her chained wrists. Since she had been arrested, the metal cuffs had been removed only a handful of times, and the skin around the restraints—and she assumed beneath—was red and inflamed. If not worse. The pain was constant: a dull throbbing in good times and a sharp stabbing fire when anything or anyone jostled them. In an attempt to prevent any serious damage, Evangeline had ripped a piece of her tunic early on and tied it around the edge, doing what she could to keep the metal on the fabric rather than her raw skin. She wasn't sure it was helping anymore—not with the filth constantly surrounding her.

Her hip ached as she walked to the back of her cell to sit and do what she spent most of her time doing: staring at the cracks in the ceiling.

She leaned her head back, closing her eyes so they could adjust to the low light level faster.

A soft tap on the bars to her right had Evangeline opening her eyes a second later. The woman in the cell next to hers nodded toward the staircase, her face and hands becoming more and more visible as Evangeline's eyes adjusted to the darkness. She started to move her hands, her lips forming silent words as she signed slowly.

"So, I take it you didn't get anything?" Odette asked, her thin eyebrow raised.

Evangeline shook her head, rolling her eyes. It'd taken a while for her to get the basic movements of signing down, but with nothing better to do, her friend had spent patient hours over the last months training her. It certainly made conversation move slower since it took Evangeline longer to get the signs right. But it was worth it, what with all the other prisoners having nothing better to do than eavesdrop.

"Apparently, they disapprove of stealing from the king's leftovers," Evangeline responded. She'd needed to spell out three of the words, and after Odette showed her the signs for them, Evangeline repeated them a few times until Odette nodded in approval.

Evangeline folded her hands in her lap when she'd finished practicing.

Odette scoffed. "The fact that the king has leftovers is infuriating enough."

Evangeline nodded, her expression pinched as she thought of how close she'd gotten to eating something without bits of mold or any sign of staleness.

"It's the Mongoose," she signed, wrinkling her nose. "Stoll." Evangeline spelled out his name, extending her legs out in front of her. "He hates me."

"He's certainly gotten worse since you arrived. But I don't think he had a kind bone in his body before you either," Odette continued, though she hesitated, her hands pausing midair. It made Evangeline wonder if the images from the Mongoose arresting Odette were floating through her mind like they were Evangeline's. "Don't take it personally. How did it go besides getting caught stealing from the king's fork?"

Despite being exhausted, hungry, cuffed, and locked in a dungeon, Odette's question brought a smile to Evangeline's lips.

"Same as the last hundred times," Evangeline responded silently, tucking a strand of hair behind her ear. She tried to avoid touching her hair, having not bathed in—well, she couldn't remember when she'd last been clean.

"I'm sure the king is getting frustrated, then."

Evangeline shrugged. "I don't care if his head explodes. I'm still not answering his questions." Evangeline hadn't told Odette about Emmalee, not because she didn't trust her, but because she didn't want to put Odette in a position where she might be questioned for what she knew. Because of that, Odette didn't know what the king wanted with Evangeline, only that she had information he wanted.

Odette remained silent, and Evangeline regarded the older woman carefully. Evangeline had not realized that Odette was still alive until she herself had been cast into the depths of the Cyanthian castle. She'd known Odette in passing from the village she'd moved to before her life became a mess, but they hadn't been close—not until they'd become neighbors in the king's filthy dungeon.

"What?" Evangeline asked, leaning her head to the side to raise an eyebrow at the woman who'd become her only friend in the wretched castle.

Odette frowned, pressing her lips together as she shook her head. She signed something, but it was too fast. Evangeline asked her to repeat it slower, and Odette complied.

"I sometimes forget to appreciate that I was arrested during King Butch's reign and not his father's."

It was Evangeline's turn to frown. "You're grateful to be wasting away in a cell?" She watched Odette carefully as she responded.

"If you hadn't noticed, I'm not wasting away." The woman let out a small smile, motioning to her curved figure. "You, on the other hand . . ."

She wasn't wrong. Evangeline found the food served to the prisoners no better than pig slop and struggled to find much to eat each day. She had lost plenty of muscle, and her clothes, which had once fit perfectly, were baggy on her. It was as if her body was withering away before her eyes. Her mind, though, remained strong.

Stubbornness was key, it seemed.

Odette tapped on the bars again, pulling Evangeline's attention back to the cell next to her. "But you misunderstand, Evie," Odette continued. "I meant that the king doesn't seem to have inherited his father's cruelty."

"I disagree," Evangeline said out loud, closing her eyes and leaning her head back again.

"Look," Odette whispered, and when Evangeline didn't listen right away, Odette tapped the bars several times. They didn't always speak in sign, especially when the conversation wasn't important. But clearly, this was, because Odette didn't say another word until Evangeline finally opened her eyes and looked at her.

Odette's hands moved slowly for Evangeline to follow. "If King Valryn were still around, you'd be dead." Odette's words had Evangeline's jaw clenching, though she kept her mouth shut. "Or worse."

"How? Look at this place." Evangeline gestured to the cells around them. It unnerved her how quickly she'd gotten used to the whimpers and crying from the others, how she could ignore them without much thought.

"Valryn either would've tortured the information he wanted out of you until you were no longer useful to him, or he would've just killed you." Odette paused, but she didn't give Evangeline time to respond. "I'm not saying the current king is the savior we were all hoping he'd be, believe me. But it could be worse."

Silence fell between them, as it often did with no warning. In the lull, Evangeline allowed the sounds of the other prisoners pacing their cells to seep into her mind. Chains scratched along the stone or clinked against the iron bars that separated them.

The first week she'd been there, she'd been chained to the back wall. But when Thorne had come down to take her to an interrogation with the king, he'd ordered the rest of the guards to leave her untethered with only the cuffs around her wrists to keep her in check.

She hated the way her mind kept finding its way back to Thorne— not because that was where it landed, but because instead of thinking of him as the guard who'd arrested her and forced her into her current position, she couldn't help but notice and dwell on the way he treated her better than the rest of the guards. Treated *all* the prisoners with more kindness and respect. Not just her.

It was infuriating.

He was the reason she was locked up.

He was her enemy.

And so was the king.

For Emmalee's sake, it was important to remind herself of that fact.

Chapter 2

LENORA

Queen Lenora rapped her fingers on the edge of the throne, her chin resting atop her other hand, which was propped up on the armrest. She had been sitting in the throne room waiting for her husband to walk through the double doors for the past forty-five minutes. And she wasn't alone.

Thirty-three courtiers milled about the room, engaging in whispered conversation. Every once in a while they would glance at her, and as soon as they met her gaze, they'd look away, sometimes choosing to "admire" the intricate painting of a field of purple flowers on the ceiling or the enormous three-story stone pillars around the room. The raised dais on which the thrones sat gave her the perfect vantage to watch and, unfortunately, be watched.

At first, she had been conflicted as to whether she should venture out to join the upper-class lords and ladies, but when her throne caught her eye, she couldn't stop herself from drifting toward it and eventually taking her place at the top of the room.

It wasn't what her father would've wanted, but thankfully, he was not currently in court, nor had he been for a while, much to her and her husband's relief. As part of the agreement that had led to Lenora's arranged marriage to Butch, Puck, her father, had also received a permanent position in the king's court—his own way of sticking his hands into other people's business whether they wanted it or not. Hopefully, though, he would continue his absence from Cyanthia for many, many more months.

Lenora just felt bad that her home and those who lived in the western part of the Black Forest—what used to be the kingdom of Haysinlin—had to put up with the nightmare of a man.

Butch would no doubt agree.

The thought of her husband drew Lenora's attention back to the throne room. Without Butch present, she could not begin the meeting the men and women in the room had gathered for, nor could she answer any questions as to where the king was. Her best guess was that Butch was locked away in his office, having completely forgotten that his presence was required elsewhere.

That was his typical reasoning, at least. Too many things to concern himself with. Orders that needed to be handed out. Laws that needed to be reviewed. A war that needed his full attention.

Lenora rolled her eyes without even realizing it, letting out a sigh.

Her handmaid Kaylene, who stood to the left of her, noticed. "Is there anything I can do, Your Majesty?" She stepped forward, curtsying before fully approaching the queen.

Sitting up straighter, Lenora shook her head. "No, unless you can make time go by faster."

Kaylene smiled. "I wish I could, for your sake." She nodded her head before stepping back.

Lenora allowed herself to be frustrated about her husband's tardiness a moment longer before taking a deep breath. In the weeks and now months following the incident in the boulder field, she had realized the grace she'd been withholding from her husband, grace he'd earned when he'd come to her rescue—something she hadn't expected of him. And he'd been busy ever since, trying to track down the woman who'd abducted her. Butch had spent what felt like every available hour trying to find where the woman had gone.

He was dealing with a lot.

Grace, not annoyance, would help him.

Lenora forced her mind to think of something else—hopefully something that would lighten her mood. She was, after all, being watched.

Thankfully, her quick conversation with Kaylene gave her just such a topic. Her mind went back several years, to before she was married, before she'd traveled to Cyanthia to wed a man she'd never met.

Lenora had grown up in the Black Forest in what used to be the kingdom of Haysinlin before her husband's father, King Valryn, combined all five kingdoms under one throne—the throne next to which she sat. And before that, her father had been a king himself, and she a princess.

It was during that time, on an outing with a few of their servants, that she'd come across a girl not much younger than she was. The girl, Kaylene—as she would later come to find out—was crying next to a tree, curled up in a ball of tattered clothing and a tangled mess of auburn hair that grew past her waist.

Lenora had stopped her horse, dismounting to speak to the stranger, knowing she was safe with the three servants she'd brought as well as the soldier her father had sent with her.

After a series of questions, Kaylene told her that her mother and brother had died within the span of a week and she was alone and lost. She'd been looking for a place to work when she'd gotten turned around in the forest—it was an easy thing to do—and had no idea where to seek shelter. When that'd been too overwhelming, she'd simply sat down to cry.

Lenora had taken the girl back to the castle, offering her a job as a handmaid. They'd grown close after that, and years later, when a letter arrived from the prince of Phildeterre addressed to her father stating that it was time for the arranged marriage between Lenora and him to take place, Kaylene had been the only friend to accompany Lenora to her new home.

Kaylene was a symbol of comfort in Lenora's mind, and when she glanced back at the handmaid, whose auburn hair was braided intricately around the crown of her head, a smile came to the queen's lips.

The double doors leading into the throne room creaked as the guards outside opened them at the same time.

Lenora bristled when the lightness in her spirit wavered for just a moment at the sudden sight of her husband. Marshal Thorne followed at his heel.

The king nodded to the courtiers, who bowed or curtsied at him, but his stride was brisk, and he took the stairs two at a time to get to the throne on Lenora's right.

"You're late," she said, her voice soft so those below wouldn't hear. She kept a pleasant smile on her lips, though it was difficult because of the returning irritation brewing in her. She tried to soothe some of the annoyance by adding, "Is something the matter?"

"Important meeting ran long," he muttered as he turned to face the courtiers. His eyes carried dark bags beneath them, as did Marshal Thorne's. The marshal took a similar position behind the king that Kaylene had taken for her.

But the bags weren't the only thing off about her husband. Though his crown rested on his head, it was crooked, and the hair was ruffled beneath it. His collar was flipped up on one side, sticking awkwardly out of his jacket. The bulge about halfway down his arm nearest her indicated he hadn't bothered to unroll the sleeves of his tunic before putting on the formal outerwear. He looked about as prepared to speak to the courtiers as the vegetation she'd planted only a week earlier was to bud and flower.

Butch cleared his throat, clasping his hands behind his back and jolting Lenora from her analysis of his appearance. "I apologize for my tardiness. The meeting may begin." His voice boomed across the throne room, and after he'd spoken, he sat down.

Lenora cast a sideways glance at her husband, willing to offer him a small smile of reassurance, but he didn't catch her eye. His posture was that of a statue. Lenora straightened her own posture, facing the courtiers with the smile she'd intended for her husband.

One at a time, the courtiers stepped forward with suggestions, requests, and sometimes complaints. Lenora remained silent, letting Butch do the speaking. Her presence for the meetings was not required, but she was grateful her husband allowed her to sit in nonetheless.

". . . be wise to host a ball or ceremony for them, especially since they have not stepped foot in Phildeterre since the beginning of your father's reign," a stout courtier said, stroking his graying beard as he spoke.

Inwardly, the queen deflated. Though they'd been married less than five years, she knew her husband well enough to recognize that if there was to be a ball or any sort of event, the king would likely pass along the burden of planning it to her. And she despised the entire process, from choosing what decorations to use to deciding the music and the menu to greeting the guests. It was a miserable process through and through.

"I agree," Butch said next to her. He glanced at Lenora. "We will greet the aristocrats of Jerr Pinn with a grand welcome. A ball is a brilliant idea."

"Thank you, Your Majesty," the courtier said, bowing as he stepped back.

Butch nodded, raising his chin as he spoke. "Who's next?"

Another man stepped up, this one younger and lankier. He bowed before addressing the king and queen.

"My apologies, Your Majesties, but those within my town have sent me to ask about the criminal woman with dark magic." At the man's words, Lenora stiffened. "Are you any closer to apprehending her?"

Butch glanced at Lenora, his jaw tightening. The smile that slid across his face looked forced to Lenora, though he did speak with a believable level of gentleness as he responded.

"It is a fair question. As of right now, I have some of the most highly trained guards searching for her. Marshal Levick is leading five captains and the guards beneath them on a thorough search of the Black Forest, and should they not find her there, they will continue their search in the other regions of Phildeterre."

Lenora tried not to snort when her husband mentioned Marshal Levick. Of all the highest-ranking officers in the royal guard, Thorne was the most capable—not Levick. Maybe in combat, but not when it came to planning.

"Next topic?" Butch said, interrupting the man who had asked the question before he could say anything else regarding the woman who had abducted the queen three months earlier.

The king's decision to continue past the subject did not, it seemed, go as unnoticed as he might've hoped it would. Lenora noted at least five of the courtiers exchanged furtive glances.

But when she looked at her husband, the only thing she saw was the normal stoic wall he wore every day.

THE MEETING DREW on, and once the final courtier left, the enormous throne room filled with pleasant silence. Kaylene had left earlier, leaving Lenora alone with her husband and Marshal Thorne.

Butch spoke next to her. "If you don't have anywhere to go right away, I have a request to make of you," he said, drawing her attention.

She had a feeling she knew what his request was, and she wished in that second that she did, in fact, have somewhere better to be.

"Yes?" Lenora responded, her muscles refusing to relax from their rigid posture until she was alone, or at least with her handmaids only.

Butch rubbed his hand over his jaw, smoothing out the beard he had started to grow over the last few weeks. With his fair hair, it gave him a more rugged appearance, and in Lenora's opinion, it did not suit him.

"I have plenty of things going on with the security of the country and the war, and it would help me greatly if you would take over the responsibility of planning the ceremony for the dignitaries arriving in three months. I know it's a lot to ask, but—"

"You're right," Lenora said, her face scrunching. It was a lot to ask. Too much. She wanted to tell him, and her hands balled into fists in her lap. But she couldn't. "You have many things going on."

"Then you'll do it?"

Lenora didn't respond verbally. Clenching her jaw, she gave a brief nod. After all, was it not her duty? Serving him how she could? Whatever he required.

Anything.

It was as if the thought was spoken in her father's voice.

"Wonderful. Thank you," he said, standing, and she copied him. He took a few steps down the dais before she stopped him.

"Before you go," Lenora said, frowning when she realized too late that despite several days of worrying over what she was about to say, she hadn't thought through the best way to say it. She rarely reached out to her husband. Maybe he would think it was strange. Or a hinderance. Or—

"Would you, I mean, if you aren't too busy . . . Would you have dinner with me tonight?" She voiced the question before she could convince herself not to.

Butch's eyebrows rose, and a second later, he was beaming at her. "Of course," he said, returning up the stairs. He held out his hand, palm up, waiting for her to take it. When she did, he squeezed her hand gently before raising it to his lips and placing a soft kiss atop her knuckles. "I'll make time for you. All you have to do is ask." Butch held her hand as he led her down the stairs.

"I know," she said. She held the skirt of her dark blue dress with her free hand, careful not to catch her foot on the hem. "I just know you've been busy." Lenora hesitated a second before adding, "I could help if—"

"Thank you," he said, cutting her off. "But it's no place for a woman." He bristled when she pulled her hand from his.

27

"I'm not just a random woman. I'm your wife. Phildeterre's queen. Shouldn't I aid in whatever ways I can?" Lenora folded her arms, glancing from Butch to Marshal Thorne behind him.

"You do plenty," Butch said, glancing at his friend. "Right?"

"It's true. Especially with everything you told us about your time away," Thorne said, his gaze on the queen.

She almost scoffed, as if her "time away" were by choice and not because she'd been held captive.

"Besides, the war is a complicated beast. The king is doing everything he can to protect you as well as the rest of Phildeterre."

"Exactly," Butch said, nodding. "I'm trying to make this country safer."

"By hunting down Estrada?" Lenora said. She bit the inside of her bottom lip as the image of the woman with dark brown hair and nearly black eyes filled her mind, the tiny house where she'd kept Lenora hostage for a month hovering just behind her. She'd told her husband and Thorne everything about her time there—everything except the location of the tiny house. She didn't know why she'd kept silent in that regard. To be truthful, she didn't know exactly where the house was since Estrada had tried to confuse her with directions. But she knew it was near enough to walk from where she'd been taken.

Why didn't she reveal that to her husband?

Why did she feel better about remaining silent?

Butch's gaze narrowed, then relaxed several seconds later. He let out a sigh. "I'm *trying* to hunt down Estrada."

"And?"

He pursed his lips, frowning as he moved his hands to his hips. He glared at the ground. "She's still out there."

Lenora kept her breath even as she asked her final question. "And when you find her?"

Butch's eyes were alight with angry fire when he looked up at her. "I'll make sure she never hurts anyone again."

Chapter 3

BUTCH

Only once he'd entered his office did Butch remove his jacket. The rolled sleeves of his tunic beneath the confining jacket had bothered him the entire time he'd held court, but years of training from a young age had kept him still as stone. Fidgeting as a prince would've earned him rapped knuckles, or worse if his father had seen. Fidgeting as a king would've earned disrespect—something he couldn't afford with a war his grandfather had started breathing down his neck each and every day.

The smell in his office was stale, which probably had to do with the fact that he'd basically been living in it for the last several weeks.

"Considering how late I was, I'd say that didn't go as terribly as I thought it would," Butch said, pausing as he frowned. "Except for the question about Estrada."

"You handled it well," Silas responded from where he stood near the door. While his friend had loosened his stance, it was clear Silas was ready to snap to attention at any second, his hands restless by his sides.

Butch scoffed, placing his crown on his desk as he ran his fingers through his greasy hair. He needed a bath. His nose wrinkled when he lifted his arms.

"That's not the word I'd use." Butch pressed his palms into his closed eyes. He was running on three hours of sleep, and it was finally catching up with him. A headache sat on the edge of his temples, threatening to spread throughout his entire skull.

"She'll break eventually."

Butch straightened, his arms crossing over his chest. "The prisoner?"

Silas nodded. "She's clearly stubborn, but she's not the kind of person who can live the rest of her life in a dungeon. She doesn't have that kind of strength. She'll be useful. We just have to wait."

"That's what I'm afraid of. Waiting. And I believe she's stronger than you think," Butch said, sighing as he slumped in his chair. He glanced out the window at the midafternoon sun glazing the treetops in a buttery light. "The longer Estrada is out there, the more chances we give her to retaliate."

"True."

"And Estrada *will* retaliate. I could see it in her eyes that night. She won't give up. It's not as if she's trying instead to live some kind of normal life now—not that she could with hordes of royal guards searching for her. No, she's gone underground to figure out the best way to poison this country."

Silas shifted, and the king's gaze returned to him. "But you do have something she wants."

"A beating heart?" Butch asked, eliciting a snort from his friend. "A head stubbornly still on my shoulders?"

"Her friend."

Butch stroked his chin, nodding. "I know, I know. It feels like we're playing with fire though." His hand went to his stomach reflexively, as it had since the night he'd almost captured the woman who'd kidnapped his wife.

According to the royal physician, he had broken three ribs. It'd been difficult to move, to even breathe. He was apparently lucky to be alive considering his other injuries. He still had moments where a fragment of one of his ribs would cause him to double over when a sharp pain shot through his chest.

But Estrada had not been the only one to cause him injury.

"I don't understand it," Butch muttered.

"What?" Silas asked. He frowned when his gaze landed on the king's hand rubbing his chest. "Do you need me to fetch Helena?"

"No, no." Butch shook his head, straightening in his chair. "I don't understand those with magic."

"Meaning?"

Butch stood, pacing around to the window to stand in the sun. "I can't stop thinking about the day we were ambushed in the gully. I saw the prisoner's magic—was nearly blinded by the flash of light, felt its heat just before I thought I was going to die. She saved me. And yet she also struck me with her magic and nearly killed me at the boulder field."

Silas bristled, his posture stiffening as he nodded. "And?"

"How?" Butch asked, clasping his hands behind his back. "How could magic be used to save, but also used to hurt and destroy? I mean"—he gestured toward the window—"Estrada is somewhere out there right now doing goodness knows what, except that it isn't good, yet I haven't convicted her friend, who has light magic. And you know why? Because of the gully. It's infuriatingly confusing."

"I'm sure it is." Silas paused until Butch looked at him. "And if you were questioning it, I think it was very wise not to spread word of the prisoner's magic. I mean, you haven't had someone with pure magic—light or dark— in the dungeon for a long time, and it would certainly cause some unrest amongst the guards." Silas's voice was strained, but Butch ignored it.

Instead, he spoke the words rattling around in his brain out loud. "She struck me, did she not? And you. Twice. I have half a mind each morning to put her on trial and be done with it. I would think you would want her to face punishment for her crimes as much as the next person. Shouldn't I do it? Do it and be done?"

Instead of answering, Silas turned toward the door, his head tilting to the side. "We have company."

"Enter," Butch said as he returned to his desk. He placed his crown back on his head seconds before a royal guard came in and saluted, first to him, then to Silas. "Yes?"

The royal guard was young, possibly a newer recruit. But he wasn't as stiff or cautious as many of the royal guards were within Butch's presence. It was almost a breath of fresh air—until he gave his reason for addressing Butch.

"Marshal Levick sent me with news," he said, his voice deeper than Butch had expected.

"And?"

"One of his men was found dead, Your Majesty. And—" The young guard grimaced. "And the marshal suspects dark magic."

"Killed?"

The guard nodded. Butch and Silas exchanged a glance.

"Was the manner in which he was killed obvious?" Silas asked, drawing the guard's attention.

"He was tracking down a merchant rumored to have runed items when he went missing, sir. There were traces of dark magic near where they found his body, but no other indications of where the attacker went after they left the village."

Butch pressed his lips together. "Does Marshal Levick have any suspects?"

"Levick thinks it's her—Estrada." The guard returned his attention to the king, standing tall.

"What makes him think that?"

"Besides the dark magic, someone reported seeing a woman with a similar description to the convict."

"Anything else?" Butch asked, trying to hold back a deep sigh until after the guard left.

"One other thing," the guard said, his brow furrowing. "Those assigned to the boulder field still haven't found Estrada's dagger, but they did find her bag."

Butch hadn't even noticed that the guard was holding something in his hands until he offered it to him.

"It's been searched for your safety, but nothing has been removed."

The bag was heavier than Butch had expected. "Thank you. If that's all, you may go."

"Thank you, Your Majesty," the guard said, saluting.

When he turned to salute Silas, the marshal saluted back. "Rest up and return to Marshal Levick in the morning," Silas said, dropping his hand back to his side.

"Yes, sir."

After the door closed behind the guard, Silas joined Butch at his desk. "Think she went back for the dagger?"

Butch let loose the sigh he'd been holding. "I assume so, but I'd hoped it was lost forever in a crevice. It looked deadly, didn't it?"

Silas nodded, then gestured toward the bag. "Let's see what's here, shall we?"

The bag itself was old, with two patches on the outside and one inside the flap.

"Random," Silas muttered, his face scrunching as he placed each item onto the king's desk.

Lavender, cinnamon and another spice Butch recognized but couldn't put a name to, and a few chips of some sort of bark. The last two items were to be expected: a canteen and a small coin purse that was nearly empty.

With everything laid out on his desk, Butch tossed the bag into the corner of the room nearest him. "This is what we're up against." He chuckled darkly, rubbing the back of his neck.

"Yes," Silas said, his attention on the items in front of him. "I have no idea how she pulled off that wall of dark magic with just these items. That's the most concerning part. It seems we need to be on our guard. This is power like I've never heard of before."

ALL HE COULD do was watch. Watch as the guards pounded relentlessly against the familiar door. Watch as they pushed past the man with the glasses, his eyes wide in terror. Watch as two guards dragged a young girl with curly brown hair out, ignoring her endless pleas and cries. Watch as they shoved her to the ground. Watch as the man with glasses stepped between the guards and the sobbing girl. Watch as a two-year-old waddled over in tears, clinging to the brave man's leg. Watch as one of the guards freed his sword. Watch as he struck down the man, the toddler, and finally the young woman.

He knew their faces.

Knew their names.

Had seen them almost every night since he'd faced the woman who blamed him for their deaths.

But the worst part was, in the midst of those dreams—those nightmares—when he was overwhelmed by the agony of loss he himself hadn't experienced, he almost agreed with her.

Butch sat straight up in bed, his skin covered in a layer of sweat that had his light tunic clinging to him. He sat there, panting, trying to shove away the images of the nightmare as he pushed his hair out of his face. Butch sat with his head in his hands for several seconds, the air of the room seeming to tremble as much as his hands were, until a light touch on his shoulder had him straightening.

"Is something wrong?" Lenora asked, her tone raspy from sleep.

Butch shook his head, taking another steadying breath before he spoke, just to make sure his words wouldn't divulge how truly perturbed the dream had made him. "No," he said, forcing a smile onto his lips before he turned to face his wife. "Just overheating is all." Butch leaned over, placing a kiss on her temple before he lifted the blankets. "I'll be back in a moment. Go back to sleep."

The second his feet hit the cold stone floor, his mind began to clear, leaving the images of murdered civilians in his bed. It was not the first time he'd left Lenora lying there since he was still unaccustomed to sharing the bed with his wife. Over the years, she'd said many times that she preferred her own room. But she hadn't argued when he'd offered for her to stay after dinner—not last night, or the many nights after he'd been cleared of injuries by Helena, the head physician.

Something had changed between Lenora and him after the boulder field. He wasn't about to complain.

Butch crossed to the bathing room, casting a glance to the large metal bath in the center of the room before settling at the bowl of water his servants kept fresh every few hours. Placing his hands on either side of the bowl, Butch leaned down, his stiff spine stretching. With a huff, he cupped water into his hands and splashed his face. It was colder than he'd expected and brought forth memories he had no desire to recall.

Flashes of Estrada's dark magic wrapping around him, biting into his flesh with freezing tendrils, flooded his mind. He'd been at her mercy more than once that night. Had been out of control.

He could've died.

Would've died if not for Silas.

Butch lifted more water to his face, his hands lingering at his brow. He pressed deeper until the images in his mind shifted to bodies scattered in the boulder field as his few remaining royal guards helped him down the hill.

His men had died.

They'd died for him.

Fighting her.

Yet she'd gotten away.

Before he could process his actions, Butch swept his hand across the counter, sending the bowl of water careening to the floor, where it shattered into pieces.

"Butch!" Lenora called, but as she rounded the corner into the bathing room, he stopped her.

"Don't," he muttered, holding his hand out to keep her from stepping toward him. "There's glass everywhere." Butch nodded toward her bare feet. "I don't want you cutting yourself."

"Are you okay?" she asked, though she stayed by the door as he'd ordered.

"I'm fine." Picking his way across the room, his own feet bare and exposed to the shards of glass, he finally made it to Lenora. "I'll find a servant to clean it up in the morning." He reached for her hand, grateful when she didn't pull away. "Come on, let's go lie back down."

Lenora took another hesitant look over Butch's shoulder at the mess he'd made before following him back to the bed. It didn't matter how long she lay next to him. Even when her breathing finally evened out as she fell back asleep, he couldn't.

Not when Estrada haunted his thoughts.

Chapter 4

EMMALEE

Emmalee's heart pounded as she wept into Ariella's hand. The catlike woman held Emmalee's mouth closed, but it didn't keep every sound from escaping. Emmalee's chest heaved, and she nearly choked trying to keep any noise from leaving her body. Her friend's body shook with silent tears as Ariella held her.

Emmalee hadn't meant to kill the guard.

She hadn't.

And the sight of the man's body lying on the ground had nearly brought her to her knees. Even now it threatened to drop her to the ground as the two women hid.

But she couldn't let the guard kill Ariella.

Not when she knew she had the power to stop him, to save her.

To do what she hadn't been able to do for Evangeline that night.

She'd made an absolute mess and had dragged Ariella right into the center of it.

"We run again on three," Ariella whispered into Emmalee's ear. "One . . . Two . . ."

"Over there!"

"Run," Ariella gasped. She pushed Emmalee in front of her as they darted around the tree behind which they'd hidden to catch their breath.

Emmalee had made a mistake in thinking the guard was alone. There hadn't been a plan. No plan, and now a mess. Not a minute after Emmalee had choked the last breath out of the man with her dark magic, two voices had started calling a name, presumably the dead man's.

They'd fled right away but had been spotted hiding behind one of the buildings on the outskirts of the village.

Emmalee had been wearing her cloak, but the guards had tracked them down nonetheless. She doubted they'd seen her face, and it was the only reason she hadn't created a cloud of mist to disappear within. If she used her magic in front of them, it would confirm she was there.

She didn't want to give the king any solid information about her whereabouts. Not while she was still trying to figure out her next move. Not while she was still planning how to save her best friend. Not while she was residing with some of the only remaining friends she had.

Ariella easily passed Emmalee as they sprinted away from the guards. Emmalee's lungs burned. She tried to keep up with Ariella's graceful movements, but her own felt clumsy by comparison as she tripped over a root and then scratched her arm on an extended branch. The sound of tearing fabric as her cloak snagged was almost inaudible as her heartbeat pounded in her head.

"This way," Ariella said, her voice being carried away by the wind rushing past Emmalee. Ducking around a tree, Emmalee followed the Pumarian through a narrow passage of brush and a boulder. Her catlike nature must've helped her see the path that Emmalee could not.

Each branch tore at Emmalee's exposed skin, and she held back tears once more, this time from the stinging sensation burning on her arms, neck, and face. Ariella didn't stop. Neither did Emmalee.

Even as the sounds of the shouts got farther and farther away.

It felt as though she was going to collapse by the time Ariella led her toward a small stream and they came to a stop.

"I think . . . they're gone . . ." Emmalee panted, leaning down and resting her hands on her knees. She felt like throwing up, either from guilt over the man she'd killed or from the forced run through the forest. Either way, she held an arm around her stomach. Her face and hands likely matched Ariella's, bleeding and scraped all over.

But at least they were alive.

Alive and free.

"Are you okay?" Emmalee wheezed, sticking her hand into the numbing water of the stream and bringing it to the back of her neck to cool herself down.

"I will be," Ariella said, glancing over Emmalee's shoulder with vibrant teal eyes slitted like that of a feline. "What you did back there to—"

"I'm sorry. I'm so, so sorry, Ari. I just wanted to protect you, and he . . . and I . . ." Emmalee gasped, clutching her hand over her mouth.

Images of the guard's body crumpled on the ground twisted Emmalee's stomach. She'd unwittingly killed before, but never that close, never near enough to see the light leave their eyes and the breath leave their lungs . . .

"I was just going to say thank you," Ariella said as she straightened, placing a gentle hand on Emmalee's shoulder. "I thought I was done for."

Emmalee stiffened, then nodded. "I'm still sorry."

Neither of them spoke for a moment, nor did they bring up the man Emmalee had killed with her magic.

"We should get back to Fae. Then we can figure out what's next," Ariella said after Emmalee handed her the canteen she'd pulled from her bag. She thanked her after taking a long drink from it.

"She's not going to be happy," Emmalee said, wiping her mouth with the back of her hand as she finished off the rest of the canteen. The cuts on her hand and face stung at the friction, and she winced.

"She was already in a mood when I left. I doubt it will get much worse." Ariella put her hands on her hips, her gaze drifting back in the direction from which they'd come. "I hope they didn't get a good look at me."

"I doubt they did."

"I suppose we'll see, won't we?" Ariella nodded across the stream. When she looked back at Emmalee, a small smile crossed her lips. "Nothing like reliving the good ol' days."

Emmalee snorted but followed Ariella. " 'Good' is the last word I'd use to describe them."

"And here I thought you liked getting into trouble with me." Ariella bumped Emmalee with her shoulder as they started toward Ajorr, where Ariella and her sister, Faeleen, lived.

Despite the unease still filling Emmalee from the inside out, she tried to let Ariella's joking comfort her. "You know, I can't say I missed running for my life."

"Well," Ariella said, pausing to pull her long blond hair up into a ponytail that covered her catlike ears on top of her head, "at least you've gotten faster. I remember you being the slowest."

"I'm not half cat," Emmalee said, raising an eyebrow.

"Could've fooled me with all the unimpressed looks you give."

Emmalee continued walking side by side with Ariella. "At least I don't throw hissy fits."

Ariella shot her a mischievous look. "I beg to differ."

"Name one time."

"My twelfth birthday. When I blew out the candles on the cake Fae managed to put together, you were so upset you didn't get to blow them out that you nearly managed to push the cake off the table. Thank goodness for catlike reflexes."

"I was hardly four years old."

"And I vaguely remember you actually hissing at me."

Emmalee couldn't stop the small smile from crossing her lips. "Well, I wonder who I learned that from."

"Don't look at me. I never hiss."

"FAE," ARIELLA CALLED as the little bell on the shop door tinkled. "Fae, we're back." As soon as Emmalee entered behind her, Ariella turned the sign of the shop to Closed.

It'd taken them a little over an hour to get back to Ajorr, but it'd been filled with the lighthearted banter Emmalee had grown up with, thanks to Ariella's incredible ability to ease the tension in Emmalee's heart.

Carved wooden figures resembling people stood all around the shop, each modeling bright clothing. Their featureless faces were eerie. Racks with colorful fabric draped over them filled the spaces where the inanimate models were not. Light came from several hanging lanterns on the walls, as well as a few on the ceiling that were a pain to light. A whirring sound echoed through a door leading to the back, opposite where they'd entered.

Emmalee wrinkled her nose at the acrid scent wafting through the shop. Ariella beckoned for her to follow to the back. Three large vats sat in the corner, and metal arms rotated around and around, mixing whatever was inside.

"Purple dye is the worst," Ariella said in a loud voice over the sound coming from the vat.

That was the smell.

"You're not supposed to be—oh! I didn't hear you," a woman with short curly blond hair said as she jogged down a flight of stairs to the right of where they'd entered. She wore a pair of round glasses. "What happened to you two?"

"We ran into some trouble," Ariella said, passing her sister, Faeleen, and starting up the stairs she'd just descended. "Em got us out of there."

"That's all you're going to say?" Faeleen spoke loud enough to be heard over the noise. "Tell me what happened."

Anyone who didn't know the sisters might think they were twins. Because they'd all but raised her, Emmalee knew Ariella was older by a few years. Faeleen's hair curled naturally, while Ariella's remained long and straight. Faeleen crossed her arms as she rested her weight to one side. She glared at Ariella, who'd paused on the steps.

"Upstairs," Ariella said, cutting in before Faeleen could argue. "I already closed the shop."

It wasn't until they were sitting in the small living area that Ariella and Emmalee explained what had happened. By the time they finished, Faeleen was chewing on a sharpened nail.

"Of course they tried to arrest you! Threatening someone while you're half transformed? What were you thinking?"

"He was going to turn me in anyway," Ariella said. "And he was going to swindle us out of our full pay. It was a lose-lose situation all around."

"So you, what, extended talons and hissed in the hope he'd wet his pants and pay without calling for help?" Faeleen sat on a chaise lounge, her legs crossed. "What if he or the guards tracked you back here?"

"We weren't followed." Ariella stood with her arms crossed. "And as far as I can tell, he didn't know where we were based."

"As far as you know," Faeleen muttered, scoffing as she rolled her eyes. By the way she scolded Ariella, she could've fooled anyone into believing she was the older sister. "Did he pay you at all?"

"Not willingly," Ariella said, a small smirk crossing her face.

"You didn't," Faeleen said, her anger slipping out of her voice as a devilish grin matched her sister's.

Ariella reached into a pocket and pulled out a plump coin purse, jingling it for her sister to hear and see. "I did."

Emmalee snorted, leaning back in her chair. It didn't surprise her. Ariella had been the best pickpocket out of the three of them when they were growing up alone and hungry in the uncaring Cyanthian streets. Faeleen had gone to other lengths, though none of them spoke about it. Emmalee had simply begged. It worked better for her since the sisters were several years older than her. They'd taught her to use her age to get pity. It worked until it didn't. Then Ariella had stepped in, showing her how to reach into pockets without being noticed.

Without being seen.

Just two shadows blending in with the indifferent world that'd nearly swallowed them whole.

Glancing between the sisters, Emmalee let go a soft smile. If it weren't for them, she would've died in the streets. If it weren't for them, she would've likely died again when a wound from a bolt had unexpectedly gotten infected. They both had a special knack for keeping her safe. She hadn't felt that way since . . .

"What?" Ariella asked, wrinkling her nose as she returned Emmalee's stare.

"Nothing," Emmalee said, dropping the smile. "I'm just glad to see you haven't forgotten your roots."

"Couldn't even if I wanted to," Ariella muttered, tossing the coin purse onto the table in front of them.

"I'll get the bandages," Faeleen said, standing up. "You two look like you went a few rounds with a sentient bush."

"The bush won," Emmalee called out, earning a chuckle from Faeleen. When she glanced back at Ariella, her feline eyes were already watching her. And by the narrowed look, it was obvious Emmalee wasn't going to enjoy whatever Ariella was about to say.

"You didn't tell us it was that powerful." She spoke quietly, but Emmalee knew it wouldn't matter. Faeleen would be able to hear her from the other room anyway thanks to the catlike hearing.

"I didn't mean to kill him." Emmalee stared at the woman who'd raised her despite barely being a teenager herself. "I told you, I just wanted to protect you."

Ariella nodded as her sister reentered the room with a small box of medical supplies. "I know." She shifted on her chair so Faeleen could sit next to her. Her sister started to dab at the blood already dried on Ariella's skin, making Ariella hiss. Literally. "Watch it, Fae, that hurts."

"And here you said you don't hiss," Emmalee teased.

"Shut up."

"Can you get me a wet cloth, Em?" Faeleen asked, not bothering to respond to her sister's complaints.

Emmalee listened, going to the kitchen, where she wet a clean rag and filled a bowl of warm water before taking them to Faeleen.

"If either of you asked me—"

"Which we didn't," Ariella huffed, cutting her sister off.

"Then I'd say you did the right thing, Em. The guards are like cockroaches. They keep coming back. The king is probably already training a new one to replace the one you killed."

The mention of King Butch left Emmalee's muscles tensing until her hands hurt from how hard she'd been clenching her fists.

"I'm not saying she should feel bad about killing a guard. I'm saying she didn't tell us her magic was that powerful." Ariella caught Emmalee's gaze, but there was no anger in it.

"I didn't want to scare you," Emmalee finally said after several seconds of silence. Her mind drifted to Evangeline, to her startled response to Emmalee's dark magic. It didn't matter that they'd been best friends. Evangeline had still looked at her as if Emmalee had grown a second head.

To Emmalee's surprise, both Ariella and Faeleen laughed.

"Em, no offense," Faeleen said.

"But you know as well as we do that not much scares us anymore," Ariella finished, though her voice wasn't as confident as Faeleen's.

As much as the elder Pumarian wanted to hide it, Emmalee had felt her tremble after she'd killed the guard. And despite it, Ariella had held her. Had comforted her. Just as she and Faeleen had done all those years ago.

"I know." Emmalee sighed, rubbing her hands over her face, then wincing as she accidentally jostled some of the more painful cuts. "I know."

Faeleen moved to where Emmalee sat, putting the medical kit between them before she went to work wiping the blood from Emmalee's skin. "We're here for you, Em. I know we went our different directions when we were younger, but—"

"It was for your protection, Em." Ariella sat on the table across from Faeleen, her knees bumping Emmalee's. "But now we're here together."

"We'll always be here for you," Faeleen added as she dipped the cloth into a water bowl.

Emmalee nodded, a sad smile flashing on her face before she cringed at Faeleen's touch. She knew the sisters had been full of nothing but good intentions when they'd encouraged her to go find somewhere safe to live out her life. But she'd only been nine. And frightened.

As an adult, she understood, especially after Ariella and Faeleen had explained to her what had really happened all those years ago to spook them into leaving the safety of their protected tiny house.

But even if the guards had seen them, even if they'd been exposed, it'd still felt like being forced to leave the only family she'd ever known. Even if it was for her own protection, it had still hurt. She knew that if Ariella or Faeleen had been caught, they'd have been executed for their magic. But Emmalee might've been too, even if her dark magic hadn't manifested until many years later.

They hadn't wanted her to fall under the same scrutiny.

Now, though, she had magic too. Now she was just as much a danger to the king as the sisters.

And even if she hadn't fully understood it as a child, something good had come out of the separation from Ariella and Faeleen.

She'd found her own sister.

Not by blood, but by the bonds they'd created from the moment Emmalee came across the young girl with white-blond hair.

She'd left these two sisters to find her own.

And now her sister was probably locked in a dark cellar drowning in chains.

Waiting for her.

Chapter 5

EVANGELINE

It'd gotten worse.

And it'd gotten worse fast.

Evangeline shivered in the darkness, her toes like icicles beneath her. It didn't matter what position she lay in, whether she was curled in a ball or sitting with her legs tucked up to her chest and her tunic around them, she couldn't get warm. And moving was exhausting.

Two weeks had passed since the last time the king had interrogated her and she'd tried to steal a roll. Odette had tried to get her to eat, but the longer Evangeline wasted away down there, the less she felt hungry. It was like every time she did take a bite of whatever disgusting food they brought, her gut turned, and twice she'd emptied her stomach—not that there was anything but bile.

She drank the water offered, but it was getting more and more difficult to move across the cell to get it.

Despite her best efforts, her wrists ached all the time, and the skin around the cuffs was angry and hot. It made signing painful enough that unless it was extremely important, Evangeline didn't sign. Odette continued to, which blocked out half of their conversations, hopefully making them confusing enough that the other prisoners didn't pick up on anything important that could be used against either of them.

In the single ray of light that shone down through the barred window in the afternoon, it was clear that the wounds from the cuffs had gotten infected, even with the strips of fabric acting as a buffer. No surprise, since everything about the dungeon was filthy.

If she were at her workshop, or even her previous employer's workshop, she could make herself medicine to fix the illness and the injuries. But there wasn't much she could do from her cell except try to slide more cloth beneath the metal. She'd cleaned out the wounds with the drinking water brought to her for a while until that proved ineffective.

Evangeline tried to turn over onto her other side, but she moaned when the metal pulled at her fragile skin.

"What is it?" Odette asked out loud, and though Evangeline could hear her friend moving closer to her, she couldn't gather enough strength to sit up and talk to her.

"I'm fine," Evangeline said, barely able to speak without coughing.

"Not the word I'd use," Odette muttered, and she shuffled around in her cell. After a few seconds, she whispered to Evangeline again. "Can you sit up?"

"I don't know," Evangeline said, her eyes still closed. Her voice sounded weak to her own ears.

"I have bread, and I've pulled off most of the moldy parts. You need to eat."

"I'm not hungry."

It was true. Her body had given up on food. The hunger she'd experienced over the months she'd spent there had dwindled and died with the rats scurrying around the dirty stone floors.

Maybe it was easier that way. As much as she hated to even consider it, if she starved to death—or if this sickness killed her first—she wouldn't be able to tell the king anything that could hurt Emmalee. Evangeline shivered again. No. She wasn't doing it on purpose. She knew she needed the bread for energy, but she could barely think of eating without feeling nauseated.

"Just a little piece," Odette said, her voice soft and motherly. "Come on, sit up."

Evangeline grimaced, her weak muscles aching and her wrists burning as she tried to get out of her huddled position on the floor. But before she could make it all the way to a seated position, the sound of footsteps echoed down the stairway.

"That's not good," Odette muttered, and Evangeline agreed.

It wasn't time for the guards to bring the next round of inedible food, nor was it time for them to clean out the sad excuse for a toilet—a bucket that sat in the corner of each cell.

45

Still struggling to sit, Evangeline managed to prop herself up in time to see two guards come around the corner to the staircase. Just as she'd expected, they marched straight to her cell. However, after they both caught sight of her, they exchanged hesitant glances.

"The king wants to speak with you," the clearly younger one said.

As was normal, Evangeline didn't respond. But she couldn't stop the cough that had her crumpling back over. It was deep within her lungs, and it stung the back of her throat as it shook her whole body.

One of the guards unlocked the cell and approached Evangeline.

"Can you stand?" he asked, his voice carrying less of a bark than normal.

Evangeline tried to get up, but she barely made it to her knees before her head swirled, and she thought she might be sick for the third time.

"I'll take that as a no. Jax, get in here," he said, motioning for the other man.

The younger guard came in and told the other guard to help lift her. Together, they gripped her on either side, using her upper arms to pull her to her feet.

Her body ached to the point of a moan slipping from between her cracked lips. The jostling was worse than the fire in her wrists. She wanted to cry, wanted them to just leave her in the cell. It'd hurt less that way.

Out of the corner of her eye, Evangeline noticed Odette watching her with wide eyes, a frown across her face. When she caught Evangeline staring, the concern seemed to double, and her friend jumped to her feet.

"She needs help. And food. Look at her, she's about to collapse. You have to get her help," Odette said, risking whatever punishment came with ordering the royal guards about.

But they didn't punish Odette. As far as Evangeline could tell, they simply ignored her.

Mentally, Evangeline thanked her friend for trying to help, even if she couldn't verbally say it because of another coughing fit and her vow of silence in front of the king and his men.

She couldn't stand by herself, let alone walk.

The stairs out of the dungeon, which she'd climbed many times before, seemed to go on forever. The two men had to drag her, and she tried to hide the pain in her face as her shins bumped into each stair, but she couldn't move her legs. Her chest hurt, both from coughing and from the pure exertion of the trek to the king's office.

It seemed like the journey would never end. The lights were too bright. The sounds too loud. The pace too quick. The only thing that came as a relief was the fresh air, some of which blew through open windows they passed in the corridors. But even with the warm cross breezes, Evangeline shivered. She'd never felt so cold in her life, even when she'd been around Emmalee's dark magic.

She trembled as she waited for the guards to be invited into the king's office, and despite the pain and exhaustion spread throughout her body, Evangeline clenched her jaw and prepared to be interrogated. Maybe the king would finally put her out of her misery.

No. She tried to stop her mind from falling down that way of thinking, but it was getting too difficult to stop the invasive thoughts. The more her body hurt, the more she wanted to be freed from it.

Evangeline glared at the door as it opened. Her body was weak. Too weak. But her mind? That remained mostly intact. Her mind—her determination— would make up for her frail body.

At least, she hoped it would.

The door to the king's office, though large, was not big enough for both guards and Evangeline to pass through at the same time. The younger guard kept Evangeline upright, the other guard following behind.

Butch had barely glanced up from his desk before he sent the guards away. The two men seemed to hesitate, but they saluted, and Evangeline was left to stand in the middle of the room by herself as they exited behind her. Her knees trembled, and the room started to turn as she blinked, fighting hard to remain standing. She would not cave. She was strong. She was . . . She was going to be sick.

Thorne's icy-blue gaze scanned over her, and Evangeline tried to keep her chin lifted. His eyes widened.

"Sit down," Thorne said, his voice commanding, but there was something else under it. Concern?

Evangeline's head swam as she tried to keep her focus on the map; however, it began to swirl, and she blinked multiple times. Her body swayed to the right, but she stumbled and caught herself before she went down.

"You need to sit—no!"

The chair was too far. Evangeline reached for it, hoping to use it to steady herself, but it remained just out of reach as she fell forward, smacking her head on the inside of her arm. She lay on her stomach and could hear two sets of footsteps thundering toward her. A large hand turned her so she stared at the ceiling.

Around the edges of her vision, the world darkened. Just before it closed in on her, she could hear a distant voice talking about a physician. The last thing she saw was the color blue.

A STAMPEDE THUNDERED in Evangeline's head when she came to, causing a moan to escape from between her dry lips. Her body ached from her head down to her toes. She blinked a few times before fully opening her eyes.

The room they'd brought her to was filled with light, both from windows and lanterns along the long walls. Beds sat in lines alongside her and across the room from her, but only a few others were occupied. She was in the bed farthest from what appeared to be the only door.

A ray of light rested over the blankets covering her, and for the first time in what felt like forever, she didn't feel chilled or cold. In fact, something else spread through her the more she awoke.

Warmth. Unnatural warmth.

Evangeline's eyes widened when she glanced down at her wrists and found them free of the magic-dampening chains that'd bound her since her arrest. Instead, her wrists were covered in bandages.

Glancing around, Evangeline checked to see if anyone was watching her. With a deep breath, she called on her magic. A ripple of heat traveled down her left arm, which she lowered beside her. Hidden away from the rest of the room, a small grin stretched across her face as an orb of light the size of an egg appeared in the middle of her hand.

Tears slid down her cheeks, and she squeezed her eyes shut as she relished the warmth of the sun and her light magic. She was grinning like a fool when she heard footsteps to her right. Her eyes snapped open.

The orb of light disappeared, and the smile vanished from her face within a second. She glanced to the side. If she'd been caught doing magic . . .

"You're awake. Good," said an older woman with a scarf wrapped around her head. The maroon scarf covered all her hair, and she wore a long robe in a light cream shade. "You were in bad shape. I've been trying to get

His Majesty to make some changes in the dungeons since he was coronated. Maybe now he'll finally listen to me. How are you feeling?"

Evangeline hesitated before responding, questioning whether her vow of silence should extend to the castle physicians as well. They did, after all, work for the king.

The debate residing within her mind must've been visible on her face, because the woman spoke again.

"You were brought in here by the king himself, and he made it clear that you were to receive whatever care necessary to bring you back to full health."

Evangeline frowned, her left hand gripping the blanket in a fist. While she figured the physician meant the words to be reassuring, a sense of dread filled her instead. If the king wanted her alive, it meant more seemingly endless months of interrogations and dungeon time. Would they chain her up again? Take away her magic?

"You aren't the first prisoner he's sent up here, you know," the old woman said as she moved a tray from a table across the room to the one next to Evangeline's bed. "Though you were certainly in the worst shape. Slept for two days straight. If he'd just make some changes . . ." The woman rambled on, oblivious to whether or not Evangeline was listening.

She wasn't.

A loud debate resounded within Evangeline's mind, and she bit the inside of her cheek. Some part of her was struck by the urge to talk to the woman. The other reasonable and hardened part of her wanted nothing more than to wield her magic and send the woman who worked for the king across the room. That part of her wanted to destroy, to leave the king's castle in a state of disarray. Evangeline quickly shoved the thought deep, *deep* within her.

The woman was helping her. Evangeline tried to focus on that as she took a shaky breath. To her surprise, her chest didn't hurt as much.

The physician motioned for Evangeline to hold out her right wrist, and she did. Grimacing, Evangeline watched the woman unwrap the bandage. It stuck to her skin, and Evangeline gritted her teeth when the woman tugged the bandage free. The skin beneath was raw and red, and a layer of white ooze covered it.

"Your wrists are infected, which is what caused your fever. It also doesn't help that you clearly haven't been eating. Was that on purpose?"

Evangeline glanced at the woman to see her staring intently at her. She shook her head, and the woman nodded.

"No, I would hope not. I doubt I'd want to eat the rubbish they send down there. Well, I'll make sure you're taken care of up here, dear. Unfortunately for you, this infection is serious, and in order to get it to go away and stay away, you'll have to take medicine." The physician released Evangeline's wrist and grabbed a small bottle about the size of a lemon. She handed it to Evangeline.

When Evangeline pulled the cork out of the bottle, she cringed away from the putrid smell. It must've been quite acidic, because it felt like a single sniff would burn all her nose hairs. But there was something else beneath the acidity, something musty. Just as she was starting to recall the ingredients in the apothecary shop owned by her previous employer, Elthia, that might contribute to a draft like the one she held, the physician spoke.

"Drink it all." The physician watched her with narrowed eyes.

Letting out a deep breath, Evangeline didn't breathe again until she had downed the whole bottle. The second she finished it, her stomach seized. She wanted to retch. The taste was worse than the smell, and she squeezed her eyes shut, clenching the blanket with her left hand while trying not to move her right as the physician held it loosely in her grasp again.

"Unpleasant, I know. But you must take it three times a day for a month or until the infection is gone."

Evangeline, eyes still closed, nodded. Having worked as an apprentice in an apothecary's shop, she knew full well that when instructions about a medicine were given, they were to be followed strictly for the full effect. Too many times people had returned to Elthia's shop claiming the remedies for their issues hadn't worked. However, when asked if they'd followed the instructions, most, if not all of them, had failed. Elthia had no pity for those who couldn't follow instructions, and Evangeline had a feeling this physician would be the same in that regard.

"Take it when you first wake, then again in the afternoon, and right before you go to bed, always on an empty stomach," the woman said, putting a greenish salve on the wound before rewrapping Evangeline's wrist. The salve burned and smelled familiar; it was probably something else she'd come across in Elthia's shop.

Having made up her mind, Evangeline waited until the woman had wrapped her other wrist and was leaving to go attend to a person moaning four beds down from her before she spoke.

"Thank you," Evangeline said, her voice still weak but stronger than it had been when she'd last spoken.

The physician stopped and offered her a small smile. "It's my job, dear," she said, then took the tray from the bedside and walked away.

Evangeline watched her go, then closed her eyes. Although she didn't feel nearly as dreadful as she had when she'd collapsed in front of the king and marshal, she still felt nauseated and her lungs ached dully, probably from coughing.

The door to the infirmary creaked open before Evangeline could fall asleep, and she cracked one eye open to see whether someone had entered or left.

She pretended to be asleep as soon as she saw Thorne speaking in a whispered voice to the physician who'd attended her. It had only been a few minutes since the woman had left Evangeline's bedside, but she hoped it was long enough that she could feign sleep without being caught.

Measured footsteps sounded down the long room, and Evangeline tried to make her breathing as even as possible. Her eyes fluttered, and she questioned how tight to close them.

"I know you're awake," Thorne said from the right of her, where the physician had stood.

Evangeline waited a few seconds longer before giving up. She opened her eyes but refused to look at him, choosing instead to stare up at the tall windows. From the angle she lay, she could only see the sky, which didn't hold a trace of a cloud amidst the sea of blue.

"How are you feeling?" he asked, pulling up a stool from the bed next to hers. It scratched across the floor and squeaked as he sat down.

Tightening her lips as well as her grasp on the blanket, Evangeline bit down on her tongue. She'd made the mistake of speaking to him a few times since her arrest, and she was bound and determined not to do it again. It didn't help that he spoke in a friendly enough way that she almost wanted to speak to him.

Enemy. He was the enemy. If only she could scrawl it across the insides of her eyelids.

"Evie."

The sound of him saying her name sent chills through her, and she clenched every muscle to keep from showing it. Unless he had told someone her name, he and Odette were the only two who knew it within the whole castle. Even during the copious interrogation sessions, the king had never called her by her name.

"Look at me."

51

She squinted even more into the light. He was maybe kinder than the Mongoose, but he'd tried to kill Emmalee, not to mention he'd been the one who'd arrested her that night.

She could still feel his rough grip on her arms as he'd pressed her against the tree.

His breath against the shell of her ear . . .

"Evie," he said again, and this time he reached forward and placed a hand on her arm.

"Don't touch me!" Evangeline rasped, yanking her arm away and scrambling off the other side of the bed. The quick movement had her head reeling, and she blinked rapidly in the hope that it would calm the swaying world around her. Leaning forward, she caught herself on the bed before she fell over, and she took several deep breaths to clear her head. But they didn't help, and she was fairly certain the floor was going to be her new bed if the slightest breeze tickled her.

Thorne had jumped to his feet, one hand on the hilt of his sword and the other outstretched as if he was trying to decide between attempting to catch her or strike her down from the other side of the cot.

Evangeline's outburst had drawn the attention of the physician, and she scurried across the room to the two of them.

"Get back in bed," she ordered, her lips tight, hiding any of the hints of compassion she'd shown before. "You'll do yourself no good by cracking your head open on the floor."

Pointing at Thorne with a trembling finger, Evangeline shook her head. Big mistake. The room swung. "T-tell him to leave."

The physician snorted. "I'll do no such thing. Marshal Thorne is here by the king's orders. Now get in bed before I *make* you."

With a wary glance at the guard, Evangeline tightened her jaw and sat back down—or rather, collapsed—on the cot as far from the marshal as possible. In the moment of panic, her magic had flared, and she was shaking trying to keep it from showing. Thorne knew about it, but the physician did not. Well, as far as Evangeline knew. Maybe Thorne had warned her.

"If you need me, holler," the physician said to the marshal before she curtsied and went back to the front of the room.

"Thank you, Helena," he said, watching the old woman. He waited until she was taking care of another person before he sat back down on the stool.

"Let's try this again, shall we?" Thorne said, straightening his jacket. "How are you feeling?"

Evangeline glared at him, and for the first time since being in the castle, she almost missed the cuffs that had infected her and made her sick. Her magic danced in flames just below the surface, scalding her in its silent demand to be freed. She was doing everything she could to keep it in check. At least with the cuffs, she could focus on hating him and the king without being distracted by the magic flaring inside her stomach.

He waited in the silence, his brilliant gaze not leaving her face for a second. She hadn't really had the chance to take in his appearance for an extended amount of time, at least not this close or with him in his royal guard clothing. Even in the interrogations, she'd tried not to stare at him for too long.

He was an enemy.

A threat to her best friend and to her.

And yet . . . he was undeniably, infuriatingly stunning. Absolutely handsome.

His hair was well-kept—brown waves that were longer on the top than the sides—and his facial hair was closely trimmed and short. It didn't hide the angles of his jaw, and a small white patch grew on the left, which was unfortunate since he probably would've had a very symmetrical face otherwise.

Her hatred for herself doubled with every second she stared in awe at his beautiful face, entranced by his eyes, the passion behind the crashing cerulean waves.

Yes, she despised herself.

And him more so.

"Evie," he said, pulling her focus back. "We need to talk."

Chapter 6

SILAS

Silas stared at Evie. Though it didn't seem possible, he knew how much power radiated through her thin frame, especially with the cuffs removed from her wrists. He understood the reason behind it—they'd caused the infection that'd nearly killed her—yet he sat as if a rod were shoved up his spine, waiting for the slightest indication that she was calling her magic.

Not because he was threatened by it—she couldn't hurt him in that moment—but because others were present in the infirmary, and he assumed they would fall prey more easily to the strength of her light magic.

At the thought, his mind yanked him back to the gully the day she'd saved the king's life, the image of her standing above them showered in blinding light. Radiant. Powerful. It was burned into his mind as surely as the burn mark she'd left on his chest the day of the boulder field.

A moment of weakness, to be sure.

"Well?" she asked, her voice tense. "Talk."

Silas lifted his chin, leveling her with his gaze—one that would've made some of the newer recruits to the royal guard shift uncomfortably.

She met it.

And matched it.

"You need to tell the king what you know about Estrada," he said, watching her narrowed eyes drop to his mouth as if she were reading his lips rather than listening to him. A thin layer of sweat was forming over her skin, and for a moment, he wondered if she was going to be sick.

"No," she muttered, squeezing her eyes shut as she leaned back into the thin pillow. "I won't."

Silas stuck his tongue into his cheek, pausing for a moment to think through his words before they passed between his lips. It was a skill he'd learned back when Butch's father was still king. And considering his position, even when King Valryn was alive, it'd been a wise skill to learn.

"She's killed his men, *my* men." He watched her for any reaction, of which she gave none, before continuing. "Even if she didn't have magic, that's still a crime that demands punishment."

Her brow furrowed, though she kept her eyes shut. Any rosiness that had been in her cheeks upon his entrance into the infirmary was gone, replaced with paleness. He had a feeling she was fighting back some sort of nausea. She coughed into her fist, her face pinching into a grimace a second later. Her white-blond hair appeared a greasy, matted mess, and dirt and grime covered her exposed skin.

Helena had looked ready to throw him out the infirmary window when he and Butch had brought her in. Though she'd waited to reprimand Silas until the king was gone.

"To think you'd allow a young woman to be at death's doorstep before you actually treated her like a human. I expect better from you, Silas. What would Lucille have said?"

He shook his head to clear the thought. Lucille, the woman who'd adopted him after his parents died, would've been disappointed in him too.

And she wouldn't have just *threatened* to throw him out the window.

She *would've*.

Silas sighed, forcing his mind back to Evie before the ghosts haunting him could add to his growing guilt after seeing the prisoner in such terrible shape.

"If you help the king find her, you'll be helping the country."

"And betraying my best friend. I won't do it, Thorne. You're wasting your time." She opened her eyes, glaring at him.

Silas stiffened. The sound of his name on her lips, even with as gravelly as her voice was, left heat rising in his stomach. He clenched his jaw. There were reactions he could control in his body, and there were others he couldn't. Best to make the ones he could control be what she noticed.

"Wasting my time?" He sneered, refusing to let the effect of hearing her say his name show. "I don't think I am." His gaze narrowed. "Rest up. The

55

king will want to speak to you as soon as you're able. And if you try to use your *magic*"—he whispered the word as he gestured toward her hands—"the magic-dampening cuffs will be the least of your worries."

Silas stood to leave, but she stopped him dead in his tracks with a single question. One that had his stomach plummeting.

"Why did you let me go those other times in the Black Forest only to arrest me that night?"

With his back to her, he wrinkled his nose. He should've known the questions would rise. It was only a matter of time.

But if she put the pieces together . . .

He replaced his pinched expression with a scowl, grasping deeply to the hope that she would be intimidated, preventing further questions. Silas turned to face her.

She met his glare with one of her own; the only sign that she wasn't as confident as she seemed was how she glanced at the sword on his belt before meeting his gaze again.

With a steady calm, Silas sat back down, leaning forward to further his intimidation after a quick glance over his shoulder. He knew his tactics were working when her cinnamon-brown eyes widened, frantically scanning his face.

"Why would I waste time with a meek little fox when a wolf lurked elsewhere in the forest?"

He expected her to wilt. Expected the same reaction he got from some of the more unruly guards when he whipped them into shape.

But her glare turned venomous. For a second, light sparked in those eyes, a flicker of the magic she hid so well.

"I am *not* a fox," she snapped, her voice strained.

Silas sat straight, pulling away from where he leaned over her—not in fear, but in surprise.

"Down there," he said, nodding in the direction of the dungeon, "in that cell, you are whatever the king tells you to be. At this point, your life is in his hands." Silas tilted his head as he stood, a small smirk crossing his face. "I suggest you start talking and give him a reason to keep you alive."

Without another word, he spun on his heels and marched out of the infirmary.

Chapter 7

EVANGELINE

It had been a mistake trying to stand up, and Evangeline split her attention between reining in her magic and trying not to vomit long after Thorne left. The medicine was not sitting well in her empty stomach, and when combined with the nauseating effect of a spinning room, she was finding not vomiting more and more difficult.

When a servant brought in a tray of food and it didn't have a trace of mold or staleness on it, she almost cried. It was nothing special: a roll, a small piece of what seemed to be boiled chicken, and a bruised apple. The portions were extremely small, yet she eagerly awaited the first bite.

Before she could enjoy her dinner, a little bottle of medicine stared up at her from the tray. She was surprised Helena wasn't there to make sure she took it. Then again, there was no reason not to take it. She hadn't intentionally gotten sick or stopped eating. And if taking the nasty draft meant her headaches and aching would go away, it was worth it.

After pulling out the cork, Evangeline pinched her nose with two fingers and downed the disgusting liquid. Unlike the first time, it burned going down her throat. She shuddered.

Besides healing her of the infection, the medicine did have one other benefit: the food was even more delectable after the putrid taste of the draft. Evangeline cherished every single bite, starting with the fluffy roll, then moving on to the tender chicken and then the sweet crisp apple. It was wonderful.

Until her stomach rolled and she emptied it onto the floor.

"You need to start slower," a physician, different from the one before, said after she'd finished cleaning the floor beneath Evangeline's bed. "If what Helena said is true, then the time you spent not eating is going to take a while to reverse."

"Helena?" Evangeline asked, pushing the tray of food away.

"The older woman who was here before me. She went home for the evening. I'm Dianna."

Dianna was likely a few years older than Evangeline. She was pale, like she didn't spend more than a few days a month in the sun. Her hair, like Helena's, was wrapped in a maroon scarf—although a curl of red hair showed just behind her ear. Dianna also wore the cream-colored robe, and it shouldn't have taken Evangeline as long as it did to realize it was a uniform.

"It's nice to meet you," Evangeline said, offering a small smile. Maybe it was the sun she'd lain in all day or the lighter environment of the infirmary, but something had put her in a better mood, especially after the marshal had left and not returned.

"How long have you been here?" Dianna asked, sitting on the same stool Thorne had.

Evangeline frowned. "Helena didn't tell you?"

Dianna smiled wider this time, revealing a large gap between her two front teeth. "She told me you've been in here"—she gestured to the room—"for a little over two days, but I mean the castle."

"Oh," Evangeline said, tucking a piece of hair behind her ear. It was still greasy and felt horrible to touch, but it was worse when it pressed against her face. "I'm not sure, but I'd guess somewhere around three and a half, maybe four months."

"Really?" Dianna asked. She'd folded her hands in her lap, reminding Evangeline of the way her stepsister, Linetta, sat when she was listening intently. "And you've been in the dungeon the whole time?"

Evangeline nodded. With the questions Dianna was asking, she was becoming more aware of the fact that she was speaking to an absolute stranger.

"And the injuries to your wrists, that was from—"

"Cuffs. Dianna," Evangeline said, offering a small smile, "could you get me some water please?" She held up the empty cup. "I'm still feeling a little sick, and I think it'd help."

"Of course!" Dianna said, taking the cup from Evangeline. She moved the tray of food to the table next to the bed. "Remember to take it slow," she said before leaving.

After being sick, whatever hunger Evangeline had felt was gone. She didn't want to look at the partially eaten apple or the few pieces of chicken she'd left behind, let alone consume them.

Instead, Evangeline curled up on her side, allowing her magic to warm her from the inside out. Her breaths drew more even as she drifted off to sleep.

A dream swept Evangeline away, and she followed what looked like a sparkling stream through a dim cave. The water was fluorescent, a mixture of bright blues and purples, and while the air around her was cooler, it wasn't unpleasant.

Evangeline ran her hand along the arched rock wall around her, intrigued by the smooth surface and the silky residue that came away on her fingers.

She followed the stream until it got bigger and the cave opened up into a pool of crystal clear water. From where she stood on the edge, she couldn't tell how deep the water was, not because she couldn't see the bottom—she could—but because she knew water could be deceiving. Especially clear water.

Still, she stared into the pool, contemplating jumping in. Curious, Evangeline stuck her big toe in, frowning when she couldn't discern whether the water was hot or cold.

Evangeline glanced around, but in the half-spherical cave room, nothing but the pool in front of her caught her attention. Finding nothing better to do, Evangeline sat down on the edge and watched as the fabric of her trousers darkened when the moisture climbed up past where the water hit her calves.

Because of the strange temperature in the water, it almost felt like her legs had detached from her body, and she glanced down just to make sure they were still there.

Evangeline blinked a few times when a face appeared at the bottom of the pool. When it showed itself again, Evangeline scrambled back from the edge, clinging to the wall.

It had been Emmalee's face. Her friend had stared back at her through the light refracting in the water. But something wasn't right. Her cheeks had been too sallow and her eyes too hollow. Like a ghost.

Evangeline, shaking, rose to her feet and wrapped her arms around herself as she looked back down. The bottom of the pool was empty. She sighed, wiping her hand across her clammy forehead. Once again, she glanced down at the pool—and screamed.

She fell backward when the distorted Emmalee burst through the water, splashing her in the face.

"Why didn't you help me?" Emmalee said, floating over the pool of water toward Evangeline. Water dripped off her, and Emmalee's dark hair looked pitch-black in its wet state.

"What?" Evangeline asked, pushing herself as far back as the cave would allow.

"You told them where I was. You betrayed me." Emmalee's voice shrieked in Evangeline's head, ringing over and over again.

"No, no I didn't!" Evangeline cried, putting her hands up to protect herself when Emmalee floated closer. "Em, please!"

Evangeline sat straight up in her bed in the infirmary, sweat pouring off her in waves.

"Easy now," Dianna cooed, wiping a cold cloth over Evangeline's forehead. "You need to lie down. Your fever got worse after you fell asleep."

With a frantic look at her surroundings, Evangeline let Dianna push her back down, wiping her forehead again.

A dream. It'd been a dream. Or a nightmare. As she tried to catch her breath, Evangeline thought of Emmalee, knowing her friend would never attack her like that.

And she would never betray Emmalee.

EVANGELINE STARED AT the ceiling. As wonderful as the sun was as it poured down through the window, spilling over the blanket covering her, it didn't do much to help pass the time. In fact, without Odette to talk to, time crawled by slowly in the infirmary.

With each meal, Evangeline took the medicine Helena had prescribed to her. Either Helena or Dianna rewrapped her wrists once a day, and by the looks of it, the infection was disappearing.

She wondered how much of her improvement was due to the sunshine. Evangeline's next breath caught in her throat, and she tried to swallow but ended up choking.

Her mother had wanted to be in the sunshine when she'd gotten sick. It wasn't possible, though, since Bowhoo was so deep in the Black Forest.

Evangeline had made the mistake of trying to convince her stepfather to take her mother somewhere to see the sun. He'd shouted at her, told her that if she wanted to take her mother somewhere, she could do it herself.

Instead, Ellayne, Evangeline's mother, had died in the darkness. Evangeline had done what she could to fill her mother's room with light, spending nearly all her money for a year on candles and lanterns to put around her mother as she lay in bed.

It hadn't helped.

Evangeline leaned back into her pillow, blinking away tears as she tried to fight the memory of seeing her mother grow weaker and weaker with each day. It had been the longest year of Evangeline's life. It didn't help that Emmalee had moved away the same year to go teach in a new school, leaving Evangeline alone with Jonathan Dipthy. Thankfully, she'd at least had a friend in Jonathan's daughter.

Linetta, Evangeline's stepsister, was a few years younger and nothing like her father. Evangeline stared at the sky through the window as she thought about Linetta. Was she okay? Was she worried about her? Evangeline snorted, knowing the answer was probably a resounding yes, especially considering the state Evangeline had left the bookshop in the last time she'd been there after sending her stepfather flying into a shelf, knocking it and all of the books onto the floor.

At least Jonathan couldn't get back at her in the castle. Evangeline rolled her eyes at the morose thought. In all actuality, she'd likely never see either of them again.

For Linetta, she mourned the thought.

For Jonathan, she rejoiced.

She'd never have to hear him call her "*lizna*," little fox, again. Never be his pawn again.

Evangeline frowned.

At what point had she resigned herself to staying in the castle forever? At what point had she decided her fate would be to never taste freedom again?

"No," Evangeline whispered, her hands clenching into fists as her magic swelled. She kept it hidden, just out of sight. If there was any time to escape, it would be while she was out of the dungeon without the cuffs suffocating her magic.

There were risks, to be sure. If she was caught, there was a slim chance the king wouldn't have her executed, especially since she hadn't given him any information regarding Emmalee. And she wasn't sure how far she could travel, as weakened as she was.

But the constant food and the lack of dampening chains had helped strengthen her, even if it wasn't back to full health. That, she knew, would take time and perhaps some sort of strength training.

Even if she could only get out of the castle walls, surely she could find a place to hide. And then she could find Emmalee. They could start over.

She needed to get out.

If there was any time to escape, it was before Helena deemed her healthy enough to return to the hopeless pits beneath the castle.

If there was any time to escape, it was while she was unattended and unguarded.

If anything, the time was now.

Chapter 8

EMMALEE

Emmalee bit the end of the rune pen absentmindedly. Glancing over the rune she'd drawn with a normal pen, she compared it to the image in the book she'd copied it from. Her lines weren't as straight, and the curve at the top was wonky. But otherwise, she could at least tell which rune it was.

As she'd always told her students, practice makes perfect.

The book she was reading, as well as a few others, had mentioned the importance of getting basic strokes down by using a normal pen. So, while she'd waited for Ariella to find her a rune pen, she'd practiced. And ever since getting the rune pen a few days earlier, she had yet to try with the actual tool.

It was almost as if all the urgency and desire to help Evangeline had disappeared and been replaced by worry. A small voice in the back of her mind whispered the thoughts she didn't want to hear. What if she failed again like in the boulder field? What if she couldn't save Evangeline in time? What if she did something wrong and Ariella and Faeleen took the fall? What if she couldn't do a simple rune?

While she had read over and over in the books that those with pure magic—light and dark—could perform rune magic, which was done out of mixed family lines and by nonhumans, it wasn't a given.

Rune magic needed to be studied, and having been a teacher, she felt as though drawing the first rune was ultimately a test. She didn't want to fail.

Taking the rune pen out of her mouth where she'd been chewing on the end, she picked up the ink pen and traced the same rune, the one for light, on a spare sheet of parchment. The first one was crooked and the second was lopsided. The third one was closer to the rune represented in the book, but the line weight was heavier on the downstrokes—Emmalee didn't know if that mattered, but she wasn't about to take chances.

After fifteen minutes of trying to get the runes to match, Emmalee slumped back against the wall. Despite the small desk in Ariella and Faeleen's guest room, Emmalee had set up on the floor. More space to stretch out, and the chair for the desk creaked with any type of movement.

Unfortunately, sitting on the floor was doing terrible things to her back and posture. She stretched, cringing when the muscles in her back spasmed. Extending her right leg, Emmalee leaned forward until she touched her toes, then did the same with the other leg.

She rubbed her right shoulder, which still ached from time to time. The place where a royal guard had hit her with an arrow had scarred, but only after a terrible infection had almost killed her. Her hand tightened around the curve of her shoulder as she rolled her neck in circles.

Emmalee had no idea how long she had been sitting, but it had apparently been long enough that her muscles thought she was never going to move again and had solidified. Her stomach grumbled as she started to move, awakening from its long slumber to remind her it was still there and needed to be refilled.

Just like when they were younger—and Emmalee had finally gotten old enough—Emmalee and the sisters had fallen into a routine of taking turns making dinner. Though, with her face still on wanted posters throughout Phildeterre, Emmalee had been limited to the supplies Ariella or Faeleen brought in from the market. It was an easy-enough task, and just like when she'd abducted the queen, Emmalee found a sort of peace in preparing meals for the sisters.

However, the happiness and enjoyment she'd once found in cooking and baking for her husband and daughter was gone, destroyed when she lost them over a year earlier. It wasn't until she was cooking for the queen during the time Emmalee had held her captive that she realized she'd just been doing the bare minimum to keep her own stomach satisfied and her body functioning.

It was different cooking just for herself.

The sisters tended to enjoy meat more often than she did, but she'd found several recipes that they seemed to enjoy and stuck to those for the most part. It wasn't her turn to cook though, and she walked out to the kitchen to find Faeleen covered in a layer of flour.

"Is this a new look, or . . . ?" Emmalee asked, drawing out the word as she leaned against the counter and smirked.

"Shut it," Faeleen hissed, flicking flour in Emmalee's direction. "I was trying to do something nice for Ari's birthday, but I didn't use a large-enough mixing bowl."

Emmalee chuckled as she crossed the room. "I'll grab a rag."

"May as well wait. I'm inevitably going to make a larger mess until this thing is done." Faeleen nodded to the bowl filled to the brim with dry ingredients.

"Want help?" Emmalee paused halfway to the drawer in which they kept the extra rags. She grabbed an apple from the fruit bowl next to her instead, chomping down. It was almost too ripe for her—not enough crunch.

"Grab the bigger mixing bowl from the top shelf, would you?" Faeleen asked, directing Emmalee to the correct cabinet. "Thanks," she responded, dumping the ingredients from one bowl into the other. "Will you make sure Ari stays down in the shop until I have all of this cleaned up? It's a surprise. I don't think she knows I'm doing this."

"Sure," Emmalee said, nodding as she headed toward the stairs leading down to the shop. She was smiling. Faeleen had made cakes for Ariella and Emmalee growing up; however, they'd chosen a random day to celebrate Emmalee's birthday since none of them actually knew when it was. It'd never bothered Emmalee though. The sisters had made a big-enough deal out of the day they'd chosen that she hadn't even known it wasn't her birthday—not until she'd asked Ariella how they knew she was turning another year older on her seventh birthday. In truth, Emmalee wasn't even sure how old she was. Not really. She'd always guessed, though, based off Ariella and Faeleen's estimations. And she'd stuck with the birthday.

By her guess, she'd be twenty-seven that year. She wondered what kind of cake Faeleen would make for her or if she'd still be with them to even celebrate. Maybe, if all went well, Evangeline would be with them too.

Maybe.

"I'll make sure she stays in the shop. See you in a bit." Emmalee took another bite from the apple as she trotted down the stairs, leaving the thoughts of Evangeline behind before they lowered her good mood.

It was strange how she'd returned to an easy rhythm with the sisters. If not for the nightmares and the dark magic reminding her of the scars inscribed on her heart, she could almost imagine what it would've been like if she hadn't separated from them as a child.

Especially when the first words out of Ariella's mouth when Emmalee entered the shop were, "Fae's making a mess, isn't she?"

Emmalee finished her bite of the apple before shrugging and saying, "Does it surprise you anymore?"

"Not when she's been doing it since the tiny house." Ariella sat at a table, a sewing needle and spool of thread in hand. "Could you tell what flavor?"

"Nope. Smelled a bit like cinnamon and cloves though."

A smile crossed Ariella's bright red lips. "Then maybe she picked up on my clues about a spiced cake this year."

Emmalee didn't respond as she sat on the edge of the table, staring at the mannequins clothed in brightly colored fabrics. "What are you working on?"

Ariella nodded toward the cream-colored fabric next to Emmalee's left hand. "The castle sent out an order for servant uniforms."

"Do you get many orders from the castle?" Emmalee asked, frowning at the material. Her stomach twisted at the thought of Ariella and Faeleen serving the king, even if he likely didn't even know about the order.

"Every once in a while. There's another fabric shop closer to Cyanthia, but when they get overwhelmed, they send extra orders to us—though they typically hoard the castle orders themselves and send us the others." Ariella paused, and Emmalee glanced at her. Her slitted eyes were narrowed, her brow furrowed. "Come to think of it, they must have quite a few other orders from the castle if they sent us such a big one."

"Wonder why," Emmalee muttered. She shook her head, pushing away thoughts of the castle and her friend trapped within it.

"Any luck with the runes?"

"No. I haven't tried with the pen yet." Emmalee took a bite of her apple.

"Scared of failing?"

Emmalee raised an eyebrow as she looked at her friend. "Speaking from experience?"

Ariella snorted, a strand of blond hair falling in her face. "Of course. Magic is always intimidating at first. At least, it is with rune magic. I would assume it's the same for yours."

After considering her words, Emmalee shook her head. "No. Not initially. It was . . . comforting." Emmalee stared at a point on the floor just in front of her boots. "In a moment of pure pain and hurt, my magic tried to help." She glanced up to see Ariella staring at her. "It was startling to be sure, but it also came naturally."

"I'm sure rune magic will come naturally after some practice too. And if you want help, I might be able to give some pointers. I'm not proficient by any means, but I've picked up a few things over the years."

"You never did tell me when you started practicing. You hadn't before we left Cyanthia." Emmalee leaned against the counter, watching Ariella sew.

Ariella shook her head. "It took a few years before I had the nerve to track down a rune pen and even longer before I found an adequate book. Nearly got arrested, but I suppose that's the risk of trying to learn something the crown has deemed illegal."

Emmalee snapped her teeth down, taking a chunk out of the apple as she wrinkled her nose. When she'd finished chewing, she bit her lip. "He's continuing the mess his forefathers made." She clearly didn't need to specify, as Ariella nodded. "These new generations are growing up without a vital part of their heritage. In Shongbay, I had children who were like us, street rats. I taught them simple things, like reading and math. Most of them came from magic lines." Emmalee paused, thinking of the young children who had saved her life after her magic had manifested and she'd been shot with a crossbow the first time. She hoped they'd gotten to the North safely. She hoped more than anything they hadn't become more casualties in the long list created by the cruel war on magic. "They didn't know runes, and when Shongbay was raided, many of them died because the crown has destroyed so much knowledge."

"Maybe once you learn, you could teach rune magic. I'm sure you'd be good at it." Ariella offered her a sad smile. "Better than me, at least."

Emmalee shrugged. "I have to think about Evie first. Then I'll think about after."

Ariella nodded. "Let me know if I can help."

Emmalee didn't respond. As usual, the accidental thought of Shongbay and her family brought in a flood of painful memories—not that they'd always been painful. Before their deaths, any memory of her husband, Anwell, and her two-year-old daughter, Hazel, had brought a smile to her lips and pride to her voice.

She rubbed her hands over her face, pausing to massage her temples.

With all the power she possessed, she couldn't stop a memory of her husband from coming to the forefront of her mind.

"You're sure it's happening now?" Anwell had asked, pushing his glasses higher on his concerned face. His bushy eyebrows frowned as he scanned Emmalee's pained expression.

"Yes." Emmalee was ready to give birth, and when a contraction came, her sentences were rarely more than a single word.

"But the midwife is—"

"Out of town," Emmalee said, breathing out as the contraction ended. They had gotten even sharper and more painful after her water broke half an hour earlier.

Anwell had just gotten home from work to find her leaning over a chair with her belly hanging off the edge—it had been the only position she could find to be semicomfortable. But as the contractions advanced, nothing was comfortable.

"What do you want me to do?" Anwell held her hand, which she knew was his way of trying to comfort her, but in her present situation, it was not helping.

She pulled her hand away, using it to push her hair from her face.

"Tub. Fill it." Emmalee closed her eyes, breathing through each contraction as they got worse.

She tried not to panic. Her midwife had told her she was traveling to a village to the west to help another woman whose delivery date was before hers, but with the baby coming early, it meant Anwell and Emmalee were left alone.

But even in that, Anwell was exactly what she needed. He had been studying to become a surgeon, and although it was different, Emmalee had that much more peace knowing her husband had some medical knowledge.

Not that it calmed *him* down.

He ran about their house, following her instructions with a look of sheer panic on his face.

When the time had come for her to give birth, Anwell had reassured her. And when he'd handed Hazel to her, they'd cried together.

And leaning against the counter in Ariella and Faeleen's shop, her back to her friend, Emmalee cried again, only this time they were not tears of joy. They were angry tears—ones that burned as they streaked down her cheeks.

The king had murdered her family.

Had destroyed countless others.

"Em?" Ariella asked from behind her, but Emmalee refused to turn around.

"I need air. I'll stay in the shadows," Emmalee mumbled as she strode toward the front door. "Back in a bit."

Chapter 9

LENORA

L enora glared out the window. It'd been over an hour since she, Merla, and Kaylene had started planning the welcome banquet for the visiting delegates from the neighboring country of Jerr Pinn. Her mood had been as high as the clouds above her while she'd been gardening until Kaylene had brought her tea and mentioned that she and Merla had laid out what they'd planned for the banquet and needed her to approve of their work.

"The order for the new uniforms for the extra servants was confirmed," Kaylene said.

"And we thought it might be wise to have delicacies from both Jerr Pinn and Phildeterre for each course," Merla said from a seat across from the couch on which Lenora and Kaylene sat.

"That's a wonderful idea," Lenora said, withholding the yawn that threatened to break free.

"I've contacted a cook who specializes in Jerr Pinn cuisine." Kaylene sat with a notebook propped up on one knee, her pen hovering above the parchment. "How many courses do you think is appropriate?"

"We've done ten in the past for the annual celebration," Merla said when Lenora did not respond right away. "Do you think twelve would be better, my lady?"

Lenora nodded, her attention on the window instead of her handmaids. "That'll be fine."

The clear blue sky mocked her from behind the panes of glass, and for a moment, she was back in a tiny house in the middle of a field surrounded by the giant trees of the Black Forest. For a moment, she was a prisoner not of the rules and regulations her father had shoved down her throat since she could walk, not even of the castle and the expectations hefted upon her shoulders when she'd married Butch; instead, she was a captive of a woman who still walked through her dreams. For a moment, she was with Emmalee Estrada.

"Your Majesty?" Kaylene laid a warm hand on Lenora's knee, drawing her attention back to the small family room on the third floor of the castle.

"Sorry, my mind was elsewhere." Lenora straightened where she sat, rolling her shoulders back just as she'd been taught as a young girl. "I think it's time for a break, don't you?" Lenora went to stand, but as the room swirled around her, she had to catch herself on the edge of the couch.

"Lenora!" Kaylene gasped, leaping to her feet. The handmaid was by Lenora's side before she'd raised her hand to calm the swirling mess in her head.

"I'm all right, I'm all right," Lenora murmured, though it was a complete lie. The room still heaved around her. "I simply stood too quickly. Just give me a moment."

Kaylene relented, taking a step back, though the look of worry on her face didn't fade a bit. Merla also stood from across the table.

"I'll get you something to drink," Merla said, not waiting for Lenora to argue before she left the room.

"Are you really all right?" Kaylene asked, sitting next to Lenora as she lowered herself back down to the couch.

Lenora wiped her trembling hand over her temple, waiting for the room to stop spinning. "I'm dizzy, but I'm sure it will pass."

As they waited, Lenora debated telling her handmaid—her friend—that it was not the first time she'd had a dizzy spell in the last few days. Far from it.

But she didn't want to let herself think—let herself *hope*—that it was anything but a coincidence.

"Remind me, Kay, how many delegates are there representing Jerr Pinn?" Lenora asked. By Kaylene's skeptical look, it was obvious the sad attempt at changing subjects did not go unnoticed.

"Twenty-one, I believe."

"And they'll all be visiting?"

"No," Kaylene said, her auburn hair vibrant in the light from the window.

Lenora nodded in approval. "Good. That would be quite a lot of people to please."

"Well, they are traveling with quite a large company. But . . ." Kaylene was silent for another moment before she cleared her throat. "Your Majesty, is it . . . Are you—"

"I don't know." Lenora cut her off before her handmaid could finish the thought she'd yet to speak aloud. "It was late, but I haven't been down to see Helena yet." Before Kaylene could press further, Lenora added, "I will. Soon, I promise. But it's been late before. I'm just waiting a bit longer."

"Are you sure that's wise?" Kaylene's typically warm and gentle features contorted into a creased brow and furrowed lines around her eyes, which clouded with worry. They reflected genuine fear. Kaylene's lips pressed together in a tight line as her cheeks paled. "I don't know what I'd do if anything happened to you," she said, reaching out her hand. Her fingers trembled, her gaze remaining fixed on Lenora.

With Kaylene's friendship spanning as many years as it had, her silent plea for Lenora to prioritize her well-being and seek the necessary attention did not need to be spoken aloud. Kaylene's expression reflected unwavering loyalty and deep concern, which no doubt lay not only in serving Lenora, but also in safeguarding her health and happiness. She and Merla had both wept with her during her previous losses, and Lenora knew well that should the dizzy spells be a sign of new life in her, her friends would be by her side in grieving when she inevitably lost another child.

Because it was inevitable.

She wouldn't let herself hope.

Not when it hurt all the more when the loss came.

LENORA'S KNEES COLLAPSED as she heaved up her dinner. With Butch still asleep in his bedroom adjoining the large bathing room, she tried to remain as quiet as she could. But with each compulsive heave of her stomach, she couldn't stop the retching noises.

"Lenora?" Butch's deep rumbling voice broke through the rushing sound in Lenora's ears. "Lenora, are you all right?"

Before she could respond, another wave of nausea overwhelmed her, and she convulsed forward. Nothing but bile came up. It burned her throat as it rose, leaving a disgusting acidic taste coating every surface of her mouth.

Lenora stilled at Butch's touch, his warm hand resting on her shoulder for a second before drawing her long black hair up and away from her face. She didn't have time to thank him before she had to lean down again. The smell rising from the garderobe was atrocious, and it sent another violent convulsion through her stomach, though nothing came out.

When several seconds passed by without her bending over to vomit, Butch—who knelt behind her—tucked a strand of hair behind her ear and said in a soft voice, "Do you need anything from me?"

Lenora forced a smile onto her face after wiping her mouth with the back of her hand. "No, I'm all right. Something from dinner must've upset my stomach." She took her hair from his hand, twisting it and looping it around the strap of her chemise. "You should try to go back to sleep. I know you have a meeting in the morning, and—" Lenora paused when she thought she might heave again, but after closing her eyes and taking a deep breath, she was able to continue. "I don't want to be the reason the meeting doesn't go well."

Butch frowned. "The only reason the meeting wouldn't go well is if Clive starts to think he runs the country. And considering that's inevitable—"

"Go to sleep, Butch," Lenora said, inclining her head when he leaned forward to kiss her forehead. "I'm fine."

"If you're sure . . ."

"I am. In fact, I'll go see if August can make a draft for me, or maybe Helena already has something for this. I'll go in a moment."

"I could go, and—"

Lenora straightened. "No, that's far from necessary." With his help, she stood, clinging to his arm for several seconds until the room stopped spinning. "Thank you," she said after he walked her to his bedroom door. "Get some sleep."

Though he looked as though he was about to argue, Lenora stopped him by squeezing his hand twice and leaving. She paused a few times on the way down to the infirmary, half considering not going at all as she passed her own suite. But a small voice in the back of her mind told her that Butch would follow up with the royal apothecary, August, and maybe Helena the next day, and he wouldn't be pleased if he found out she'd lied to him.

The infirmary was farther than she remembered it being, and it didn't help that the hallway continued to swirl whenever she looked anywhere but straight forward. She had no reason to be looking over her shoulder, but some part of her was afraid of running into Merla or Kaylene. She didn't want either of them to worry, and the more she thought about it, the slower her steps became. She didn't want Helena or Dianna to worry either.

Lenora paused in the middle of the hallway, leaning against the brick wall. Something about the coolness flowing into her temple left her body more relaxed than it had been a moment earlier. She'd felt a similar coolness when she'd been with Estrada—

She jolted upright, pushing the thought from her head, but not before it left an image in her mind: the woman with shoulder-length wavy black hair sobbing on her knees, mourning the loss of her family, of her daughter.

No.

Lenora pinched her lips together. The woman had abducted her and taken her from her home. She'd held her against her will. And yet Lenora couldn't stop the small swell of sympathy from sucking her down a dark hole. It was one she found her mind traveling to more and more since returning to the castle, one where she was free to do as she pleased in the warmth of the afternoon sun, with no responsibilities, no rules, no regulations, no—

"Your Majesty? Is everything all right?"

She hadn't realized she'd resumed her walk to the infirmary until one of the two guards posted outside spoke to her.

"Yes." The word sounded breathy to her own ears. "I need to speak to Helena."

They saluted, and one of them opened the door for her before they could ask any questions as to why she was there.

"My lady?" Helena, the head physician, frowned at Lenora. The older woman smoothed out the creases on her cream robe.

Lenora knew Helena well because she had been one of the people in whom Lenora had confided when she'd lost two babies to miscarriages and the third to a stillbirth. Helena had been there for the first miscarriage and for the stillbirth, and she'd checked on Lenora after Butch had brought her back from her time with Estrada.

Her time as Estrada's *captive*, Lenora reminded herself as she offered Helena a small smile.

"I was feeling nauseated and thought it best I come to see you," Lenora said, following Helena into the room of beds.

"Sit," Helena said, motioning to the nearest cot.

The room only held three other occupants. The two nearer to her were both male, and one she recognized as a royal guard she'd passed in the hallways on occasion. She didn't recognize the second, which meant he was probably a servant who stayed in the lower levels of the castle or one of Marshal Thorne's new recruits.

In a bed at the far end of the room lay a woman with blond hair, and although Lenora couldn't see her face—she was lying with her back to the door—she could tell they were of a similar age.

"Is it a random occurrence, or has this happened more than once recently?" Helena approached her with a cool rag and a few poultices of herbs.

Lenora bit her lower lip, wondering whether to tell Helena about the dizzy spells or the fact that she'd thrown up in her own garderobe multiple times in the last two weeks.

"It really isn't that bad," Lenora said, her attention turning back to the door. "I shouldn't have bothered you at this hour, and—"

"Your Majesty, I'm the last person you should be hiding your well-being from." Helena spoke in a firm tone, though her gaze held nothing but reassurance. "It's been more than once?" When Lenora nodded, Helena rolled her lips inward, pinching them together. "How often?"

"A few times a week for the last few weeks. But it could just be a change in the season, or maybe—"

"Have you been with His Majesty?"

The question felt innocent and invasive in the same moment.

"Yes." Lenora started to question why that felt strange to admit when Helena placed the back of her hand against Lenora's forehead.

"You don't seem to be warm, but that doesn't rule out a fever or sickness. What about your cycle?"

Lenora glanced down at her hands. "It's late."

"Doesn't guarantee it, but you could be—"

"Test for everything else first, please," Lenora said, cutting her off.

"You know that's not the way we do things here. If you've been with—"

"Helena, I'm not asking." Lenora leveled Helena with what she hoped was a commanding look, though she doubted it was anywhere near as intimidating as her husband's.

Helena grunted as she walked away from the cot.

Trying not to dwell on what her dizziness might mean, Lenora turned her attention back to the woman on the bed near the large window.

There were too many servants to keep track of in the castle, and while there were quite a few women with fair hair, Lenora was sure the woman wasn't a servant, especially with the filthy tunic the young woman wore. It wouldn't have been the first time her husband had offered the castle as a safe haven for civilians affected by the war—the other physician, Dianna, was proof of that. But before she could come up with any other reasons, Lenora's mind went back to the guards outside the door.

Glancing over her shoulder to where Helena had disappeared, Lenora checked the rest of the room before rising from the cot and walking to the end of the infirmary. She stood beside the woman's bed for a second, her brow creasing as she tried to place her. She wasn't familiar at first, but as Lenora crossed to the other side of the bed and studied the frail woman's sleeping face, a memory wiggled, trying to free itself from the back of Lenora's mind. She recognized the woman's face.

But why?

Not a servant.

Not a scullery maid.

Not someone from the castle.

Lenora leaned closer, her gaze tracing the contours of the woman's gaunt face. She had shoulder-length white-blond hair that was matted and clearly unwashed. Her cheekbones were stark against her pale skin, and dark circles hollowed out beneath her closed eyes. The tunic she wore, which peeked out from beneath the thin wool blanket, was filthy and torn, covered in dirt and grime. Bandages covered her wrists.

Who was she?

And why did Lenora already know her face? Know that beneath her sleeping lids, her eyes were brown? Know what the woman looked like when she was terrified and in despair?

The realization hit Lenora like a bolt of lightning, and she took a step back in response. A pair of glasses and a crimson-stained tunic fluttering in the breeze next to a little girl's wooden doll. A reminder of the atrocity that had taken place in that village. The pain of a heart tearing in two. The cold relief of hidden dark magic surfacing. And the woman before her sobbing, pleading, comforting as best as she could.

75

Lenora clasped a hand over her chest. Estrada had shown her the memories she had of the day she learned her entire world had been destroyed. Her husband and two-year-old daughter. She had used magic in that tiny house to show Lenora the pain she'd experienced at the order of Lenora's husband. And in those memories, this woman's face emerged. She'd been a safe haven for Estrada. Her best friend. Estrada's source of solace.

And now she lay, vulnerable and broken, on death's doorstep before Lenora. What had her husband done?

At the same time her heart broke for the woman, Lenora's gaze softened, and she took a step forward. Gently, she brushed a stray lock of hair from the woman's forehead.

"Who are you?" Lenora whispered, a deep sense of urgency and a fierce wave of protectiveness sweeping through her. She needed to know more about the woman, to understand the bond she shared with Estrada. And more than anything, she wanted to help her before it was too late.

"Your Majesty." Helena's harsh whisper had Lenora stepping away from the cot, her wide eyes meeting Helena's. "Come here." The physician stood next to the cot Lenora had been sitting on earlier.

Lenora cast a glance back at the woman before returning to Helena, who looked like she was ready to both scold her and determine whether she'd been harmed. Her narrowed gaze scanned Lenora for any sign of injury.

"Who is she?" Lenora asked, lowering her voice to a whisper.

Helena had brought a small tray of various medical items, and she fiddled with one as she pinched her lips together. "A prisoner who got sick. The king sent her here a few days ago."

"A prisoner?" Lenora repeated, frowning from both the new surge of dizziness and the curiosity she felt toward the woman. "What was her crime?"

But in her heart, she already knew. At the thought of the war, at the thought of Estrada, Lenora's thoughts jumped to the most logical answer.

Magic.

It had to be.

But was it a pure magic, either light or dark? Dark maybe, like Estrada's? No. Lenora searched the memories Estrada had shown her. Her friend had light magic. She'd displayed it that day in Shongbay.

"Whatever it is, it's important. The king had Marshal Thorne come in to check on her."

Of course he had. The woman was Estrada's friend.

When Helena continued, Lenora struggled to pay attention to what the physician was saying.

"I've treated prisoners before, but the king has never shown interest. I expect this one has something to do with the woman with dark magic the king is after." Helena had no idea how right she was. "If the king would just change some of the conditions in the dungeon, maybe I wouldn't have had to bring the poor girl back from the brink of death," Helena muttered under her breath. It didn't matter though, because Lenora had barely heard her.

An image of Estrada's wavy black hair and dark magic forced its way to the front of Lenora's mind, and the queen couldn't help but shiver. Maybe the prisoner knew what had happened to her after the night in the boulder field. Maybe she knew where Estrada had gone after being injured. When had her husband arrested her?

"I would like to speak with her," Lenora said, watching the way the prisoner's figure hardly moved as she breathed. She was all but a silhouette with the great looming window darkened by the night outside.

"I'm sorry, Your Majesty, but the king has ordered that no one apart from Marshal Thorne may speak to her."

Lenora frowned but did not argue. She waited until Helena was finished, promising more answers in the morning, before thanking her. With one last look at the woman at the back of the room, Lenora left the infirmary.

If the king was refusing to let anyone speak to the woman, the only person she could take that up with was her husband. He certainly had answers, and with things warming up between the two of them since they'd returned that night from the boulder field, he might just tell her why Estrada's friend was lying in the infirmary next to death itself.

Chapter 10

BUTCH

"And you're sure that's how they're getting past our lines?" Butch leaned back in his desk chair, his focus still on the map spread out before him. One of Marshal Aldrich's captains and two of his commanders stood across from him.

"Ice skimmers have been seen in the distance, but they're already gone by the time we are heading out to check them," the captain responded.

"How many?" Butch asked.

"It's hard to say," one of the commanders said, wrinkling his nose. "They aren't individualized, so they all look the same."

The other commander nodded and continued after the first paused. "For all we know, it could be the same four or five."

"Or it could be thirty of them," Butch muttered, rubbing his hand along his chin. "Very well. I'll have to think on this, unless the marshal has any suggestions already?"

The captain shook his head. "No. Just the report."

Butch stuck his tongue into his cheek as he frowned at the map. "It's too risky having a post out on the ice. Let me think on it."

"Yes, Your Majesty." The captain and the commanders saluted before departing his office.

Sighing, Butch ran his hands through his hair and stared at the ceiling. Silas would have an idea. He was almost sure of it.

But Silas was busy training recruits.

Necessary recruits if the reports from the war fronts were as dire as they'd been made out to be.

A knock at the door pulled Butch's attention away from Marshal Aldrich's report on his desk.

"Enter," he said, standing in the hope of returning some blood to his legs. He'd been sitting for hours, and his stiff limbs creaked as he stretched.

Butch's eyebrows rose when his wife walked in. Without thinking about it, his gaze went directly to her stomach. He would've been lying to himself if he said the first thought in his mind when she'd been sick early in the morning was not that she might be pregnant again. However, he let the hope die as he had before, remembering the agony the three losses had brought upon her.

And, if he was honest, him.

Lenora bowed her head. "I apologize for the interruption, but I need a word with you. Now." Her face was no paler than normal, but there was something about her tone of voice, as if she was about to tell him something important, just like when she'd told him about . . .

"Of course." Butch forced a placating smile onto his lips, sitting back down in the chair behind the desk. "Please sit," he said, gesturing toward the chair before him. "Are you feeling better?"

He slipped the parchment with the warfront report under a less important one. No need to worry his wife with the bad news it bore.

He waited until Lenora had fixed her skirts and returned her attention to him.

"Much, thank you."

"And the welcome ceremony planning? How has that been? Have you made much in the way of progress?" Butch leaned forward in his chair to rest his hands on his desk.

Across from him, his wife sat straighter, lifting her chin. "That isn't what I came to discuss," she said, her words clipped.

Butch held back a frown and inclined his head. "All right, what is it?"

"The woman in the infirmary. Who is she? Tell me truthfully."

The question had Butch fighting for neutrality on his face.

His shoulders tensed, and to cover the change in his demeanor, he leaned back in his chair. Before he could ask why she knew about Estrada's friend, the image of Lenora bent over the garderobe vomiting returned to his mind.

She'd visited the infirmary.

Just like he'd suggested.

That was how she'd found out.

It was his fault.

"She's a prisoner," Butch said, keeping his voice even.

"Why?" Lenora raised an eyebrow. "What did she do that caused you to nearly kill her?"

"Excuse me?"

"Have you seen the state of her?" His wife raised her voice, gesturing to the door behind her. "She's a wraith at best."

"Lenora," he said, trying to keep the warning tone in his voice from revealing the sudden anger squeezing his chest. "Careful."

Did his wife truly think so little of him?

The last thing he wanted was to drag his fragile wife into more issues with the woman who'd abducted her and held her captive for a month, even if Lenora was poking him with a glowing cattle prod. The best thing for her would be to remain ignorant, but since that no longer stood as an option . . .

Butch steeled himself, clearing his throat before he spoke. "I apologize, Lenora, but other than noticing the woman in the infirmary, I don't see how this is relevant to you."

"Helena said only you and Thorne are allowed to speak to her. Why? What has she done?"

Butch squinted at the wall just over his wife's shoulder, his mind reeling as he tried to determine how much to reveal.

With a glance at her, Butch rubbed his temple and sighed. "The prisoner is believed to be a close friend of the woman who held you hostage. I have been trying to determine where Estrada is by questioning her."

Lenora scoffed, then quickly leveled her expression. "So, you've been torturing the poor girl?"

"No," Butch said, the word abrupt and sharp as it came out of his mouth. "I simply ask her questions." His palms sweated, and he dried them off by smoothing the fabric of his trousers.

"How did she end up in the infirmary, then? She looks . . . Butch, I don't understand how she's still alive with how thin she is."

Butch bit his cheek. Helena had been bothering him about the dungeon for a while, and if he had just listened to her, maybe he wouldn't be having this conversation. As soon as he had the capacity, he was going to speak with some of his guards about the conditions in his dungeon. It seemed like a problem he could fix by delegating.

If only he'd listened to Helena sooner . . .

"The prisoner grew very ill, and when she collapsed during an interrogation a few days ago, I sent her to the infirmary. I don't want her dead, Lenora. That's why she's in Helena's capable hands. I'm making sure she gets the care she needs to recover." Butch paused, rubbing his hand over the back of his neck. The narrowing gaze his wife was shooting him did not bode well, and he searched for words that might appease her curiosity without pulling her into the nightmare that was Estrada's continual destruction of peace.

"The woman in there is believed to be a close confidante of Estrada, and if we can convince her to aid us, we stand a better chance at finding the true threat and ridding Phildeterre of her dark magic and the danger she poses. I don't even want to think about what would happen if Estrada found her way north and joined the war against us. The reason I'm not allowing anyone to speak to the prisoner is to prevent her from finding a way out of the castle and back to Estrada. If we lose this woman, we might lose our chance at getting an upper hand on a very, *very* dangerous enemy. This woman can't be trusted, and we need to keep our guard up."

"So, she's spoken to you about Estrada?" Lenora shifted in her seat.

"Unfortunately, no." Butch removed his crown for a moment, running his fingers through his hair. "She hasn't spoken a word since she arrived."

"And if she remains silent?" An air of hesitation filled Lenora's voice, her wide eyes showing a hint of concern that made his stomach turn. How could she care about a criminal?

"She'll remain in the dungeon."

"And if she helps?"

Butch pinched his lips together. "I haven't yet decided."

"So, you're quick to punish her down in that horrid place, but not to give her any sort of hope at freedom?"

Irritated by his wife's questioning, Butch waved away her words. "You can't see the full picture, for which I can't fault you. Either way, the woman is a prisoner and is not to be approached. Is that clear?"

Lenora stood before answering. "Crystal, Your Majesty." She curtsied, though it was obvious it was out of a sense of duty rather than true respect. "Thank you for your time."

He dismissed her with a wave of his hand, waiting to slouch until the door closed.

"Well, I wasn't expecting that," he muttered, pinching the bridge of his nose between his thumb and pointer finger.

He supposed it was bound to happen at some point though. There'd been too much luck in keeping the prisoner's presence a secret thus far, and as he'd learned the hard way, luck only lasted so long when it came to his war against Estrada.

A WHILE LATER, Butch filled Silas in on his meeting with Marshal Aldrich's men as well as the surprise visit from his wife.

"I don't want her anywhere near the prisoner," Butch said, leaning against his desk. He rolled up his sleeves as he watched his friend fold up the report in the chair across from him.

"Understood."

"Is the prisoner still without magic dampeners?"

Silas's brow furrowed, as if he followed the king's line of thinking. "Yes. But Helena won't allow me near her wrists until they've healed."

Butch wrinkled his nose. If he ordered the physician to allow the prisoner to wear the magic-dampening cuffs, Helena would let him hear about it for the rest of time. Not that the physician scared him, but she certainly wasn't someone to test. Being on Helena's bad side was like a death sentence.

"As soon as she's able, I want the prisoner surrounded by the metal." Butch sighed again, straightening his crown. "And get one of your captains to come up with a list of ways to improve the conditions of the dungeon. I'd prefer my prisoners stay down there and not be brought up to create more headaches. If it means better food, then so be it. Whatever is necessary, I trust you to approve the changes."

"I think you just spared yourself the wrath of Helena by saying that." A smile pulled at the side of Silas's mouth. "She's been lecturing my ear off every time I go check on the prisoner."

"Dodged a bolt, then."

Silas grinned, then inclined his head. He gestured toward Butch's desk. "Shall we discuss Levick's report?"

82

Butch sighed as he nodded. Marshal Aldrich's report wasn't the only bad news he'd received that day. "Another failed search."

"No sign of her?"

"None." Butch read from the report he slid off his desk. "How is this possible?" He crunched the parchment in his hand, a swell of frustration filling him. "There are posters everywhere, and over half of the guards who are meant to be off duty are in the field instead."

"She's smart."

Butch sighed. "Too smart." The room fell into silence, and Butch leaned against his desk, staring at the ceiling. He still hadn't changed it from his father's reign, though he'd meant to. It was the last piece of the office still stained with the memory of his father. And in fact, it was quite literally stained. Speckles of dark brown spread over the stone.

The sight of the dried blood and the haunting thought of his father led Butch's mind down another path, toward the looming shadow of a château. Butch clenched his jaw.

"What?" Silas raised an eyebrow, his blue eyes holding Butch still with a solemn gaze.

"We need to get information we can use to capture Estrada."

"Yes."

Butch ran his fingers over his jaw as he processed what he was about to say. "Interrogating the prisoner here hasn't gotten us anywhere."

Silas straightened his posture as if he were about to jump to attention, but he remained quiet.

"What if we took her to Lavfor?" The name of the château left what felt like a coat of grime on Butch's tongue, yet he steeled his features and waited for his friend's response.

"Are you serious?"

"Are we at war?" Butch kept his voice level but lifted his chin as he stared Silas down. "If we are in as grave a situation as we seem to be," he said as he pointed toward the correspondence with his other marshal, which he had placed back on his desk after his wife's departure, "we need to take this matter seriously."

"You mean torture the prisoner." Silas's voice fell flat, his hand tightening into a fist at his side. "Hasn't she essentially been tortured in the dungeon? You saw her when she collapsed."

Butch clenched his jaw, narrowing his eyes at Silas. "She's a prisoner, not a guest. And besides, she hasn't spoken a word since you arrested her." He wrinkled his nose, his gut already twisting in anger at the mere thought of the prisoner staring right past him as if he weren't standing before her asking her simple questions. As if he were nothing more than a fly buzzing around with only the purpose of annoying her. "Maybe she needs motivation."

"And you're willing to reopen Lavfor? To continue your father's experiments, which you were so strongly opposed to before?" Though his tone did not change, Silas's stature did, even as he rose to his feet.

Silas's brows knitted together, forming a deep furrow as a flicker of anger flashed in his bright eyes. A vein in his temple bulged as if he was holding back his true reaction out of formality. His chest rose and fell with uneven breaths, and despite all the training Butch knew he'd undergone as a guard, he shifted his weight from one foot to the other.

"You know better than most that I have no intention of reinstating the atrocities of which my father was so fond," Butch growled, narrowing his eyes at Silas. "But I cannot allow this prisoner to best me. I cannot let Estrada continue to make a mockery of my men. And I cannot allow magic to reside alongside those who are nothing but prey in the eyes of magic wielders. I must protect my people."

"I understand," Silas said as he took a deep breath. He closed his eyes briefly, and a war of emotions flashed across his face in a second before they dissolved back into granite. "Is this woman, this prisoner, not one of yours to protect as well? Is she not a citizen within Phildeterre?"

Butch tried—and failed—to hide his annoyance. "If I spared every magic person who walked through my doors, I would be nothing but a laughingstock and a failure in the eyes of my predecessors, my people, and all the leaders of our surrounding countries." Butch puffed out his chest, embracing the phantom ache in his ribs from where the prisoner had struck him with her magic. "Besides, she attacked me and my guards and freed the woman who abducted my wife."

"Of course," Silas said, lifting his chin. The stone expression on his face did not change, but he did unclench his hand at his side. "My apologies, Your Majesty."

"So, you approve of me sending the prisoner to Lavfor?" Butch raised an eyebrow.

"No, but you do not need my permission to do so."

"You'll support my decision if I do?"

Silas nodded his head but said nothing. An emotion clouded the marshal's eyes. He cleared his throat, and his gaze locked on the parchments in Butch's hands. "Maybe I should go."

"You have somewhere better to be?" Butch asked, raising an eyebrow when Silas frowned.

"I meant go to the Black Forest, see if there's anything I can do to aid Levick, even if it's simply to give him a break."

The room fell silent as Butch switched his thoughts back to what they'd been discussing. He processed what his friend was suggesting. It made sense, and in theory, it was a good plan; however, the longer he dwelled on it, the more unsettled his stomach twisted inside him.

"How long were you thinking?" Butch questioned, stroking the side of his jaw.

Silas's posture loosened, and he shrugged, saying, "Long enough to take a stab at finding Estrada myself."

"How many will you take?"

"Three commanders and their men."

Butch nodded once in approval. "All right. Take a new group and replace Marshal Levick and those who have been out on the field the longest. But before you send them back, question them. They're bound to have seen or heard something that might be useful."

"I'll spread the word, and we'll leave in two days," Silas said, his shoulders rolling back as he saluted.

"And before you go, check with Helena in the infirmary. If the prisoner is healthy enough, send her back to the dungeon. I don't need my wife or anyone else engaging with her," Butch said as he sat back down in his desk chair.

"Of course," Silas said, but he bit his lower lip. "Your Majesty?"

"Go ahead." Butch gestured for Silas to present whatever was giving him pause.

"Will you wait to send her to Lavfor until I return?"

"You have some desire to go back there?" Butch couldn't keep the surprise from sneaking into his tone. If anyone hated the château and all that it stood for more than Butch, it was Silas.

"Of course not. But I believe it's wise to have a marshal escort her, and I'd like to be the one who does it."

Butch rubbed the side of his head, his eyes narrowing at the chair in front of his desk. "Very well." He pinched his lips together. "I'll continue to think on Lavfor, and you can rest assured I won't move her there until you return."

"Thank you, Butch." Silas offered him a small nod. "I'll check on her, and if she can be moved, I'll make sure she gets to her cell."

Butch shuffled through the correspondence with his other marshal, holding one letter up before responding. "Levick will relieve you after a few weeks. Hopefully you'll be more successful than him and find her in that time. Then all of this could be over, and there would be no need to reopen that nightmare of a place." Butch muttered the last part, but Silas clearly heard it, because he nodded.

"I need to go make preparations," he said, lifting his chin. "We'll figure this out, brother." He saluted, and Butch watched him turn on his heel and leave the office.

As much as he didn't want to send his best friend into a situation where he might fall prey to Estrada, he knew Silas would be as efficient, if not more, than any of the other marshals. If anyone was going to get a lead on Estrada, maybe even catch her, it was going to be him.

Chapter 11

EVANGELINE

Evangeline's heart relentlessly beat like a pounding drum in her chest. Anticipation flooded through her veins, a storm breaking free from its confines.

Soon.

She'd have to act soon.

Otherwise, she'd lose her opportunity. It wouldn't be long before they would deem her healthy enough to return to the dungeon; Helena had as good as told her earlier that day without realizing it. She'd muttered about the irrationality of "sending her back" when she wasn't fully recovered yet.

But she was recovering. The strength Evangeline had lacked was returning, and with it, her drive to leave. She wasn't anywhere near the healthy state she'd been in when she'd first been arrested, and she wasn't sure if she would be able to do more than stumble along the wall, but she didn't have a choice. There would be no escaping when she returned to the dungeon.

Evangeline bit her thumbnail as she stared up at the dark sky out the window.

Not long now.

Just another minute or so . . .

"Everything all right?" Dianna asked as she approached Evangeline's bedside. She'd just finished helping a man—likely a guard—who lay in the bed two down from Evangeline's.

"Yes, thank you," Evangeline said, mustering a smile. She didn't realize how intensely she must've been staring until she glanced over at Dianna to find the kind woman's brow furrowed. Evangeline's teeth ached from how hard she'd been clenching her jaw, and it felt unnatural to be smiling— especially when she'd likely get Dianna in trouble.

She shouldn't care.

Evangeline knew that.

But both Dianna and Helena had shown her a gentle and even friendly kindness she'd not experienced in months besides Odette. Certainly not from any others who worked for the king and weren't kept in dark and filthy parts of the castle.

"Actually, Dianna." Evangeline took a deep breath. "Do you mind checking the wrapping on my right wrist? It feels a bit tight."

"Of course." Dianna smiled, grabbing a stool and sliding it next to Evangeline's bed. She took Evangeline's extended hand, holding it closer to her face.

Sleep.

Evangeline closed her eyes to the bright light that flashed from her hand. Dianna collapsed forward, her head landing next to Evangeline's hip before she slid off the bed and landed on the floor. Before the other two occupants in the room could question what was happening, Evangeline flashed her magic once more, effectively putting them to sleep as well.

"I'm sorry," Evangeline mumbled as she slid off the bed. Her legs trembled, and she held the cot for stability. The room spun, and for a second, she questioned whether she'd be able to take more than a few steps. She had to try though.

Evangeline stepped over Dianna's slumped form. "I really am sorry." Not that the sleeping woman could hear her.

Emotions surged within her chest, but she buried the tumultuous wave deep within, determined to keep it concealed.

Her freedom was at stake, after all.

It didn't matter how she felt, just that she continued to follow the plan she'd spent hours laying out in her mind.

The chill of the floor prickled her bare feet. She wasn't sure how much time she had before the spell keeping the other three asleep would wear off, so she didn't bother with her boots. Besides, it'd be easier to trip with the heavier boots on her feet. At least this way she could feel the solid floor beneath her, whether she felt solid or not. And she did not feel solid in the slightest. Every step had her head spinning, and she nearly emptied her stomach by the time she reached the door.

It was hard to tell how long she had, considering she'd done the sleep spell in a calm moment this time rather than as a reaction, like the day she'd mistakenly saved the king's life.

And there was still the guard outside the door to put to sleep as well.

Not to mention any others she may come across as she tried to escape.

Tried.

A layer of sweat built on the back of her neck, and she tried to focus on her breathing rather than the twisting sensation in her gut and the weakness threatening to topple her over.

Evangeline took a deep breath as her hand hovered over the door handle. Her stomach squeezed. For yet another time, she regretted eating dinner only an hour earlier. It would not benefit her to be sick in the middle of her escape.

Before she could turn the handle, though, the door opened, and one of the king's royal guards nearly walked straight into her.

"My apologies, my—wait, what are you—" He dropped to the floor before the light in her hand had faded back beneath her skin.

Evangeline clung to the doorframe to remain standing. The hallway outside the room seemed so large and threatening. How was she supposed to know what was around each corner? How was she supposed to navigate a part of the castle to which she'd never been?

The rapid breaths she sucked in made her head even lighter, and she forced her eyes closed as she tried to slow her breathing. She couldn't panic. Not now. Not even if every fiber of her being begged her to collapse to the ground and curl up in a pitiful ball. No. She needed to move the guard, and she needed to escape.

Emmalee needed her to escape.

Blinking her eyes open, she let out a shaky breath and did a quick check to make sure the hallway was clear and none of the guard's brothers-in-arms were nearby. She had to move the man's sleeping body, but considering she could hardly move her own, she needed another way to move him.

"Think, E, think," she muttered under her breath. There was no way she'd be able to lift the man, let alone drag him—not unless there was something to ease the friction. An image flashed through her mind of Evangeline pulling Emmalee around the hardwood floors of the little apartment in which Evangeline had lived as a child. They'd used her bedsheets and had gotten in trouble when Evangeline's stepfather had caught them. Thankfully, Evangeline's mother had stepped in before Jonathan Dipthy had punished them.

A bedsheet could work.

Evangeline spread a sheet out on the floor, then grunted with the effort of rolling the guard on top of it. She was out of breath by the time she stood, gripping two corners of the sheet. With a silent prayer, Evangeline pulled. The guard slid easily over the floor, so easily that Evangeline lost her balance and toppled backward. She landed hard on her hip, catching herself just before her head hit the floor. Scrambling back to her feet, she checked the others in the infirmary to make sure they were still asleep. They were, and after checking the hallway, she confirmed it was still empty.

She dragged the man just inside the infirmary door. Evangeline didn't bother to prop him up against the wall. She left him lying to the side so that if the door opened, he wouldn't be noticed right away. After muttering an apology to the guard, just as she had Dianna, Evangeline approached the door again.

With a tremulous breath, Evangeline stepped into the corridor.

As if the castle wanted to aid in her escape, the hallway outside the infirmary remained void of others, and more specifically, guards. Evangeline stayed near the wall as she closed the infirmary door behind her. She used it to keep herself upright, pausing to catch her breath when she quickly became winded. At least if she kept to the edges, it would be easier to dive behind a pillar or into a doorway should she hear someone coming.

That was the hope.

Considering she had been unconscious when the king and Thorne had brought her there, Evangeline had no idea where in the castle she stood. However, she had overheard Helena speaking to one of the people who'd come in for one reason or another. She'd mentioned going up to the servants' quarters and using that entrance to bring in supplies.

With little to go off, Evangeline set her focus on finding the servants' exit. She'd make her escape there instead of casually strolling through the main hall where anyone might see her. Not that she knew where that was either . . .

Evangeline glanced down the hall in both directions before she made a decision. Each step on the cold brick floor left her feet tingling and her heart pounding. Her legs trembled beneath her, threatening to give out if she had to run. The pressure in her ears built until it felt as though she was deep beneath dark waters, though she wasn't sure if that was from the anxiety sprouting from moving through her enemies' home or some residual effect of her infection turned sickness.

Either way, it was unpleasant, and it left her feeling vulnerable to being caught. How was she supposed to hear footsteps when all she could hear was what sounded like rushing water pounding down just inside her ears?

Evangeline kept looking over her shoulder every few feet, only releasing the breath in her lungs when the sight behind her remained the same.

Distracted by what was behind her, Evangeline crashed into a small table holding a vase. Before she could react, the vase tumbled to the floor and shattered. The sound echoed down the corridor, and the blood in Evangeline's veins ran cold. Without another thought, she ducked into a small servants' staircase and climbed the stairs as fast as her weakened body would allow.

Her lungs throbbed in her chest, and she felt as though they'd caught on fire by the time she reached the top. Evangeline leaned forward and tried to give her breathing a moment to calm. Her hands trembled. She pressed them into the tops of her legs as she bent over.

"Breathe," she begged her lungs as she closed her eyes. The sweat that had been building trickled down her face until she wiped it away. When she could breathe at least a little more normally, she checked around the corner.

Voices echoed below from the entrance into the stairway. She couldn't make out their words, already moving out of the staircase and down the next hallway.

She didn't make it more than a few feet before footsteps echoed along the same corridor in which she stopped. Evangeline threw an anxious glance over her shoulder, not noticing the movement behind her before a hand clasped around her neck, another around her waist.

Someone far stronger than her dragged her backward, and something cold wrapped around her throat. The next instant, her head slammed back into the stone wall of a dark room, causing bright stars to flash in her sight. Evangeline let out a grunt at the impact, but before she could say anything, or even scream—which was what her body was telling her to do—the hand around her waist slid up to cover her mouth completely.

The room the man had yanked her into was dark, lit only by the moonlight streaming in from a partially covered window to Evangeline's left. But it was enough to reflect light off the man's brilliant blue eyes.

As soon as she realized who had grabbed her, Evangeline bit down as hard as she could.

Thorne hissed, yanking his hand away and shaking it. "Really?" he spat, growling as he leaned in closer. The cold chain around her neck tightened under his fist, keeping her pinned to the wall. He towered over her, his eyes narrowing with each second he glared down.

"Let me go," Evangeline said, begging her speeding heart to calm. It wasn't until she concentrated on the adrenaline coursing through her that she felt the absence of warmth. It had to be the chain Thorne had wrapped around her neck as he'd pulled her out of the hallway. She was sure of it. It was likely made from the same metal as the cuffs that had nearly killed her.

"I'm glad to see you're well enough to stand." Thorne's voice revealed anything but actual relief at her recovery. "But I do remember warning you not to try to run."

"I was . . . going . . . for a walk." Evangeline gritted her teeth, matching his glare with one of her own. She pressed up onto her tiptoes to ease some of the tension from the chain he held around her neck.

Thorne must've noticed her struggle to breathe because he loosened his grip. "In other words, you were trying to escape."

Evangeline tried to wedge her fingers between the chain and her throat, allowing for even more breathing room, before she answered. "What else would I be doing?"

"Trying to harm the king or queen?"

At his words, Evangeline froze. "What?"

Thorne regarded her, tilting his head to the side. "I think you heard me."

Evangeline scoffed, her breath moving a few strands of his hair from his forehead. It was then that she noticed his clothing. He wore a loose tunic and linen trousers; it was the farthest thing from a uniform she'd seen him in since the first time they'd met. Thorne had rolled the sleeves of his shirt up past his elbows, and the gap in the top of the flowy fabric revealed a glimpse of a toned chest.

"Well?"

It was difficult to swallow, though she wasn't sure if it was from the chain or her gaze, which lingered a few seconds too long on him.

What was wrong with her?

The man had her pinned to a wall with a chain threatening her air supply, and she was staring. At. His. Chest.

Or rather his muscles.

Delirious. She had to be delirious.

Evangeline cleared her throat, peeling her gaze from his body. "I have no ill intentions toward either the king or the queen." She lifted her chin as she met his vibrant eyes. "I *just* want to be free. I'd even leave this wretched country if I could cross the border. But no, the king has even managed to make that near impossible."

Thorne stayed quiet for a moment, his gaze trailing over her face as if searching for any hint of a lie. "You have magic."

"You have blue eyes."

"It's illegal."

"It's hereditary."

"You're going back to the cells," he muttered, pulling her away from the wall with a single tug.

At his words, panic flooded through her body, threatening to sweep her legs out from under her. Evangeline's chest tightened. Not the darkness. Not the cells. Not the magic-dampening metal that suffocated her the longer she was there.

"No, please no." Evangeline hated the pleading tone in her voice, but there was nothing she could do to keep it from bleeding into her words. "No," Evangeline repeated, keeping one hand between her neck and the chain. With the other, she dug her fingernails into his bare forearm. "Either send me before a trial, as you should've done months ago, or kill me. Better yet, let me go free. Just don't take me back there."

He stopped pulling her toward the door, turning to face her until she had to tilt her head up to look him in the eye. His brow was furrowed, and hesitation wound around his eyes. "You're in no position to request such a thing. You're lucky the king is merciful. Anyone else would've tortured the information they desired out of you and then put you to death."

"Why hasn't he, then? And you don't think that dungeon is torture enough?" Evangeline didn't want to push too far. Physical torture was the last thing she wanted to accidentally inflict upon herself by opening her mouth, but his declaration sparked enough curiosity that she couldn't keep the words from spilling between her lips. Why hadn't the king just killed her? She'd given him nothing—and intended to continue her same routine.

"Because he's a good man."

Evangeline couldn't stop the sharp laugh before it barked through the silent room. " '*Good*'? That is the last word I'd use to describe your king."

"He's your king too."

"My jailor. The cause of my headaches. Maybe my executioner someday. But *that man* will *never* be my king."

Thorne remained silent, his jaw clenching and revealing taut muscles in the light coming in from the window. "Very well. I'll take you back to the infirmary, and at first light, you'll return to your cell."

The mention of her cell—of that dark, freezing prison—had her heart thumping wildly in her chest again. How close had she been to freedom? How close? If she could get the chain off her neck . . .

Evangeline forced air into her lungs, difficult as it was with her nerves and the chain. She needed to think, to be smarter than him. It couldn't be that hard.

"Fine, but remove this chain. I'm not a pet to be leashed." She lifted her chin, trying to exude as much dignity and pride as she could.

"Yeah, right." Thorne snorted, shaking his head. "How foolish do you think I am?" He lifted a thick eyebrow. "You'll use your magic the second I remove it."

"I will not." Evangeline forced an air of offense into her voice. She'd once been able to fool the nobility into thinking she was of their class; she hoped enough of those skills—skills she'd once hated—might be enough to convince the marshal to release her. All it would take was one second . . .

"I'm not removing the chain." Thorne started to pull again, but Evangeline dug her heels into the floor and leaned back.

"And here . . . I thought . . . you weren't . . . as bad . . . as the rest." The metal pinched her skin, closing her airways the more she struggled.

"Stop fighting me and it won't be as uncomfortable," he muttered, but he loosened his grip again—not enough to release the chain, but enough that he wasn't strangling her.

That gave her an idea.

"I can't . . . b-breathe . . ." she said, fluttering her eyes. The last thing she wanted to do was beg again and show any further weakness, but if that's what would do the trick . . . "Please, I can't breathe . . ." Evangeline thrashed about, her hands frantically gripping the chain, which was certainly not threatening her life. But Thorne didn't know that. "Please, I c-can't . . . Please . . ."

Something like panic flashed through his brilliant blue eyes, and he seemed caught off guard. He hesitated for a moment longer, and then after what felt like a lifetime, he finally released the chain around her neck.

The second the warmth came back, she focused on the marshal, unable to keep the triumph from gleaming behind her eyes and the grin from her lips.

Sleep.

Chapter 12

SILAS

Silas recognized his mistake a second too late. The room, once enveloped in the cloak of midnight and coated only in a few beams of moonlight, exploded into painful light that made Silas's eyes burn even after he closed his eyelids. The heat from Evie's magic flashed through him, a soft caress that brought with it an otherworldly warmth. It seeped into the very marrow of his bones. His ears filled with the distant echo of a forgotten lullaby his mother had once sung to him in what felt like another lifetime, a haunting melody that tugged at the edges of his consciousness, urging him to slip into a blissful sleep.

His muscles relaxed for a moment, and he stumbled backward. If a burning sensation just above his heart hadn't started throbbing, he would've collapsed to the floor, deep in the sleep his body so desperately needed. Instead, his mother's final gift snapped him back to the room and held at bay the heaviness in his bones, the drowsiness clawing at his eyelids. The throbbing in his chest mimicked his own heartbeat, coursing through him like a lifeline as he tried to summon his wits to push through the remaining haze. Evie's spell lingered though, slowing his thoughts to a crawl.

That didn't stop him from reacting.

He was, after all, the king's marshal.

The light faded beneath Evie's skin, and before it was gone, he had her pressed back against the cold stone wall with his dagger against her throat. The moonlight traced the contours of her face, highlighting her wide eyes as they met his. He read the question behind them before a single word slipped through her pink lips.

"How?"

Silas kept his voice neutral as their breaths mingled in the air between them. "I couldn't tell you. But what I can say is that from now on, there will not be a moment outside of your cell where you don't have magic-dampening metal on you."

Her defiant glare cut through him. The worst part, though, was that even with the dagger resting steadily in his nimble hands, he knew he couldn't use it. Not on her. Not according to the sketchbook hidden in his room.

Even at his mercy, the woman before him had somehow walked away triumphant in the altercation. Did she know? If she did, he couldn't tell.

Silas held back a yawn. "Come on," he growled, keeping the dagger at her throat as he gripped her by the upper arm. He pulled her from the wall, releasing a breath of silent relief when she didn't fight him again.

The shine of the chain on the floor caught his attention, and he scooped it up as he passed it.

Evie's nose wrinkled when he wrapped it around her arm just above where he held her. Neither spoke, and Silas was grateful for that and the chain. She may not have realized it, but with his lack of sleep, if she had tried to put him to sleep again, it might've worked. And that was thanks to the dreams of her attempt at escape that had started when he'd first taken her to the infirmary.

With her lean long legs, she had no problem keeping stride with him, and he didn't slow down as he led her back to the infirmary. She did, however, seem quite out of breath by the time they stopped.

"They're not dead," Evie said under her breath before Silas could ask about the bodies in the infirmary.

Silas paused in the doorway, glancing to the right, where a guard lay passed out. His gaze scanned the room until he noticed a woman's foot hanging out in the aisle, where he assumed she was also fast asleep.

"Ouch!" Evie snapped, and Silas relaxed his hand, which had tightened the chain around her arm at the sight of the damage the prisoner had caused with her magic.

"How long will they be out?" he asked, forcing the muscles in his shoulders to relax, which seemed to be the last thing they wanted to do. Silas leaned over the guard at his feet.

"I don't know," she replied, her gaze locked on his free hand, which was unclipping the set of cuffs on the guard's belt.

Silas watched her reaction as he straightened and nodded toward the back of the room. When she didn't move, he nudged her toward the bed she'd been in since he and Butch had brought her to Helena. "Move, Evie."

"You're not going to—"

"Oh yes I am," he growled in her ear as he tugged her closer to his side, tilting his chin as he glowered at her. "Unless you'd like to go directly to your cell now?" The threat worked as he'd hoped it would, and she moved voluntarily toward the bed, a scowl on her face.

"Helena is going to be angry when she sees the cuffs on my wrists," she said, pausing at the end of the bed.

Silas refrained from rolling his eyes at her sorry attempt at talking him out of the magic-dampening restraints. With a gentle shove, he pushed her backward until she sat on the bed. He stood over her for a second longer before nodding for her to scoot back.

"I'm not putting them on your wrists," he said. For some blasted reason, Silas struggled to keep his facial expression neutral as he lowered himself to one knee before her.

"What are you—"

Silas tensed at the small breath that escaped her lips as he lifted her foot and shifted the hem of her trousers up several inches. Her skin was soft, and he gritted his teeth as an ounce of guilt trickled through his veins at the thought of the cuff breaking her skin there as it had on her wrists. He wouldn't allow it. As soon as she was back in the cell, he'd make sure no cuff hurt her.

Why did he care?

He cleared his throat as he clamped the cuff around her ankle, securing it with a key before attaching the other cuff to the end of the bed. With a yank on the chain to make sure she was secure, Silas stood.

"I'll return in a few hours to collect you. I recommend getting some sleep while you can." He spoke as he turned to leave, pausing only when she responded.

"You're taking me back?"

Silas bit his lip, taking a moment to collect his thoughts as he tilted his chin back and stared at the ceiling. Why did he care that every single part of her question was dripping with audible fear? Why did that make him want to promise he'd never let her go back to the dungeon? Why? Why did she matter?

When he didn't respond, she spoke again. "That's it?"

He took a deep breath before he faced her. "I'm going to put Dianna and the guard you attacked in two of the beds."

"I didn't attack—"

"Then I'm going to go tell the king about your attempt to escape." That shut her up.

And without another word, Silas left her lying in the infirmary.

"SHE DIDN'T GET FAR THOUGH," Silas said, covering his mouth as yet another yawn threatened to break free during his conversation with the king.

"And you just happened across her?" Butch didn't try to hide his skepticism as he took a sip from his tea. The two of them sat in the empty council room. The king had a meeting with his council members regarding the war efforts in the North in only a few minutes, but he had agreed to meet with Silas at his insistence.

"I can't explain it," Silas said as he shook his head. "I couldn't sleep, and there was a bad feeling in my—" He stopped speaking, his hand hovering just above his stomach.

Butch raised an eyebrow at him. "Well," the king said matter-of-factly after a few seconds of silence, "I'm glad you caught her. And I want her returned to the dungeon as soon as possible. I don't want to risk her getting free again and wreaking havoc in my home."

"I'll go now." Silas pushed up from his chair, nodding briefly at the king before heading toward the door. He paused when Butch called his name.

"Silas, take someone with you. Two are better than one, especially when facing someone with magic."

"Of course," Silas said, holding back a grimace until he'd closed the meeting room door. The small amount of guilt he swallowed each time his best friend mentioned magic—the very same magic that ran through Silas's veins—choked him more and more ever since he'd first pulled out his rune pen to save Evie.

Silas yawned, covering his mouth with the back of his hand as he headed back toward the infirmary. After preventing Evie from escaping, he'd gone to change into his uniform before meeting Butch, but when he caught a glimpse of himself in one of the many mirrors along the hallways, he noticed one side of his collar was popped up and his buttons on the jacket were gapping. What he wouldn't give for a few more hours of sleep. Sleep that didn't include a repeated dream of Evie sneaking down the very same hallway in which he'd caught her. Sleep that didn't include dreams that left her face etched into his mind hours after waking. Sleep that lasted more than an hour.

With each step he took, the sleepless night weighed heavier on his eyelids. He stopped in the middle of the hallway, moving to lean against the wall to balance himself as the corridor swam around him. He'd never felt so exhausted in his life, and he wondered how much of it had to do with his multiple sleepless nights and how much was owed to Evie's magic.

As if closing his eyes summoned the memory, he watched the dream he'd had every night since bringing her to the infirmary flash across his mind. Her hesitant footsteps. The sight of her clinging to the walls to stay upright. The glances over her shoulder. Panic flashing across her lovely eyes as the vase toppled to the floor. The winding staircase she climbed as if she hadn't been sick and lying in a bed for days or been locked in a cell for months. The anger and desperation in her face when he caught her—trapped her with the chain.

He'd experienced it all. Over and over and over again. And with fear of it coming true keeping him up at night, he'd waited. Waited in the small study for her to try to sneak past.

Waited.

And caught her. Just like in the dream.

Maybe that meant he wouldn't have the blasted dream anymore.

Maybe he'd get some sleep.

He chuckled darkly.

For some reason, the idea sounded more outlandish than his dreams coming true exactly as he'd seen them.

Silas rubbed his fingers over his temple before continuing through the castle halls toward the infirmary. The sun was only just beginning to ascend into the sky, occupying the space the moons had not a few hours ago.

When she'd been sitting there on the bed, looking down at him with those wide eyes and—

Coming to an abrupt halt, Silas pressed his palms into his closed eyes.

"She's a prisoner, Thorne," he muttered under his breath. "An enemy of the royal family. An enemy to you, idiot."

And yet . . .

It felt like he knew her. He'd known her face, her eyes, long before he'd seen her that day in the gully. He'd watched her age within charcoal-covered pages.

He took a shuddering breath before gritting his teeth and marching toward the room his thoughts often traveled to: any room she occupied.

It was that accursed sketchbook. It had to be. Some foolish part of him had started to believe that everything in those pages would happen. Maybe a few had, but that didn't mean the rest would.

He never should've accepted the sketchbook, let alone looked inside. Without prompting, a single sketch flooded his mind until it was clearer than the corridor before him.

The wall. Her hands around his shoulders. The flush of her cheeks. The look in her eyes as her—

This. This was why he'd offered to go to replace Marshal Levick in the Black Forest. This was why he needed some sort of physical space that would allow him to think clearly.

Because he couldn't think clearly.

Not when Evie was involved.

Not with those stubborn brown eyes watching his every step.

Not when he'd seen them staring at him in black-and-white detail, as if she knew every part of him and still wanted more.

Chapter 13

EVANGELINE

Evangeline couldn't bring herself to meet Dianna's eye when the woman finally woke up on a bed near the exit door. In fact, her stomach was twisting so much that she feigned sleep just to avoid talking to the woman. But it wouldn't take a genius to notice the new accessory around Evangeline's ankle.

Just the thought of the cold metal suffocating her magic summoned the image of Thorne on his knees before her.

Now *that* twisted her stomach.

But not in the way she expected.

Her heart began to race faster with every second that passed, and she forced herself to take a deep breath, choosing to focus on the heat of the sun shining down on her instead of the warmth that had filled her at Thorne's gentle touch on her ankle, his cerulean eyes meeting hers, the way she'd almost wanted his hands to linger against her skin.

Evangeline froze. Heat radiated from her cheeks, and it quickly became one of those few moments when she was grateful for the cuff on her ankle preventing the blush she knew was darkening her face from lighting up with her magic.

"Are you awake?" Dianna's soft voice roused Evangeline from her thoughts, and with an inward sigh, Evangeline turned over and met the physician's gaze.

"Is something wrong?" The words barely made it out of Evangeline's lips before the weight of her actions settled upon her like the thin wool blanket had turned to lead. The tension in her muscles coiled tighter with each passing second.

She should apologize for what she'd done, but that would mean she'd reveal her magic. There was no telling how Dianna would react or who she would tell.

"I just . . . I should rewrap your wrists with new salve." Dianna pulled the stool toward the bed. She avoided meeting Evangeline's gaze, but that didn't stop her from asking a question Evangeline should've been ready for but wasn't. "Did you try to run?"

Evangeline's breath caught for a moment before she sighed and glanced toward the wide windows. "Yes."

"Why?"

"Isn't it obvious?" Evangeline studied the window. "I'm a prisoner in this awful place."

Dianna remained quiet for a moment, her focus on the cloth bandage she unwrapped from Evangeline's wrist. When she spoke, her voice was soft. "It's a refuge to me."

Evangeline caught her gaze, surprise flooding through her at the sight of moisture filling Dianna's eyes.

"Dianna, I'm—" Before Evangeline could apologize, Dianna shook her head.

"He's a good man. The king. You just . . . You don't understand." Dianna tugged at the bandage around Evangeline's wrist.

"Why do you hold him in such high regard?" Evangeline asked after a moment of silence. It took Dianna a second before she sighed and responded.

"My husband and I lived in the Glass Fields. Neither of us expected the war to come to our village, and we weren't ready when we were told to evacuate. It took us a day to pack what we could. Many others were going to leave the next day too, but . . ." Dianna's words faded as she pinched her eyes shut and took a shaky breath. "But the fighting came early. Whatever line the royal guards held broke, and the battle trampled our village beneath its boots.

"My husband and I tried to leave, but a stray arrow struck him. I wouldn't—I couldn't leave him. All we could do was hunker down. I tried to save him. I tried—" Dianna's resolve cracked, and tears flowed freely down her freckled cheeks. "A guard found me a while after my husband had died. The sounds from the battle had started to fade, but I was too distraught to leave my love and seek safety. The guard was injured, and after he reassured me that he wasn't going to hurt me, I used the supplies I had left to help him. In exchange, he brought me to his captain, and they offered me safe passage with an escort of guards who were returning to Cyanthia.

"When I arrived, King Butch asked to see me because I had helped one of his men. He's not an evil king. He's not. He . . . He offered his deepest apologies for my loss, as well as to compensate for my husband's death. He could've stopped there, but instead he offered me sanctuary here, working under Helena." Dianna met Evangeline's gaze again, and this time there was a fierceness that radiated through her, straightening her posture.

"He chose to take care of me, as he has done for many others in his employ. I'm certainly not the only one he provides housing, food, and pay for. He is our king, and he deserves respect."

Evangeline pinched her lips together, restraining the words she wished to say. *He's not* my *king, nor will he ever be.*

She couldn't stop her thoughts from trailing down a path she knew well. Respect needed to be earned, and the best way the king would do that would be to end the ridiculous war on magic. Simple as that.

As if reading her thoughts, Dianna continued. "I don't know what you've done, nor do I care to. But I do know that the king is protective of those he cares for, and if you had anything to do with the queen's disappearance—"

"I didn't." Evangeline lifted her chin, her jaw tightening at the thought of Emmalee's foolish act. "Are you finished?" She glanced down at her wrist, which Dianna had rewrapped.

The physician did Evangeline's other wrist in silence, which weighed heavily on Evangeline as she refused to look anywhere but the window.

It was a while after Dianna had left Evangeline's bedside that the door to the infirmary opened, and a few seconds later, Thorne's voice carried over the room.

"It's time for her to return to the cells, by order of the king."

She'd been expecting it, but his arrival still sent a wave of chills through her that her magic couldn't prevent because of the cuff around her ankle.

Evangeline didn't take her attention from the window until multiple sets of footsteps stopped next to her bedside.

"Marshal Thorne," Helena said, drawing Evangeline's attention when the physician came around to the side of the bed closest to the window. Evangeline had been so focused on the freedom lingering outside that she hadn't noticed when Dianna had left and Helena had replaced her.

"You're taking her back already?" Helena asked, resting her hands on the bedside. Though she didn't look down at Evangeline, her protectiveness radiated through her stature and tone.

"I apologize, but the king has decided she needs to return to her cell." Void of all emotion, Thorne's voice did not betray what had happened during the night.

"Her wounds are healing and the medicine is fighting off the infection, but she's far from *healed*." Helena narrowed her gaze at a spot over the bed, and it was only when she switched it to something else that Evangeline glanced at where Thorne stood.

With the Mongoose.

It took most of Evangeline's willpower not to groan when her gaze landed on her least favorite guard, who was regarding her as if she were horse manure sticking to the bottom of his polished boots.

Evangeline tightened her jaw, reminding herself to remain quiet in the new company. She'd made the mistake of speaking with Thorne, but she would not repeat it with the Mongoose. Evangeline kept her eyes on the two men, matching the Mongoose's glare with one of her own.

"He's quite insistent," Thorne said, his formal posture contrasting with the man who'd pinned her to a wall the night before and prevented her escape.

He looked rough, with dark circles gathering beneath his eyes and his uniform gapping in weird spots. She wondered if he'd had the chance to sleep. Or where he slept. Did he live in the castle or somewhere in Cyanthia? Was he married? Did he have a family? A wife?

Evangeline bristled. Foolish little thoughts pecked at her mind, but she wrote them off as being brought about by the small amount of sleep she herself had gotten. Even though she'd managed to nap a little since he'd returned her to the infirmary, she wished she could've slept again before returning to the dark abyss.

"Very well," Helena said, shifting beside the bed. "But she will need to continue to take the medicine, and either I or Dianna will visit her to redress her wounds each day."

"Of course," Thorne said, nodding. "We want the continued progress in her health as much as you do."

Evangeline held back a scoff, knowing Helena's motives to see her healthy were far less selfish than Thorne's and the king's. Recovering likely meant she'd only have more grueling hours of pointless interrogation to look forward to.

And she doubted the Mongoose wanted her to heal at all.

"On your feet," the Mongoose barked at Evangeline, his hand reaching to his belt where a pair of cuffs dangled.

At the same time Evangeline widened her eyes, Helena spoke.

"You can't put this girl in chains again—not with her wrists in this condition." Helena's voice was firm.

"With all due respect, she's a prisoner, and—"

"Helena is correct," Thorne said, cutting Stoll off. "Her wrists are off-limits when it comes to the cuffs." He nodded toward Evangeline's ankle. "That'll suffice."

Helena must not have noticed the chain because her face contorted into something like disdain when she moved her gaze from the metal to Thorne and Stoll. She kept her lips pressed tightly together, though, and did not argue.

"Rest assured, she'll remain uncuffed in her cell. We have no intention of seeing her fall ill again. Right, Commander Stoll?"

The Mongoose's beady gaze fell on Evangeline, and he sneered at her as he responded. "Yes, sir," he said through a clenched jaw.

Evangeline didn't even try to hold back her smirk, knowing it'd irritate him more, just like it had the king.

Thorne wiped it from her face as soon as he approached her ankle and pushed back the fabric of her trousers again, just as he had when he'd knelt before her. With nimble fingers, he unlocked the cuff looped around the bed, though he left its partner attached to Evangeline.

"Stand, please," Thorne said, his crystal gaze resting on her.

Evangeline shifted, glancing back at Helena, who nodded. Evangeline rose from the bed, the floor cold on her bare feet. Unlike during her escape attempt, Evangeline took time lacing up her boots, which had been left by the end of the cot.

A smile threatened to cross her lips when she could tell that her slow movements were causing irritation to rise in the two men. They didn't force her to move any faster though—not with Helena standing there ready to speak out on her behalf, unless it had to do with her remaining aboveground. Apparently, the physician had only so much pull.

When Evangeline finally got both boots on, she walked to the other side of the bed. She wanted to thank Helena once more, but she kept her mouth closed. Instead, she inclined her head toward the physician, offering a small smile. But it felt weighed down, and the smile fell quickly from her lips when the Mongoose gripped Evangeline around the upper arm. She couldn't keep the glare from leaving her eyes as she looked at him. His meaty hand clamped tighter, the rough glove irritating her skin.

He was leading her toward the door, Thorne trailing behind them, when Helena spoke up one last time.

"If I see that her injuries worsen down there, I'll have to request that she return to the infirmary."

Evangeline glanced back over her shoulder, noting the intensity behind Helena's eyes.

Thorne bowed his head. "Of course, Helena. Thank you."

The Mongoose tugged Evangeline's arm, and she glared at the ground as they led her out of the infirmary. She tried to think of something positive about returning to the cells, but the only thing she could come up with was that she'd see Odette again.

"Thank you, Stoll. I'll take it from here," Thorne said when they reached the top of the stairs leading down to the dungeon.

"Of course, sir," the Mongoose replied, releasing Evangeline to salute.

Once the guard left, Thorne nodded to the two guards at the top of the stairs and led Evangeline down. He did not, however, lay a hand on her. The clanking of the loose cuff around her ankle was reminder enough that she wouldn't be able to overpower him—with or without her magic.

The fear that trickled through her veins nearly exploded when Thorne stopped halfway down the stairs and cleared his throat. She froze when he turned to look at her.

"We need to talk."

Chapter 14

EVANGELINE

Evangeline glanced over her shoulder, taking a step back up.

"I don't suggest it," Thorne muttered, nodding in the direction she had looked. "I'd wager I'm faster."

Evangeline held back the comment threatening to slip from her lips: if his wide shoulders and muscular neck were any indication, he hadn't been wasting away in a prison cell for months like she had. Instead, Evangeline pressed her lips together as she crossed her arms, a silent indication for him to speak since she had no intention of doing so.

"I'm leaving for a while." Thorne rested one hand on the hilt of his sword, but it didn't seem to be a threat by the tone of his voice.

Evangeline held back the question, knowing he might continue. Instead, she studied his face, which rested at the same level as hers since he stood a few steps down. The crease in his brow led her to believe he wasn't thrilled at the opportunity to leave. Even more surprising, *she* wasn't pleased about him leaving.

"I'm going to go replace a marshal who's been searching for Estrada."

His words made Evangeline lift her chin, and she shifted her gaze to the side. It was just another one of his ploys to try to get her to talk.

She wouldn't let it work.

"I thought I'd give you a warning," Thorne said, raising an eyebrow. Despite the prideful gleam in his eye, there was something else, something darker, lurking beneath. "The king has grown tired of your silence and is considering other means of making you talk. It is in your best interest that you don't force his hand in this matter."

"Force his hand?" Evangeline retorted, not bothering to play her silent game anymore. She'd already failed in regard to him—truly, epically failed, if she really thought about it. "And since when do you bother yourself with *my* best interest? I will not speak to that man."

A shadow fell over Thorne's face, darkening his features from one side as he took a step up, his face drawing nearer to hers. "I recommend you use the time I'm away to consider what you might be able to tell the king."

Fire burned in Evangeline's belly despite the magic-dampening cuff still clinging to her ankle.

"I know exactly what I would tell the king," she said, making him raise his eyebrows.

"And what would that be?"

"That he's wasting his time holding me here. It's been months. Even if I knew where Emmalee was that night, I've been locked in a dark hole since then." Evangeline crossed her arms over her chest, glaring at him. "But clearly, neither of you are bright enough to realize that."

Thorne took a deep breath, his chest puffing out. But he didn't seem surprised that the words she spoke were not at all beneficial to the king or him.

"He and I have considered that," he said, and without another word, he continued a few steps down before Evangeline stopped him.

"Then why am I still here? What do you want from me? Why am I still breathing?" Evangeline asked, not moving. "You know I have—"

Thorne shot back up the stairs. In one swift motion, he covered her mouth with one hand and braced the other behind her head before shoving her against the wall. She let out a muffled squeak. His body flush against her, feeling as unmovable as the cold stone pressed against her back, just as it had the night before. Evangeline didn't dare breathe as she watched him with wide eyes. Didn't dare expand her chest, didn't dare push back against him.

She did, however, consider trying to bite him again.

"Don't," Thorne whispered, his voice taut as he scanned her face. "I told you to stay quiet about that."

The shock from his quick movements and close proximity was wearing off. Fast. It was replaced by a growing sense of annoyance. With a smirk, she opened her mouth and licked the inside of his hand since it wasn't close enough to bite.

He growled, pulling away and rubbing his palm down the front of his trousers. Thorne backed down a few stairs and glanced up at her with narrowed eyes.

"You licked me."

"You deserved it." Evangeline wiped her mouth with the back of her hand, stepping away from the wall. She reined in the cocky grin she so desperately wanted to display, instead choosing an air of annoyance.

Thorne surprised her by letting out what almost sounded like a snort instead of getting angry like she'd expected. Pressing his lips together, he shook his head and placed his hands on his hips. "Only the king and I know." There was a pause before he continued in a lower voice. "About you. What you can do. Others may have their suspicions, but we haven't said anything, and unless you've spoken to anyone . . ."

Evangeline frowned, not adding that the cuff on her ankle had all but told the two physicians about her. Instead she asked, "Why?"

"Because you saved him."

"What?"

"That day in the gully. He remembers that you saved his life." Thorne copied her when she crossed her arms.

"I also struck him," Evangeline said, her voice quiet on the off chance they could be overheard.

"*That* he also remembers clearly, as do I." Thorne's low voice rumbled as he narrowed his eyes at her. But he shook his head, and the edge was gone when he spoke again. "He's seen what people like you can do. He's seen the bad—plenty of it—but when you saved his life, I believe you showed him it isn't all that way."

"But why does that matter? I'm clearly a prisoner," she said, gesturing at her filthy clothing. "Why keep my"—she pointed to the cuff on her ankle—"secret?"

Thorne's lips tightened, and he frowned as he reached up to a thin chain around his neck. He didn't pull it out and rubbed the side of his face instead.

"There are those in this castle who are not as patient as the king and would rather see every single person with magic slaughtered first and put on trial afterward, which makes this complicated."

Evangeline scoffed, rolling her eyes. "Lovely."

When he looked at her, his gaze had softened, and something like fear crossed over his face. "This is complicated, unfortunately. More than I wish it were." He exhaled, his brow furrowing.

She wasn't sure what it was, but something about the way he stood and the tone of his voice had her believing him. Before she could ask what he meant, he straightened his posture.

"I'll send someone down with a new tunic. Yours is . . . Well, you should have a new one. I'll make sure it happens before I leave." He glanced down at her dirty ripped tunic before meeting her eyes again. "Come. I have other things I need to attend to before I leave." He nodded for her to follow.

Evangeline considered the stairs winding up for a moment, but with a sigh, she surprised herself by not resisting his command.

He'd catch her anyway.

He seemed to have a knack for it.

Chapter 15

LENORA

Lenora stared at the wall across from her, avoiding Helena's knowing gaze from where she sat beside Lenora's bed. She couldn't speak. Couldn't move. Couldn't breathe.

"Your Majesty?" Helena spoke in a gentle voice, one Lenora knew the physician didn't employ often. Only when things were dire. When her patient was about to receive terrible news. "How are you feeling?"

"Tell me," Lenora said, her voice trembling despite her best efforts to maintain an easy façade. "Am I . . . ?"

Helena nodded when Lenora finally turned to face her. "Yes, Your Majesty. You're pregnant again."

Lenora's world seemed to waver. For a mere moment, a glimmer of joy flickered—a spark that could ignite even the dampest of wood into a blazing fire. Her breath quickened as excitement took over, and her hands instinctively moved to cradle her thin stomach.

But as quickly as the fragment of happiness appeared, it was shattered by a wave of panic. Her heart raced, a drumming rhythm in her ears that drowned out the other sounds in her room. The calming aroma of her favorite incense lit on her desk became strange and stifling. She choked when it became hard to breathe.

Her vision blurred. Flashes of her past losses came back to her—relentless wave after wave that made the room around her spin. The colorful tapestries on the walls twisted and whirled into a dizzying pattern as her palms grew clammy. Lenora shivered.

In her now brightly lit chamber in the castle, Lenora resisted the overwhelming pull of one of her worst memories until she could no longer stand it. It sucked her in, and she succumbed to the images flashing before her mind. Her room had been a bloody chamber of agony and despair.

She'd lain on the same ornate bed, but the covers were stained by crimson. The scent of blood lingered heavy in the room, metallic and acrid, mingling with the distant smell of flowers and leaves fading in the autumn air wafting in from the open window. The room was awash in muted light from the dark gray clouds covering the sky, casting eerie shadows upon the plush silk curtains.

The memory remained veiled in a suffocating fog of despair, each detail shrouded by the weight of the past. The weight of her loss. Lenora's body trembled as if she were reliving it in the present moment. Her heart thudded in her chest, a pounding drum threatening to drown out the world.

She remembered the distant figure of her husband bursting through the door. But it'd been too late. The babe hadn't even taken a single breath outside her womb. Couldn't. She'd failed her. Butch's voice had been a ghostly whisper in the dense fog surrounding the memory, and his hands, desperate and trembling, had tried to comfort her. But even his presence felt far as she'd faded in and out of consciousness.

The memory tormented her as she now sat across from Helena. In it, a surge of pain and loss overwhelmed her. The moment should've been nothing but a joyful start to a new pregnancy, but the wounds felt as fresh as if they'd happened that morning. The day she'd given birth to her dead daughter. She was trapped within the room, unable to escape the visceral haunting memories. Every detail. Every sensation. It was all etched into her consciousness, a reminder of her failure to her child. To her husband. To her country.

She needed air.

Air that wasn't fraught with overwhelming memories of copper and iron, wilting flowers, and salty sweat.

Lenora's chest tightened as she scrambled out of her bed, lurching past Helena when the room spun.

"Your Majesty!" Helena said, catching Lenora under the arm when the walls shifted and the floor quickly approached. A jolt of pain shot through her shoulder, but at least she hadn't collapsed.

As soon as the dizziness ended, Lenora pulled free from Helena's grasp and crossed to the balcony. She couldn't get the door open fast enough, her fingers fumbling with the lock.

"Open . . . Open . . ." Lenora mumbled under her frantic breath. Only when the doors blew open and she was able to stumble out onto the balcony and grip the edge of the marble railing was she finally able to fill her lungs.

The war coursing through her swelled. How could the joy of finding out she carried new life be so at contrast with every acidic drop of anxiety within her? And then the guilt spilled in. How dare she feel any negative emotion about having a child? That was her sole purpose: bear an heir. How could she feel anything but relief at finally being pregnant again?

But the memories.

The pain.

The nightmares.

Helena wouldn't understand.

Butch wouldn't understand.

No one would understand.

Well . . . not *no one*.

Someone else had experienced the loss of a child. Someone else had felt the devastation afterward. Someone else might be able to fathom the utter confusion storming within Lenora's mind.

Lenora shivered. A cool breeze swept around her, almost as if it were echoing the thoughts in her mind, mimicking the chill that had followed that woman, her captor, around constantly.

Estrada would understand.

"Your Majesty." Helena cleared her throat.

In her panic, Lenora had not noticed the physician following her out onto the balcony.

"Is there anything I can do for you?" Her gaze flicked to the edge of the balcony, to the drop beneath it. Did she think Lenora was going to jump?

With her breathing slowing down, Lenora fully faced the physician. Lenora even took a step forward in the hope that it would reassure Helena that she hadn't come outside for that purpose.

"Thank you, Helena, for telling me. If you wouldn't mind, I'd like to keep this to myself for a little while."

"You don't want me to tell His Majesty?" Helena paused, and when Lenora shook her head, Helena nodded. "Of course. I'll leave it to you to tell him, then."

"Thank you," Lenora said, her fingers still gripping the white marble railing behind her despite the rest of her body relaxing bit by bit.

"I will be telling August though. I want you to start on some drafts to strengthen you and the baby as early as tonight."

Lenora considered what she'd said. The old apothecary was harmless, but the more people who knew . . . "All right. You may tell him. Please make sure he knows not to spread the news though."

"I'll make sure he uses the utmost discretion." Helena curtsied, cast the balcony one last glance, and left without another word.

Lenora turned back around to stare out at the castle and the town below. The wind caressed her with gentle fingers, moving dark tendrils of her hair from her face as she tried to remember to breathe.

Time slipped by without Lenora paying much attention to it. Whether it was two minutes or thirty, at some point Kaylene and Merla entered her room while she still stood on the balcony.

"Lovely day, isn't it, Your Majesty?" Kaylene said, but she stopped short at the door. "Lenora?" Her voice softened, but Lenora did not turn to face her.

"Helena came to see me," Lenora said softly, her hands beginning to tremble on the railing again. With a deep breath, Lenora turned toward the door.

Kaylene and Merla stood just inside, both sets of eyes on her. Merla held a tray with tea and a few biscuits, but she placed it on the short table nearby before walking past Kaylene and drawing Lenora inside by the hand. Merla's own hands were calloused and warm as she tugged Lenora away from the railing.

"Sit down, Your Majesty, and tell us what she said." Merla sat Lenora down on the settee, allowing Kaylene the seat next to her before she herself took the empty chair across from them.

Lenora took the cup of tea Kaylene offered her. After another moment of silence, Lenora was barely able to whisper the news.

"I'm pregnant again." Her voice wavered as she spoke, the words emerging like fragile glass. She fixed her gaze on the ornate carpet at her feet, unable to meet their eyes. Her chest tightened as the memories she'd been barely fighting off threatened to return.

The room seemed to hold its breath in the silence.

Lenora's gaze finally lifted to meet her handmaids', and she did all she could to hold back the overwhelming rush of emotion. Her jaw ached from how tightly she clenched it.

The air in her bed chamber sparked with the collective emotions of the three women. Tears welled in Kaylene's eyes, and fear rested just behind

Merla's. As she held their gazes, silent understanding passed between them. Her handmaids held both joy and the reminder of her past losses.

"And? How are you?" Kaylene asked, breaking the silence with her gentle tone.

"Is there anything we can do to help?" Merla added

Lenora took a shaky breath before closing her eyes again. "Please keep it a secret for now. I . . . I don't want to get ahead of myself again. And I don't want to trouble Butch with it—not before I have to, at least."

Frowning, her handmaids exchanged a look. However, by the time they returned their attention to Lenora, the concerned expressions had been replaced by agreeable ones.

"Of course, Your Majesty." Merla nodded. "Did Helena say anything else?"

Lenora explained the physician's visit, and when both her friends offered to get the tonic from the royal apothecary later, she thanked them but denied the help. "I'd like to go myself for today just to see how he makes it."

Though it wasn't a complete lie, it also wasn't the full reason. The infirmary was down the hall from August's laboratory, which meant she'd have the opportunity to slip in and see if the prisoner her husband had mentioned was still there. If she'd recovered at all. Lenora hoped she had.

She was Lenora's only connection to Estrada.

A connection her husband had specifically told her to stay away from.

Lenora glanced between Kaylene beside her and Merla sitting across from them. They cared. She knew that. But they didn't understand her loss.

In fact, the longer she spent sitting with them and listening to them talk, the more she craved the company of someone who would understand.

Someone who knew the loss of a child.

Someone she couldn't be with.

In some twisted way, she wanted to tell Estrada about her pregnancy.

And her best bet was Estrada's friend.

She just needed to find a way to get to her, to make sure she was okay.

Better yet, maybe she could even get the prisoner out with a message for Estrada.

See her taste the freedom Lenora so desperately missed.

But what risks would she have to take, and would it be worth it if freeing Estrada's friend meant betraying her husband? Her country?

Chapter 16

EMMALEE

Emmalee stood in front of a mirror and glared at the rune she'd drawn on her throat as it faded in front of her eyes. She'd been thrilled when it had worked, transforming her voice into one she didn't recognize. But it'd only lasted half an hour before it wore off and revealed her identity.

Since it'd worn off, she'd gone back to the books to look for other ones to practice. Emmalee sighed as she flipped through the rune book. While she had gotten good practice with some of them, she was no closer to figuring out how to save Evangeline than when she'd gotten the rune pen over a month earlier.

The runes scrawled in inky black lines blurred together, and her eyes focused on the yellowed pages rather than the symbols. She couldn't remember the last time she'd had a full night of sleep without waking up from a nightmare, either about Anwell and Hazel or about Evangeline.

Her shoulder ached, and she pulled the fabric of her tunic back to rub her scar. Each time it throbbed, she was reminded of two things: her enemy was more cunning than she gave him credit for, and she wasn't immortal.

The next time she made an attempt at getting justice from the king, every detail needed to be laid out and every eventuality planned for. In the meantime, though, there were other people who might play very important roles in giving her information she needed in regard to her final target: the king.

And that meant hunting down guards—preferably the ones who'd also played a part in murdering her family—and figuring out all the cards the king had in his hand so she could free Evangeline and have another ally on her side.

But even that would require the right timing and a flawless plan.

She needed to know where the king was keeping her friend, how to get there unnoticed, and how to get out without being caught. While she could assume the king was keeping her in the dungeon of his castle, that was a guess, and it offered the small percent of failure should Evangeline not be there.

No, she needed certainty.

And to do that, she needed more information.

"ABSOLUTELY NOT!" Faeleen hissed, her vibrant green eyes bright as her pupils narrowed to slits. She crossed her arms over her chest. "You are not bringing a royal guard in here to interrogate him. Not only is that stupid and irresponsible, it's also—"

"Idiotic and foolish and dangerous and—"

"I get it," Emmalee said, cutting Ariella off. Emmalee held her hands up in surrender. "That's why I asked. I'll find someplace else to take them."

"The whole idea is ridiculous! You'll get yourself killed!" Faeleen continued, throwing her hands up in frustration. "You're smarter than this, Em."

"I need information on the castle, and there's no one better to give it to me than the king's men themselves." Emmalee sat back on the small couch, hiding the fact that she agreed with them. If there were any other way . . .

Besides, it would be two birds with one stone should the guard be one of the ones who had been responsible for the deaths of her husband and daughter.

Emmalee shoved the thought aside. Her focus needed to be on Evangeline—on getting her out of the castle. Justice for her family would come afterward with Evangeline's help. They'd do it together, just like they'd spoken about when Evangeline had saved her that day in the boulder field.

The thought of Evangeline sent a pang through Emmalee's chest. She missed her. Missed talking to her. Missed baking with her. Missed simply sitting next to each other in silence. She'd sent Evangeline a few messages with her magic, but there had been no response.

It left Emmalee feeling emptier each time she sent one.

"We know this is important to you, Em," Ariella started to say.

"But we want to make sure nothing happens to you," Faeleen finished for her sister. "You know how much we care for you."

"We don't want you to get hurt. Or worse," Ariella said, concern wrinkling her brow.

"I appreciate that." Emmalee sighed, rubbing her right temple. It had started to throb, and the more she pressed against it, the worse the ache became. "But I need to get Evie back. There's no telling what the king has put her through already."

Or if she was still alive.

Emmalee stiffened as the distressing idea invaded her thoughts. There was no preventing it, and it rested on the edge of her mind constantly. But Evangeline had to be alive.

She had to be.

"That's true," Faeleen said in regard to something Ariella had said.

"At least he shut down Château Lavfor," Ariella added, causing her sister to nod in agreement.

Emmalee didn't respond. She'd known about the castle of horrors, but she hadn't thought about it as a threat.

Not until now.

Because now *she* had magic.

Of course it was something the sisters had thought about; they'd been at risk of being taken to Lavfor when they were younger and King Valryn still reigned. Emmalee wondered how much the sisters had worried over their safety growing up right under the king's nose in Cyanthia. They'd done a very good job of shielding her from their fears when she was young. She was only now starting to see how many precautions they'd taken to keep each other and her safe.

"What?" Faeleen asked, and when Emmalee glanced at her, Faeleen's green eyes narrowed. "Why are you making that face?"

She hadn't even noticed that she was clenching her jaw and that a wave of cold was trickling through her. Emmalee reined her magic in before it could manifest in an ominous dark cloud, but Ariella's gaze had already dropped to Emmalee's clenched fist.

"What is it, Em?" Ariella spoke in a softer voice than her sister. She wrapped a straight strand of her long fair hair around her finger over and over again.

"It's not important." When neither of the sisters dropped their intense gazes, Emmalee continued. "I'd never considered Lavfor. I just . . . I guess I was never worried about it. Not until now. I know it's no longer in operation, but I suppose it's still a threat."

Ariella shook her head at the same time Faeleen spoke.

"It's not. When King Butch took the throne, he shut the entire château down. It's covered in ivy, and no one has been there in ages—at least, no one except the guards left to watch it for any intruders."

"How do you know?" Emmalee asked Faeleen. The mention of the king by name had her gritting her teeth as her stomach tensed. Strange how the mention of a person's name could cause such a visceral reaction.

"We had an order from a nearby village and went past it a few months ago. It looks intimidating from the outside, but it's worn down and harmless."

Ariella glanced at Emmalee and nodded. "And for that you should be glad. It makes your job easier."

"Easier?"

"The Cyanthian castle is hard enough to enter, but Lavfor was *made* to keep magic folk helpless," Faeleen said, sending a hesitant glance toward Ariella.

"That's the last place any of us would want to wind up," Ariella added, a small shiver passing through her.

Emmalee leaned back. They made a fair point, and it wouldn't benefit her to focus on anything not related to Evangeline.

They sat in silence for a while, not meeting one another's eyes. Finally, Emmalee shifted on the couch, tucking her feet beneath her.

"You mentioned an abandoned village not too far away, right?" Emmalee asked. She watched the sisters carefully and gauged their reactions.

Faeleen bit her lip, wrinkling her nose as she remained silent. Ariella moved as though she was uncomfortable in her seat before nodding.

"It's northeast of here," Ariella said. "But please be careful, Em. There are a lot of people who still lurk around that area, and I'm sure not all of them are friendly to our kind."

"By that she means there are bounty hunters who would happily turn you in to the king for their heaping reward." Faeleen crossed her arms over her chest, a sour expression still painted across her youthful features.

"I'm sure they would try," Emmalee said, and while it seemed to ease the tension written across Ariella's face, it only made Faeleen sit straighter. "I'll be all right, Fae. I won't do anything until I'm ready. You know that."

119

"I know that's always your *intention*," Faeleen muttered. "But I also know that you nearly got one of the other kids arrested in Cyanthia out of spite because you thought she was going to take your territory."

Emmalee held her tongue, refraining from pointing out that she had been a child at the time. *And* she hadn't been wrong. The older girl *had* wanted Emmalee's streets for her own pickpocketing and thievery, and she would've gotten it had Emmalee not stood her ground.

It hadn't been impulsive.

It'd been what she needed to do.

That was a lesson she'd learned early on from the two women sitting with her. She would do what she needed to in order to survive.

"I'll be careful," Emmalee repeated before standing. "I'm going to walk there now and see if I can get an idea of which buildings are usable. I'll stay out of sight."

Before the sisters could argue, Emmalee grabbed her dark violet cloak and left.

Evangeline needed her, and no bounty hunter, royal guard, or pompous king would stand in her way.

She'd do what it took to make sure Evangeline survived too.

PART TWO

Chapter 17

EMMALEE

Emmalee's legs ached from the walk back to Ariella and Faeleen's from the abandoned village. It was the third day in a row she'd made the two-hour trek back and forth, but at least she'd found a place that would allow her the space she needed to interrogate a guard without having to worry about the sisters getting sucked into her dealings. The last thing she wanted was to have them fall into the king's hands after so many years of trying to protect each other.

When Emmalee wasn't making the trek back and forth, she had managed to successfully draw a special rune that prevented sounds from leaving a room. It was temporary but would give her more than enough time to interrogate the royal guards.

There was only one hiccup in her plan.

She had no idea what to do with the men after she'd finished questioning them.

Despite the night in the boulder field and the mistake in the village with Ariella, she didn't want to kill any of the guards. Evangeline wouldn't want that, even if some of them were murderers themselves.

Especially the ones who'd killed her family . . .

Emmalee shook her head. She didn't want to kill them.

But what to do with them?

It was a question she pondered all the way back to Ariella and Faeleen's.

Letting them go was completely out of the question. They'd run straight back to the other guards, and an army of the king's men would descend on Emmalee—and quite possibly Ariella and Faeleen—in no time. There had to be a way of subduing them without killing them. Perhaps a rune or a spell.

If only she still had the grimoire. There certainly had to have been a useful spell in the book from the banshee—not that it could help her now that the king had most assuredly gotten rid of it.

"Just like all the other books he and his ancestors have destroyed," Emmalee muttered as she rounded the corner to the fabric shop.

She was already through the front door and halfway to the back of the shop by the time she lowered her hood and pulled out her dark waves. It was time for a trim—her hair had grown long past her comfortable shoulder length and was nearly down to the middle of her back. Maybe Ariella could remove a few inches without making it look hacked off. Hopefully she'd improved since the last time she'd cut Emmalee's hair. Emmalee grinned at the memory of the horribly uneven cut Ariella had given her. Faeleen's hair was at least a bit forgiving with the tight curls. Emmalee's . . . not as much.

The sisters weren't down in the shop when Emmalee arrived, though that didn't surprise her. It was almost time to close according to the dimming lights out in the streets, and that typically meant the sisters were setting up for work the next day.

Sure enough, Faeleen stood on a ladder and was leaning over one of the large vats wiping down the inside when Emmalee entered.

"We weren't sure when to expect you," Faeleen said without looking at her. Her catlike ears were exposed with her short hair pulled back into a half-up ponytail. It made her look younger somehow, even from the side.

"Is Ari upstairs?" Emmalee asked, glancing over her shoulder at the staircase.

Faeleen shook her head, finally turning to look at Emmalee. "She's out shopping. We ran out of flour and oil but didn't have time to go to market earlier today. She'll be back soon though." Faeleen tossed the rag in her hand into a dirty bucket on the floor before hopping down from the short ladder.

"Can I help with anything?" Emmalee asked. "I could clean off—"

The door to the shop slammed open. Emmalee and Faeleen ran out of the back room in time to see Ariella shut the door behind her.

"What is it?" Faeleen asked as Ariella turned the sign in the front window from Open to Closed, hurriedly shutting the curtains a second later.

Ariella's cheeks were flushed, and a frantic look glistened in her slitted teal eyes. Strands of hair flew loose from the two blond buns she'd braided to cover her feline ears on the top of her head, having forgone the scarf that normally covered them.

"Ariella?" Faeleen's voice came out as a sharp squeak, her posture straightening as she watched her sister continue to move around the shop, blowing out the lanterns until the front fell into darkness.

"Royal guards," Ariella said, taking her cloak off and tossing it to Faeleen. Her younger sister caught it and shoved it behind the counter. "They're checking Ajorr for a woman with dark magic. A sorceress." Ariella's wide eyes found Emmalee's own dark ones. "Em, they're in the village searching for you."

Before Ariella could say anything else, Faeleen sprinted past Emmalee to the back of the shop. As soon as she was out of the room, Ariella turned to Emmalee.

"We need to hide you," Ariella said, her voice hushed as she grabbed Emmalee by the upper arm and pulled her away from the front door. But they stopped at the entrance to the back.

Emmalee bobbed her head in agreement but fell short of finding any feasible options. "Where? They'll check the apartment if they come in, and there's no point in—"

"In the back, under the vats. There should be enough space." Ariella's eyes, like her sister's, were vibrant, though hers held a bluish tint when compared to Faeleen's.

"Are you sure they won't—"

Voices shouted outside the door, and Ariella pulled Emmalee to the back. The three clean vats shone in the remaining lantern light, and Emmalee eyed them warily.

"You have to hide," Ariella said, urgency filling her voice. She let go of Emmalee so she could race to the other side of the room to pull a lever on one of the mixing machines. The arms started to turn on all three despite the fact that they were empty. Ariella pulled a different lever lower to the floor, and a hatch opened on the side of the farthest vat.

Emmalee stepped in front of it, bending down to peer inside. Gears turned and pipes crisscrossed over one another. But if she was able to contort her body, she might be capable of squeezing into the back, which was shrouded in semidarkness.

Despite the mechanical noise coming from the machines, Emmalee could just make out the sound of the front door crashing open, followed by impatient shouts. She glanced over her shoulder in time to see Faeleen letting her hair down to cover her feline ears as she raced to the front of the store. She paused for only a second to motion for Emmalee to hide.

"I'll let you out as soon as they finish searching in here. Stay silent," Ariella whispered, waiting until Emmalee was all the way in before she shut the hatch.

Emmalee bit her lip as she hit her head on a pipe, trying not to make a sound. It smelled musty, as if the air beneath the vats was never circulated. She scrunched her face when she put her hand in a slimy puddle. Her cloak got stuck twice, and she didn't think about the threat of the turning gears until one almost caught her hand. She felt it rotating and pulled away only a second before it would've minced her fingers. Her body squirmed at the mere thought of the metal crunching her bones.

It didn't help that as soon as Ariella had closed the little door, all the light had gone away except for a sliver that leaked out from a crack in the metal. But even then, she was forced to use her memory from the brief look she'd gotten of it. And there wasn't enough of a memory to avoid bumping random parts of her body against the machinery, some of which were extremely hot. She couldn't risk lighting a fire with her magic; the guards might see it and become suspicious.

The air was muggy, and she was already sweating after only being inside for a minute. Tiny droplets formed on the back of her neck, dripping to the front and down her chest as she bent over.

When she ran into the back of the small space, she turned around to face where she assumed the entrance was. Her pale violet tunic seemed to be a beacon shining out in the darkness even with the lack of light. She pulled her dark cloak tighter around herself.

If only she'd stayed in the abandoned village a little longer . . .

Emmalee shoved the useless thought away. If she'd stayed longer, she may have walked in *during* the search. That would've been worse.

The bass of the male voices carried and rang into Emmalee's hiding space. She listened, trembling from head to toe.

She couldn't get caught—not when Evangeline was depending on her.

Not when it would surely mean Ariella's and Faeleen's quick arrests. Or deaths.

She had to protect the sisters.

". . . required to let us search your back room," an unfamiliar voice said, and Emmalee stiffened at the sound of it.

"I understand that, and I'm not trying to stop you. I'm just saying that this machinery is extremely expensive, so please don't break anything." Ariella must've been close because her voice was louder than the man's.

Holding her breath, Emmalee tensed as the guards began to move things around and bang on some of the vats.

"How do these run?" a guard asked, his voice closer to Emmalee than she was comfortable with. He followed his question with a bang on the vat Emmalee hid beneath.

"Steam," Ariella responded, and she must've patted the vat. "We probably dyed the material used to make those very uniforms." Pride filled her voice, but the guard merely grunted.

"Can a person fit in them?"

Ariella let out a high-pitched laugh Emmalee recognized; her friend was scared. Truly scared. When Ariella spoke again, her cadence was off, and her volume was louder than normal. "Take a look. We're heating them now for the next batch, and you'll see just how dangerous it would be to sit inside while the arms are turning. I wouldn't recommend the swim. Not to mention that when the liquid is in there, it could very well burn your skin off given enough time."

Another bang rang next to Emmalee's ear, and she cringed away. Her hands trembled, and she struggled to swallow as the guard asked his next question.

"What about underneath?"

"Underneath?" Ariella's voice was once again too high.

"They're bolted to the floor," Faeleen said when her sister failed to answer the question. A perfect team, the two of them. Always had been. "There isn't really an underneath."

The noise of the machines mixing above and around Emmalee filled the air, and she waited for the guards to move on to the next shop, or at least back to the front of the store. She wanted to be able to breathe deeply again without fear of bumping into something and making noise.

"Open the hatch," a guard said, sending chills through Emmalee. As far as she knew, there was only one hatch—and it led directly to her hiding place.

Ariella didn't argue, which Emmalee knew was wise, as it would've been suspicious. But as soon as Emmalee heard the hatch opening, she couldn't help but panic.

Her dark magic swelled within her as if trying to calm her down. In her mind, she begged it to hide her, to cloak her in darkness and make her invisible to the guard's eyes. While she could feel her magic going out from her, nothing seemed to change in the dark space.

The hatch opened, and a man bent down. She could see him clearly, and she waited for him to call out that he could see her too—even she had been able to make out the back of the small space when she had first looked in. And though she had felt her magic go out from her, there didn't seem to be a barrier protecting her from the guard.

The man tilted his head, his gaze roaming over the moving parts. But when he looked directly at her, he didn't stop. Instead, he took one more scan of the space and stood back up.

"Not enough room to hide," he said to the other guards.

Emmalee only released the breath trapped in her lungs when the hatch closed again. She inwardly thanked her magic for saving her life. However, her blood ran cold when the guard spoke again.

"Do I know you? I could've sworn I've seen you somewhere."

"Me?" Ariella asked. "I don't think so, unless you've come to collect the fabrics for the castle."

Emmalee's chest tightened. She doubted that was what the guard had meant. They wouldn't notice a poor fabric dyer—not unless she was doing something that would catch their attention, like flashing her eyes or hissing at a merchant.

There were only so many guards assigned to the area. If he recognized her . . .

"There's a second floor, yes?" a guard farther away from Emmalee's hiding spot asked. The first guard hadn't said anything else, and something about the abrupt end to the discussion left Emmalee's stomach turning.

After another too-long silence, Faeleen said, "Yes, it's this way."

Emmalee couldn't tell how many guards there were, only that there were enough to cause a thunderous sound when they marched up the stairs to the apartment above.

Her mind raced. What if they found the books on runes? She'd just left them out like a fool.

Raising a shaking clammy hand, Emmalee focused on sending her magic out as an extended set of eyes. It crept along the floor in serpentine movements, an invisible squirming thing that traveled up past the last few guards stepping up the final flight of stairs.

Emmalee's breath stopped short. Seven, eight, nine. There were nine of them by the time her magic slipped past them undetected into the farthest room on the left. Why were there nine royal guards in the sisters' shop? How many more were outside in the village? And even more startling, how had she gotten back to the shop without seeing them storming through buildings? Emmalee's stomach twisted, and her extended sight went blurry for a moment when a sickening thought filled her mind.

Had they seen her?

Was that why they were there?

Had *she* brought danger straight to Ariella and Faeleen's doorstep?

Emmalee forced herself to take a breath of the acrid air. She needed to hide the evidence of her presence. But how? Her mind raced through the spells she knew, the ones she'd practiced. A mist would be too obvious. She couldn't put the guards to sleep. Her heart pounded in her chest. Maybe if she could force her magic to cover the room like it'd cloaked her beneath the machine. That had worked. But it was so far to extend that amount of magic . . .

It had to work.

She couldn't let Ariella and Faeleen get into trouble—not after the years they'd spent protecting her and the efforts they were going through to protect her now.

Emmalee regained her focus and control, forcing the extended tendrils of dark magic to wrap around and conceal the books lying out on the bed. And the desk. And the windowsill. And the floor. By the time she'd covered each with her magic, she was panting and sweating, pushing herself to her limit. It was more magic than she had used since the night at the boulder field. Her mind and body ached, her magic straining against her hold.

How could she have been so careless? If she'd just put the books away, or better yet, taken them out of the house, far away from her friends—

The door opened, and three of the guards entered the room. Emmalee held her breath as she urged the magic to hide the convicting evidence just a bit longer. Each second felt like an entire lifetime.

Stay hidden, she thought as her hand trembled. She considered raising her other hand in the hope that it might strengthen her spell, but she was currently using it to keep herself upright.

A guard approached the desk as the others filed in and started going through Emmalee's things. "Whose room is this?"

To Emmalee's horror, Ariella answered with a blatant lie.

"It's mine."

Foolish. So foolish. If the guards found anything—if Emmalee's magic failed and the king's men were able to see the illegal books on magic she was hiding—Ariella could be arrested and end up just like Evangeline.

The guard who had asked the question opened his mouth to say something else, but Ariella beat him to it.

"I have two rooms because I have too much stuff. At least, that's what my sister says. And we sometimes use this room for our family when they're visiting." Ariella kept rambling, but the guard silenced her with an irritated flick of his wrist.

"That's enough," he said, his attention still on the desk. A frown crossed his face, and for one terrifyingly long moment, Emmalee wondered if he saw through the haze she had placed around the room to cover her sins. But a second later, he nodded toward the other men. "Nothing. Move on."

Emmalee held her magic in place until she was drenched in sweat and sure that all the guards had left back through the front door.

It felt like hours, though it was probably only a few more minutes at most, until Ariella returned to the vat and opened the little hatch. When she peered in, she frowned.

"What did you do?" she asked, squatting in front of the opening. "I mean, how did he not see you? You're hard to see, but you're definitely—" Ariella's jaw dropped, and her eyebrows rose as Emmalee sent her magic out the same way she had when the guard had looked in. "It's like you're not even there. And the books in your room?"

"I covered those too."

"That's incredible," Ariella said, standing back as Emmalee let go of the spell and started to exit.

After a few complicated seconds of navigation, she was out, though it wasn't nearly as difficult as going in blind.

"Thank you for hiding me." Emmalee sighed, noting new dark stains on the knees of her trousers as well as on her hands. "But you shouldn't have claimed my room as yours. If my magic had slipped—"

"They're gone now. That's all that matters," Ariella said, closing the hatch. "Besides, if they had found your books, Fae and I would've handled it."

Faeleen scoffed as she walked into the conversation from the front of the shop. "You've got a bigger head than I thought if you believe you and I could've taken on nine royal guards."

Emmalee nodded. "It wouldn't have ended well."

"You look awful," Faeleen said to Emmalee, twirling a curl of her blond hair around in circles.

"I was just in a sweltering crawl space for at least half an hour, clinging to a spell to keep us all out of trouble."

"You were only hiding for fifteen minutes, tops," Faeleen said, shrugging. "Either way, we need to figure out what we're going to do. They were talking about sending for more guards. They're convinced you're in the area or something."

"They're not wrong," Emmalee muttered under her breath.

"It'll be harder to get in and out of the village once they arrive. We need to start planning, and we should make backup plans on top of those," Faeleen added, glancing at her sister.

Ariella scratched the back of her head. "Well, obviously, Em can't leave the house anymore—not even to go to the abandoned village. It's going to take a long time for this to blow over."

"That leaves you and me to run errands. That's doable. We'll keep the curtains shut from now on."

"Em, you need to stay upstairs where the windows aren't as easy to see through should a curtain slip," Ariella said, nodding in response to her sister's suggestion.

Emmalee's ears started to ring the more the sisters talked until her head felt as though it were going to vibrate off her shoulders. She'd brought a small army of guards into the home Ariella and Faeleen had worked so hard to build over the years. In mere months, she'd turned their world upside down. *She'd* done that. It was her fault.

And what if the guards returned unexpectedly? What if they wanted to question Ariella and Faeleen further? What if something terrible happened to them?

Heart racing, Emmalee steadied herself on the wall as she closed her eyes. She couldn't be the reason they were in danger.

She understood.

She understood *exactly* why the sisters had sent her on her way as a little nine-year-old girl. Now she was the threat to their safety, just as they had been to hers.

"And when we—"

"That's enough," Emmalee said, her voice a whisper as she shook her head. Unwanted tears started to burn within her eyes as she took a shaky breath. "You're both ignoring the problem. I'm the danger here. To you. To your lives." She held up a hand when Ariella started to argue. "You both know just as well as I do that it'd be safer for all of us if I left."

Faeleen's curls bounced as she shook her head, her brow furrowed. "No, Em, we're not going to let you just—"

"It's my choice, Fae. I already got one adopted sister into trouble by being close to her. I refuse to put your lives in jeopardy too—not after this," she said, nodding to the vat and then the front of the shop.

"Emmalee, I know what you're trying to do, but you don't have to protect us." Ariella stepped forward and grabbed one of Emmalee's hands in hers. A second later, Faeleen did the same, taking Emmalee's free hand. "We're in this together."

Squeezing both their hands, Emmalee gave a small smile before pulling away. "I'm not bringing my war with the king to you. Not anymore, at least. I can't . . . I can't undo what danger I've already put you in, but I can at least lessen it for the future."

"Em," Faeleen said, her eyes filling with matching tears to Emmalee's own. "Please stay."

"Please," Ariella added. "We can keep you safe here."

"Maybe that's true, but I need to get Evie out of the castle. I don't . . . I can't stand to think of what the king has already put her through because of me. I can't just abandon her." Emmalee wrapped her arms around herself. "And I need information to do that." She sighed.

"We can figure that out when this all dies down," Ariella said, glancing at Faeleen, who nodded in agreement.

"And if it doesn't?" Emmalee asked. Her gaze drifted around the back of the shop. "This could've been a lot worse." Emmalee pinched her lips together, then offered a small smile. "And when I finally am ready to start asking guards questions, it's going to draw even more attention. I can't be walking back and forth from Ajorr to the abandoned village. It's too obvious. I need . . . I need to leave. For you two and for Evie." Emmalee held back her tears, but it made swallowing difficult. "I'm sorry." She reached forward and pulled Ariella into a hug, then Faeleen afterward. "I'll gather my things."

Not half an hour later, they said goodbye. Both sisters continued to argue with her, trying to convince her to stay. In some ways, it reminded Emmalee of the tearful farewell they'd given her many years earlier when they'd split ways and the roles had been reversed. It wasn't any easier, except for the ever-present reminder that Evangeline needed her. And the sisters needed her to leave, not that they'd ever be rude enough to tell her. But they'd see. They'd understand. Just like she had.

Emmalee pulled her hood over her head as she left through the front door. It would've been ideal to leave through a back door, but one of the vats was directly in front of it and prevented the owners, or Emmalee, from accessing it.

As she made her way out of their village, Emmalee couldn't help but check over her shoulder to make sure she wasn't being followed. But to her delight, none of the guards noticed her as she bathed herself in darkness, blending in with the shadows using her magic.

Some part of her heart cracked when she left Ajorr for the last time, at least for the foreseeable future. Ariella and Faeleen were the closest thing besides Evangeline that Emmalee had to family, and leaving them now felt almost as terrible as it had the first time. Only this time, it was her choice. And it was for their good.

Even if it hurt.

Chapter 18

SILAS

Silas dropped his pack to the forest floor, the sound swallowed by the mossy surface beneath his boots. "We camp here," he said to the captain who came to a stop next to him. "Tell the other captains and the commanders under you to set up the tents."

"Yes, sir." Captain Malkim saluted, turning on his heel. He started barking orders, his voice bouncing around the mammoth trees of the Black Forest.

Though his men were nearby, Silas took a deep breath for what felt like the first time since they'd marched from Cyanthia. He'd ridden a horse most of the time but had walked alongside his men for the last four hours of the journey. It seemed only fair since they'd walked the rest of the multiple-day trek.

Hopefully it'd be worth it.

Hopefully, by choosing to forego the location Marshal Levick had occupied for months, he might make more progress than his counterpart.

Hopefully he'd return to the castle with Estrada arrested and the largest threat to his best friend out of the way.

Then, maybe, he could break whatever was keeping him from ending the other threat—Evie.

That was, if he wanted her dead.

Silas ran a hand through his short hair, shaking his head as he growled low from his throat. Of course he wanted her dead. He'd seen the sketches, had seen her standing above the king while he looked on the verge of death.

And yet something protective had seized him when Commander Stoll had treated the prisoner with anger on the way to the dungeon. And when she'd collapsed in the king's office, an undeniable streak of concern had struck him like lightning in the Glass Fields. And—

Why couldn't he think of anything but her? Why was she always on his mind, traipsing through his thoughts as though she belonged there? As if she weren't a deadly prisoner? As if she weren't a threat to his king? As if she weren't—

"Marshal, the men are setting up camp. How soon should I prepare them to gather for orders?" Captain Malkim emerged from the darkness, saluting as he approached Silas.

"Half an hour should suffice," Silas responded without a second of hesitation. "It won't be a long briefing. In the meantime, I want lookouts patrolling each side of camp. We are sitting between three abandoned villages, and I would wager they are not as vacant as they appear."

"Understood, sir." Captain Malkim nodded, clicking his boots together as he saluted once more. He turned to leave, but Silas stopped him.

"And Captain, I don't want anyone going off alone." He waited for the captain's nod of approval before returning the salute, dismissing him.

No one, that was, except for him.

Chapter 19

EMMALEE

Despite her careful steps, leaves crunched beneath Emmalee's boots. Her hands trembled, one resting on the hilt of her dagger just within her cloak. She'd been crouching for over two hours, waiting for a lone guard to pass her hiding spot within a twist of enormous tree roots. She was certain she had at least eight spiders crawling on her from the number of webs she'd walked through.

And yet every guard she'd seen had been with a partner.

Could she take on two lone guards? Yes.

Did she want to? No.

It'd cause too much of a commotion, especially if things went wrong. But if one isolated guard went missing, it might take longer for it to reach the higher-ranked officers.

Apparently, a single oblivious guard was too much to ask for.

Frustration finally gnawed at her, along with aching muscles from crouching for so long. After checking the coast was clear, Emmalee left her hiding spot and started back toward the abandoned village. She could refresh the silencing runes on the house she'd chosen and try again tomorrow. Emmalee forced herself to take a deep breath.

She wasn't quitting.

She wouldn't. Not on Evangeline.

It'd already been a week and a half since she'd left Ariella and Faeleen. If she'd waited that long, she could wait another day.

The hair on the back of Emmalee's neck stood on end as the sound of a man humming traveled on the wind toward her. She froze. Using her magic, which snaked and slithered on the forest floor, Emmalee found the source of the sound. With the ability to see through her spell, Emmalee watched as a guard with his back to her magic focused on wetting the ground in front of him.

Before she could get too excited, Emmalee searched the area. No other guards were around—at least, none that she could see. If there were, they'd gone far enough to give the man some semblance of privacy as he relieved himself.

How kind of them.

Emmalee grinned.

It was too perfect an opportunity to let pass her by.

Retracting her magic, Emmalee snuck up to the guard just as he was fixing his trousers. Emmalee struck, using her magic to put him to sleep and catch his falling body before he hit the ground and made a noise.

Keeping a steady stream of magic wrapped around the guard to levitate him back to the abandoned village, Emmalee split her focus. Despite the success with her first step, panic was already beginning to creep in as she considered what she would do next. Or maybe it was adrenaline. Either way, it had her heart racing and her hands getting clammier and clammier.

She was an outlawed criminal, yes. But a torturer? No. She'd been a teacher, for goodness' sake. How was she supposed to interrogate one of the king's men?

She needed to breathe. She knew that. Panicking would get her nowhere.

Emmalee glanced at the guard, taking in his face for the first time as she tied him to the chair she'd prepared in the center of the empty house. Her stomach twisted. He was young. So young. Probably still a teenager.

For a second, she considered letting him go. Her hands hesitated on the last knot around his left wrist. He was someone's son. Maybe someone's brother.

Her heart pounded in her chest, and despite her best efforts to remain calm, she felt like the thin strings holding her together were slowly but surely unweaving.

As soon as he was secure, Emmalee started pacing. She couldn't stop. Back and forth she walked behind the guard, mentally reciting the questions she needed to ask. She didn't want to think what would happen afterward.

She wasn't sure how much time had passed—long enough for her to consider returning the boy and trying someone else at least four times. Finally, though, the guard began to stir.

Emmalee took a deep breath and steadied herself. With a quick check over her shoulder, she made sure the silencing runes she'd drawn were still illuminated. They were.

"Wh-what's . . . ? Where . . . ?" The young man's words trailed off as he craned his neck to look around. He pulled at the restraints, but Emmalee was relieved to see they held.

The floor creaked as Emmalee shifted her weight, and the guard began squirming even more. "Who's there?" It was clear by his loud voice that he was trying to be strong, but the trembling beneath his words gave him away.

Emmalee stepped around so he could see her. His eyes widened.

"I take it you know who I am?" she asked, her voice calm despite the storm raging inside her.

The guard blinked, confusion and fear flashing across his young face before his gaze darted to the door. "The sorceress. The woman with dark magic everyone's looking for."

Nodding, Emmalee sighed. "That's very true. Do you know why I brought you here?"

He shook his head.

"Not even a guess?" Emmalee asked, raising an eyebrow.

"N-no, I d-don't know."

Emmalee stopped directly in front of him, turning until she faced the guard. "I want to ask you questions. Will you answer them?"

Something like steel flashed in his eyes, then disappeared a second later. "No. No, I-I won't."

"You just did."

He pinched his lips shut. She tilted her head, watching his body language. He still pulled at the restraints despite not making any progress with them. Given the obvious flicks of his gaze toward the door, he was very clearly trying to think of a way out.

Emmalee stepped to the side, blocking his view of the front door.

"You know what happened in the boulder field with the king a little over four months ago?"

He didn't respond. His attention flicked to the dagger at Emmalee's waist.

Emmalee tried to hide the shakiness of her hands as she unsheathed the gift she'd given her husband, letting the black metal glint wickedly in the light. She had no intention of cutting the man—she could hardly stomach the thought—but a little intimidation could work.

Was working by the wide-eyed look he gave her.

"The boulder field?" she asked again.

He nodded, wetting his lips as he flicked his anxious gaze from her to the dagger and back.

"Good. There was a woman there that night. Short blond hair. She was arrested. Is she . . . Is she still alive?" Emmalee choked on the question.

What would she do if he didn't answer her? What if Evangeline was dead, *had* been dead all this time and Emmalee didn't know?

Her grip tightened on the hilt of the dagger.

"I-I don't know who you're talking about."

Emmalee frowned at him, taking a step nearer. "A woman. Blond. Arrested. Is she alive or dead?"

"I didn't . . . I wasn't . . . I don't know. I don't know of any woman arrested that night."

"Don't lie to me. I saw that marshal arrest her."

The guard sank back into his chair, his attention fixed on Emmalee's hands, which were darkening with magic as her emotions rose.

"I'm not. I promise. I-I don't know of any woman arrested that night." He flinched when she took a step forward. "Please!"

Emmalee struggled to swallow. "She has to . . . has to be alive. Where is the king keeping her?" Emmalee's voice grew more urgent, her nerves fraying by the second. He had to know. He worked for the king.

Evangeline had to be alive.

The guard looked even more confused. "I don't know what you're talking about," he said, his voice barely a whisper.

"Tell me!" Emmalee tried to hold back the swell of hysteria threatening to overwhelm her, but by the dark mist pouring out of her hands, she was failing miserably.

"I don't know!" the guard cried, his panic evident as all the color drained out of his face. "I haven't spent much time at the castle. I'm new. I just . . . I just finished training a few months ago. Please, I don't . . . I don't know anything about any prisoners."

Emmalee's heart sank. She tried to think of another question, something that might help her. "How do I get into the castle? What's the least guarded entrance?" she demanded, her voice trembling. The room seemed to be spinning. He had to have something useful to say. This couldn't be a waste—not after everything she'd done to set it up.

The guard hesitated, then glanced toward the door when something cracked outside. His eyes widened at the same time Emmalee's gaze darted to the silencing runes.

"No," she muttered as the rune nearest her started to flicker and fade. "No, no, no." She turned back to the guard to tell him to be quiet, but it was too late.

"Someone, help! Help me. Someone, hel—"

Without thinking, Emmalee extended her hand, allowing her magic to encircle the guard. Dark tendrils wrapped around his mouth and nose, stifling his cries.

The guard struggled, his eyes wide with terror. He shook his head, trying to get her magic off, but she held on tightly. Emmalee found her rune pen where she'd left it in her bag, and with her heart racing, she knelt near the door and retraced the runes. Her hands shook. It took a delicate amount of focus to write the runes, all the while keeping the guard silent.

When the runes glowed steadily again a minute or two later, Emmalee let out a wavering breath. She'd done it.

Letting her magic return to her hands, Emmalee stood and brushed off her knees before turning around to face the guard again.

She dropped her rune pen.

Emmalee stared in horror at the young man. He still sat in the chair, bound and tethered to the spot. His head was slumped back, lifeless eyes staring at the ceiling, mouth agape in a silent unending scream.

Emmalee stared at the body. Her hands trembled. She'd done it by accident. An accident. She'd killed him. He hadn't been much older than some of the students she'd once taught.

She stumbled backward, and bile rose in her throat. He was just a kid, and she'd taken his life. He'd been tied down. Helpless. And yet she'd still killed him. She hadn't been threatened. He'd been defenseless. She'd killed before, but always in the heat of battle, often in self-defense or the defense of someone else. Never like this. Not once. This . . . This was deliberate. Cold. And it made her sick.

Forgetting all about the sound that'd sparked the boy's panic, Emmalee tripped over her own feet getting to the door. She flung it open. Her stomach churned. She rushed outside, missing the last step and landing painfully on her hands and knees.

Tears blurred Emmalee's vision as she heaved up the contents of her stomach outside the small shack in the abandoned village. She hadn't meant to do it. It'd been an accident. It'd just happened. She hadn't mean to. She hadn't.

The world shrank as she heaved again. Nothing but bile came up, scorching her throat with acid. Snot ran down her nose. She was sure her eyes were red from crying.

And even when she started to calm down, she couldn't bring herself to reenter the shack—not when the young guard's body still sat tied to a chair in the middle of the living room. A teenager. A child.

She'd killed him.

And for what?

He'd given her nothing. Not a single snippet of information she could use to save Evangeline. Nothing that would help to reunite her with her friend.

What else was she to do?

She couldn't leave him there—not when she needed to reuse the shack for a more forthcoming guard.

Emmalee's stomach turned once more at the thought of going through the whole ordeal again.

"I'm so s-sorry," she cried as tears dripped off the tip of her nose. She wasn't sure to whom she was apologizing. The boy. His family. Evangeline.

She covered her mouth to stifle her cries.

She couldn't give up on Evangeline. But she didn't want to do it again. She couldn't.

Emmalee choked on another sob.

What was she meant to do with the body?

Bury it?

Burn it?

She couldn't just leave him somewhere for someone to find and recognize him.

Emmalee leaned over and vomited.

Again.

Chapter 20

SILAS

Silas leaned his elbow against the rickety desk that one of the guards had set up in his tent. Unlike the rest of his men, he had his own space in which to sit and give orders. It was nice . . . ish. Better than sleeping on the cold hard ground.

Frowning at the map in front of him, Silas traced the lines indicating well-traveled paths. The three abandoned villages that surrounded them were on the outskirts of other thriving villages. He'd sent word to the commanders and captains present in the area, most of whom were men Marshal Levick had left behind when they'd switched places. Over the past two weeks, the men in charge of the areas surrounding Silas's guard post had met with him, informing him of the activity they often faced in the area.

If he could figure out from the local captains and commanders what was normal, then anything outside of that could be worth investigating, especially if it had to do with dark magic.

However, nothing had come of it. Yet.

Silas had spent the week entrenched in their reports and routines, noting every discrepancy, no matter how small.

He ran a hand through his hair. Only a week and he already regretted offering to leave the castle. He hated the Black Forest. Hated not being able to see the changing of the sun to the moons. Hated the constant buzzing of insects. Hated the uncomfortable cot. Hated the isolation. Hated being away from Butch. Away from his home.

Away from her.

Silas groaned, pinching the bridge of his nose.

Once again, Evie had managed to infiltrate his thoughts, just like she did several times an hour every moment he remained awake.

And sleeping? Well . . . that was no better.

Worse, even.

"Sir," a voice called from outside the flap of his tent. "You need to come quickly."

Silas sighed, grabbing his jacket from where he'd left it on the cot. If this was about another fight breaking out because his men were bored and rowdy . . .

"What is it?" Silas asked, straightening his jacket collar. He fell into step beside the young officer.

"A body. We've found a body."

"Whose?" Silas's brows knitted together.

"We're not sure, sir. It's burnt, but we think he's one of ours."

A knot tightened in Silas's stomach. As best as he could, he kept his face impassive, nodding slowly. "Where was he found?"

"Between two abandoned villages to the west and the north. Someone noticed smoke and told one of ours."

Silas didn't ask any further questions, instead letting the conversation fall silent. They walked for at least fifteen minutes, striding down a clearly marked path until the guard turned left.

He led Silas through dense thickets to a small clearing where a group of men had gathered. The acrid smell of charred flesh and fabric hit as Silas approached, and he swallowed hard to maintain his composure.

The body lay on the ground, and while it was severely burnt, the tattered remnants of a jacket did indeed mark him as one of the king's men.

Potentially one of his.

Silas clenched his fist.

"I want the body brought back to camp and examined for an identity and for any traces of magic." Silas gave the order with a steady voice despite the surge of anger and disgust swelling within him.

"Sir," one of the men said, his voice strained, "I know who it is. It's my cousin, Officer Michael Reynard. I recognize the tattoo on his neck."

He recognized the name from the new recruits who'd recently passed training. The guard was just a boy, barely out of school. Silas's stomach turned, and he fought tooth and nail to remain unfazed for the sake of his men.

Silas glanced at the marking the guard indicated and gave a brief nod. "I'm sorry for your loss, Officer. Truly. I still want Reynard brought back to the outpost and examined. Who was supposed to be with him?" Silas flicked his attention around the group of men, their solemn faces watching him with careful eyes.

When no one spoke up, Silas clenched his jaw. "Was he alone, then?"

More silence.

Silas ran his fingers through his hair, shaking his head. "Get his body to the outpost. I want groups of two and three searching the area. We need to find out what happened here. Report anything unusual immediately, and *do not* go off alone. That is an order."

As the guards dispersed, some accompanying the body back to the outpost while others searched the area, Silas knelt by the burnt section of vegetation. He reached out, fingers hovering just above the scorched earth. An unnatural coolness lingered, sending alarming shivers up his spine. The presence of dark magic was unmistakable.

The chill seeped deep into his bones, and Silas closed his eyes to focus on the residual magic. It was faint but palpable.

Opening his eyes, Silas scanned the area, searching for any clues that might reveal more. The vegetation around the burn mark had wilted and blackened, unnatural in its decay.

The earth should've been hot, still radiating warmth from the fire.

With a deep breath, Silas stood.

Either Estrada had done this for a reason only she knew, or someone else was walking around setting the king's men on fire.

Silas frowned.

Both options left him with a growing headache as he made his way back to the outpost alone.

Chapter 21

EMMALEE

Emmalee paced the floor of the broken-down shack, her eyes never leaving the bound figure in the center of the room. It'd taken her over a week to shake off the accidental death of the first guard. It wasn't until she'd repeated Ariella's and Faeleen's words to herself that she finally started to prepare for the next round of questioning.

"Do what you must to survive," she'd whispered to herself as she left the shack.

It'd worked.

At least, it had until the next guard she'd taken woke up tied to a chair and started hollering. The silencing runes on the walls held though. However, the sound did set Emmalee on high alert.

The flickering light from a single lantern cast long shadows on the walls and on the young man. He couldn't have been much older than eighteen.

Survive. She was doing this to make sure her friend survived. That she herself survived, at least long enough to make the king pay.

"Let's try this again," Emmalee said, her voice calm even as she gritted her teeth. "Where are they keeping the young woman with blond hair and light magic who was arrested?"

Despite the fact the guard seemed just as nervous as the first one had been, he'd yet to answer a single question. Instead, he stared straight ahead with a determined gaze and a clenched jaw. He refused to meet her eyes, though he did seem to notice the dagger and her dark magic. Emmalee had a feeling his staring was the easiest way for him to hide the fear lurking just behind his defiant eyes.

She took a step closer, her magic simmering just beneath the surface. "I don't want to hurt you. All you have to do is tell me where she is. Tell me what I need to know. Then I'll let you go."

The guard scoffed, remaining silent.

Patience wearing thin, Emmalee raised her hand, grateful it wasn't shaking and revealing how terrified she was about what she was about to do next. She hadn't gotten that far with the first guard since he'd answered her questions, albeit unhelpfully. Emmalee allowed a tendril of her magic to curl around her fingers, its inky blackness stark against her pale skin.

For Evangeline—for her best friend—she would do what she had to. But even as she thought them, the words tasted sour in her mouth. They came out even more bitter.

"I can make this rather unpleasant," she warned, her voice dropping to a whisper as she circled behind him. He flinched as she let her magic trail over the exposed back of his neck. "But I'd rather not."

Still, the guard said nothing.

Evangeline's face flashed across Emmalee's mind. Was she being interrogated? How cruel was the king being to her? Was she even still alive?

Emmalee clenched her hand into a fist as frustration churned within her. She focused on the guard, letting her magic seep into the air around him. The temperature in the room dropped, the shadows deepening, pressing in on him from all sides.

The man trembled, the chair creaking as he shifted to look at the darkness surrounding him.

"You're scared," she said softly, striding around to stare into his eyes. Could he tell how much she was trying to remain calm? Could he tell that she was likely just as terrified as him? Could he tell how inexperienced she was? Emmalee clenched her jaw. "Tell me where she is. How do I get to her?"

The guard shivered as she wrapped the chill of her magic tighter around him. Emmalee's gaze hardened as he remained silent.

"Tell me how to get into the castle," she demanded, her voice filling the small room. "Where are they keeping my friend?"

The guard's breathing grew labored, sweat trickling down his face despite the cold.

147

"I can show you nightmares you can't even imagine," she said, her magic weaving around his mind, threatening to plunge him into a world of terror. Her terrors. The horror she'd experienced in Shongbay. Seeing her family killed after she'd finally brought them back. Losing her chance to make the king understand in the boulder field. She could shove her memories into his mind just as she'd done the king. "Or you can tell me what I need to know, and this can all end."

The guard's eyes darted to hers, fear finally breaking through his resolve. He swallowed hard. One second he opened his mouth as if he were about to give her what she so desperately needed in order to rescue Evangeline, and the next his lips clamped shut in stubborn defiance.

Her frustration boiled over. "So be it."

Chapter 22

SILAS

Silas stood at the edge of his guard outpost, his gaze scanning the forest that surrounded them. Since they'd found Michael Reynard's body, his men had confirmed the use of dark magic in the man's murder. With each day that passed, Silas's frustration grew. Estrada continued to remain in the shadows of the forest.

The sound of twigs breaking behind him pulled Silas from his thoughts. He turned to face the approaching guard.

"Captain Orin," Silas said, matching the officer's salute. Orin had been one of Levick's captains who'd stayed behind after his commanding marshal took Silas's spot in Cyanthia.

"Marshal Thorne." Orin gave a small nod of his head. "I think I have something that might be of interest to you."

Silas gestured for him to continue.

"A while ago, we were conducting a thorough search of a nearby village for Estrada. We checked each building but found nothing. Well, I thought we found nothing." Orin gave a small smile. "Do you remember when the guard was killed earlier this year? Someone thought they saw Estrada. I was there. I saw two women fleeing the scene. One matched Estrada's description. The other, well, I thought I recognized the owner of a fabric shop we searched. I think she was with Estrada when the guard was killed. Long blond hair. Bright teal eyes. Almost feline."

Silas raised his eyebrows. "That death was a while ago. Are you sure this woman is the same person?"

"Sure enough to warrant an arrest and interrogation."

"Very well," Silas said, nodding. If there was the slightest chance the fabric shop owner knew of Estrada, it would be worth speaking with her.

THE SMALL VILLAGE was quiet when Silas and his men arrived.

"I want this done quickly and quietly. No reason to cause a commotion." Silas gestured toward the fabric store, which sat on the end of the main street.

"And if there's resistance?" Captain Orin asked.

"I'll handle that if the situation requires it." With a nod toward his men, Silas entered the fabric store.

A woman stood at the counter with a sewing needle in one hand and a panel of cream fabric in the other. She had long blond hair and a brilliant teal scarf tied around the top of her head. As soon as she looked up, her eyes, a similar shade to the scarf, widened in recognition.

"Officers," she said, inclining her head. "What can I do for you?"

Silas glanced around the shop before raising an eyebrow at Orin. The captain gave a short nod.

Confirmation.

"What's your name, miss?" Silas asked, keeping his tone light.

"Um, Ari. Ariella."

"Well, my name is Marshal Thorne. I believe you might have some information that would help us. If you wouldn't mind coming with me, we—"

"Information?" Her voice rose an octave as she frantically glanced between Silas and the four men who'd followed him inside. The other eight remained out in the street. "What information?"

"We can answer that if you come with us." Silas offered her a small smile but dropped it when she shook her head.

"I don't have any information. I don't." She lowered the needle and fabric.

With a single look, Silas calmed his men, who'd been reaching for their swords.

"It's just to chat," Silas continued in an even tone. "Nothing to be concerned about."

Unless she had magic.

And was friends with Estrada.

Evie flashed across his mind. Pale and underfed in the back of her cell. Collapsing to the floor in Butch's office. Near death in a bed in the infirmary. And all the other prisoners who'd been mistreated in the dungeon because of their magic.

Silas cleared his throat.

"Will you come willingly?" he asked.

"I—"

"Ari? What's going on?" A voice came from the back of the shop, and a second later, another woman stepped into the shop. She had a similar shade of blond hair, but hers fell in tight curls.

"Fae, this is Marshal Thorne." Ariella's voice shook, but it was obvious, at least to Silas, that she had shoved whatever fear she had behind a wall.

Fae was important to her. That much was clear.

Silas nodded to the new girl before returning his attention to Ariella. "Your decision?"

Ariella's face went pale. "I don't have any information."

Silas sighed. With a curt nod, he stepped back, positioning himself between the two women. With another nod, this time to Orin, the four guards surrounded Ari. Just as he'd predicted, the other girl, Fae, reacted. And not in a good way.

"What are you doing?" Fae shrieked. Silas caught her as she tried to pass him to get to Ariella, who he assumed was her sister. She thrashed in Silas's grip, causing him to grab her other arm, pinning them both to her sides.

Behind him, his men arrested Ariella, moving her toward the front door of the shop. Metal cuffs clinked, and Silas's stomach clenched at the panic scrawled over Fae's face.

"You can't do this! She hasn't done anything!" Tears streaked down Fae's cheeks as she continued to pull against Silas. "Stop! You can't take her!"

"Fae, that's your name, right?" Silas spoke quietly, angling himself so she couldn't watch as his men pulled Ariella—who was surprisingly silent— from the shop.

"Please!" she cried.

"Listen to me, Fae," Silas continued. "You're making this worse for her. For you. We want to ask her some questions. If we don't find anything, she'll be returned unharmed. But you need to calm down." He grasped her tighter when she tried to pull away. "Fae, stop." He tried to keep the pained expression from his face. This was the part of being in the field he did not miss. "I don't want to have to arrest you too."

That made her freeze.

"If you fight this, it won't be good for either of you."

The sheer panic in her eyes twisted his stomach. But the stakes were too high. If Ariella had information on Estrada, they needed it, and he couldn't let sympathy cloud his judgment—not when his best friend's life could be at risk.

"Promise me you won't do something rash as soon as I let you go," Silas said, hoping his men had already started back toward the outpost.

"She's my sister. Please, you can't hurt her."

Silas nodded. "I don't want to hurt her. I don't want to hurt either of you. All I want is to have a conversation with Ariella. Can you promise me you will stay here if I let you go?"

The front door had long since closed, leaving just the two of them in the shop, yet Fae still looked over his shoulder as if she might catch another glimpse of her sister.

"Don't hurt her."

Silas nodded once. He released her, hesitating one second to see if she would react. But she stayed where she was, her shoulders slumping.

Silas backed out of the shop, not taking his eyes off Fae. It wasn't that he didn't trust her, but grief caused people to act against better judgment.

It wasn't until the front door shut between them that Silas released the air trapped in his lungs and let his posture slouch.

Yeah.

He hated being in the field.

SILAS SAT IN the dimly lit makeshift interrogation room at the guard outpost. He tapped his fingers rhythmically on the wooden table that separated him from the empty chair. It'd been a few days since they'd arrested Ariella, and while she continued to say she knew nothing, he could tell she was lying. Her body language and rise in pitch while speaking gave it away. His patience waned with each day. He needed answers about Estrada, and he was willing to bet Ariella had them.

The tent flap opened, and Orin escorted Ariella inside. She looked tired and wary, but resolute. Silas gestured for her to sit, and she complied.

"How did you sleep?" Silas asked, deciding it was best to keep the conversation light, at least at first. He passed a cup of water across the table to her, along with a plate of food.

"Fine," she replied, her attention on the cup and plate instead of him.

Silas nodded to Orin, who left the tent with a salute.

"All right, I want to make this quick. Tell me why you were seen with a deadly convict earlier this year after the woman killed a guard with dark magic."

"I don't know what you're talking about," Ariella said, her voice already rising in pitch.

"You were seen, Ariella. We've already been over this. We know you have connections to Emmalee Estrada. Help us, and this will all go easier for you."

Ariella's teal eyes flickered with a mixture of fear and determination. "I wasn't there."

"Sources say otherwise."

"Well, your sources are wrong."

Silas filled his lungs, inhaling a deep breath and releasing it as a sigh in the hope that it might help his patience hold out for a little longer. He rubbed his temples. "You're protecting a dangerous woman. I just don't understand why. Help me understand."

Ariella pinched her lips together.

All right. Time for another tactic. One he didn't enjoy employing.

"Does your sister know anything? Fae?"

Ariella stiffened.

"Orin," Silas called, and he only had to wait a second before the captain stepped into the tent and saluted.

"Marshal."

"I need you to round up a group of men and go back for Ariella's sister." Silas watched Ariella in his peripheral vision.

"No," Ariella whispered.

Orin turned to leave.

"No! Please. Don't involve her. She doesn't know anything."

"Maybe." Silas held out a hand to stop Orin. "But she might give me more than you have. It's worth a shot, you see, because I know you aren't telling me something. Maybe your sister will."

Ariella's nose wrinkled as she glared at Silas. "Don't you dare involve her."

"Then give me something," Silas said, his voice low and threatening.

A tense silence followed, and then Ariella spoke, her voice barely above a whisper. "You don't understand. Emmalee . . . She never wanted any of this. She's gone through so much. She's just trying to survive."

Silas straightened. "Hold off on the sister," he said, dismissing Orin. When he'd gone, he turned back to Ariella. "Where is Estrada?"

Ariella shook her head. "I don't know."

"You're lying," Silas said, frustration creeping into his voice. "How long have you known her? How do I find her? Were you harboring her? How did she—"

"Sir," a guard said, stepping into the tent and saluting. "I apologize for interrupting, but I have the reports from Ajorr." The guard glanced at Ariella, then back to Silas.

"Get Captain Orin in here," Silas growled to another guard, who'd followed the first. "I want her prepared to be taken to Cyanthia. The king will want to speak with her."

He hoped he could get more from Ariella when he returned to the castle, because if he was sure about anything, it was that he wanted out of the Black Forest.

Chapter 23

EMMALEE

Two days. Two days she sat with the second guard and tried to get him to answer her questions. She'd had to refresh the silencing runes eight times. She'd even left to get more supplies and fully expected the guard to have found a way out of the house after waking from the sleeping spell she'd put him under. But no. He'd simply managed to tip the chair over. She'd been pleased that the silencing runes had been so effective that she hadn't heard his hollering until she crossed the threshold.

He hadn't given her what she wanted.

Her patience had worn thin.

And the image of Evangeline broken and chained somewhere in the darkness of a dungeon cell haunted Emmalee like an overly attached ghost.

It was time. She needed someone new. But this . . . This was the part she didn't want to do, and her stomach was already upsetting at the thought.

"This is your last chance to give me something worth the last forty-eight hours you've wasted." She raised an eyebrow, far past the point of repeating the request twice.

The man glared at the wall behind her.

That alone was infuriating.

Emmalee raised her hand, dark magic flowing from her fingertips. It enveloped the guard in a shadowy haze before slinking into his nose, mouth, and ears. She kept her hand steady. She'd studied the spell over and over but hadn't tested it on anything bigger than an unlucky squirrel. It required absolute control. Emmalee let out a low breath, ignoring the slippery feeling of anxiety sliding through her veins.

Control.

Absolute control.

The guard's body went rigid, his eyes wide with terror as her magic seeped into his very bones.

Slowly, his muscles locked into place, and his breath slowed until it was barely perceptible. Emmalee watched despite the horror writhing around in her stomach like a pit of vipers.

The guard's face slipped from defiance to fear and finally to a blank stare.

"At least I didn't kill you," she muttered as she strode over to his chair and leaned down until she was merely inches from him. The spell trapped him inside his mind. He wouldn't be able to tell anyone about her, but he was alive—if it could even be called living. To her dismay, it didn't feel any better than accidentally killing the first guard.

She sat down across from him, leaning her head against the wall as she extended her legs out in front of her.

Another failed interrogation.

Another sick and horrible feeling in her gut.

And not a single step closer to saving her best friend.

Emmalee didn't realize how blurry the room had gotten until she wiped the first tear from her eye. She wasn't even sure why she was crying. Maybe it was because she'd failed again. Maybe it was because she'd all but taken another man's life up close. Maybe it was because she missed her family, including Evangeline. Maybe it was because she was tired. Maybe it was all of it.

Either way, she sat there long after the tears subsided, her mind blank as she stared at the evidence of her stained soul.

"What do I do with you?" she whispered, though she wasn't sure if she was talking to the guard, who wouldn't respond in his state, or if she was asking herself the question—not that she had an answer.

With a sigh, Emmalee pushed off the floor and stood in front of the guard. He couldn't stay there. She needed to leave him somewhere someone would find him. Hopefully they'd take care of him, but that wasn't something she could control, so she didn't dwell long on the thought.

Emmalee grabbed the back of the guard's chair, relying on her magic to help her drag him across the creaky floorboards. The scraping sound echoed through the empty shack. She could've levitated him if she'd had the energy, but she felt empty.

For the first time in a long time, she felt cold.

As she stepped outside, the chilly night did little to help.

She knew that she needed to find someone else to get the information from so she could rescue Evangeline, but she just couldn't find the motivation. Maybe it'd return. She hoped it would. If not, well, both she and Evangeline would likely meet the same fate.

The guard was deadweight, and Emmalee struggled with his chair. She was halfway through the abandoned village when the sound of hurried footsteps approached. She stiffened, dropping the guard and preparing for a fight. If other guards had tracked her down—

"Em? Emmalee!" a voice called out, frantic and breathless.

Emmalee turned just as Faeleen rounded a corner. Her feline eyes were wide, panic etched on her face. Anxiety clenched Emmalee's heart in its iron fist.

Without a second thought, Emmalee sprinted toward her friend.

"Fae, what—"

"It's Ari!" Faeleen wailed, her voice breaking as she smashed into Emmalee and wrapped her arms around her in a desperate hug. Emmalee clung to Faeleen, grasping at her cloak and the back of her head.

"What happened?" Emmalee's lungs forgot to function as Faeleen sobbed onto her shoulder.

No, not Ariella. Not after Evangeline. No, no, no. Breathe, she needed to breathe, but she couldn't.

Faeleen sobbed louder. "They took her. They just showed up and . . . and I couldn't—They took her, and . . . She's gone!"

Chapter 24

LENORA

Lenora stared out her window. She'd contemplated the decision for days, but after returning to the infirmary and finding that the prisoner had been moved, likely back to the dungeon that had caused her to get so sick, Lenora had made up her mind. She couldn't bear the thought of the young woman wasting away in such a place. She had to do something, even if it meant going behind her husband's back.

Hopefully he'd never know the role she played.

Lenora turned away from the window and walked to the small sitting room. She took her place on the chaise longue, tapping her fingers on her leg until Merla and Kaylene finally knocked on the door and entered. She motioned toward the other seating and watched as they sat across from her.

Both looked at her with expectant expressions, and Lenora's mouth became very dry. "Tea?" she asked, gesturing toward the tray a servant had brought in earlier.

Merla and Kaylene exchanged worried glances, then nodded. After they each had a cup in hand, Merla finally broke the silence.

"You wanted to speak with us about something? Is it—" Merla stopped abruptly, her gaze dropping to Lenora's midsection.

Lenora quickly shook her head. "No, nothing like that, thank goodness."

Of course that was where their minds had gone. She offered a small smile, sipping her tea as Merla and Kaylene relaxed a bit.

"No, this is . . . I need your help," Lenora began, her voice steady despite the nerves churning in her stomach. "It's . . . Well, it's quite possibly very illegal for all of us should we get caught."

Kaylene's brow furrowed at the same time Merla straightened in her chair.

"I want . . . I want to reach out to a prisoner—a woman I saw in the infirmary when I went to see Helena. She's no longer there. I checked. I have to assume she's been moved back to the dungeon."

Her handmaids remained silent, but they both seemed uneasy in their chairs.

"I plan to send a note to her in the dungeon," Lenora explained. "But I can't do it myself. I need to make sure it gets to her though."

"Your Majesty," Merla said, biting her lip. "This is risky. We could be arrested for interfering with a prisoner."

Kaylene nodded in agreement. "It's dangerous."

"I know. Especially since Butch has deemed this prisoner off-limits. He believes she's extremely dangerous. I . . . I don't. I mean, I think she has magic, but you didn't see her in the infirmary. She was nearly dead. I don't . . . I can't just let her waste away. If I could help her, maybe—"

"Help her how?" Merla asked.

"I want to find a way to free her."

Kaylene and Merla froze.

"Free her?" Kaylene's voice was a whisper. "How do you plan to do that?"

"I'm not sure yet. But she was so pale and thin. I can't just stand by and do nothing while she suffers. She's not a threat. She's just . . . broken."

The women remained silent.

Lenora's nerves continued to grow until Kaylene finally spoke.

"I'll help you." She placed a hand on Lenora's. "However I can."

Merla sighed, then nodded in agreement. "But we have to be careful. We can't afford to make any mistakes."

A surge of gratitude and relief washed over Lenora, driving away most of the apprehension she'd held not a minute earlier. "Thank you," she said softly. "I feel guilty about putting you both in this position, but—"

"We wouldn't want you to do this alone," Kaylene said.

"What do you plan to achieve with this note?" Merla asked, setting her teacup down.

Lenora hesitated, the unspoken hope of contacting Estrada lingering in her mind. "I want her to know she has allies. That there's hope."

That maybe someday she'll be free.

Lenora held back the words—words she clung to herself, not that it was a possibility for her.

Not as long as the crown and title of queen chained her to the castle.

Chapter 25

EMMALEE

Emmalee gave another disgusted look at the guard who sat unconscious in the middle of the shack. Faeleen had easily lured the man away from his partner with a single look.

The pig.

Maybe it was a good thing she found the man to be so repellant. It likely meant there would be less guilt when she inevitably turned him into a giant vegetable. Still, though, her stomach was unsettled at the thought of her third interrogation.

Faeleen had wanted no part in the questioning and instead took up a post outside to watch for any sign of trouble. Emmalee didn't blame her. She didn't want to interrogate the guard either—not after the first two attempts.

But now, with Ariella having been arrested too, it wasn't just Evangeline depending on her.

And it was her fault Ariella was gone. Even after separating from the sisters, Emmalee had not been able to spare them from the danger the king posed.

She glared at the back of the guard's head. The man wore a gray collar. He was some sort of leader in the king's military, she just didn't know which one.

And what did it matter?

The less she knew about him, the easier it would be when she inevitably finished questioning him. Her hands clenched into fists, then released a second later when she forced herself to breathe.

Ariella needed her to question the man.

Evangeline needed her to question the man.

So she would question him, even if it felt like some part of her withered away with each guard she took.

Running her fingers through her hair, Emmalee walked around toward the silencing runes by the door. They were fresh. They'd hold.

Besides, the shack was far enough away from the rest of the other buildings that even if there were others around, it was doubtful they'd be nearby.

She wanted to get the interrogation over with. The sooner it was over, the sooner she could make moves toward rescuing Evangeline and Ariella. What awful fate did the guards have for the elder Pumarian? Emmalee shuddered. Faeleen had been in such a panic that it'd taken over an hour for either of them to calm down and another long while before Faeleen had been able to explain what happened when the guards came to the shop.

Emmalee straightened when the man groaned. She hadn't bothered with the voice-altering rune she'd been practicing or a blindfold since the guard had seen Faeleen before she could use her magic to knock him unconscious.

"Pleasant nap?" she asked, her voice light as she watched panic fill his face. Maybe it was because he'd clearly had nefarious intentions toward Faeleen when he'd followed her, or maybe it was simply because he was one of the king's mighty guards tied to a chair in a broken-down shack, but the sight of his blanched face and wide eyes gave Emmalee a sort of prideful satisfaction.

He struggled against the restraints, but he didn't pose any sort of threat. Even if he did get free from the ropes, there was always her magic to stop him.

"You're her," he said. His nose wrinkled, and his eyes narrowed at her. "I saw you that night in the boulder field. You're Estrada."

"Emmalee," she said, shrugging. She tried to hide her trembling hands by putting them in her trouser pockets. He didn't need to know that she was likely more nervous than he was. "So, we've met?"

"You threw me off the hill."

"I'm sure I did. If your king had obeyed my instructions, I wouldn't have needed to do so." Emmalee watched as his features darkened. "What? Have I insulted your king?" She spoke in a singsong voice.

"You killed my brother," he growled.

Emmalee froze, her muscles tensing at his words. "That night?" The words were tight as she pictured the odd angles of some of the bodies she'd passed when she and Evangeline had fled the hill. And she'd known she'd been the cause of it then too. And then there were the two other guards she'd killed accidentally. The guard's brother could've been one of them.

"You threw him off the hill too. He wasn't as lucky as me. I was the one who found him."

"Oh." Emmalee bit her bottom lip, startled by the guilt wriggling within her.

She spun so her back was toward him. Breathe, she needed to breathe. The king was at war with magic folk, and casualties were a part of war. But still, she'd taken the man's brother. She wasn't a monster. She wasn't.

"I-I'm sorry." Emmalee spoke in a low voice filled with more honesty than she'd expected. It seemed to surprise him as well.

"Sorry?"

Emmalee inhaled deeply before she nodded and turned back around. "I know what it is to lose family. I'm sorry I was the reason for that."

The guard scoffed. "Sorry? You think that'll bring my little brother back?"

She shook her head. "I know it won't."

Silence filled the room as they stared at each other. She pressed her lips together. The next question left her lips before she had time to process it.

"What's your name?"

She hadn't meant to. She didn't want to know. Why had she asked the question in the first place? Just as she was about to tell him it didn't matter, he spoke.

"Why do you care?"

"I don't." She walked over to her bag. Emmalee reached in and pulled out her canteen, her throat feeling dry. "I also don't apologize all that often."

"Stoll. Kendrick Stoll." His voice wavered, and he seemed reluctant to give his name. "My brother was Corwinn."

She wished he hadn't answered.

Emmalee put the canteen away after wiping her mouth with the back of her hand. The guard was glaring at the floor as if he could set it on fire. It was as if she could see the hatred coming off him in waves.

"You were close?" Again, the question spilled from her mouth before she could prevent it. She moved to the wall, leaning against it as she had when he was still unconscious.

Maybe these questions were good though. She could use them, at least. He was certainly being more talkative than the other two. And with him being more than a lowly officer with a tan collar, maybe he would have the answers to her questions. It was just a matter of getting him to answer them.

"Winn followed me from our parents' farm in the Level Plains to become a royal guard. He hated violence, but he did it to be with me." Stoll narrowed his eyes at her. "And you killed him."

Emmalee crossed her arms over her chest. "That night, after the wall of magic fell, the king and one of his marshals almost killed me. And—"

"They should've."

Emmalee refrained from arguing and instead continued. "A friend of mine saved my life, but she was arrested. Do you know—"

Stoll sneered at her. "The blond woman. I knew she was a friend of yours. The brat." He wrinkled his nose again. "She's been nothing but a headache."

Trying to hide the relief at hearing that Evangeline was still alive, Emmalee spit out another question. "Where is she?"

The man snorted. "If you'd asked a couple weeks ago, I would've told you she was as good as dead. Deserves it, too, for being friends with a murderer."

Emmalee couldn't restrain her magic as it shot from her hand and wrapped around the man's neck. He made a gurgling noise, his eyes widening as Emmalee stepped closer.

"But she's not," he choked out, gasping for air when she released him.

"Where is she?" Emmalee repeated, glaring down at him. Her stomach twisted when his lips curved up into a sneer.

"Your little friend wasn't doing well last I saw. She's probably still wasting away in the dungeon, thin and broken." His large eyes glinted at her as he continued to gloat. "Lucky for her, I doubt the king will interrogate her with Thorne in the field. King Butch typically wants his pet marshal in the room when he questions her. Not that she's a threat. Just bait for the actual beast."

Emmalee held very still as she gleaned bits of information from his words. Evangeline was alive. She was being kept in the dungeon and had been questioned what sounded like multiple times. While she trusted her friend, Emmalee felt the unpleasant sensation of anxiety stirring in her stomach. What if Evangeline couldn't handle the interrogation and gave up something that might lead them to her?

As soon as the thought crossed into her mind, Emmalee shook it out. The guards hadn't found her yet, and she was sure that was because Evangeline hadn't given up on her. And even if they could get her to talk, Evangeline wouldn't know Emmalee's location. They'd been separated for too many months.

Far too many months.

Then there was the "pet" marshal—Marshal Thorne. He was the one who'd come to the king's rescue just as she was about to kill him in the boulder field. The one who'd almost killed her—and would've if Evangeline hadn't saved her. He was the one who'd arrested Evangeline.

And he was somewhere in the Black Forest with her.

That thought both excited her and sent a new wave of fear through her. The man was capable—that much he'd proven. A new dark thought clouded her mind, and she turned her ire on the guard.

"Another woman was arrested a couple days ago from Ajorr. Were you there?"

The guard didn't answer.

"Don't go silent on me now, Stoll." Emmalee lifted his chin with a wisp of her magic.

His eyes widened, but he clenched his jaw. Fear was scrawled over his face, and Emmalee wondered how quickly his bravado would crack if she stole the air from his lungs.

Worth a shot if it meant saving Ariella.

Emmalee held his body still with her magic, letting tendrils snake into his mouth and nose. It was a much weaker version of the spell she'd used on the second guard, and she kept her own breathing constant as she wrapped her magic around his lungs. She didn't squeeze hard—not at first. But soon Stoll's eyes bulged, and he made a faint choking sound.

"If I let you breathe, you'll talk to me again?" she asked, using a voice she'd saved for the troublesome children in her classroom. He needed to know who was in charge.

Before he could pass out, she released him. He coughed as he sucked in air, his head hanging low.

"Well?" she asked, crossing her arms over her chest. "Feeling chatty?"

"I h-hope you b-burn."

Emmalee sighed.

It was going to be a long night.

Chapter 26

SILAS

Wide-eyed, Silas stared at the sketch he'd drawn while half asleep. He didn't remember reaching for the charcoal from the fire. Didn't remember pulling the top report off the pile on his lopsided desk. Didn't remember sketching the lines of her face, of her hair, of the flames surrounding her.

He'd only seen the woman a few times, if he didn't count the drawings of her in the sketchbook.

But staring up at him with dark eyes containing enough hatred to fill an ocean was Emmalee Estrada.

Silas struggled to swallow.

He'd woken in his chair to find his hands covered in dark stains from the charcoal, and it wasn't until he noticed the sketch on the desk beneath him that he realized what had happened.

Without a second thought, Silas crumpled the paper.

It couldn't be happening.

It was impossible.

His mother had made sure of it.

Silas stomped out of his tent and tossed the paper into the firepit nearest him. The parchment caught flame, and Silas watched as it charred and eventually turned to ash.

Good.

That was a good sign.

If the parchment could be destroyed, that meant it was just a coincidence.

That was, if sketching his best friend's number one enemy while being completely out of it could be considered a coincidence.

Silas rubbed his jaw and then the back of his neck. The sooner he found Estrada, the sooner life could go back to normal. Then maybe he could sleep without some sort of nightmare waking him or waking to find that he'd started doodling in the middle of the night.

At least he hadn't drawn Evie.

Silas's cheeks warmed at the mere thought, and he ducked back into his tent before one of his men noticed him. He did *not* want questions as to why he was blushing like a twelve-year-old girl.

It took a few minutes, but he finally got all the charcoal off his hands and was drying them when Captain Orin entered his tent.

"Sir, I have an urgent report."

Silas nodded, unrolling the sleeves of his tunic. "Go ahead."

"Commander Stoll has gone missing, and another body was found."

"Where's the body?" Silas asked, pinching the bridge of his nose.

"In the medic tent. He's not dead, but . . ." Orin's words trailed off. "He may as well be."

"And the commander? When was the last time Stoll was seen?" Silas asked as he followed Orin to the medic tent.

"At his post several hours ago. His partner came back alone saying he'd lost Stoll."

"You've informed them to stay together, no?"

"Yes, sir," Captain Orin said, clearing his throat. "Many times. Stoll can be . . . Anyway, do you want to speak with his partner?"

Silas nodded. "Send the partner to the medic tent. I'll speak with him there."

Captain Orin saluted and rushed away to carry out Silas's orders.

Silas took a deep breath and steeled himself. If Estrada was the person who was abducting his men, the best way to find her was to find Stoll.

Chapter 27

EMMALEE

Emmalee wanted nothing more than to go to sleep. Stoll's head lolled to the side, exhaustion written over his face as much as she was sure it was on hers. It'd been hours. Maybe a full day. Faeleen had checked on her twice, bringing her dinner the second time, but she hadn't stayed long.

While the guard seemed to put on a brave face, he had broken multiple times after a bit of persuasion on her part—persuasion in the form of dark magic.

She'd finally worked through her questions, some of which he'd answered. Sometimes, like now, she had to go back to questions she'd asked multiple times.

Stoll's gurgling turned into fits of coughing as Emmalee released his lungs for what felt like the thousandth time.

"I . . . I wasn't there. In Ajorr," he finally spit out, glaring at her from beneath his lashes. He chuckled darkly before he spoke again. "Took her to the camp. Caught a glimpse of her though," he sneered. "Hope I get to play with her first before she's broken like your other little friend."

Even though she knew he said things to hurt her or rile her up, after all the hours spent in the shack with him, Emmalee's control still snapped.

She let out a scream of rage and sent a wave of dark magic coursing through Stoll's body. He writhed and screamed in pain, but all Emmalee could see and hear were her friends—Evangeline and Ariella, bruised and battered in dark cells crying out for mercy. Mercy.

"Mercy!" Stoll screamed.

Emmalee's breaths came in ragged gasps, her hands trembling as she fought to rein in her magic.

Stoll was still sputtering when Emmalee stomped forward and gripped his chin, forcing it up until he met her fiery gaze.

"Tell me where they took her," she demanded, her voice low and deadly.

Stoll's eyes were wide, but a second later, he grinned that infuriating sneer. "This hurts you, doesn't it? Knowing they're in chains because of you. That the pretty one in the dungeon is withering away because you couldn't save her. That the other one is going to face the same—" Stoll's head snapped to the side when Emmalee backhanded him. He chuckled.

Her stomach curdled.

She turned away, trying to steady her breathing. Hating that he had successfully gotten under her skin, Emmalee paced the floor behind him, her hands on her hips as she ran through the questions she still needed answers to. It wouldn't help Evangeline or Ariella if she lost her focus.

"The castle. How do I get in?"

Stoll let out a loud huff that sounded a bit like a laugh. "You don't. Actually, by all means, try. You won't survive, and I'd so like to see your head mounted on the wall."

"How?"

"Well, first you'd be arrested, and then they'd cut your head off, and then—"

Emmalee released a whip of dark magic that shot out and lashed the back of his left leg. Stoll howled and swore.

"Tell me."

"Not a chance. Besides, security is heightened."

Frowning, Emmalee strode around until she faced him again. "Heightened?"

Stoll clenched his jaw.

"Why is it heightened? Because of me?"

He looked away, glaring at the wall.

"Fine, have it your way."

AN HOUR LATER, Stoll told her all about the visiting dignitaries and the welcome ball. Of course the king and all the upper-class sycophants were hosting a ball amidst a devastating war. Probably just a normal weekday for them. He'd even been kind enough to tell her through coughing fits when the welcome ball was to happen.

However, much to her chagrin, Stoll still wouldn't tell her how to get into the castle. But it was more to go off than she'd had before, which she considered a success.

"Tell me about the king. His weaknesses. His marshals' weaknesses. Better yet," she said, tilting her head as she regarded him, "tell me about the marshal in charge of the attack in Shongbay when the king murdered my family. What's the marshal's name?"

The question hadn't been in her original list, but since Stoll had given her more than the other two guards, she wavered from her list.

He raised an eyebrow. Apparently, the question had caught him off guard after being asked the same questions over and over.

"Why?"

"Because I want to know, obviously," she said, sending a wisp of her magic to caress the side of his face. He flinched away, glaring at her as if he could skewer her with his eyes.

"No."

"Come now, Stoll. It's a simple question with a simple answer. A name. Just a name," Emmalee crooned. Her mind flashed an image of the marshal she'd bumped into before she'd left only to return a day later to find her family murdered. The man had been there when her magic had manifested too. She wasn't sure why she was asking, other than having the satisfaction of knowing the man who'd likely given the king's orders to the guards who'd murdered her family. She wanted—no, *needed*—to know.

Emmalee took a deep breath before sending a string of her magic toward Stoll. Just like the many times before, her magic slithered into his ears, his nostrils, his mouth, not inhibited in the slightest as he wriggled and tried to move away. Emmalee clenched her hand.

He gasped, making a choking sound for several seconds before Emmalee released him. And just like the many other times, it took several suffocatingly long rounds of smothering him before his wide bright eyes turned pleading.

"Levick," he whispered, his head tilting forward. "Marshal Levick."

"And where might he be?" Emmalee asked, cocking her head to the side. She gave him several more seconds to catch his breath.

"I-I shouldn't have—"

A commotion outside the house interrupted Stoll. Not a second later, Faeleen ran inside, closing the door behind her.

"Guards," Faeleen said, gasping. "They're looking for him." She pointed to Stoll.

Emmalee spun and glanced at the silencing rune next to the door, which was still glowing faintly. Carefully, she crossed the room and lifted the side of one of the tattered curtains covering the windows.

Emmalee stumbled away from the window. Eleven. eleven royal guards stood outside the front door, quite possibly with more around the back. She glanced back at Stoll, who must've been able to read the panicked look on her face because he started laughing.

"In here!" Stoll shouted, a wide cocky grin on his face. Apparently, he didn't recognize the rune on the door, but then again, why would he?

Emmalee didn't bother shushing him. The rune would hold—at least until she and Faeleen were long gone.

"Grab my bag. There probably aren't as many in the back. You can handle one or two, right?"

"Probably," Faeleen said. "And you?"

"Leave out the back window. I'll catch up to you," Emmalee said as she grabbed her belongings and shoved them into Faeleen's hands.

Both women jumped when a fist banged on the front door. It was locked, but it wouldn't last long, and she wasn't going to stay to hold it.

Emmalee ushered Faeleen to the back window. Before Faeleen could leave through it, Emmalee let out a dark mist, hoping it would give her friend enough time to escape unnoticed. How long, though, she wasn't sure. She was already tired and feeling more than a bit drained.

"Be careful," Emmalee whispered before Faeleen disappeared over the edge and into the darkness.

Spinning around to face Stoll, she narrowed her eyes.

He'd told her so much, and with a bit more, she knew he would likely continue to give in to the interrogation. But there wasn't time. And she couldn't just leave him. He'd run straight back to the king and tell him everything she'd asked him. She knew it. But she didn't have time to do anything about it. The spell to paralyze him would take too long, and the frame on the door was already cracking. Her fingers brushed the top of the dagger on her belt. It would be messy. There would be nightmares . . . well, *more* nightmares than she already had.

But he would talk.

Unless . . .

Emmalee's hands trembled as memories of Shongbay flooded back into her mind. She could hear the screams, smell the charred flesh of the guards she'd set on fire. But it was fast. At least, it had been then.

Before she climbed out the back window, she extended a shaky hand. Flames stretched upward in a circle around Stoll, nearly reaching the ceiling. The room started to light in a blaze, and she tried to block out the sound of Stoll screaming and the front door being broken down as she scrambled out the window. As soon as she was out of the building, the screaming stopped. Well, she doubted it stopped. But the silencing rune did its job well. She lowered herself onto the forest floor and took off running.

She would not think about the man burning alive.

Another man she'd condemned to death.

Not until she could get far enough away to vomit up the dinner Faeleen had brought her.

"There, she's there!" a male voice shouted from her left.

Emmalee's magic reacted before the guard could take a step toward her, sending him flying backward. But he was heavy. So heavy. And her body felt as though it'd collapse with much more of it.

How long had she been awake?

How long had she been using her magic to question Stoll?

Exhaustion weighed her down as she took several steps from the shack.

Another guard charged her, and this time her magic did little more than knock him down.

She needed to run, and fast.

Scanning around her, Emmalee determined that most of the guards must've been at the front, because she didn't see any more movement around her.

Without looking back, Emmalee disappeared into the trees, doing what she could to ignore the guilt of ruining yet another life. For Evangeline. For Ariella and Faeleen. For her family.

Chapter 28

SILAS

Silas kicked the door to the shack down in one try, then backed up as flames licked at his face.

"Stoll?" Silas called before taking a step in.

As soon as he crossed the threshold, he heard it. The screams. The absolute agony.

"In here," Silas called, gesturing for the other guards to follow him. The flames were concentrated in the center of the room. Two more guards filed in behind him, covering the lower half of their faces. "Jackets. Give me your jackets!" Silas shouted, blinking as the smoke made his eyes water.

The guards complied. A moment later, Silas pushed through the fire, having wrapped his face enough to protect himself from most of the flames. He reached the center of the room and threw the extra jacket over Stoll, who was coughing and moaning. The flames licked at Silas's hands, but he dragged the chair out of the center of the room.

"Get the flames out," Silas ordered, tearing the jacket off his head and throwing it over Stoll. He patted at the flames, trying not to look directly at the damage already done to the commander. "Free his hands and legs. You," he said, pointing to one of the guards nearby. "Go prepare the medic." Then to Stoll, he spoke again. "Who?"

"Back . . . window . . ." Stoll's voice came out raspy. "Estrada."

Silas tensed. "The rest of you, get him back to the medic tent. Now!" Silas barked before sprinting around the side of the house, not waiting for a response. He reached the back of the broken-down shack, his gaze scanning the dark forest. A flash of movement caught the corner of his eye. He ran.

"Stop!" Silas shouted, his voice cutting through the night air.

Ahead of him, Estrada glanced back, her eyes wide as she ran faster. She dropped her hand by her side, letting mist leak to cover her trail.

Silas pushed harder, closing the gap between them. A second later, he tackled her to the ground.

The impact knocked the wind out of him, but he forced air into his lungs as Estrada struggled beneath him.

"Stay down!" he commanded, his voice harsh and authoritative.

Warning bells went off in Silas's head as the temperature began to drop. He ripped the magic-dampening cuffs off his belt, closing one over the wrist he already held in his hand. The temperature stabilized instantly.

She must've noticed too, because she twisted and writhed beneath him on her stomach. Silas tried to grab her other wrist, forcing it behind her back to secure it with the other cuff.

Pain exploded in Silas's nose when Estrada slammed her elbow back into his face. Coppery blood covered his tongue as it trickled into his mouth. He staggered. It was only a second. But it was enough for him to lose control just long enough for her to squirm out from under him.

She freed a dagger he recognized from the night in the boulder field from her belt.

His pulse thudded in his ears as he unsheathed his sword. He highly doubted she'd been trained in any kind of combat, but he wasn't going to risk not removing his weapon.

A look of recognition crossed her face as she stared at him.

"Marshal Thorne," she said, taking several steps backward. The cuff and chain jangled at her side.

Silas wiped the steady stream of blood from his nose, his eyes narrowing. "Surrender, Estrada. This doesn't have to end in more bloodshed."

Estrada's grip tightened on the dagger, her knuckles turning white. "I'd happily spill more of your blood," she spat, lunging forward with the blade aimed at his chest.

He wasn't sure what had compelled her. Anger? Fear, maybe? Either way, it was clear by her sloppy footwork and unbalanced stance she hadn't been trained. Not like him.

Silas dodged, grabbing her wrist and twisting it. She let out a cry, but she gritted her teeth a second later and kicked his shin. Remaining steady, he grunted at the impact, which would most certainly bruise. He didn't care if he returned to the castle black-and-blue. He would see Estrada arrested.

Yanking her off-balance, he prepared to catch her other wrist, the one still holding the dagger. He did not expect her to move with him.

The momentum was too much. He loosened his grip to catch himself, and it was enough for her to break his hold. He stumbled back, and she took the opportunity to swipe at him again. The blade nicked his arm, and he hissed in pain.

His sword swiped through the air only an inch from where she'd been standing. If only she'd been closer. Just a bit. Silas lowered his sword and changed tactics.

"Oof." Estrada clutched her stomach as she staggered backward. She fought to keep her balance after his swift punch hit her in the torso.

Silas didn't hesitate. He closed the distance between them, abandoning his sword. In a desperate move, she slashed wildly, grazing his cheek.

"You're under arrest," Silas growled, catching her arm. With a swift move, he twisted her arm behind her back and shoved her forward, pinning her to a tree trunk.

A faint memory played at the edge of his mind. He'd arrested Evie in a similar fashion, only he'd made sure he hadn't hurt her. With Estrada, though, he had no such qualms.

The metal chain jingled, and the cuff brushed her free wrist. Just as it was about to click into place, securing the arrest both he and Butch had been hoping for for over a year and a half, Estrada managed to twist her body enough to loop her ankle around the back of his leg. With a shift of her hips, they both tumbled backward, Silas dragging her with him.

For a second time, the wind left Silas's lungs. Next to him, Estrada groaned. She must've landed wrong on her arm because she cradled it as she lay on her back.

Before she could react, he had her pinned again. He leaned over her, straddling her waist to keep her from moving.

A flash of metal caught in his peripheral vision as he reached for the second cuff still attached to her by one wrist. Estrada had somehow found her dagger on the ground.

Silas caught her wrist just as the blade sent a flash of fire across his side. Using the advantage of his strength, he wrestled it from her grip. A moment later, he pressed her own blade into her skin along the column of her neck.

Estrada clenched her jaw, glaring up at him.

"As I said," Silas panted, his breathing just as labored as hers. "You're under arrest." He tried to ignore the pain coursing through his cut and bruised body. No wonder she'd managed to escape his men so often. She wasn't just cunning; when forced into a corner, she was downright savage.

But he had her.

And it was over.

"Get off her!"

A streak of green and yellow flashed to Silas's right. His weight shifted off Estrada as someone tackled him to the ground.

The two of them rolled until Silas ended up with a familiar face above him. Ariella's sister, Fae, glared down at him with slitted pupils with unnaturally green irises and pointed teeth. Her fingers had grown claws, and they pressed into his throat until he was sure he was bleeding there too.

"Where's my sister?" Fae shrieked, pressing harder into his neck until he had to clench his jaw to keep from crying out.

Silas grunted but did not answer. At some point, he'd lost his grip on the dagger, and out of the corner of his eye, he watched Estrada crawl over to where it lay. She reattached it to her belt, favoring her injured arm.

Voices echoed from nearby. Male voices.

No doubt his men searching for him.

However, he didn't dare call out for two reasons: he didn't need more of his men getting injured, and he was fairly certain Ariella's sister could rip his throat out before he even got a sound out.

"Fae, we have to go," Estrada said, still catching her breath as she scrambled to her feet.

Fae hissed at her. Actually hissed. Silas's eyes widened.

"Not until I know Ari is safe. Where is she?" Fae lifted Silas by the collar and slammed his head back onto the ground.

The world above him swam. He groaned, closing his eyes against the swirling surroundings that threatened to make him sick.

"Faeleen!" Estrada pleaded as footsteps came closer. "Now!"

"But—"

Estrada rushed over and pulled Faeleen off Silas, and before he could get up, Estrada kicked him in the ribs. Silas crumbled, covering his midsection. He blinked several times to clear his vision.

Estrada glared at him one last time before she tugged Faeleen into the shadows, their footsteps fading in unison.

Chapter 29

EVANGELINE

Evangeline listened to Helena complain about the terrible lighting in the dungeon for what felt like the hundredth time in a row as the older woman squinted down at Evangeline's wrists. They had scabbed over since they'd stopped wrapping them, and the skin around the scabs was constantly itchy. However, Evangeline knew better than to scratch it, even if it did feel like it was driving her mad at times.

"Higher, boy, hold it higher," Helena said, her voice exasperated as a guard adjusted the lantern above them.

It'd been three weeks since Thorne had locked her back up in her cell. As soon as he had left, Odette had gushed over how much better Evangeline appeared and how lonely it had been when she was gone.

And while Evangeline missed the cot in the infirmary, Odette's company quickly made the brick floor a worthy bed.

Better yet, Silas had stayed true to his word, and a servant had brought down a fresh, albeit simple and oversize, set of clothes for Evangeline. Did they fit properly? Not even close. But were they torn and filthy? Well, not when she first got them.

Several weeks later though . . . They weren't torn, per se, but filthy? Yes.

Thankfully, the food didn't revert to masses of inedible mold, as she'd expected. That, she found out later, was because Helena had requested that the food brought with the medicine be appetizing so Evangeline would continue to gain her strength back. And according to Helena, the king was making some of the changes

Helena had suggested to the dungeon. Didn't seem like he'd changed much, but at least the food seemed more edible and there weren't as many rats. She wasn't sure how he'd accomplished that, but she wasn't complaining.

When the first tray of food had come and it wasn't stale, Evangeline had even spoken a word of thanks to the servant girl who'd brought it. Odette hadn't seemed surprised and had told her it'd gotten better after she'd left. Evangeline still split her food with Odette, though, insisting her friend take part because her stomach still could not consume an entire meal without being somewhat sick.

The medicine, while disgusting, did seem to be working, and Helena mentioned that she was pleased with Evangeline's progress every time she came down to check on her.

Evangeline hadn't realized how much she'd missed Odette until her friend went back to filling the empty stretches of time with conversation. In the dungeon—unlike in the infirmary, where Evangeline had counted on the physicians to provide her with company—Evangeline didn't have to weigh what she was going to say, considering most things spoken between her and Odette were through signing.

"Another week or two of the medicine and I might just be done with you, Lia," Helena said, brushing off her apron as she packed up the bag of supplies she carried with her.

Evangeline nodded, thanking her without words since the guard holding the lantern stood nearby—not that he seemed to be paying attention.

Helena bid Evangeline goodbye and left with the guard. As soon as they disappeared up the winding stairs, Evangeline went to sit down in the back of the cell, and Odette tapped on the bar.

"So, is it Evie or Lia?" Odette signed when the dungeon returned to its dark and silent state. A few of the cells that had been occupied around them before Evangeline had left were empty now, and when she'd asked Odette about it, the answer seemed grim.

"Evie. But I don't—"

"Want it to get back to the king. I know. Where did Lia come from?"

"It's my middle name. Came from my father's mother."

"It's pretty." Odette paused, a smile on her face. "I'd name a daughter that."

"Did you want other children besides your son?" Evangeline recalled the conversation that had happened early on in her time in the dungeon.

179

Odette had explained that she knew how to sign because her son, who was eighteen, was deaf and couldn't speak without signing. He'd left when he was fifteen to go apprentice under a blacksmith in a different village, leaving Odette to run her shoe shop alone. She'd written him for a while before she was arrested, but Kristopher—or Kris, as Odette lovingly referred to him—likely didn't know what had happened to her.

"I wanted a daughter, but that never happened. Honestly, I just hope I get to see Kris again someday." Odette offered Evangeline a sad smile.

"Hopefully not down here," Evangeline responded.

"Definitely not. What about you? Have you thought about children?"

"Me?" Evangeline let out a surprised laugh. "Not married. No children. I don't . . . I don't know if I'd ever have a child."

"Really? Why?"

"It's not that I wouldn't want them." Evangeline bit her lip, trying to put into words what she'd once written in a journal when her magic had manifested on her twenty-first birthday. "This country . . . It's a terrifying place to raise children, if you think about it."

There it was—the fear of passing her magic down to another person, one she loved more deeply than herself. It was easier to be selfish, to keep the child from grief and struggle by never bringing the child into the broken world.

"Well, if you did have a child, what would you name it?"

"I haven't thought about it, really," Evangeline signed, her thoughts still wrapped in a layer of fear. She shook her head, trying to free it of the feeling.

"What comes to your mind first?"

"Ellayne, after my mother." Evangeline raised her eyebrows when the answer came easily.

"And if you were lucky like me and had a boy?"

Evangeline snorted. "I honestly have no clue."

"You don't like your father's name?" Odette teased, but she stopped grinning when Evangeline's face fell.

"He left my mother and me out of nowhere. His name was Wren, and as far as I know, he's a coward and probably dead."

"I didn't know. I'm sorry."

Evangeline forced a smile onto her face. "Of course you didn't know. I've never told you. It was a fair question. What would you have named your son if he had been a girl?"

The two of them continued to talk for several more hours, and every once in a while Odette would explain an unfamiliar word she signed, letting Evangeline repeat it a few times after her. But eventually the conversation drew thin, and they fell into a comfortable silence.

Evangeline leaned her head back against the wall. With the topics of the previous conversation still swirling through her mind, she thought of her family—or what was left of it.

When her mother died, she'd been left in the care of her stepfather, a complicated and often unkind man. Evangeline had never considered Jonathan Dipthy part of her family. As for his daughter, Linetta, Evangeline considered her a sister even though they did not share blood.

Maybe, like Odette's son, Linetta thought Evangeline was dead. What kind of dread would fill her sister when she learned of Evangeline's disappearance? She wondered if Emmalee had filled Linetta in on what had happened, though she doubted it. Emmalee would hopefully not risk venturing into Bowhoo, where Evangeline, and later Linetta, had grown up. Hopefully Linetta was still safe. And Emmalee.

Footsteps down the stairway drew Evangeline from the stomach-churning thoughts, and she sat straighter. The steps were light, too light for a royal guard. It was most certainly a servant bringing down Evangeline's medicine and dinner.

When the young woman rounded the corner, Evangeline furrowed her brow. Typically, a girl in her teenage years with short brown hair brought the tray. This servant not only dressed better, wearing a light blue dress under her apron, but she appeared much closer to Evangeline's age. A curl of auburn hair peeked out from beneath the scarf in which her hair was wrapped.

When she got to the bottom of the stairs, she glanced to the left and right before her gaze landed on Evangeline, who was staring at her. She carried a tray like the other servant, but something was off about her. She glanced over her shoulder at the staircase before making her way to Evangeline. She startled when one of the men a few cells away rattled the bars and called out to her, but she regained her stance and quickened her pace.

"You're the one who was in the infirmary, right?" the woman asked, her gaze flicking to Odette for a second after she asked Evangeline the question.

Evangeline nodded but didn't reply, watching the woman from the back of the cell.

The woman bent down and slid the tray through the gap at the bottom of the door, which was tall enough for a tray of food but too small for a person to slip through—not that Evangeline had tried.

They stared at each other for a few seconds before the servant cleared her throat. "Should I stay until you're finished, or . . . ?"

Evangeline refrained from snorting, rolling her lips inward as she pushed herself to her feet. The other servant girl typically left after she delivered the tray, and the fact that this one was staying left Evangeline's mind tingling with curiosity.

Keeping her eyes on the servant, Evangeline crossed the cell and squatted next to the food. It didn't appear any different than normal, and she unplugged the cork from the small bottle of medicine. Holding her breath, she downed it. The taste was still horrendous. Evangeline shuddered as she replaced the bottle on the tray.

However, something peeked out from beneath the plate, and Evangeline tilted her head to the side. It looked like the corner of a piece of parchment.

Brow furrowing, Evangeline glanced up at the servant.

"Is everything all right?" the woman asked, her gaze flicking to the tray and back to Evangeline a few times.

Evangeline's thoughts whirled as she tried to decide if she should point out the obvious parchment. But if the servant didn't know she'd been a messenger, it could get the sender in trouble as well as Evangeline.

"It's fine. Thank you," Evangeline said, grabbing the tray and taking it to the back of the cell.

The woman glanced once more at the tray before nodding and leaving the dungeon. When her pattering footsteps disappeared, Odette chuckled next to her.

"Well, that was strange."

Evangeline mumbled a word of agreement as she angled her body to hide the tray from the rest of the dungeon. She directly faced Odette's cell as she picked up the plate and removed it from the tray. A small folded piece of parchment remained.

She held her breath. Her fingers fumbled as she picked up the message and unfolded the crease.

It was difficult to examine in the low light, especially since she had her back turned to the only light source in the dungeon—the window didn't let in any light because the sun had already descended behind the horizon and the moons weren't out yet.

"That's new," Odette whispered, scooting closer to the bars that separated them.

When Evangeline glanced at her, Odette pointed to the paper and then signed something she could only guess was a question about what was on it.

Evangeline squinted at the scrap of paper, and she had to blink a few times as her eyes strained to read the small cursive. She didn't dare read it aloud and instead mouthed the words with a frown creasing her brow. *"Be patient. Be prepared."* Evangeline read the four words over again in her head before passing the note to Odette.

"Vague," Odette signed, sending it back through the bars. "No name."

Evangeline nodded and mouthed the words as she responded silently. "It's neat. A woman's, most likely."

Her stomach had leapt when she'd first seen the note because for a second, she thought Emmalee might have managed to get it to her. But that hope sank when she saw the handwriting; it looked nothing like her friend's.

Evangeline turned her attention to the food. For the first time in a while, her stomach growled, and she ripped off a part of the bread.

"Do you trust it?" Odette asked, thanking Evangeline when she passed a piece of bread to her.

"Maybe, or maybe it's a trap." After she'd seen it wasn't Emmalee's handwriting, the possibility that it could be the king or someone else leading her into a false sense of hope was the next thought that popped into her head.

"Could be," Odette said, nodding.

With her mind distracted by the writing, Evangeline didn't respond, and the two women shared her dinner in silence. If the note was a trap, it was best not to think much more of it. But the problem lay in the fact that she didn't know whether or not it was meant for her downfall. Even if it had truly come from an unknown ally, though, there was not much she could do to be prepared for something completely unknown.

And with that thought in mind, Evangeline wadded up the small piece of parchment, dipped it into the water from her cup, and swallowed it. At least that way she wouldn't get in trouble when the guards searched her cell.

Chapter 30

LENORA

Lenora continued to wring her hands as she paced across her bedroom. She was supposed to meet her husband for dinner in less than ten minutes, and Kaylene still hadn't returned from the dungeon.

It'd taken longer than she'd hoped to reach out to the prisoner, but that was because Lenora and her handmaids had spent a long time figuring out the best way to send a message without being caught. They'd considered using a servant, but there was no promise they wouldn't talk. After too much debating, Kaylene had volunteered.

Merla stood by Lenora's armoire, her arms crossed over her chest as she watched Lenora's progression back and forth across the room. She remained silent. Unnervingly silent.

"You don't think someone noticed, do you?" Lenora asked, not stopping as she turned on her heels again to pace toward the window. Though she was starting to feel dizzy from each switch in direction, she didn't stop. She couldn't sit still. It was better to get it out before she did something during her dinner with Butch that would make him curious—or worse, suspicious. Her stomach twisted with the guilt of going behind her husband's back.

"I'm sure she's fine, Your Majesty." Merla spoke with certainty, but not enough to calm Lenora's racing heart. "We should go to dinner now though. We don't want to keep the king waiting."

"Of course. You're right," Lenora said, nodding.

Merla offered Lenora her gloves, helping slide the silk fabric up past Lenora's elbows. Though the servants kept her room warm, the hallways and other rooms in the castle tended to be quite drafty—one of the bigger complaints Lenora had about living in the castle. Even in the middle of summer, the castle clung to its draftiness enough to keep perpetual goose bumps on Lenora's skin.

Lenora walked arm in arm with Merla down the corridors of the third floor, though her mind wandered to other parts of the castle, namely the dungeon. Had Kaylene passed on the note? Had she gotten caught? Where was she?

And what spirit had possessed Lenora to write the note in the first place? If her husband found out she had defied his direct orders to leave the prisoner alone, he'd be furious.

The guard outside the smaller family room cleared his throat, still holding the door open for Lenora and Merla.

"Right, thank you," Lenora said before Merla or the guard could ask what had caused her to stop as though frozen before the room.

"I was beginning to wonder if you'd forgotten about me," Butch said with a grin as he rose from the table and met her halfway into the room. He reached for her hand, and she inclined her head as he leaned down to place a soft kiss against the fabric covering her knuckles. The heat from his skin sank in through the glove, warming Lenora's hand as he led her to the seat across from his. He pulled out her chair, then pushed it in as she sat down.

"I'm sorry we're late," Lenora said, taking a sip from her cup. "I lost track of time."

"Making plans for the welcome banquet, I presume?" Butch took his seat across from her, nodding toward two servants waiting on the side of the room. They approached the table and began lifting the silver cloches covering the trays of food.

Lenora simply nodded, slicing into her chicken and taking a bite to avoid responding. When she looked up, he was watching her.

"And . . . you? How are you?" Lenora covered her mouth as she spoke.

"I've been better." Her husband leaned back in his chair, sipping from his cup as he stared at a spot just behind her.

"Is everything all right?"

Butch's expression pinched together, his brow furrowing as he lowered the cup to the table. "Yes. I mean, no. Yes, I'm all right, but I haven't heard anything from Marshal Thorne. And . . ." He sighed, running his hand down the side of his cheek. "I've hit a rather large dead end. It's—I don't—" He rubbed his fingers along his temple, massaging the spot for several seconds before finishing the thought. "I'm not sure where to go from here. I have options." He tapped the table twice, his attention somewhere far away by the glazed look in his eye. His jaw clenched. "I don't like some of them, but if I don't have a means of finding Estrada soon, it may come to them."

"What options?" Lenora asked, forcing her voice to remain pleasant while her mind descended to the dungeon, where Estrada's friend had supposedly been moved. Maybe that was why Kaylene hadn't returned yet. Maybe the prisoner was somewhere else. Maybe—

"Options I would prefer to keep as options rather than only choices." He wrinkled his nose, straightening when he met her questioning gaze with his own. "I'm not getting what I need from the prisoner you saw. She's more stubborn than I gave her credit for." He muttered the last part under his breath, scratching his chin absentmindedly.

"What options, Butch?" Lenora twisted the fabric of her skirt in her hands beneath the cover of the table.

Silence hung heavy in the room. Lenora kept her gaze fixed on her husband, but his distant stare locked on to some invisible point across from him. It was as though he was seeing horrors visible only in his mind, and she longed to reach for him, to understand what was causing his body to tremble.

Her heart ached as she noticed the subtle tremor in his once-steady hand as he ran his fingers through his hair.

As Butch took a deep, almost inaudible breath, Lenora waited for his response.

"I'm considering moving the woman to the château."

Her blood turned to ice. "Lavfor?" Lenora asked, the word a mere whisper.

She'd only heard stories of Château Lavfor, having never been there herself. But she remembered the agonizing nights during the first few months of their marriage when Butch had been determined to bring down what he himself had described as a "castle of horrors" created by his predecessors.

Butch cleared his throat as he sat straighter, shifting his weight to lean on one arm of the chair. "Forgive me, Lenora. I shouldn't have brought it up. Let's change the topic, shall we? Have you—"

"You can't, Butch. You worked so hard to put an end to Lavfor." Not to mention it would be harder to help Estrada's friend if she was in an entirely different location. Lenora tried to keep the fear from trickling into her expression, and she forced her muscles to relax, as she'd done many times in court. "What makes you think she'll give you anything under duress? And are you sure you want those kinds of responses? Wouldn't you rather have the truth than be told whatever you want to hear to make the torture stop?"

"I don't *want* to have her tortured. I don't want to have *anyone* sent there." Butch's voice came out as a low trembling whisper. "But if it comes down to my people and—"

"She's a person too. And from what I've heard—" Lenora placed a hand over her racing heart. When had it started to beat so quickly? And her face felt warm, as if she'd been working in the sun all day instead of staying in the cold castle. "From what I've heard, Lavfor would kill her before you got anything out of her."

"It depends on who's in charge of things there, but—are you all right?" Butch asked, leaning forward in his chair when Lenora wiped away a drop of sweat forming on her temple. "You look as though you're going to faint."

"I'm all right, I just—"

But Butch was already pushing back from the table and was by her side before she could finish her sentence. He slid her chair back and knelt before her, placing the back of his hand on her forehead.

"You're burning up," he muttered, glancing over his shoulder toward the door. "I'll get someone and—"

Lenora cut him off, catching his hand in hers and pulling it toward her chest. "Don't. I'm fine." When he tried to pull away, Lenora gripped him tighter. "Butch, please. Don't reopen Lavfor."

"This isn't about—"

"Please don't." She stared into his eyes, pleading with him in the silence that followed. Once more he looked back at the door, and with a shaky hand, she caught his cheek and pulled his attention back to her. "I *need* you not to reopen it." With every part of her being, she hoped he would not ask her why. She couldn't—wouldn't—tell him why.

Butch stared up at her for a second longer before something changed, the warm brown color of his eyes deepening.

"All right," he whispered, his voice gentle as he squeezed her hand. "All right."

"Thank you." Lenora breathed out, letting her forehead fall forward and rest against his, her eyes fluttering shut. "You'll figure this out," she said, stroking her thumb across his cheek. She opened her eyes to see him studying her.

"I hope you're right," he mumbled, turning his head to kiss the inside of her palm before sitting back on his heels. "I really do." He stood up, leaning down to kiss her on the forehead, his lips lingering for a moment before he sat back down in his chair across from her.

Butch rubbed his hand over his face. He looked tired, as though he hadn't slept in weeks. Maybe months. He pinched the bridge of his nose as he sighed, sprawling out his legs. "I suppose we ought to change the subject," he said, his eyes closed.

"I suppose so." Silence followed as Lenora tried to slow her racing heart. She took a sip from her cup, letting her body sink into the chair. "Are we going to host a ball for the annual celebration for Cyanthia?" She hoped not. "It'll fall right around the time the Jerr Pinn delegation will arrive."

"The thought hadn't crossed my mind. Maybe we could combine the welcome ball and the annual celebration ball into one."

"That's brilliant." And it meant she only had to plan one obnoxious ball for the time being.

Butch changed the topic again, and Lenora pushed her food around her plate as she tried to listen, though not much made it to her mouth.

Since Helena had confirmed that Lenora was pregnant, it continued to feel as though each thought had to slog through a field of fog. Conversations tended to wander off as she lost her thoughts, or she struggled to focus on what had been previously said. Multiple times she stopped in the middle of a response entirely, not able to complete whatever thought had previously filled her mind.

Butch continued to regard her with a wary eye, especially when she asked him to repeat himself for the third time.

"Are you sure you're all right?" He frowned over the rim of his cup.

"Yes, just a bit tired."

In a matter of seconds, he was on his feet and offering his arm to her. "I'll walk you to your room."

Lenora thanked him, taking his arm. He was warm beneath her cold hands, and he didn't say anything as he led her out of the room. Despite the warmer weather, a chilly wind went through the hallway, and to Lenora's surprise, she found herself snuggling closer to her husband.

Even more surprising, when she glanced up at him, Butch was smiling at her.

"What?" Lenora asked, her brow furrowing.

"Nothing. I'm just glad you came tonight." He patted her hand still wrapped around his arm.

His words caused her to pause. Lenora hadn't anticipated such warmth in the genuine smile on his lips.

At what point had she started noticing the sparkle in his chestnut brown eyes? When had his gentle grins started making her stomach flutter?

A flicker of realization ignited within her—she wanted to tell him. Butch wasn't just the man, the *king*, she'd been forced to marry. At some point, he'd started to become a person she trusted.

He'd just decided to forego his decision to reopen Lavfor simply because she'd asked him not to.

He'd *heard* her.

And she wanted to tell him.

He needed to know.

"Let's take the long way through the portrait hall tonight." She didn't know what she was saying until his brow furrowed.

"Are you sure?" An air of hesitation tainted his voice. Butch's gaze met hers, and when she nodded, he sighed. "All right."

They continued in silence, entering the hall adorned with generations of royal portraits. Lenora couldn't remember the last time she'd been in the portrait hall. It was out of the way, and honestly, she wasn't fond of looking at the faces of the people who'd started the war on magic. By the growing tension in Butch's grip, he wasn't particularly fond of it either.

The faces of queens and kings stared down at them, frozen in time.

Lenora tore her gaze from the Maudit line, turning instead to look at her husband. With a shaky breath, she placed a hand on his chest.

"I need to tell you something."

His fingers tightened around hers, though she couldn't decide if it was meant to be reassuring or a source of grounding for him.

Just as she was about to speak, a weight held her tongue down. They had suffered so much before, each pregnancy leaving invisible—and in her case quite visible—scars. The fear of disappointment and heartache lingered, and Lenora's breath quickened.

What if she'd read him wrong? What if he didn't respond well? What if . . .

Lenora's voice emerged as a quiet murmur, nervously breaking the silence in the portrait hall.

"I'm pregnant."

Chapter 31

BUTCH

Time stopped. Every sound became muffled. The faces in the frames around them blurred.

Lenora's whispered words lingered in the air.

Pregnant.

She was pregnant.

Fear coursed through Butch's body, clenching his pounding heart firmly in its grasp. Bloody images flashed across his mind. Lenora lying in the bed, her delicate face twisted in agony. Terror streaking across Helena's face. The small lifeless body of the child that had never taken her first breath.

He'd almost lost Lenora.

And when the stillbirth hadn't killed her, the grief from multiple miscarriages almost had.

And now, if they had to go through either of those again . . .

They stood together in the heart of the room, surrounded by the scrutinizing and watchful gazes of past rulers. He knew he should be overjoyed that there might be an heir, but if it meant losing her . . .

Lenora's hand rested gently on Butch's chest, her fingers cold as ice. Her dark eyes seemed wholly focused on his face as she flicked her gaze from his eyes to his lips and back up. Her features, touched by the soft incandescence of candlelight, held a vulnerability that she'd rarely shown in the years of their marriage. She looked radiant—glowing, even—in the low light that accentuated her porcelain-doll features: her large eyes, her rounded face, the faint blush that had all but leached out of her pale skin when he'd mentioned Lavfor.

How long had it been since she'd spoken? He needed to speak. To say something. Anything.

Butch's fingers instinctively found hers and intertwined with them. "You're sure?"

"Helena said—"

"How are you? Are you feeling all right? Should you be on your feet?" At the mention of the physician, it was as if Butch's mind doubled in speed. He pulled her over to a bench near one of the grand windows, urging her to sit down before he knelt in front of her. Butch's fingers trembled as he wiped his hand across his forehead. "When will the—are you—how can I—I'm not sure—" Words spilled out of his mouth, sentences without end, until her touch stilled him.

To his surprise, a small smile crept across Lenora's lips as tears welled in her eyes. With tenderness, his wife grasped his face and leaned down to kiss him softly on the forehead.

"I'm just as terrified as you," she whispered, tilting his chin up to look into his eyes. He grasped her hands on either side of his face, interlacing his fingers with hers.

"But you're—"

"I'm all right. A little sick here and there, but that's normal."

Butch's heart thundered in his chest. "How long until . . . ?" He wasn't sure how to ask. What if he said the wrong thing?

He didn't need to finish his thought.

"Helena thinks I'm about six or seven weeks in. Enough to be sick most days."

"You said that's normal though, right?" He couldn't keep the fear out of his voice. "It's not a sign that something's wrong?" He brought their hands down, resting them in her lap.

Lenora shook her head but didn't speak. She rubbed soft circles into the back of his hand, and the longer she stared down at him, the more a fire began to build in his stomach.

His wife, carrying his child.

Though a small voice in the back of his mind warned him not to cling to the newfound hope, he couldn't stop the growing warmth from within. As he knelt before her, the initial fear that had gripped him slowly dissolved and was replaced by a flame that flickered and danced with the prospect of fatherhood.

Somewhere in the deep sea of her gaze, the same emotion reflected in the mirror of her eyes—a small glimmer of anticipation bubbling beneath the lingering weight of loss.

Lenora's touch on his hand was both grounding and electrifying. A silent reassurance. The fire in his stomach spread, engulfing the remnants of fear.

"You're really pregnant?" He couldn't keep his voice from trembling, and despite the anger his father would've shown him at his weakness, moisture filled his eyes.

"Yes."

He couldn't stop himself as he leaned forward and pulled her into a tight embrace. The faint hint of her lavender perfume enveloped him as he shoved his face into the crook of her neck.

"Thank you," he said, his voice breaking. "Thank you."

She remained still as he hugged her, stroking his back in small circles as if it might soothe him. Out of the corner of his eye, he noticed his father's scowl in one of the paintings. It felt as though his father's eyes were burning a hole through him; as if to show him how disgraceful he was, a weeping mess on his knees.

Butch cleared his throat, sitting back on his heels as he tried to calm his beating heart. "Things will need to change. I don't want you putting yourself or the baby at risk."

"There isn't—"

"I'll make sure the security in the castle is doubled, and we'll make sure the patrols on the third floor are timelier."

"That's nice, but—"

Butch straightened his jacket as he cut her off again. "And I'll have someone else plan the welcome banquet for the Jerr Pinn delegation. Are there any other things that are causing you stress?"

Lenora bit her cheek as if she was about to say something, then thought better of it. He waited a moment longer until she shook her head.

"If you think of anything else, don't hesitate to tell me. Are the cooks aware? We should make sure they don't serve anything that could affect—"

"I'll speak with Helena, but Butch, I don't think we should spread the news—not yet, at least. Not until . . ." Her words faded away, and her face fell. "Something could happen again. I want to be hopeful, but I'm also—"

"Me too," he said, taking a seat on the bench next to her. He leaned back against the wall, letting his eyes flutter closed. "And you're probably right. We'll put off telling people until we can't keep it quiet anymore."

"Thank you for understanding," Lenora said, and another second later, she placed her hand on his. "And thank you for wanting to make things easier on me."

"Of course."

BUTCH DRUMMED HIS fingers rhythmically against the polished wood at the head of his council table. The dignitaries from Jerr Pinn would be arriving in just a few weeks, and Butch watched as his council members discussed the boundaries and logistics of the new trade agreements he was to present to the delegation upon their arrival. The trade agreements could fortify their alliance and bring prosperity to both nations, and while Butch wanted to be hopeful, a small voice told him to be realistic. Jerr Pinn had shut down trade routes into and out of Phildeterre during his grandfather's reign because of the war on magic within Phildeterre.

"I believe that would be the best way to phrase the section on magic folk crossing the borders," Councilman Clive said, and several others nodded. In fact, for the first time in what felt like forever, there had been little arguing between the council members.

"And we are in agreement on our stance with monitoring the boundaries?" Councilman Macaw asked.

More nods.

Butch forced a smile, trying to focus on the discussion. His mind kept drifting back to the previous night. How was he supposed to focus on legislation and politics between nations when all he wanted to do was spend time with his pregnant wife?

"Your Majesty?" Councilman Clive's nasally voice cut through his thoughts. "Do you have any thoughts on the trade agreements?"

Blinking, Butch refocused on the faces peering down the table at him. "Yes, of course," he said, clearing his throat as he sat straighter in his chair. "The proposals are solid. As long as they feel welcome and see the benefits of our collaboration, I'm sure everything will go smoothly. We will be tightening security, given the tensions with magic-related incidents. I'll speak with my marshals to make sure they keep disruptions to a minimum."

The council members murmured in agreement.

Just as one of the members began outlining the itinerary for the dignitaries' visit, the door to the council chamber opened, and a young messenger entered, his face pale and drawn.

He approached Butch, bowing deeply.

"Your Majesty, I have urgent news from the Black Forest." He spoke quietly, casting a nervous glance over his shoulder at the council members.

"Of course," Butch said, his stomach twisting. If something happened to Silas . . . Butch nodded to his council as he rose to his feet. "Continue without me. I'll be back shortly."

When he and the boy were out in the hallway with the doors closed behind them, the boy spoke.

"There's been another death, sire. A guard was found in the Black Forest, burned by what appeared to be dark magic."

Dread settled over Butch. He clenched his jaw. "Who?" Butch asked, pleading over and over in his mind that whatever name the boy said wouldn't be his best friend's.

"Officer Michael Reynard, Your Majesty."

Butch closed his eyes for a moment, trying to refrain from releasing a sigh of relief. There was no reason for the pressure to be easing from his chest when Reynard was as much one of his men as Silas. And while he sensed guilt rising in him, he couldn't stop the relief.

"Marshal Thorne is aware, I assume?"

"Yes, sire."

"All right, thank you for informing me. If there are any developments, please let me know." Butch dismissed the messenger with a nod and returned to the council chamber.

"Your Majesty?" One of the council members nearest the door addressed him, and Butch stood taller.

"I apologize, but I'm cutting this meeting short. I have some things to attend to. You've made great progress, and we will reconvene tomorrow at the same time. Good evening," he said before giving a slight bow and exiting through the same door.

As he strode through the castle corridors, his mind churned with dark thoughts. The constant threat of dark magic, the loss of his men, the potential danger to Lenora and their unborn child. It all pressed down on him until he was suffocating under a heavy shroud.

He made his way to the third floor and entered his private chambers. Only a low fire in the hearth lit the room, and with the curtains drawn tight against the sinking sun, Butch sat on a chaise longue in quiet darkness. However, he didn't stay long.

Soon enough, he was pacing the length of the chamber from door to window and back again, his hands clenching and unclenching at his sides.

He needed to find Estrada and put an end to her.

For his country.

For his wife and child.

For himself.

But he needed to find her. Needed to know how she thought. How she planned. What she feared and her weaknesses. And to do that, he needed to get the blasted prisoner to speak. If anyone could answer his questions, it would be the infuriating blond woman who now haunted his dreams as much as Estrada.

The thought that Estrada could very well be planning her next move made his stomach churn.

His mind flashed to Lenora, her face pale and strained over supper the night before. He could still hear her voice echoing in the back of his mind, pleading with him not to reopen Château Lavfor. He'd promised her he wouldn't. But with another guard dead . . .

Desperation gnawed at him.

He couldn't bear the thought of losing his wife, or their child, to the insidious threat of dark magic.

To the insidious threat of Estrada.

Butch stopped pacing and stared at the ornate mirror on the wall across from him. When had the dark circles under his eyes become permanent? What startled him more, though, was the hollow look in his own eyes. In the low light, he almost looked . . . He looked like his father.

He lifted his chin, glaring at his reflection.

He was the king.

His duty was to protect his kingdom.

He was a husband.

His duty was to protect his wife.

He would soon be a father.

Butch's jaw clenched.

He would speak to the prisoner, and she would answer his questions, even if it was in the midst of begging for mercy.

The stakes were too high.

Chapter 32

BUTCH

Butch took a shaky breath before he pushed open the creaky door to the dimly lit interrogation room at the heart of the dungeon. He hadn't stepped foot in the room since his father had been alive, and the sight of the iron chains and dark stains that covered the walls unsettled his stomach.

Weak. That was what his father would've called him.

Butch forced his attention to the person who seemed completely out of place in the dark room. Even with her greasy hair and filthy clothing, Estrada's friend radiated a light that made him double-check to make sure she was in fact wearing magic-dampening chains. Unlike the cells in the dungeon, the interrogation room had not been built with the same magic-dampening metal.

Her stoic expression never wavered, even as he closed the door behind him. The harsh sound of metal grating against metal echoed in the small space as she adjusted her posture on the chair to which she was chained.

The woman didn't speak—not that he expected her to start a conversation with him after months of silence.

Butch paced in front of her, his anger simmering beneath the surface as he recalled all the hours spent staring at her from across his desk.

"Do you know why you're here?" he asked, watching her watch him.

Nothing.

Butch glanced at the table sitting against the wall. It held metal instruments he had no desire to use.

But Lenora.

And his child.

And his country.

He crossed the room and picked up a tool, examining it in the light of a torch hanging on the wall.

"Do you know what Château Lavfor is?" Butch watched her for any reaction, but the only change was a quickening of her breathing. She didn't even crane her neck to look at him. "Do you know what my father had me do there?" Butch tried to keep his voice even, but the memories of bodies strapped to tables and unending sobs filled his mind.

He turned to face the prisoner, still holding a small curved knife. "Where would Estrada hide after committing murder?"

The prisoner's eyes widened, and for a second, she flicked her gaze to him before focusing back on the door. She remained silent, her hands tightening on the arms of the chair.

Butch walked behind her, if only to hide how much his hands were shaking. He let the knife rest with the flat side on her shoulder as he leaned down over the back of the chair.

"Does she have other friends she would run to? Ones who would hide her?" he asked, keeping his voice low.

When she didn't respond, her attention still straight ahead, Butch forced air into his lungs.

"Speak!" he shouted, slamming his hand down on the back of her chair.

She flinched.

Butch stormed around to the front, flinging the knife back onto the table, where it clattered against the other torture instruments. He put his hands on the back of the chair, caging in her head and forcing her to look at him as he got in her face. Only, she didn't look at him. Her attention dropped to his chest as soon as he was face-to-face with her.

"Speak!" he shouted again.

She winced, closing her eyes.

Was she trembling?

And . . . were those tears beginning to spill out of her eyes, still pinched shut?

Butch took a step back.

And another.

Memories flooded into his mind, unbidden and painful.

A different face. A young boy with blond hair. A prince. Sobbing in a closet after being forced to cut out the tongue of a siren. The ears of an elf. The eyes of a dryad.

The screams.

The blood.

The look of satisfaction on his father's face as he stripped his son's innocence away piece by piece.

Cruel laughter echoed in his mind.

His father's laughter.

Butch's heart pounded in his chest. He could almost feel his father's hand on his shoulder, could almost hear his father's voice berating him for his weakness.

Coward.

Weak.

Deficient.

Pathetic.

His vision blurred. Turning away from the prisoner, he forced himself to walk, not run, out of the interrogation room. He let the door slam behind him.

Leaning against the cold stone wall of the dark hallway, Butch trembled with the effort it took to hold himself together, as if the scars in his memory, on his heart, were threatening to pull apart at the seams, if not the physical scars on his back. He pressed the heels of his hands into his eyes, as if that could push away the haunting images.

The lessons had been designed to break him and mold him into his father's image. To be a ruler like King Valryn. Like King Kylian before him. To be merciless and feared.

To be anything but weak.

Funny how the lessons had left Butch pleading for mercy and fearing for his own well-being.

He pressed his back against the wall, sliding down until he sat upon the cold floor. His head rested in his hands as he took a deep shuddering breath.

He'd made others in Lavfor feel the same way. Had tried to block out their pleas for mercy. Had ignored the look of true fear in their eyes.

The image of his father loomed larger in his mind. Cold unfeeling eyes. Hard unforgiving mouth. Cruel unbridled hands.

The heavy door to the interrogation room seemed to mock him. He'd failed. Failed to break the prisoner. Failed to protect his men. Failed to end magic in Phildeterre. Failed over and over again.

A whip cracked somewhere in his thoughts.

He flinched.

Footsteps approached, and Butch quickly wiped any moisture from his face as he grasped the wall to stand. He straightened, lifting his chin.

"Your Majesty," a guard said, saluting. "I was told you were down here. Marshal Thorne has returned from the Black Forest."

Butch cleared his throat before he spoke, not trusting his voice not to betray him. "Is he hurt?"

"Yes, but not as bad as Commander Stoll. They're both being tended to in the infirmary now."

Nodding, Butch thanked the guard. "I'll be there soon enough."

The guard saluted again and retreated, leaving Butch alone. He took a deep breath, trying to steady himself.

And when he was ready, he left the dungeon and the memories that threatened to drown him, stopping at the top of the long spiral staircase to alert one of the guards posted there to take the prisoner back to her cell.

She'd talk. If not by torture, then by some other means.

But it could wait until he tended to his best friend.

BUTCH'S HEELS CLACKED along the floor as he made his way to the infirmary. Partway there, Marshal Levick found him and fell into step behind him.

"Your Majesty," he said after he'd saluted. "I heard Thorne is in the infirmary. I assume that's where you're headed."

Instead of responding, Butch nodded.

One of the physicians, Dianna, was waiting by the infirmary door and opened it for them without a word. Clearly, they were expecting him.

Helena welcomed the men when they entered. "Thank you for coming, Your Majesty," she said, bowing her head in respect. "The marshal and commander are this way."

Butch followed her through the rows of beds. The sharp scent of drafts filled his nostrils, and he braced himself for what he might see.

Silas lay on one of the last narrow beds next to another bed occupied by a man Butch barely recognized as Commander Kendrick Stoll. Silas's face was pale and drawn, though it seemed more out of frustration than pain. His cheek was bandaged, his nose was swollen and discolored, and his arm was wrapped tightly. Despite his condition, as soon as his gaze landed on Butch, he offered him a small smile.

"Just a few scratches," Silas said in greeting, attempting to sit straighter but wincing in the process.

Butch's heart clenched at the sight of his best friend in the infirmary bed. He forced a smile, trying to mask his concern, especially in front of Marshal Levick and the others. "You've had worse."

"That's what I tried to tell her," Silas said, nodding toward Helena.

Shifting his gaze to Stoll, Butch stiffened. His injuries were more severe, and Butch wasn't sure the man was alive until the commander opened his right eye—his left was covered by a bandage, as was most of his body. The parts of his flesh that weren't covered in bandages were burnt. The sight of charred flesh made Butch's stomach churn, and the smell almost had him retching.

Stoll's breathing was shallow, and he regarded the king with a weary gaze.

"Commander Stoll," Butch said softly, stepping closer to the bed. "How are you?"

"It was her," he rasped, his voice barely audible. Butch didn't want to consider that the guard hadn't answered his question.

Butch turned back to Silas, his expression serious. "Estrada?"

Silas took a deep breath, wincing as he did. "Yes. She took him. Interrogated him. And when we interrupted her, she set him on fire and fled. I tried to arrest her but clearly didn't succeed."

Butch's jaw tightened. Seeing the guards lying in the infirmary beds felt like a reminder of the threat he was supposed to be ridding his kingdom of. Butch glowered at the wall.

"Your Majesty." Stoll's voice was rough, and when his words sent him into a coughing fit, Helena rushed to his side and helped him drink water. The concerned look in the physician's eyes, a look she rarely gave, set Butch on edge. The scent of smoke still wafted from Stoll.

"Can you tell me what you saw? What did she—"

"Information," Stoll wheezed before Butch had finished his question.

"What kind?" Butch asked, putting his hands on his hips. "And how did she manage to capture you?"

Stoll glanced down at the blanket, his jaw clenching. "Saw a woman . . . in the distance. My partner and I were checking the outside of a building." He paused, catching his breath with his eyes closed. When he continued, his voice was hardly a whisper. "Went in different directions, and when I saw the stranger, I-I followed."

"And your partner?"

"Don't know. I got distracted, and then I-I messed up. Everything went black. When I woke up, I was tied to a chair and Estrada was there."

"Then you disobeyed a direct order," Marshal Levick cut in. "You were supposed to alert others and *not* go alone."

"Marshal," Butch chided. While he didn't disagree, there was also a time and a place, and standing at the commander's bedside while he lay immobile from burns was not it.

"I know that," Stoll said, his voice taut. "Paid the price for it, didn't I?"

Butch clenched his hands behind his back. "And the information she wanted?"

"She asked questions. . . about the prisoner. The blond one," he said, sneering. "Wanted to know where she was being kept." Stoll glanced at Marshal Levick, and something of a glint showed in his eye. "And she asked about you."

Next to Butch, Marshal Levick straightened. "Why?"

"Don't know, but she wanted to know where you were."

"What else did she say?" Butch asked before Marshal Levick could speak again. The marshal almost appeared to be trembling, which would've been comical considering Marshal Levick was a mountain of a man.

"She asked about the ceremony for Jerr Pinn." Stoll averted his gaze as he answered.

"How does she know about that?" Butch narrowed his eyes at Stoll, who didn't verbally respond. "What did you tell her?"

"She tortured me, and . . ."

"What does she know?" Butch said, stepping forward when Stoll's sentence fizzled out.

"I told her it was in a few weeks. That's all I know anyway, and—"

Warning bells rang in Butch's mind. The dignitaries would arrive soon, and while he was already planning to reinforce security because of Lenora's pregnancy, it would have to increase even more if Estrada knew about the arrival of the Jerr Pinn dignitaries.

"You're going back into the field," Butch said to Marshal Levick. "I need her found before the welcome ball for Jerr Pinn. Marshal Thorne, when you're recovered, I need you to . . . Why are you shaking, Levick?"

"I apologize, Your Majesty, but I . . . I don't . . . If Estrada asked for me by name, I believe I'm a target in her eyes." Marshal Levick bowed his head in submission. "You remember, sire, that I was the one in charge of Shongbay when her family was executed. She probably—"

"Fine," Butch said, waving his hand to the side. "We'll discuss this at a later date. For now, I want the two of you to have your lead captains out searching with their men for Estrada. You can remain at the castle until after the Jerr Pinn dignitaries leave, Marshal Levick. It'll be wise to have more protection anyway. I want preparation on my desk by tomorrow, Levick." He nodded when Marshal Levick saluted and left.

Butch's resolve hardened. Seeing his men, especially Silas, like this fueled the fire in his stomach. He couldn't let Estrada continue to wreak havoc.

He laid a hand on Silas's shoulder, careful not to press on any injuries. "Rest and recover. I need you back on your feet as soon as possible. We'll need to rethink some of the security for the castle."

"Of course," Silas said, his brow furrowed.

Butch nodded, then turned to Helena. "Keep me updated on their progress."

"Yes, Your Majesty," she replied with a respectful bow.

"Your Majesty," Stoll said, drawing the king's attention. "What will you do with the prisoner? The one Estrada cares about?"

Butch sighed, rubbing his temple with one hand. "She's to remain in the dungeon for now, at least until after the trade agreements with Jerr Pinn are signed and taken care of. Estrada's interest in the ceremony is not something to gloss over. I have a feeling Estrada will try something to free her friend during that time. Should Estrada try to come rescue the prisoner, we must be prepared, and that means having the most capable hands available. Rest up. We've got plenty of long nights ahead." Butch turned to leave, but Silas stopped him.

"There's something else," he said, his blue gaze focused on Butch as he turned back toward the beds. "A prisoner. One who knows Estrada. One who might just talk with the right motivation."

PART THREE

Chapter 33

EVANGELINE

Evangeline sat huddled in the corner of her cell, her body trembling as she tried to stop the tears that wouldn't cease leaking from her eyes. Though she'd been returned to her cell after the interrogation room, she couldn't shake the king's shouts and the cold metal of the chains biting into her skin from her mind. She hardly noticed the cold stone floor beneath her with the numbness that had settled into her bones.

The king had been livid. She'd seen it in his eyes. And then . . . then something had switched. She had thought for a second that she'd seen something else. A different emotion.

Desperation.

She hadn't been able to stop the flow of tears when he'd left abruptly. And now the tears still persisted.

For the first time since she'd been arrested, she'd been truly afraid. Was that what others had felt during Butch's father's reign?

In the cell next to hers, Odette watched her with concern in her eyes.

Odette caught Evangeline's eye and began signing. "Are you all right? Did he hurt you?"

Evangeline hesitated before responding, her shaking fingers fumbling slightly. "I'm fine. Not hurt."

Odette's expression softened, and she reached through the bars separating their cells, her fingers brushing Evangeline's shoulder in a comforting way.

"It's okay to be scared," she signed. "What happened?"

"The king . . . He tried to make me talk. He was so angry . . . I thought . . ."

Odette's eyes filled with understanding. "But he didn't hurt you?"

"No. But what if he tries again? Or someone else . . ."

Odette started signing, then stopped at the approaching sound of footsteps echoing down the corridor. Both women froze.

Evangeline sat straighter, wiping any residual moisture from her face. Chains rattled down the hallway. She quickly glanced to her right, and it was clear Odette was just as alarmed by the sudden arrival of the guards.

"Are they here for me?" Evangeline signed as she mouthed the words.

Odette shook her head, gesturing to the figure walking between the two guards. The person—a woman with light hair—sagged between the two as if she depended on them to remain standing.

"What are you looking at?" one of the guards spat at Evangeline, who wrinkled her nose when they stopped at the cell directly across the hall from hers.

Evangeline lowered her gaze, focusing on the new prisoner as they tossed her into the cell and locked the door. The woman stumbled but caught herself on the side wall, glaring at the guards with bright teal eyes as they walked back the way they'd come.

Once the guards were out of earshot, Odette crossed to the front of her cell, pressing against the bars. "Are you all right?" she asked, keeping her voice lowered.

The woman looked up, her eyes weary but alert. "Fine," she said, her voice barely above a whisper. "Just . . . tired."

"I'm Odette. What's your name?"

"Ari."

Evangeline stepped closer, her ears perking. The woman regarded her, and as Evangeline got closer to the front of her cell, she noticed the catlike ears peeking out of the woman's straight blond hair. Pumarian.

"What?" Ari asked, raising an eyebrow.

"You know Em," Evangeline whispered, the words barely audible.

But Ari clearly heard them. "You're her. You're Evie."

Evangeline gave a small nod. Odette caught Evangeline's attention, signing, "Who is Em?"

"I'll tell you later," Evangeline signed back. Then to Ari, she said, "Is she all right?"

"She's trying to find a way to you."

"No," Evangeline whispered, clutching the bars for support. "It's too dangerous."

"That's what Fae and I tried to tell her. But you know her. She wouldn't listen."

Evangeline's breath caught. The idea of Emmalee risking herself to save her sent a mixture of hope and dread through Evangeline. She glanced at the cells, where there could very well be others listening.

But she had questions.

"Why are you here? And be careful what you say," Evangeline whispered, tilting her head to the left to indicate the cells.

Ari sighed, her shoulders sagging. "A guard recognized me. He saw me with . . . her. And when the marshal threatened to bring Fae, my little sister, in for questioning, I panicked and told him I knew our friend. I think that's why they brought me here."

Fear gripped Evangeline by the throat. If they had already extracted information from Ari once, they would undoubtedly succeed again, especially if they used her loved ones against her.

"Ari, listen to me," Evangeline said, dropping her voice even lower, hoping the cat ears weren't just for show. "You cannot tell them anything about *her*. It puts *her* in danger."

Ari's bright teal eyes filled with guilt and what was probably determination. "I know. I'll try, but if they threaten Fae . . ."

Before Evangeline could respond, heavy footsteps echoed down the corridor.

"Already?" Evangeline muttered.

Another set of guards appeared at the bottom of the staircase, their expressions grim. Evangeline moved to the back of her cell as they approached, their attention fully on her.

"The king wants to see you," one of them said, his tone leaving no room for argument—not that she would argue.

Silence was her friend.

"Get up," he said, standing in front of her. The other guard blocked the exit until his partner had Evangeline's upper arm in a viselike grip.

"Cuffs?" the guard at the door asked, his hand already at the pair dangling from his belt.

Evangeline's heart raced. Her wrists had all but healed, and Helena had long since stopped sending her medicine with her food. But the memory of the cuffs alone sent tremors through her.

"Thorne said no," the man holding Evangeline responded, pulling her out of the cell. "Besides, what's she going to do?" He leaned down over her. "Run?"

Evangeline clamped her mouth shut, already feeling the warmth from her magic filling her as soon as she stepped foot out of the cell. It urged her to use it to fight back, to free herself.

Could she run?

Not without Odette and now Ari. She couldn't leave them. Wouldn't.

The guards started yanking her toward the staircase with unnecessary force.

She glanced over her shoulder at Odette and Ari as the guards hauled her out of the dungeon. For the first time since the guards had brought her to her cell, Ari looked worried.

Good. Maybe she'd stay quiet.

WHILE SHE WAS out of breath by the time she got to the top of the stairs, the thought of trying to escape was still circling in the forefront of Evangeline's mind.

Which way could she run?

Where was the exit?

How many more guards were there patrolling the halls?

Not without Odette and Ari, she reminded herself. Yet the temptation remained.

Her magic thrummed inside her. She was sweating trying to keep it from showing. With each step, she had to focus on keeping the magic hidden— keep it from burning the hands of the guard manhandling her.

"Jax and Hulbert, stop for a minute." The familiar voice echoed down the hall, and Evangeline turned her head to see Thorne striding down an intersecting hallway toward them.

To her utter confusion, relief flooded through her body at the sight of the marshal. Before she could determine why, Thorne reached her and her unwanted entourage.

Both guards saluted to Thorne, who did it back before looking down at Evangeline.

His bright eyes blazed through her. He had a cut on his cheek, and by the discoloration around his nose, it'd been broken recently. Evangeline glanced at the rest of him, checking for more signs of injuries. If he had them, he hid them well.

"Sir?" the guard holding Evangeline said, a questioning tone filling his voice.

"I assume you're taking her to the king?" Thorne asked, splitting his gaze between the two men, both of whom nodded. "Then I'll take her from here. I was just on my way to see His Majesty."

"Of course, sir," the other guard said, saluting again.

"Would you like us to accompany you to the king?" the guard who'd been holding her asked when Thorne replaced him by her side, though he did not grip her arm as the other man had.

"That won't be necessary. Thank you," he said, nodding to them before they saluted and marched down the hallway from which he'd come.

As much as she didn't like or trust Thorne, he was a better option than the other royal guards. She rubbed her upper arm, glaring down the hallway where the two men had disappeared.

"You seem better," Thorne said, his voice light. "How are you feeling?"

Evangeline turned her attention to him as he stuck his hands in his pockets. "Why are you back?"

"That's not an answer to my question."

"Nor is that."

Thorne raised an eyebrow, something glittering behind his icy eyes. She wasn't sure what it was until he spoke. "I'm needed here."

Evangeline held back the comment she wanted to make, which had something to do with loyal dogs rolling over at their master's first whistle. Instead, she shifted her attention to the corridor behind him.

Despite not being forced around by one of the guards, her magic was still shifting uncomfortably within her, and she rubbed her thumbs over the hem of her tunic to distract herself.

"Thank you . . . for this, I mean," she said, pulling the fabric of the tunic away from her body to indicate his departing gift.

"You should've received one sooner. That's my fault. I apologize."

She pressed her lips together, not meeting his eyes as she nodded. An awkward silence settled upon them until Thorne cleared his throat.

"And the food? Have you been eating?" he asked, and when she finally glanced up and met his gaze, his brows were knitted together.

"Yes."

"And sleeping?"

She frowned at him. "Careful, Thorne. You almost sound like you care." She watched his reaction with discerning eyes, and he surprised her when he chuckled softly and rubbed the back of his neck.

"I suppose it does sound like that, doesn't it?" He looked her up and down once more, his gaze lingering on her scarred wrists for a little longer than necessary. "You're healed though, right? No longer sick?"

"Helena says so."

"But how do you feel?"

Evangeline shifted her attention back to the floor. "Why do you care, Marshal?" She didn't speak the question with as much venom as she could've. Instead, it sounded genuine. It *was* genuine, she realized as she waited for his response. Why was he checking on her like he would a . . . a friend?

"Because, for some reason, I do."

Her gaze shot to his, her eyes widening at his words. He stared down at her, his posture rigid and his jaw clenched. And yet something soft lingered in his eyes. In the way he let his attention flicker around her face as though he was checking for injuries. In the way his tight expression loosened the longer he regarded her.

"Why?" It was barely a whisper.

"I don't know. I can't explain it. I just—" Thorne stopped talking when a set of footsteps clicked down a nearby hall. By the time the patrolling guards passed them, saluting to the marshal and giving her dirty looks, Thorne's softened edges had sharpened again.

"I saw her," he said, his voice low.

Evangeline snapped her attention to him, eyes narrowing. All easiness of the past few minutes vanished at his words. "You're lying."

He pressed his lips together and shook his head. "I didn't do this to myself," he said, gesturing to his face. "She disappeared out the back of the house she'd been using to torture one of my men. Left right after she lit him on fire. She seems to enjoy that." He glared at the floor before chuckling darkly. When he finally met her gaze again, something bitter filled his eyes, though some tiny hopeful part of Evangeline hoped it wasn't meant to be directed toward her. "Did she take pleasure in lighting ants on fire with glass as a child? I'm just curious." His voice was taut, lacking a lightness despite his sad attempt at a joke. "If I'd arrived a second later, the commander would've died. And if I'd been earlier—"

211

"Don't," Evangeline said, cutting him off as she crossed her arms over her chest. "I know she's stronger than you."

Thorne lifted his chin, but he didn't respond right away. "You underestimate me, Evie."

"I think I estimate you just fine, Thorne." She glared at him, wishing she'd thought of something more intimidating to say. Unfortunately, most of her concentration was centered on hiding her magic. She'd all but forgotten it during the first half of their conversation because, for some reason, his gentleness had lulled it to sleep within her. However, in the single mention of Emmalee, he'd managed to rile it back to the surface.

Thorne stepped closer to her, his chin tilted down as he scowled at her. Evangeline wanted nothing more than to take several steps back. The man was in her space. But she didn't move. Instead, she lifted her face and matched his glare.

"Your friend is a criminal."

"And so is everyone with magic to you people," she said, scoffing. "Doesn't matter that she was born with it." Lowering her voice, Evangeline glared at him. "That *I* was born with it."

At her words, Thorne looked over the top of her head, scanning the empty hallways around them. He straightened, though when Evangeline checked, they were the only two around.

"The king is expecting us. We should go," he said, his tone formal as he gestured for her to walk in front of him.

At the mention of the king, Evangeline's mind sucked her back into that dark and gruesome interrogation room.

Chained to a chair.

Trembling as she waited for torture that didn't happen.

The last thing she wanted was to face the man who'd ordered that she be brought there.

Evangeline dragged her feet as slowly as she could, trying to expand the time before she'd stand in front of the king.

Had Thorne approved the interrogation room and the threats of torture? He probably had. Yet why was she struggling to believe that? Ari had even said the marshal, likely Thorne, had used her little sister as leverage to get her to speak. Maybe he approved of torture. That'd be good. It'd give her a legitimate reason to hate him. She wanted to hate Thorne, wanted to hate him more than the king, because then maybe she wouldn't think about him so much. Wouldn't dream about him. Wouldn't think about those gorgeous eyes every time silence fell around her.

It frustrated her to no end that she'd grown comfortable speaking to the man walking behind her—the man who'd arrested her, the man who wanted her best friend, and maybe even her, dead.

"I won't talk to him," she mumbled, wondering if she'd said it to be heard or to remind herself of her stance. Thorne didn't respond, and she glanced over her shoulder to see if he had even heard her. "You're the one who told me to stay silent."

"I did." His voice matched hers in volume.

"Why?"

"Why what?"

Evangeline stopped, turning to face him. "Why did you tell me that?"

Thorne once again checked the hallways, and when his gaze landed on two servants carrying baskets with bedsheets in them, he nodded to them with a grin, waiting until they rounded a corner. With one more scan of their surroundings, Thorne nodded toward a door to his right.

"I'm not going in there with you," Evangeline said, crossing her arms as she shook her head.

Thorne put his hands up in front of him. "I'm not going to hurt you. But I'm also not going to answer that question out in the open." He lowered his arms to his sides. "Your choice."

Evangeline cast a sideways glance at the door. How important were the answers to her questions? Hadn't they kept her awake in her cell multiple times since she'd been arrested?

Her magic filled her with warmth, and she let it give her the reassurance that it would protect her. Sighing, she walked toward the door, listening to Thorne's footsteps as he followed her.

It was a small sitting room with large bookshelves filling up the right side of the room. Three armchairs and a small couch sat in the middle on top of an ornate rug. Evangeline crossed the room to the bookshelves, drawn in by the elegant spines and scrawling letters. How long had it been since she'd sat down and read for fun? Too long.

Distracted by the books, Evangeline forgot why she'd gone in there until Thorne closed the door behind him. He cleared his throat as she turned around.

"Well?" she said, her hands on her hips.

213

"I said what I said to protect you." His voice was flat, but his face—it flickered with too many emotions to count. Confusion, confidence, calmness.

Evangeline's eyebrows rose as she took a step back, bumping into the bookshelf behind her. "What?" Her voice was a whisper.

"There are people here who would see every person with magic killed and yet still want more blood." Thorne lifted his chin, catching her in his diamond gaze. "I'm not one of them."

"But you serve one," Evangeline said, her heart beating in her ears. "The king would see me dead if I didn't have something he thought he could use."

Thorne shook his head. "You're wrong about him." His voice was gentle, and he took a step toward her. "He's a good man. A good friend. A good king. Better than his father and grandfather."

"Why?" Evangeline asked, her voice trembling.

"He's wiser than—"

"No," she said, shaking her head. "Why do you want to protect me?"

"I . . . I think you're the key."

Evangeline's ears perked up, and she frowned. "What?"

"I think you hold the answers to this conflict with Estrada," he said, his voice soft.

Evangeline tensed. "She's my best friend. I will not turn my back on her."

"And if she isn't who you think she is?"

Evangeline stepped toward him, crossing her arms over her chest. She glared defiantly at him. "And what if she's not who *you* think she is?"

"Do you really believe that? I told you the truth. She has tortured and killed my men and very well could've killed me. Is that who your friend is? If so, I have to question your choice in companionship."

Evangeline barely kept a grasp on her magic as anger flooded through her. "And you? What about your best friend?"

"What about him?"

"Did he tell you he chained me to a chair in an interrogation room and threatened me with torture? What kind of companionship do *you* keep, Thorne?"

Thorne stiffened. "He what?"

"Guess you should take a look at your own choices before you start judging mine." Evangeline didn't realize she'd stepped closer until she had to crane her neck to look up at him. Her heart beat frantically in her chest.

His face void of emotion, Thorne stepped to the side, leaving the path to the door open. "We're already late." He spoke in a monotone voice.

"Yeah, that's what I thought," Evangeline said, brushing past him.

Chapter 34

BUTCH

Butch paced back and forth across his office as he waited for the guards he'd sent to collect the prisoner to return. His thoughts were a tangled mess of guilt and determination. The image of the prisoner's tear-streaked face haunted him. He couldn't shake the memory of nearly crossing a line he'd vowed never to cross again after the death of his father. Not to mention he knew Thorne would be angry with him if he found out.

Voices spoke outside the door, and Butch crossed to the other side of his desk.

"Enter," he said, straightening his collar as the door opened. "Where are Jax and Hulbert?" he asked when Silas entered with the prisoner.

His marshal saluted to him, then gestured for the prisoner to take the seat in front of the desk. "I ran into them in the hallway and figured I'd save them the trip."

Butch grunted in response, his gaze shifting from Silas, who was closing the door, to the woman, who seemed incapable of doing anything except glare at him. Just looking at her made his muscles tense, especially around his torso where she'd struck him with her magic months ago.

Not a word. After months of questioning, she'd somehow remained silent. Even now, her jaw clenched. His did the same in response.

And yet some little droplet of guilt niggled the back of his mind. He'd nearly tortured her. Nearly cut into her skin to get answers. Nearly become his father.

He didn't realize how long they'd been staring at each other until Silas cleared his throat next to him.

"Helena tells me you're healed of your ailments. Is that correct?" Butch asked, unable to keep his voice light.

Nothing. No response. No words. Just a never-ending glare.

"You at least appear to be healthier."

She blinked at him, a defiant look in her eyes. She'd braided her hair back into a thick braid, and strands fell out of it around her face.

"Well then," he said, already irritated enough to clench his hands behind his back. "I suppose we should begin."

Her gaze shifted to Silas for a second before moving to the map behind Butch, as if she didn't care to pay attention.

Butch took a deep breath before speaking. "It appears Estrada has been trying to get information out of my men. Can you tell me what she might be interested in learning?" He raised an eyebrow. Of course, thanks to Commander Stoll, he knew some of the answers to the question he'd posed. He hoped, however, that Estrada's friend might understand more of how her friend's mind worked.

The prisoner tightened her lips, her focus still on the map rather than on him. Her hands clenched into fists in her lap. But still no response.

"People are dying. Good men. Do you understand the gravity of the situation?" He leaned forward on his desk. "If you don't start talking, more innocent lives will be lost. Is that what you want?"

Nothing.

"Do you want to know what I think?" Butch tilted his head. "I think she wants to find you."

While it was a subtle change, he noticed the way her features softened for just a second. Then it was gone, and she went back to glaring at the wall.

"Do you think she'd be foolish enough to try to find you here?" He tried to keep the tone of his voice conversational; he didn't want her to know how important it was that she answer the question. The prisoner's response, whether verbal—which he doubted—or nonverbal, would determine how much more security he put in place at the quickly approaching welcome ceremony.

"Do you think she'll come for you?" he asked again, watching her closely.

The prisoner shifted her focus to him, her eyes still narrowed. But her brow furrowed for just a moment as she lowered her gaze to the floor. When she looked back up, her expression was neutral.

"If I may," Silas said next to him, and Butch motioned for him to speak as he took a step back. It was the break he needed to calm down before he exploded.

Silas stepped around to the front of the desk and leaned back against it. While Butch couldn't see his face, he knew his friend well enough to know that the man was not smiling as he crossed his arms over his chest.

"You are not doing yourself any favors by staying silent, nor are you doing any for your country."

Butch watched the prisoner's reaction to Silas's words, but the only thing it seemed to do was pull her glare from the king. She lifted her chin, narrowing her eyes at Silas as he continued.

"Your friend is a criminal. Whether she has magic or not, she must pay for her crimes against the throne. The longer you stay silent, the more opportunity you provide for her to rack up additional offenses." Silas uncrossed his arms, putting his hands in his pockets. "If you care at all about this country, I suggest you tell us everything you know about her so we can save innocent lives."

Butch frowned when a drop of sweat trickled down his temple. The temperature in the room had increased, and when he wiped his forehead with a cloth from his desk, he glanced at the prisoner.

"Speak," Butch growled, willing the stubborn woman to open her mouth and give him what he wanted.

She had squeezed her eyes shut, her hands clenching the fabric of her trousers.

Silas reacted before Butch could, removing the pair of cuffs that hung on his belt and snapping one around her left wrist. The temperature in the room lowered, and she opened her eyes again.

But they were not filled with anger, as Butch had expected them to be. Instead, relief filled her face as she stared up at Silas. He did not put the other cuff on her wrist, letting it dangle instead.

"I'm sorry," Silas muttered, stepping back to the desk again. "I didn't want to, but—"

"I know," she said in a soft voice. Her eyes widened at the same time Butch's did.

Butch straightened, stepping around his desk so he stood in front like Silas. "You spoke."

The prisoner turned her attention to him, her chin lifted and her glare present once more. "I did. I *am* capable." She spoke in an insouciant tone, though her voice bore a musical sound, like a stringed instrument.

"Why haven't you spoken before?" Butch gripped the desk behind him, clenching it as he leaned on the edge.

She didn't respond immediately, and for a moment, he thought she would return to her silence. But after sticking her tongue into her cheek and glaring at him, she responded.

"I have spoken, just not to you."

Butch glanced at Silas, but his friend's attention remained on the woman. His posture was rigid, and something about his tightened jaw brought forth a thought.

"You two. You've spoken, haven't you?" Butch asked, his gaze flicking between his most trusted ally and a woman who sided with his greatest enemy.

"Yes," she said, her focus on Silas. A hint of a smirk pulled at the corner of her mouth but never fully showed.

Something twisted in Butch's stomach until he felt sick and red lined his vision. His best friend and worst enemy's best friend were, what? Allies? Friends? The feeling in his gut worsened. Were they something more? How had he not realized?

He took a deep breath. If he exploded, it would surely cause the prisoner to revert to silence. He couldn't afford that.

"About?" Butch growled, directing the question to Silas, who opened his mouth to respond but didn't get the chance before the prisoner answered.

"Your loyal guard dog has been trying to get me to answer your questions since he arrested me." The two of them stared at each other until Silas looked away.

"It's true," he said, glancing at Butch.

Butch pinched his lips together, resisting the urge to shout at the marshal in front of the prisoner. He tried to rationalize how Silas could keep the fact that the woman had spoken to him a secret. What else was he hiding from him?

Focus. He needed to focus. At least she was finally speaking. It'd taken long enough. He knew he needed to deal with his anger toward Silas later.

"Will you tell me?" Butch asked, crossing his arms over his chest as he stared at her.

"What do you think?" She scoffed, shaking her head once. "I won't."

"You—"

"Let me rephrase," she said, closing her eyes for a moment. "I *can't*. You've kept me here long enough that I couldn't even begin to guess where she is or what she's doing. The only thing I can tell you is why."

Butch stiffened. "I know why."

The images Estrada had forced into his mind on the boulder field, the ones he continued to have nightmares about, flooded his mind unbidden. Even that morning he'd woken up in a cold sweat calling out the name of a little girl he'd never once met.

"Of course you do," the prisoner said, her tone curt. "You killed her family."

"I didn't." Butch shook his head. "Their deaths were not my fault."

She snorted, rolling her eyes. "I'm sure you never do anything wrong, *Your Majesty*," she muttered, moving her glare to the floor. "I'm sure apologies are a foreign concept and the words 'I'm sorry' aren't even in your vocabulary."

"That's enough," Silas said, his voice low. A clear warning.

"Is it?" the woman asked, a fake smile on her lips. "Then I'll just be quiet again."

Before Butch could argue, it was as if she'd not spoken a word. She clamped her mouth closed, as she had in all the previous interrogations, and returned her gaze to the map once more.

Butch rubbed his forehead and then the side of his face. "Take her back, then find Levick and meet me in the council meeting room. We have some things to discuss."

BUTCH WAITED IN the council room, pressing the heels of his hands into his eyes. He needed sleep and wanted nothing more than to find Lenora and curl up next to her in bed. But there were things that needed to happen first, conversations—particularly one—that needed to take place before he could have any sort of rest.

Silas entered the council chamber first, closing the door behind him.

"Levick is on his way and will be here in half an hour. But before he gets here, I wanted to discuss something with you, if that's all right." Silas approached the end of the table, taking the chair next to Butch's.

Butch had fully planned on letting Silas have the full weight of his anger after learning that his best marshal had been hiding his relationship with the prisoner for who knew how long. Instead, though, he nodded sharply to Silas.

"Go on."

"Did you take the prisoner into the dungeon interrogation rooms and threaten her with torture?"

Butch's shoulders tensed, and he clenched his fists. "So, you really do chat with her, don't you? I figured if we were keeping secrets, why not? How long were you going to wait to tell me she'd been talking to you? Hmm?"

"Butch." Silas's tone held a warning, but Butch ignored it.

"Tell me, Silas. Why did you hide that from me? We *need* her to talk, and yet you've spent how long concealing that she has been talking, just not to me?"

"She hasn't told me anything useful." Silas crossed his arms over his chest. "You think I'd hide vital information that could help protect you and this country?"

"I don't know. Clearly, you're better at hiding things from me than I gave you credit for."

At Butch's words, Silas blanched. "You are my priority, brother. Nothing she has said is useful. It's insults about me. About you. And most of all, she's reiterated that she won't tell you anything about Estrada. I've tried to convince her, but she won't hear it." Silas took a deep breath that shifted into a sigh as he rubbed the back of his neck. "I'm sorry, Butch. I shouldn't have hidden that she was talking to me."

Butch stuck his tongue into his cheek, casting an assessing glance over his friend. "How deep does it go?"

"What?"

"Are you fond of her?" Butch settled back into his stance.

"No, I mean—" Silas bit his lip, his focus on the table. "I am concerned about her health."

"Just her health?" Butch waited for Silas's response, and when it didn't come right away, Butch rubbed his jaw and shook his head. "How deep, Silas?"

"I don't know."

"Will this interfere with your ability to do your job?"

"My job is to protect you."

"*And* my country. Can you do that while juggling whatever this is?" Butch gestured to Silas, a frown on his lips. "Or should I start bringing Levick to the questioning sessions?" He said it purely to get under his friend's skin.

"That depends, brother," Silas said with a bit more bite in his tone than Butch had expected. "Are you planning to torture the information out of the woman? If so, you'd better speak with Marshal Levick, because I want *no* part in that. How could you, Butch? After all the nightmares you experienced, how could you even consider that? And you want to discuss going behind backs? Why did I have to learn about it from the prisoner? Why didn't I hear about this from you?"

"Because I had to try something, *brother*." Butch shook his head, his words vibrating as they rose in volume. "Estrada is a threat to everyone. My country. My people. My family. I *need* answers."

Silas lowered his voice as he tapped the table with a pointed finger. "You know better than anyone that *this* is not the way. We're supposed to be better than this, Butch. Better than torture. Better than your father."

Butch's resolve faltered, and he closed his eyes, running a hand through his hair. His anger fizzled out, replaced by the infuriating knowledge that his friend was right. It didn't justify his actions with the prisoner, but Silas knew better than most the nightmares King Valryn had inflicted upon him.

"I know," Butch admitted, his voice barely above a whisper. "I know. And I couldn't go through with it. But I need to know . . . I have to protect . . ."

Butch's mind flashed to images of his wife, of the hesitant hopefulness that he saw on her face every time they discussed the pregnancy. If all went well—he knew better than to assume it would—he'd be a father soon and would have the responsibility of protecting not just his wife and country but a child. A baby.

And if he couldn't rid the threat Estrada posed, what kind of world would the baby enter?

He knew the answer.

A broken one.

Silence had filled the room, and Butch didn't realize he was staring at nothing until Silas cleared his throat. His friend leaned forward. "There's something you're not telling me. What is it?"

Butch let out a short dark laugh. "Plenty, brother. There's plenty you don't know. But . . ." Butch regarded his best friend, catching and holding his gaze. He hadn't told a soul about the pregnancy. Lenora had asked him not to. But the weight of the secret had worn him down over the weeks.

He needed to tell someone. No, he *wanted* to tell someone; he wanted to tell his brother.

Taking a deep breath, Butch let his shoulders droop. "Fates, Lenora is pregnant. After everything we've been through—the stillbirth, the miscarriages—I just . . . I can't bear the thought of losing her or another child. And I can't . . . I can't do anything to help her physically. I can't control what's going on there. But I can do everything in my power to stop this threat, and any threat, that could put her or the child in danger. *That* I can control. I need her to be safe. I *need* to get Estrada out of the picture and make this world safer for my child."

Silas's expression softened, and he squeezed Butch's shoulder. "You've been carrying this by yourself, haven't you?"

Butch's next laugh sounded more like the offspring of desperation and exhaustion. "What else was I supposed to do? You were busy following orders to chase after an evil sorceress in the woods. I don't exactly have a lot of friends."

"It must be the prickly personality." The way Silas said it, in a monotonous tone quickly followed by a smirk, had Butch laughing a true laugh.

"Must be."

As their chuckles died down, Silas watched Butch with his steady gaze. "I know it's difficult to hope sometimes, especially after all you've faced. Because brother, you've dealt with more than most. But you have to remember that hope is what keeps us moving forward. It's what gives us the strength to face another day, to fight another battle. Without it, we are lost."

Butch sat silently for a moment, his eyes trained on the table. "How do you do that?"

"Do what?"

"How do you always know what to say?" Butch snorted, shaking his head before he glanced at Silas and offered a small smile. "It's infuriating and reassuring at the same time."

"It's certainly a talent," Silas said, shrugging. "Listen, brother. You are a good king. A good leader. A good fighter. A good brother. A good husband. And soon, a good father."

Silas stood, and Butch copied him. A second later, Silas grasped Butch by the shoulders, a large grin spreading over his face.

"You're going to be a father," Silas said, yanking Butch forward into a bear hug. "Congratulations!"

Butch's eyes glistened with unshed tears as he pulled back to meet Silas's gaze. "I'm terrified. What if I can't protect them? What if you're wrong and I'm not a good father? What if I'm like him?"

Silas's grin faltered, replaced by a look of concern as he studied Butch's face. "You're not your father, Butch," he said firmly. "You're a kind and compassionate man. You'll be a wonderful father."

"And if I'm not? What if . . . I don't want to hurt . . . If I'm like him, I might—" Butch choked on his words as Silas gave his shoulder a gentle squeeze.

"You think I'd let you turn into him?" Silas's voice held a hint of amusement, likely put there on purpose to reassure Butch.

"No, but—"

"Then have faith, Butch. You're not alone in this. You never were, and you never will be." Silas clapped him on the shoulder, pulling him in for another hug before shoving away from him. "And I think we should get drinks and celebrate tonight. You and me. What do you say?"

Butch sat back down in his chair, taking a deep breath—the first one he'd been able to take since Lenora had told him.

"I think . . ." he said, a small grin spreading across his lips. "I think I can still drink you under the table."

Chapter 35

LENORA

Every muscle in Lenora's body locked at the sound of his voice.

Kneeling over the soft earth in the royal garden, Lenora had been completely relaxed with her fingers gently tucking new flowers into their beds. The act of planting, of coaxing life from the soil, brought her a sense of peace. It was a refuge. A haven. Her small rebellion against the world that would see her pristine and perfect at all times. The fresh scent of flowers brought a calm through her like nothing else.

At least, it had.

Until a shadow loomed over her and a voice that sent chills down her back spoke.

"Well, if it isn't my daughter, the *queen*, playing in the dirt like a common peasant."

Lenora's hands stilled, her body tensing instinctively at the sound of his growl.

Beside her, Kaylene had already frozen, and she cast a wide-eyed glance at the man behind Lenora before bowing her head in submission. A warning would've been nice, but she supposed her friend hadn't realized until it was too late.

Hiding the shaky breath she took, Lenora looked up. Her eyes met her father's disdainful gaze as he stood there, his arms crossed over his chest and his glare meant to set her on fire. The smell of bitter alcohol clung to him, as familiar and unwelcome as ever.

"Father," she said softly, trying to keep her voice steady. "I didn't realize you'd returned to court."

"Clearly," he snapped, his eyes narrowing more, if that was possible. "Have you lost all dignity? I certainly hope this isn't how you've started presenting yourself as queen to the king's court. You're filthy and covered in mud. You look like a disgrace."

Lenora glanced down at the single stain of mud on her skirt. The gloves covering her hands were a different story, but they would be washed. Still, though, she didn't argue.

Instead, she bowed her head. "I was just . . . planting some flowers," she explained, her voice weaker than she wished it to be.

"Of course you were." He wrinkled his nose. "You played in the dirt as a child. Why should anything change now that I've gotten you the highest seat of power in the country?" Puck sneered at her. "You spent far too much time in the garden at my home, wasting your time with that good-for-nothing gardener boy. Of course you're doing the same thing here."

At the mention of Leo, Lenora pinched her lips together. Every part of her silently argued. He hadn't been good-for-nothing. It hadn't been a waste of time. What did her father know of how she'd spent her time when he was off doing goodness knew what with goodness knew who?

But she lowered her head farther.

"You're queen, Lenora. Start acting like one. Stand up, get inside, and clean yourself up. You're making a fool out of me."

"Of course," Lenora murmured, begging the tears stinging her eyes to hold on a little longer before falling. She pushed herself to her feet, brushing off her skirt.

Puck's eyes followed her movements with disdain. "How does your husband tolerate you?" he muttered, and while it had been low, he'd clearly meant for her to hear the insult.

Lenora bit her lip, turning her back on her father for a moment of reprieve as she pulled off the gardening gloves. She handed them to Kaylene, who quickly squeezed Lenora's hand. The reassurance wasn't enough.

"Please return these and then meet me back in my suites."

"Of course, Your Majesty," Kaylene said, curtsying before walking toward one of the nearest sheds. Lenora didn't realize she'd sent her only buffer away until it was too late.

She was alone with her father.

After another shaky breath, Lenora steadied herself.

Turning, she led him back to the castle, her heart growing heavier with each step away from her safe haven.

As they walked through the corridors, Puck continued his tirade, berating her for her poor posture, for the light dusting of freckles on her cheeks, for the lack of grace with which she stepped. Lenora remained silent, her mind racing with thoughts of how to keep him as far from her as possible.

"My accommodations in upper Cyanthia are being renovated. I will be staying here for the next few months."

Lenora's stomach dropped, and for a moment, the hallway swayed.

"Oh," she managed to say before the click of heels in the hallway saved her from having to respond.

"There you are. I—oh, Puck." Butch, her knight in shining armor, rounded the corner and paused. He opened his mouth, forcing a fake smile onto his face. "Welcome back," Butch said, his face becoming a mask of steel before Lenora's eyes.

"Your Majesty," Puck said, bowing deeply and for far longer than necessary. "A true pleasure to be in your presence again."

Lenora's skin crawled at her father's oily tone. It wasn't new to her though. She'd heard him use it many times over the years, especially when he wanted something. But she knew what he wanted, and she knew her husband wouldn't give it to him. The closest thing her father would receive to his returned crown was a place in the king's court.

A position her father would never be satisfied with.

It had been that or war between her father's Haysinlin and King Valryn's Cyanthia and allies.

A war her father couldn't win.

"I didn't realize you'd returned," Butch said, drawing Lenora's attention away from her thoughts.

"Of course not, my liege. I didn't realize I was returning so soon either. Thankfully, my work out west went smoothly, and I was able to return to court sooner than expected. I was just telling Lenora that I need to take residence here for a while, as my accommodations in Cyanthia are under heavy renovation at the moment. It seems they were not prepared for me either."

Butch's gaze flicked to Lenora, and she pleaded with him silently to save her. Unfortunately, he was in no position to refuse, and Lenora knew it.

"I would be more than pleased to set you up in a room on the second floor," Butch said, shooting Lenora a brief apologetic look as he pressed closer to her. His pinky brushed Lenora's, hidden within the fabric of her skirt, and a wave of relief passed through her. Without hesitation, she linked her smallest finger with his, using him as a lifeline to keep her standing.

"That's very kind of you, Your Majesty. I hate to bring this up, but your father always offered a room on the third floor. Is that not how things work anymore? I was, as you well remember, a king too."

Butch's pinky tightened on Lenora's before he responded. "I remember. However, things have changed since my father's passing, as *you* well know. The best I can offer is a room on the second floor. Or, if you prefer, I'm sure I can arrange for a room at one of the inns nearby."

For just a second, Puck's mask slipped, and the anger he hid well showed in his eyes. When Lenora blinked, it was gone.

"A room on the second floor would be lovely. And dinner. Together. I believe that would do quite nicely as well. It has been a long time since we've had a family dinner, don't you think, Daughter?"

Lenora struggled to swallow. She knew she was clinging too tightly to her husband, but it was the only thing keeping breath in her lungs. "I-I—"

"We have plans, but I'll make sure you receive dinner in your room. We must be going, but please let my servants know if you need anything. Otherwise, we'll be seeing you, Puck."

Without another word, Butch took Lenora's hand in his, intertwining their fingers, and tugged her down the hallway. It wasn't until they were in Butch's office with the door shut that Lenora took a full breath. A second later, Butch turned and pulled her into a bear hug.

"I am so sorry," he said into her hair. "I didn't know he was coming, otherwise I would've warned you."

"You have nothing to apologize for." Her voice came out muffled because of his jacket. "You all but saved me out there."

"If I could put him in a room down in the dungeon, I would."

That made Lenora snort, and she nodded as she pulled away. "I'd have preferred that. But I suppose it was a win keeping him from the third floor."

"It certainly was." Butch kissed her forehead before releasing her fully. "In fact, I'm going to let the patrolling guards know to keep an eye out for him and make sure he doesn't go upstairs."

"You are a wise one, Butch Maudit," she said, a smile crossing her lips.

"I'll keep him away from you as best as I can," Butch said as he walked around and took a seat at his desk. "If anyone knows how to avoid unwanted fathers, it's me. I'll take care of it, Lenora." He returned her smile, and warmth filled her chest. "I'll protect you."

Chapter 36

EMMALEE

Emmalee bit her thumbnail as she peeked around the corner of a modest building with an apartment on top. She and Faeleen huddled in the shadows, waiting for the right opportunity. Their breath fogged in the cool night air. They'd been watching the servant for days, learning her routines and times she would be most vulnerable.

"Are you sure?" Faeleen whispered, her green eyes reflecting the light from the street torches.

Nodding, Emmalee reiterated what she'd been saying since Faeleen had decided to join her in her rescue attempt. "We need that map, Fae. It's the only way we'll be able to get in and out without attracting unwanted attention."

Faeleen swallowed hard but nodded in agreement.

Movement drew their attention toward the street, where a young woman in a servant's uniform made her way to the building. As soon as the girl opened the door and entered, Emmalee and Faeleen slipped inside, closing the door quietly behind them. Emmalee wore a dark cloak with a hood that hid her face and hair; Faeleen didn't since her likeness was not plastered in every village.

The servant made her way up a flight of stairs in a narrow hall, and it wasn't until it was too late that she noticed the two women behind her.

By that point, Emmalee's magic had already returned to her hand and Faeleen had caught the young woman's unconscious body.

Upon entering the servant's apartment using her own key, Faeleen and Emmalee deposited her on the couch. Faeleen searched the rest of the apartment while Emmalee drew silencing runes on the walls. They had to get this right. If they were caught, they'd risk the king learning of their plans.

Emmalee peered around the window curtain. Her gaze darted to the unconscious servant sprawled on the sofa. The room was dim, and the flickering candle Emmalee had lit cast eerie shadows on the walls.

After checking the other rooms, Faeleen took a seat near the woman, waiting for her to wake.

A few minutes later, the young woman stirred, a soft groan escaping her lips. Emmalee almost felt bad. Almost. Except the woman worked for the king.

Kneeling next to the couch, Emmalee prepared her magic in case the woman reacted violently.

The servant blinked, confusion clouding her eyes as she took in the room. When her gaze landed on Emmalee and then Faeleen, her eyes widened, and she scrambled into a seated position.

"Who are you?" the servant asked, voice trembling.

"Relax," Emmalee said, her tone as soothing as she could manage. "You're safe. We just need your assistance with something."

The servant cast a nervous look toward the front door. As if Faeleen could read the woman's thoughts, she placed a firm hand on the servant's shoulder, keeping her in place.

"Please," the servant whimpered. "I don't know anything. I don't have a lot of money, but I'll give you whatever you want."

Emmalee felt sick. It felt wrong. It all felt wrong. But when she thought of Evangeline, she steeled herself for what she had to do.

"We just need information," Emmalee said, her voice firm. "We need you to draw us a map of the castle floors."

"What?" The servant's gaze darted between Emmalee and Faeleen. "Why?"

"Not your concern," Faeleen replied. "Just draw the map."

Emmalee pulled parchment and a pen from her bag and placed them on the small table across from the couch.

"Each room needs to be labeled in detail," Emmalee said, pushing the materials toward the servant.

Tears welled up in the young woman's eyes, but she nodded, wiping them away with the back of her hand. The servant's hands shook as she began to draw.

231

As she worked, Emmalee and Faeleen exchanged glances. They needed to ensure they knew every nook and cranny of the place. There could be no room for mistakes. Emmalee had already had her fill of failed plans.

"What happens when I finish?" the servant asked a little while later as Emmalee examined her partially finished work of the first floor.

"You'll stay here," Emmalee replied. "You'll be safe, and we'll leave once we do what we've come to do."

The servant's eyes widened in fear again, but she didn't protest.

Emmalee chewed the edge of her nail as she paced the room. While her plan had worked thus far, needing to rescue not just Evangeline but also Ariella threw a new collection of obstacles into the mix. That meant another person to hide. Another risk of being noticed.

When Emmalee glanced up to find Faeleen watching her with fear in her eyes, her stomach twisted. She had to save Ariella. It was her fault she'd been taken in the first place. Emmalee turned back to the servant, watching her draw every detail.

They had to succeed.

Too many lives depended on it.

Chapter 37

LENORA

Lenora's heart raced as she ran through the maze, the towering hedges casting long menacing shadows that reached out to ensnare her. Her breathing came in ragged gasps, panic clawing at her chest as she called out for him.

"Leo! Where are you?" Her voice echoed off the walls of green foliage.

The place that had once been her sanctuary, her safe place with her love, closed in around her and became a cage.

She stumbled over twisted roots and uneven ground, her desperation mounting with each passing moment alone. Tears blurred her vision as she frantically searched for any sign of him, but the maze seemed to stretch on endlessly.

A flash of silver eyes and brown hair disappeared around a corner up ahead. Lenora called again.

When she rounded the corner, she came to a halt.

Leo stood in the center of the maze, his hands in his pockets. The tips of his pointed ears, which he typically kept under a hat, peeked out from beneath his chestnut hair.

"You found me," he said, his voice flat.

"I've been looking for you everywhere," Lenora said, closing the distance between them.

She wrapped her arms around his waist, but to her surprise, he did not return the gesture. Instead, he pushed her back by the shoulders.

"Get off me, Lenora." The harshness in his voice made her cringe.

"Leo, what—"

He let out a long dark chuckle. "You honestly believe I loved you? Wow." He shook his head as he looked down at her. "You're more pathetic than I thought."

And then, just as suddenly as it had begun, the nightmare shifted.

Lenora sat on her bed, cradling her swollen belly, her hands slick with blood as she screamed for help.

The doors and windows remained shut. And the longer she stared at the walls, the closer they got until her spacious room was no larger than a chicken coop.

With a gasp, Lenora jolted awake, her heart pounding in her chest as she struggled to catch her breath. Sweat dampened her brow, clinging to her skin like a second layer of sticky clothing. She shivered despite the warmth from the glowing fire in the hearth.

Beside her, Butch stirred. When had he gotten there? She'd gone to bed alone. His movements were slow and groggy as he awakened. His arm, cast idly over her midsection, tensed.

"Lenora? What's wrong?" he asked, his voice low and husky from sleep. He'd been lying on his stomach, and he pushed himself onto his side. "Talk to me." He brushed a strand of her hair behind her ear, his touch gentle and reassuring. "Is something wrong with—"

"No," Lenora murmured, pushing the rest of her hair from her face. She hesitated to say more, her heart still heavy with the weight of her nightmares. She had no desire to tell him about Leo or the horrible image of the second nightmare. "Nightmare," she finally whispered, her voice barely above a breath.

Butch didn't press her further. Instead, he held open the duvet, letting her slide back down until her back was pressed against his chest. He wrapped an arm around her stomach, pulling her close. When he kissed the back of her neck, murmuring reassuring words into the shell of her ear, she almost smiled. Lenora intertwined her fingers with his, matching her breathing with her husband's until she fell back into a dreamless sleep.

"THEN HOW ARE WE GOING TO GET HER OUT?" Merla asked as she brushed Lenora's hair.

Through the mirror, Kaylene frowned as she hung Lenora's clean clothes in her wardrobe.

"If there are more men to guard the castle, I don't see a way to get the girl out. I mean, it was going to be difficult with the number that already patrol." Kaylene paused, glancing up at them through the reflection in the mirror. "Are you sure you still want to do this?"

In all truth, she wasn't. Guilt had started to creep through Lenora's mind like vines the more time she spent with her husband. Freeing the prisoner he was depending on to protect their country felt like more and more of a betrayal with each passing day. But she'd already reached out to the prisoner, and the memory of the half-dead woman lying in the infirmary replayed in Lenora's mind. And if she could get her out with a message to Estrada about Lenora's pregnancy, maybe she wouldn't still feel so alone while she was surrounded by so many people who cared but didn't understand.

Lenora bit the inside of her cheek, rubbing her cold hands together in the hope they'd warm up. "You've seen her, Kay. They've sent her to the infirmary with the way they've been treating her. All because she's friends with Estrada."

Kaylene nodded, but the frown remained on her delicate features. "I know, but she looks better. Healthier. And it's just . . . That woman, Estrada, she captured you. Held you hostage. I just don't see why you'd want to help a friend of hers escape the castle."

Merla had remained quiet, silently working on braiding Lenora's hair. But when she'd finished, she caught Lenora's gaze.

"What is it" Lenora asked, pulling the braid around her shoulder. "You don't think we should save this girl either?"

"It's not that, Your Majesty. I understand where you're coming from. There are just so many unknowns. The king didn't tell you what the prisoner is capable of. For all we know, she could be just as much a threat to you as Estrada was."

Lenora bristled at the mention of her captor. But as her mind brought forth images from her memories spent in captivity, she struggled to picture anything but the pure grief written all over Estrada's face. The freedom Lenora had experienced. The peace.

"She never hurt me. She didn't want to," Lenora said, her voice soft as she stroked the end of her braid. "She just wanted her family back."

The handmaids exchanged glances before Kaylene joined Merla next to Lenora.

"She attacked our entourage and took you from us. And her magic—"

"Her magic was passed down from generation to generation, and there was nothing she could do to keep from receiving it." Lenora's voice was sharp, and Kaylene bowed her head as a sign of submission.

"I'm sorry," Kaylene said, her voice wavering. "I didn't mean to—"

"I know," Lenora said, lifting her chin as she caught Kaylene's gaze. "I'm sorry for snapping at you."

Kaylene offered a weak smile. "Let's figure out how to save her."

Chapter 38

BUTCH

Butch sat across from the prisoner Silas had brought from the Black Forest. His patience continued to wear thinner and thinner as the feline woman stared back at him with steely resolve. He'd been hoping for an easier interrogation than Estrada's other friend, but it appeared Estrada chose her companions wisely. Ariella remained frustratingly tight-lipped.

"Look, Ariella," Butch began, his tone firm. He had gotten her name from Silas, who stood at attention behind him. "I know you're trying to protect your friend. I respect that, I do. But considering her criminal behavior, it would be safer for my people if she was found and arrested."

Every moment of silence only fueled his growing impatience. He glanced at the parchment in front of him, where he'd jotted down questions in the hope that it would keep him organized in the interrogation. Thus far, though, the only thing it'd served to do was grow his anger with each unanswered question on the page.

"I've been informed that you have a younger sister. Is that true?" Butch watched for a reaction and was pleased when her pupils narrowed into slits. "Faeleen, isn't it?"

"You're all alike," Ariella hissed. "Lies and threats."

"Believe me, Ariella," Butch said as he leaned forward. "If I threaten your sister, it will not be a lie. I carry out my word. Tell me how you know Emmalee Estrada."

Ariella hesitated, and her resolve faltered for a moment. "You won't pursue my sister?"

"I give my word."

"Your word isn't worth the horse dung on my boots. I want it in writing."

Butch refrained from rolling his eyes as he pulled out a fresh sheet of parchment and jotted a quick statement. He turned it to face her, and she scanned it briefly.

"Make it official," she said, nodding toward his signet ring.

Smart girl.

Butch did as she said, pouring wax and sealing the document with his ring.

"Now answer my questions."

"I found Emmalee roaming around the streets of Cyanthia as a toddler. Fae and I took her in and taught her how to survive. We parted ways when I was fifteen and Fae was thirteen. We lost touch after that."

"What about her family?"

Ariella scoffed. "You killed her family."

As if he hadn't seen the nightmare enough when he was asleep in his bed, the image of Estrada's husband and two-year-old daughter being killed by his men flashed in the back of his mind. The memories of the nightmares weren't nearly as gut-wrenching, but they did bring on a headache, as always.

Butch gritted his teeth. "I mean parents or siblings. An uncle, aunt, cousin?"

"She's an orphan. She had no one but us, and then her husband and daughter."

That wasn't entirely true—at least not if the other prisoner in his dungeon had anything to say about it. But maybe Ariella didn't know about her. Maybe Estrada had met her after Ariella and her sister.

Butch continued to ask questions, and with great reluctance, Ariella answered them. But the more he asked, the more he realized she didn't have the information he needed. She'd only known Estrada as a child.

That Estrada, for all he knew, no longer existed.

"What do you know about her plans?" Butch asked, rubbing the bridge of his nose.

Ariella's gaze hardened, and she pinched her lips shut.

"Well?"

"I've told you everything I know," Ariella said. Her lips curled into a defiant smile. "And you know what? It won't be enough."

Butch tensed. "What do you mean?"

"You think you can protect anyone? Your wife, your country, yourself? Em will find you, and when she does, she won't hold back."

"Are you threatening me?"

Ariella shook her head. "I don't have to. You willingly put that noose around your neck the moment you took your father's mantle."

Butch stood, placing both hands on his desk as he leaned forward. "Consider this your trial, Ariella. For possession of magic, aiding and abetting a known criminal and murderer, and threatening the royal family, you are hereby condemned to execution by beheading." The words tasted bitter in his mouth, and Butch hated the sound of them spoken in his voice. But she'd threatened his wife. "Take her back. Alert the executioner that his presence will be necessary tomorrow morning at dawn."

As Silas summoned guards to take Ariella back to the dungeon, Butch couldn't shake the feeling of dread settling on his chest. A necessary price to pay, it seemed, for the protection of his wife, his child, and his kingdom.

Chapter 39

EVANGELINE

Evangeline and Odette waited for Ariella's return.

In the silence, Evangeline had finally told Odette about Emmalee, from the moment Evangeline had met her as a little girl to the last time she'd seen her after the boulder field. Odette had listened and only asked a few questions at the end. Evangeline had left out the parts about her own light magic though. She wasn't sure why, except that there was some small part of her that was concerned her friend wouldn't look at her the same way.

She wasn't sure she'd be able to bear that.

Gentle footsteps coming down the spiral stairs interrupted them. Since she'd received the strange note weeks earlier, the servant girl with the red hair had not returned, nor had there been any other secret letters—and Evangeline had checked thoroughly.

Evangeline shifted on the floor, squinting through the darkness. She waited for the usual servant girl to come around the corner.

The servant with the red hair descended the last few stairs and carried the tray of food to Evangeline. Before the girl reached the cell, Evangeline crossed to the door, wrapping one hand around the cold metal bars.

She had decided not long after receiving the first note that if the girl returned, she would speak to her, ask her who had sent her. In a whisper, of course.

The servant stopped a little farther from the door—far enough that if Evangeline reached between the bars, she would be a hair's breadth out of reach.

"What's your name?" Evangeline asked in a low voice.

The woman glanced at the cells around them, but Odette was the only one within hearing range—unless any of the prisoners were elves, fairies, or Pumarians, though the only Pumarian Evangeline knew of was being interrogated.

"Why?" the young woman asked.

Evangeline, noticing the way the servant backed up, took a step away from the door in the hope that it would make the woman feel more comfortable—comfortable enough to answer her burning questions.

"Curious, I guess," Evangeline said, retreating another step when the servant approached the cell door. "You don't dress like the other servants."

"I'm not a servant," she said, keeping her eyes on Evangeline as she bent down and slid the tray through the slot at the bottom.

Evangeline raised her eyebrows. "Who are you?"

"A handmaid." Without another word, the woman turned and left the dungeon.

Evangeline stood a moment longer at the door, her breath catching in her chest at the woman's words.

"Handmaid?" Odette signed out the letters as soon as Evangeline looked back at her. She stood and walked closer to Evangeline. "As in a handmaid to the queen?"

Evangeline's gaze fell on the tray at her feet. "Who else would have handmaids here? No princesses. So unless they're hosting company, she has to work for the queen," she signed, checking over her shoulder to make sure no others were paying attention.

"Is there a—" Odette stopped signing in the middle of her question when Evangeline stopped watching and squatted down and lifted the plate from the tray.

A little piece of paper fluttered down to the ground from where it had been stuck to the bottom.

Neither woman spoke as Evangeline unfolded the paper and squinted at the looping handwriting.

"The time is coming," Evangeline signed, not daring to utter the words aloud. "What's that supposed to mean?"

Odette lifted her hands to respond but dropped them to her lap again at the same time heavy footsteps resounded in the stairway. Evangeline's eyes widened. She grabbed the cup of water, wadded up the note, and swallowed it just as the first guard came around the corner.

Evangeline moved the tray to the back of the cell, sitting down as two guards came to the bottom of the stairs. But they weren't there for her.

Between them stood Ariella, and by the look on her face, something had gone terribly, *terribly* wrong.

"TOMORROW MORNING?" Evangeline covered her mouth with her hand as she gasped. "That's so soon!"

Ariella nodded, her face pale. She wasn't crying, and Evangeline wasn't sure how the young woman had enough strength to keep the tears at bay. "At dawn."

Evangeline's heart pounded. She glanced at Odette, who looked equally horrified. Evangeline wanted nothing more in that moment than to be able to hug Ariella, to comfort her.

"We have to do something. We can't just let them . . ." Evangeline's words died off at the despondent look on Ariella's face.

"There's nothing we can do. The king is determined, and I . . . I made it worse. I just . . . I couldn't help it. Thinking about Fae and Em . . ." She trailed off, her eyes glistening with unshed tears. "I should've stayed quiet."

Evangeline's mind raced. "If we can get a message to her, maybe . . . I mean, she's clever. She might—"

"You said it yourself: it's not a good idea for her to be here. Besides, she'd never get the message in time."

Evangeline knew she was right, but it didn't fix anything. "I'm so sorry, Ari. I wish . . . I wish there were something I could do." Evangeline slammed the palm of her hand against the cell bars. If they weren't there, maybe she could use her magic to save Ariella.

"What did you tell him? When he asked you about her, what did you say?" Evangeline asked after a little while.

Ariella sighed, slumping down against the wall. "I told him we grew up together. I don't think . . . I don't think he can use any of it. I just wanted to protect Faeleen. I had to—"

"I understand," Evangeline said, nodding as a small sad smile crossed her lips. "She's your sister." Evangeline didn't add her second thought: Emmalee was her sister, and if Ariella had said anything that could hurt her . . .

Evangeline wrapped her arms around herself at the sudden chill spiking through her.

The three women fell silent, and in the morning, the guards came and took Ariella away.

Chapter 40

SILAS

Silas stood at the edge of the executioner's platform, his face a mask hiding his disgust and fear. The crisp morning air carried with it the murmurs of the gathered witnesses, which consisted mainly of the king's councilmen and a few high-ranking guards. He felt each whisper like a lashing, the weight of his role in Ariella's execution suffocating him from the inside out. He'd promised her sister she'd be returned, that she wouldn't be hurt. And just like all the other promises he'd made to other magic folk, it'd folded in on itself and failed. He was a liar. A traitor.

And the worst part? No one knew.

Ariella knelt in front of the executioner's block, her hands bound behind her. She cast a sidelong look—or rather a glare—at Silas.

One he fully deserved.

If he'd just left her alone . . .

Silas struggled to swallow. It did not do well to deal in what-ifs. That was something his adoptive mother had told him while she raised him in the castle.

Fear hid in shallow waters beneath Ariella's teal eyes—fear he'd seen many times before in the eyes of those who stood accused of possessing magic, of those he'd led to the executioner's platform.

When he'd led Ariella there, he'd experienced a pang of guilt so sharp he'd nearly tripped.

Ariella's composure only deepened his shame. Had she expected her life would end like this? Growing up alone and starving on the streets of Cyanthia? It could've very well been his own fate if his parents hadn't left him with Lucille.

But Butch's decree was absolute.

So Silas stood by, reminding himself over and over that the allegiance he'd sworn to Butch had been worthy. Justified. Right.

Butch wasn't his brother by blood, but by bond.

Yet his sworn allegiance to Butch felt like it chained him to a traitorous fate of watching magic folk die for the magic in their veins—the magic in *his* veins—just like the chains that bound Ariella to her place before the sharpened ax.

"Last words?" the executioner asked after her crimes had been repeated out loud for the witnesses to hear. A warning, rather, for them to witness. The executioner's voice reverberated as a low hollow echo in the courtyard.

Ariella lifted her chin, her gaze sweeping over the people who'd come to see her blood water the ground. "You all should be ashamed of yourselves. Every one of you. You're blindly following a blind king. And the only thing I regret is that I won't be around to see him trip and fall from grace."

Silas's heart lurched. Defiant and stupidly brave. He silently commended her.

The executioner looked up to the balcony where Butch stood with several guards. Butch nodded. The executioner raised his ax. The group fell silent.

Silas forced his eyes to unfocus and inhaled sharply as the metal fell through the sky, glinting in the early-morning sun.

The dull thud that followed made Silas's stomach churn.

It was over, and yet Silas remained rooted to the spot.

Ariella's body lay lifeless, her illegal blood staining the wooden platform. The witnesses began to disperse, their twisted morbid curiosity clearly satisfied.

When others arrived on the platform to clear the body and the mess, Silas finally descended, his steps heavy. He chuckled darkly to himself as he made his way to the training room to take out his self-disgust on new trainees.

At least then he could do something productive with all the hatred flooding through his illegal magical veins.

SILAS STOOD ON the platform, dressed in the black robes of an executioner. The crowd below was a faceless mass. Their whispers reached him in a deafening cacophony that made him cringe.

In his hand, he held a deadly sharp sword, but that wasn't what caught his attention. His hands were covered in burn scars, raw and painful.

Before him knelt Evie, her eyes wide with fear. The chains binding her glinted in the harsh light.

Dread settled in Silas's stomach. He knew what was to come but was powerless to stop it.

He lifted the sword, surprised by how heavy it felt. Silas wanted to scream, to throw the weapon aside. But his body moved of its own volition.

"Please," Evie whispered, her voice breaking through the roar of the crowd. "Please don't."

The sound of her pleas cut through him like the sword in his hand. He tried to speak, to tell her he was sorry, but no words came. He raised the sword higher until it was even with her chest.

He pulled back, and before he could process his action, he ran her through. Her lovely face froze in a silent scream until he freed the blade from her chest. She twisted to the side and collapsed, unseeing eyes still open as a blossom of crimson spread over her tunic.

Silas jolted awake, his body drenched in sweat. His hands clenched the sheets, his breath coming in ragged gasps. The vividness of the nightmare left him disoriented, and he swung his legs over the side of his bed, scrambling to his side table.

A second later, he lit a candle and studied his hands, half expecting them to be littered with burn scars. But they weren't, nor were they stained with Evie's blood.

He couldn't clear his mind of the image of Evie, the fear in her wide brown eyes, and the sense of helplessness that had overwhelmed him.

Silas buried his face in his hands, trying to steady his breathing.

He had to know.

Was it true?

He couldn't remember.

With frantic movements, he tore open his trunk and dug through his belongings until he found the leather-bound sketchbook. For several minutes, he flipped through until he was satisfied the dream he'd seen wasn't determined as reality in the book.

When he'd finished skimming through a second time, he stopped on the page he'd often turned to and kept it open on his bed. Then he grabbed a clean tunic and left the room, slamming the door shut behind him.

Chapter 41

LENORA

Lenora stood before the ornate mirror in her chambers, her attendants bustling around her with focused urgency. Merla and Kaylene worked deftly, smoothing the delicate fabric of her dark-blue-and-silver gown, as well as arranging her hair with meticulous braids and jewels. A few other servants flitted in and out, bringing various accessories and cosmetics.

The dignitaries from Jerr Pinn were arriving within the next hour or two, and Lenora felt as though she'd been sequestered in her chambers for more than a couple lifetimes.

Her baby bump, a small tender curve just beginning to show, had been hidden beneath the folds of the dress to camouflage it as much as possible. Lenora placed a hand over her abdomen. The news of her pregnancy had not yet been made public, and she wanted to maintain some semblance of normalcy for the important diplomatic events of the next few days.

"Are you comfortable, Your Majesty?" Merla asked, her voice gentle as she secured the final pin in Lenora's hair.

"As comfortable as I can be," Lenora replied with a small appreciative smile. She glanced at her reflection again. They'd done a wonderful job at concealing her condition. She looked almost well rested despite copious sleepless nights as of late—for her and her husband. The arrival of her father hadn't helped either of them with their sleeping habits.

Her raven hair was arranged in an elegant updo, and her dress, a deep ocean blue with silver flowers lining the hem and growing up the pleated panels of the full skirt, complemented her fair complexion.

Kaylene stepped back, a grin on her face. "You look absolutely radiant."

Lenora gave a soft laugh, trying to ease the apprehension she felt. "Let's hope the dignitaries from Jerr Pinn agree."

Once they were ready, Kaylene and Merla accompanied Lenora to the front entrance of the castle. Lenora descended the grand staircase, her heart beating a little faster as she spotted Butch waiting at the bottom.

He was absolutely dashing. The sight of him stole the breath from her lungs. Or perhaps that was the child in her belly and the corset working in collaboration to leave her lightheaded. Either way, she nearly swooned, which of course made her smile larger.

Butch stood tall and regal in his formal attire. A rich velvet doublet of deep green embroidered with golden threads had been perfectly tailored to his broad shoulders. His blond hair was neatly combed, and the crown atop his head gleamed under the flickering torchlight.

As she approached, their eyes met. For a mere moment, it was as if the entire castle faded away, leaving only her and her husband. Butch's gaze traveled over her with unabashed admiration, his usual stern expression melting into something a bit more tender.

"Lenora," he whispered as she reached him. "You look like a vision. I don't think I've ever seen anything more beautiful."

A blush heated her cheeks, and a soft smile played on her lips. "Thank you, Butch. You look rather handsome yourself."

Butch took her hand and raised it to his lips, brushing a gentle kiss across her knuckles. When he rose and leaned in, she held her breath. His voice dropped to a whisper meant only for her.

"If we didn't have these dignitaries to welcome, I'd whisk you away right now and show you just how much I appreciate that dress."

Lenora's stomach fluttered. Or, again, maybe it was the baby. And maybe it was their child that made her lean into him and whisper, "Show me later." She kissed him softly, her fingers brushing his clean-shaven cheek.

Butch's expression darkened. "I'll hold you to that, you know," he said, a gleam in his eye as he caught her hand and pressed her palm to his lips. He lowered her hand to his arm. "Thank you for giving me a reason to get through this," he said out of the corner of his mouth. With a smirk and a wink, he led her to the double doors.

The sun cast a warm glow over the castle walls as Butch and Lenora paused at the edge of the staircase. The lords and ladies of the court waited in fine silks and velvets. They stood on either side of the stairs, leaving an aisle for the Jerr Pinn delegation to pass through.

A line of carriages pulled in through the main gates, each stopping to let the passengers depart before pulling forward to unload trunks and belongings by the side entrance.

The attire of the people approaching the castle differed from that in Butch's court. Their clothing appeared vibrant and flowing, with men and women alike wearing brightly colored robes and tunics made of shimmering lightweight fabrics. Many of the men sported beaded braids or elaborate topknots, while the women wore their hair loose, some with flowers and jewels. To Lenora's shock, and likely the shock of many others in the Phildeterre crowd, some of the women had bare midriffs, their clothing fashioned in two pieces.

Even more surprising, there were clearly magic folk traveling in the company. A man with short hair, pointed ears, and silver eyes accompanied a young woman with pointed teeth—an elf and a vampire.

Butch stiffened beside Lenora. Together, they approached the delegation, their crowns catching in the light and shimmering on the marble steps as they moved.

One of the leaders of the Jerr Pinn oligarchy, a distinguished man with matching salt-and-pepper hair and beard, stepped forward and bowed deeply. "King Butch, Queen Lenora," he greeted in a deep voice.

"Lord Aric Dalton, I presume?" Butch said, inclining his head when the man nodded. "It is an honor to host you and the Jerr Pinn delegation. We welcome you to Phildeterre and to our home here in Cyanthia."

Lord Aric straightened, a warm smile spreading across his face. "We have much to discuss, Your Majesties. Jerr Pinn looks forward to the time spent here."

As the formalities continued and Lord Aric started to introduce the other members of the oligarchy, along with their family members—a group numbering fifty-six in total—Lenora's mind wandered off. The presence of magic, so openly accepted, twisted her heart in a way she hadn't felt in a while. Her thoughts wandered to that tiny house in the middle of the Black Forest where, for a month, she'd lived with magic.

She missed it.

Lenora couldn't tear her gaze from the elf, who reminded her so much of Leo with his pointed ears and silver irises that a pang radiated in her chest. Her grip tightened on Butch, who glanced sidelong at her. Concern flashed on his face for a second before she gave a subtle shake of her head.

Finally, after a lifetime standing in the sun, and with the initial greetings concluded, Butch led the way back into the castle with Lenora at his side.

"Were you expecting . . . ?" Lenora left out the rest of her words, knowing the elf and surely others in the delegation behind them would be able to overhear if she started discussing that their new company was filled to the brim with magic folk.

Thankfully, Butch understood.

"No. No, I was not. Don't worry," he said as he pressed a kiss to her forehead. "Everything's under control."

Chapter 42

BUTCH

Everything was *not* under control. Not only had the delegation from Jerr Pinn arrived with many magic folk in tow, but Puck had decided to join the festivities.

"I was sure this boy would've burned the country to the ground by now." Puck spoke loudly to a few of the Jerr Pinn residents as he clapped Butch on the shoulder. "You've surprised me. Well done." His breath reeked of alcohol.

Butch flinched.

If he wasn't careful, the country would start burning as soon as word got out that he was hosting magic folk in the castle.

Puck's presence was like an impending storm cloud over the otherwise stately and orderly throne room. The delegates from Jerr Pinn stood in their vibrant robes, their curious eyes scanning their surroundings, many lingering on the painted ceiling. Across the room, Lord Aric and his wife and daughter were engaged in conversation with Councilman Clive. The councilman kept casting glances to a man with bright green hair and tattoos lining his exposed torso and arms who was speaking with Councilman Macaw.

"Your hospitality is almost decent this time, Butch," Puck continued, a buzzing gnat in Butch's ear. "Though, I must say, I'm surprised to see my daughter looking so . . . plump. Lenora, my dear, have you finally outgrown your picky eating habits?"

Lenora's face turned pale, her gaze darting nervously to Butch. She'd endured her father's cutting remarks her whole life, but it wasn't until the boor was present that Butch remembered just how much he should admire his wife for surviving his criticisms.

Butch stepped closer to Lenora, placing a protective arm around her waist.

"She looks perfect, Puck," Butch said, his jaw tightening. He forced a smile. "And as much as we appreciate your presence, we have important guests to entertain. If you'll excuse us." Butch didn't wait for a response before tugging Lenora away. She kept her head bowed, her steps hesitant. Butch could almost feel the tension radiating from her, and it pained him to see her so distressed.

"If he ruins this for me, I'm dragging my father's old stocks out from the storage house and putting him on display," Butch whispered into Lenora's ear.

That, at least, brought a small smile to her face.

"Thank you," she whispered, giving a slight nod before turning a semiforced smile to Lord Aric and his family.

Butch tried to keep a confident and welcoming demeanor, even as he kept his peripheral vision on his father-in-law. The last thing he needed was for a war to break out with Jerr Pinn because Puck went and opened his large mouth.

"Lord Aric," Butch said, inclining his head. "I trust you and your delegation are finding everything to your satisfaction?"

Lord Aric smiled warmly. "Indeed, Your Majesty. Your hospitality is most gracious. We are eager to discuss your proposals. You met them outside, but let me reintroduce my wife, Layanna, and my daughter, Akina."

The women curtsied, though it was a little sloppy, which made Butch think it wasn't a custom in Jerr Pinn.

"Of course, a pleasure to meet you both." Butch offered his hand and greeted both women.

"Your presence here is an honor," Lenora added softly from beside him. "We hope to forge a strong and lasting relationship between our countries."

"Your wife is magnetic, King Butch," Layanna said, grasping Lenora's extended hand. "You are very lucky to have her on your council."

Butch tensed. Clearing his throat, he gave a short nod. "She is, isn't she? Unfortunately, or maybe fortunately for her, Lenora is not a part of my council."

At this, Aric and his wife frowned. "Why not?" Aric asked.

Butch opened his mouth to reply, but nothing came out. For several long awkward seconds, silence surrounded them.

"Your Majesty," Silas said from behind Butch.

"Ah, Lord Aric, Lady Layanna, and Miss Akina, let me introduce you to one of my marshals, Marshal Silas Thorne. He is one of five, all of whom run my military." Butch silently thanked Silas for the interruption.

"An honor." Silas bowed. "If I might have a word, Your Majesty," Silas said, nodding to the side.

"I'll return in a moment," Butch said, giving Lenora's arm a quick squeeze.

"Your father-in-law is berating a werewolf," Silas growled through a forced smile. "What would you have me do?"

"I suppose running him through with a sword is out of the question?" Butch rubbed his temple. "Show him to his room. Make sure to do it discreetly. And I'm sure the servants already know, but please reiterate that the Jerr Pinn guests will be in the *opposite* wing from him."

"I'll do my best," Silas said, grimacing as he glanced over to where Puck was insulting a man with bright yellow eyes that seemed to be glowing brighter by the second. "Wish me luck."

"Luck," Butch muttered, patting him on the shoulder before returning to Lenora. "My apologies. One of our, ahem, guests seems to be enjoying the drink too much. But I believe it's being taken care of."

Butch's protective instincts flared when Puck glared in their direction. Silas was leading him out, wisely with the support of a few other guards.

"You're doing great," Butch whispered to Lenora, his lips close to her ear.

Lenora nodded, taking a deep breath. "If you'll excuse me, I'm feeling a bit fatigued. I believe I'm going to retire to the women's room. If either of you would like to join me, you're more than welcome. And Lord Aric, I'm sure I will see you again at the welcome ball tomorrow night." Lenora smiled a genuine smile, first to Lord Aric, and then to Layanna and Akina, both of whom surprised Butch by accepting the invitation.

Before she could leave, though, Butch pulled Lenora to a quieter corner of the throne room behind one of the giant pillars. With some semblance of privacy, Butch cupped her face gently, looking into her eyes.

"Are you okay?" he asked, his voice tender.

Lenora nodded, covering his hands on her face with her own. "I will be. Thank you for taking care of my father."

"The only one I want to take care of is you. I'd like to show *him* how narrow the balcony railings are in the west tower." Though he was joking, Butch half considered how much drink Puck would need to consume to be convinced he could fly. Butch shook his head, clearing the thought. "You're brilliant, and capable, and more wonderful than I deserve. Remember that when he opens his fat mouth."

She smiled, kissing the inside of one of his hands. "Thank you."

Butch pulled her closer, brushing the softest of kisses on her lips.

"Don't think for a second I've forgotten about your promise earlier," he said against her mouth, a smirk pulling the edge of his lip. "I'll see you later, minus the stunning dress."

Stepping back, Butch admired the blush crossing from one cheek to the other as his wife hid her smile. He leaned against the pillar, hands in his pockets, as he watched her leave with some of the other women.

And as he bit his lower lip, smirking, he couldn't help but feel like a vital piece of him was walking out the double doors.

Chapter 43

EVANGELINE

Evangeline sat in the dim light of her cell, her knees drawn up to her chest. The cell across from hers had remained empty since the guards had taken Ariella several days earlier. She hadn't seen the execution, but the sight of the guards dragging Ariella away was burned into her mind. The days since had been a blur of grief and quiet tears.

She'd lasted, well, she wasn't sure how many months locked in a cell as a prisoner to the king. She'd been interrogated multiple times and was regularly mistreated by the guards, and she'd hardly cried. But something about Ariella's death had affected her. Maybe it was because Ariella had been a connection to Emmalee—one Evangeline hadn't known she'd been missing. And with Ariella dead, it was like losing Emmalee all over again.

Evangeline sniffled, wiping her cheeks with the back of her hand. Odette had tried to comfort her, but there was little that could be said. Her friend had seen her fair share of people leave and never return.

It likely wasn't something someone could get used to.

At least, Evangeline hoped she never grew numb to it.

The sound of footsteps broke through the silence. Evangeline lifted her head, her eyes, raw from crying, narrowed as she tried to make out who was approaching. It certainly wasn't a guard—they tended to be quite loud—and it didn't sound like any of the normal servants or even the red-haired handmaid either. With nothing better to do, Evangeline had made note of the different footsteps from those who frequented the dungeon the most.

And with the last note Evangeline had received coming an hour after Ariella had been taken, Evangeline hadn't thought much of it.

Three days.

That was what it'd said.

The handmaid had left it for Evangeline three days ago. How had time moved so quickly and yet so slowly? Evangeline tapped her fingers against her knees, sitting in the back of her cell.

For the first time, the message had been concrete. It wasn't vague, something that gave her false hope.

And she'd all but forgotten it between mourning Ariella and replaying the last interrogation with Butch. She'd spoken. For the first time, she'd uttered words in front of the king, and she couldn't help but regret it every time the nagging thought entered her mind.

The footsteps drew closer, pulling Evangeline's mind back to the notes the handmaid had given her. She'd thought they'd been from the queen, but the longer she pondered it, the more she questioned whether it was a trap.

Evangeline thought of the queen. She'd only ever seen Lenora in person once—if you could even consider it that. On the week of the king's coronation and wedding, Evangeline had slipped into Cyanthia to join the festivities. At that point, both she and Emmalee had hopes that King Butch would be different from his father, that he would lead the country into an era of peace. Of course, thus far they'd both been wrong in placing their hopes in the youngest king in history.

The streets had been packed, and Evangeline had struggled to elbow her way through the crowds. The merchants took advantage of the extreme increase in foot traffic, selling triple the number of wares as normal, as well as sending the delicious scents of food into the titanic crowd.

It was midday when the luckiest people, including Evangeline, managed to squeeze into the castle courtyard, where the new king and his wife were waiting on a tall balcony to address the people.

Evangeline stood near the back. She recalled her trembling hands, which she curled into fists, and the swirling mix of nerves in her gut, not because of the new king and queen, but because her magic had manifested several months earlier.

The security at the events was heightened, making the number of royal guards roaming throughout the excited crowd even more intimidating. Evangeline had slipped behind other citizens multiple times as a way to stay out of sight—not that anyone there knew of the light magic warming her from the inside.

From near the back of the throng of people, Evangeline watched as the new royals stepped up to the edge of the balcony. Her first impression of Butch was completely different than how she saw him now. Having seen him snap into anger, striking his desk and raising his voice, it was harder to remember the initial thoughts she'd had upon seeing him years prior. She tried to picture him as she once had. Part of her remembered thinking he seemed gentle, possibly even kind, especially after the way in which he spoke to the people, as if they were more than just his subjects.

And though she hated that the thought had ever crossed her mind, she had once considered him handsome. His fair hair was darker where he let it grow on his face, framing his jawline nicely. He was quite tall, though not scrawny and not overweight. She didn't doubt for a second that the man was solid rock beneath his expensive clothing, seeing as how he'd grown up in a time of war. He was probably in a similar shape to Thorne—though when her mind drifted in that direction, she yanked it back by remembering her initial thoughts of the queen.

Queen Lenora was a smaller woman, certainly shorter than Evangeline, who stood as tall, or taller, than most of the other girls her age. The queen had worn a large silver crown with a few dangling jewels that rested along her forehead, but from the distance Evangeline had stood, it appeared that the piece wore her rather than the other way around. She hadn't spoken once during the entire address, and it hadn't escaped Evangeline's notice that she stood a few feet away from her husband.

In a way, the queen reminded Evangeline of the little gray mice she sometimes caught scurrying out of the corner of her eye when she'd been living in the first village after moving out of her stepfather's bookstore. Lenora didn't smile. Not once. Her gaze would dart over the crowd before flicking to her husband and then down to the ground.

It wasn't that the queen wasn't attractive. She had beautiful dark hair, almost like Emmalee's but straighter. The tendrils that were intentionally left out of the intricate braided bun were clearly meant to be curled, but they'd lost the spiral and were wavy at best.

As Evangeline tried to remember the queen—tried to put a possible face to the person who'd built her up with hope only to tear it down—the footsteps slowed.

"Evie," Odette whispered, but Evangeline was already rising to her feet.

By the time the person came around the corner, Evangeline stood at the front of her cell. The woman, draped head to toe in a black cloak, was older and taller than all the servants and even the handmaid who'd come before.

257

The woman approached Evangeline's cell, keeping the hood of her cloak pulled down to conceal her face.

"Who are you?" Evangeline asked, stepping back from the door. The woman did not have a tray of food. Something jingled in her hand, and Evangeline's eyes widened when the woman pulled out a set of keys—the set of keys the guards unlocked her cell with.

"It's time," the woman whispered, trying a key, which didn't work.

"For?" Evangeline asked, glancing at Odette, who stood next to Evangeline on the other side of the bars separating their cells. The woman didn't answer as she tried another key, then another. "Who are you?" Evangeline repeated, her voice low as she took another step back.

The door screeched open, and out of the corner of her eye, Evangeline saw movement. A few of the other prisoners were watching what was happening at the far end of the dungeon—and no doubt eavesdropping. The woman was wise not to reveal her name, the more Evangeline considered it.

"Come," the woman said, stepping back from the door, leaving plenty of space for Evangeline to leave.

But she didn't.

Evangeline shook her head as she crossed her arms. "How am I supposed to know this isn't a trap?"

The woman glanced over her shoulder toward the stairs and in doing so revealed part of the clothing under her cloak. It was the same as the other girl's—a handmaid's dress.

"You're wasting time you should be using to leave the castle," the woman whispered.

Evangeline glanced at Odette. "She's coming with me," she said, nodding toward her.

"No. Just you."

"Go, Evie," Odette whispered, and when Evangeline glanced at her, the older woman had a small smile on her lips. "You don't deserve to be down here."

It wasn't true. If anyone deserved to be a prisoner in the cells, it was the woman who had used her magic to attack the king and one of his marshals, not to mention had freed a woman they considered to be one of the current largest threats. But she didn't argue with Odette. Instead, she argued with the woman.

"She's coming with me, or you can lock that door back up and leave."

Evangeline held her breath when the woman looked down at the ring of keys she was still holding. It was a risk to challenge the person trying to free her, but after the countless days and sleepless nights, Evangeline had grown close to her cell neighbor, and she wouldn't lose someone else. Not after Ariella. Not when she had a chance to save Odette.

The handmaid sighed. Thirty seconds later, Odette's cell door opened with a similar screeching sound.

"Thank you," Odette said to the woman, and for a moment, Evangeline almost laughed. She hadn't even thought to thank the woman for releasing her from the cell.

"Take this and follow me," the handmaid said, shoving a piece of paper into Evangeline's hand. "Stay quiet, keep your head down, and don't get caught."

Before Evangeline had time to see what the parchment had written on it, the handmaid strode to the stairway and started up, not waiting for either of them.

"She's pleasant," Evangeline muttered, clutching the folded piece of paper in her fist.

"Be grateful," Odette whispered back as they reached the bottom of the stairs. "She's risking everything right now."

Instead of responding, Evangeline started climbing the stairs, and though it left her out of breath, she was not nearly as winded as Odette.

"When was the last time you were out of your cell?" Evangeline asked when they paused halfway up. She continued to keep her voice low, glancing up the stairs where the woman had disappeared.

"Can't remember," Odette wheezed, leaning over as she caught her breath.

Each step up sent a ripple of excitement and a tremor of terror through Evangeline. She knew from the multiple times she'd been interrogated that there were always two guards at the top of the dungeon. They may have let the handmaid out, but there was no chance they would let two prisoners escape.

However, when they reached the top of the stairs, the two guards were slumped against the wall. Food was spilled on the floor, and what Evangeline thought was growling at first turned out to be a snore from one of them, though she couldn't tell which one.

The handmaid stood at the end of the corridor on the left, apparently checking to see if it was clear around the corner. Other than the two unconscious guards, the hallway appeared empty.

When she noticed them reach the hallway, the handmaid strode over to them, motioning for them to gather close. In the light of the hallway, her appearance was less ominous, though she still didn't smile.

"The parchment," she said, nodding toward Evangeline's hand. "It's a map. Take this left hall, then follow the map and stay out of sight."

The woman appeared to be in her mid- to late thirties, and wisps of her tightly curled dark brown hair peeked out from the hood of her cloak, which she wasn't wearing as low.

"Okay, but how do we get out of the castle gate?" Evangeline asked. Though she had been exhausted and weary from her forced walk through the forest the night she'd been arrested, she had tried to make note of things that would make an escape attempt more difficult. The numerous guards and the castle gate were both on the list she'd made, along with limited ways in and out.

"Once you get outside the castle through the exit on the map, you'll find a servant's outfit to put on. There's only one," she said, shifting her gaze to Odette. "I was only told to come for you." The handmaid narrowed her eyes at Evangeline, clearly trying to emphasize the mistake she seemed to think Evangeline had made.

"All right," Evangeline said, ignoring her response. "Thank you."

The woman nodded. "One more thing," she said, pulling a sealed envelope from a pocket in her dress. "Give this to your . . . friend. I assume you know who I mean?"

Emmalee. It had to be Emmalee. Had she organized this? How had she influenced the queen's handmaids?

Questions raced through Evangeline's head as she took the envelope and slid it into her undergarment, where it was safe against her chest. "Yes."

"Good luck, then." Without another word, the woman went down the hall opposite the one she'd indicated they should take.

"The map?" Odette said, drawing Evangeline's attention from where she'd watched the stranger disappear.

"Right," Evangeline said, shaking her head. Her hands trembled more than she would've liked as she unfolded the paper.

The map was hand drawn, and the same handwriting from the secret notes Evangeline had received marked certain areas, such as the entrance to the dungeon where they stood.

"That looks fairly straightforward," Odette said, looking over Evangeline's shoulder at the parchment. "If we're here, there are only a few corridors before we're out of the castle."

"But there's only one servant outfit to get through the gate." Evangeline frowned at the paper. It seemed too easy, and the nagging feeling that it was all a ploy to manipulate her rose in her stomach.

"We'll figure that out when we get there," Odette said, patting Evangeline on the arm.

Evangeline bit the inside of her cheek, then nodded as she tucked the map away into the strap of her undergarment. At least that way the map wouldn't fall out of her pockets.

She followed Odette as the older woman led the way, peeking around the hallway to make sure it was still clear. They paused halfway down the hallway because the path they were supposed to take was meant to lead to the left.

"Look at it again," Odette whispered, glancing down the hall. "There should be a corridor right here." She pressed her hand against the wall on the left. "Or maybe it was right?" She shifted her attention to the intersecting hallway as Evangeline pulled the map out again.

"No," Evangeline said, shaking her head as she stared up at the two-story wall. "You're right, it's supposed to be here." She looked back down at the paper, pulling it closer to her face, and noticed a smudged section next to where they were supposedly standing. "Wait," she said, squinting at the parchment. "I think there's a line of instruction here that got messed up."

Odette waited as Evangeline tried to read the tiny handwriting.

"Do you hear footsteps?" Odette whispered, looking back and forth from one hallway to the other.

Evangeline glanced up from the paper, closing her eyes in the hope that it would boost her hearing. She did hear footsteps, lots of footsteps. But the sound wasn't echoing from the hallway they stood in or the intersecting one. She tilted her head and then opened her eyes.

"It must be coming from above," Evangeline said, though she kept her voice low. "It doesn't seem to be getting any louder or softer, and I don't think there's much below us at this point since the dungeon didn't stretch this far." She nodded in the direction they'd come.

Odette nodded. "You're probably right." She gestured toward the map. "Sorry to interrupt."

Evangeline returned her focus to the paper, and after a few seconds, she glanced around. "Do you see a stone with a small diamond carved into it anywhere? I think it says that we have to find that stone and press it."

The two of them started scanning the wall that was supposed to have an entrance into a secret stairway. Every once in a while one of them would press a stone, but nothing would happen.

"Here," Odette finally said, pushing a brick. Unlike all the others they'd pressed, this one scraped along the ones around it until it was inset by about an inch.

For a second, everything in the hallway seemed to fall silent.

Evangeline scrambled backward when the stones started to move. They shifted, rearranging until a doorway a few feet taller and several feet wider than her opened into darkness.

"Incredible," Odette said, a look of awe on her round face. "I've never seen rune magic used like that."

"Let's go," Evangeline said, putting the map away as she started into the dark corridor.

Odette followed behind her, and they both stopped on the other side. "How do we close it?" Odette voiced the question Evangeline already had in her head.

"Maybe there's another stone," she said, feeling around on the wall, though it was hard to see. By chance, she found a stone that—like the one on the outside—moved farther in when she pressed it. The door closed, taking all the light with it.

"Now what?" Odette asked.

Evangeline hesitated, her mind racing. Darkness pressed in from all sides, and there was no way but one to see. She knew she could trust Odette, but fear still haunted her. What if her friend reacted poorly? What if she feared Evangeline and her magic or, worse, rejected her?

Taking a deep breath, Evangeline tried to calm her racing heart. She couldn't hesitate—not when they needed to move forward. Without light, they would likely be trapped in the stairway.

Evangeline squeezed her eyes shut, sighing as she made her decision. "Odette, there's something you need to know." She paused, her voice trembling. "I-I haven't told you everything."

Warmth filled her right hand, and as it did so, a small orb of light formed.

"You . . . You have . . ." Odette's voice trailed off as she flicked her wide-eyed gaze between the light and Evangeline's face.

"I'm sorry I never told you," Evangeline whispered, her stomach twisting. "It's not that I don't trust you, but . . . it was a risk—one I didn't want to take. Not with everyone listening down there. And even with the sign language, I—"

"I understand, Evie. I understand." Odette didn't say anything else as she stepped closer and peered down at Evangeline's hand.

"We need to go," Evangeline said, nodding toward the corridor.

She took a few steps backward in the direction they were supposed to head, and when Odette followed her, she turned to face the new corridor. The walls were made of the same bricks as the rest of the castle—or at least the parts she'd seen. And while there were torches lining the hallway, they were all unlit and covered in dust and some in cobwebs.

"Your magic—it's why you were arrested?" Odette asked in a low voice after a minute of walking.

Evangeline sighed, shaking her head. "No, I—well, maybe. Partially."

"Meaning?" Odette's voice wasn't condescending or judgmental. It was gentle, the same she'd spoken to Evangeline with when she fell ill.

"My friend, the one I told you about."

"Emmalee."

"Yeah. She was in trouble. I helped, but in doing so, I . . . I attacked the king and Thorne."

Odette's footsteps stopped resounding, and Evangeline turned to see why she'd stopped. Her friend had a look of horror scrawled over her kind face.

"You should be dead," she whispered.

"I know. After Ariella . . ." Evangeline sighed. "I know."

"Why has he kept you alive all this time?"

Evangeline pressed her lips together, glancing over her shoulder at the darkness. "He thinks I'm useful. Em is the one he's after. He wants me to lead him to her."

Odette started to nod as if what Evangeline was saying made sense. "You're protecting her."

"Yes, well, as much as I could from inside a cell," Evangeline said, her gaze lowering to the light in her hand.

"And the king knows you have magic?"

Evangeline couldn't help but snort, watching the subtle shifting of the light in the orb. The glow wasn't too bright that she had to squint, nor was it making her eyes water, but when she looked at Odette, it did leave a residual spot of light in her vision for a few seconds.

"I hit him in the chest with my magic. He knows."

"Then we need to get you out of here," Odette said, her brow furrowing. "I've seen too many leave and never return from the cells, and I don't want that to happen to you."

"Better yet, let's get out and never have to see the cells again," Evangeline said, offering a small smile before turning to walk down the corridor again.

Chapter 44

EMMALEE

"This feels like it's going to go horribly wrong," Faeleen said, her hands on her hips as she stared down at the map the servant girl had drawn them. It lay spread out on the table before them, its lines and markings meticulously studied by both Faeleen and Emmalee.

Standing next to her, Emmalee stared at the symbol she'd sketched over and over with a normal pen. It was an old rune, one more complicated than any she'd ever tried—more than the one that altered her voice. This would change not only her voice but her entire appearance. And Faeleen's. At least, that was what the book said.

"We've planned this with every possible outcome in mind."

Even the most painful ones, Emmalee thought as she fixed a wrinkle in the servant's clothing laid out beside the map. They'd use it to blend in once their appearances were altered.

Emmalee bit her lip. The rune was an important part of her plan, but it was also one of the most intimidating parts. The instructions in the book said not to perform it too often because it could alter a person's appearance forever in terrible ways, so she hadn't practiced it with the rune pen.

Out of her entire plan, this was the biggest unknown, and she hated the way the sight of the rune twisted her stomach.

Emmalee glanced at Faeleen. The young Pumarian stood with a look of determination radiating in her slitted eyes. Emmalee's heart swelled with a mixture of fierce protectiveness and deep affection for her. The bond she and the sisters shared had been forged in the fires of hardship and survival during the rough years on the streets of Cyanthia, and as she watched Faeleen study the items on the table in front of them, Emmalee decided there was nothing she wouldn't do to keep Faeleen safe. And to rescue Ariella. And find her other sister, Evangeline.

To put the last remaining scraps of her family back together.

Faeleen caught her looking. "Let's hope we get them out before the king even realizes we're there."

Emmalee nodded, but the anxiety-riddled knot forming in her chest wouldn't completely dissipate. "We have to be careful. The place will be crawling with guards."

Placing a warm reassuring hand on Emmalee's shoulder, Faeleen said, "I trust you, Em."

A lump formed in the back of Emmalee's throat. She reached out and pulled Faeleen into a tight hug, holding her close. "I promise you, Fae, we'll get Ari out." Emmalee pulled back. "Stay close to me. If anything goes wrong, we stick to the plan. Get to the exit points we mapped out."

"No heroics."

A small determined smile curved Emmalee's lips. "No heroics."

Faeleen glanced toward the back bedroom where the young servant girl lay unconscious in her bed. "How long until she wakes up?"

"Probably twelve hours, give or take."

"Then we need to be long gone by then, because she's definitely going to go straight to the king."

Emmalee nodded. They'd discussed what to do with the girl, but Emmalee had refused to cause her any harm. They'd likely already traumatized her enough for a lifetime over the last few days with all the questions they'd asked as well as invading her space. The least they could do was let her live.

"If you're ready, let's do this," Faeleen said, rolling her sleeve up and presenting her wrist to Emmalee. "Don't draw it wrong."

Clenching the rune pen in her hand, Emmalee took a deep breath and pressed the tip to Faeleen's exposed wrist. She followed the movements of the rune exactly as the book had described, and the closer she got to completing it, the more Faeleen fidgeted.

"What's wrong?" Emmalee asked, fear trickling through her.

"It's itchy," Faeleen replied. She wrinkled her nose. "Keep going though. I don't want to know what happens if the rune isn't completed."

Emmalee sighed in relief. "The book mentioned that altering one's appearance could lead to some discomfort. I tried a voice-changing rune once and my throat was sore until the rune wore off."

Completing the final stroke of the rune, Emmalee took a step back. The intricate design began to glow faintly, the lines shimmering with a soft incandescent light.

"It definitely tingles," Faeleen said, staring intently at her wrist.

Emmalee sucked in a breath as Faeleen's appearance began to shift right in front of her. The tightly curled shoulder-length blond hair straightened and darkened into a sleek chestnut brown that fell to her mid back. Her bright green eyes shifted to a rich hazel. Her soft features altered as her cheekbones and nose seemed to sharpen. Even her height changed, adding just enough inches to be about the same height as Emmalee.

"Fascinating," Emmalee murmured as she walked around Faeleen. "It worked perfectly. You don't look like you at all," Emmalee said, her voice filled with awe.

Faeleen turned to a small mirror on the wall and gasped. "This might actually work." A grin flashed on Faeleen's new face as she touched her hair and the edge of her jaw. She caught Emmalee's gaze in the mirror and spun around. "Your turn."

Emmalee bit the edge of her thumb, staring at Faeleen a second longer before she nodded. "My turn."

Her friend hadn't lied. The rune *was* itchy.

When she finished, she placed the rune pen on the table and glanced down at her hands. Emmalee frowned. They were tanner than she remembered them being, especially with all the time she'd spent in the Black Forest. And her fingernails had grown out from where she'd bitten them down to the nail beds.

Emmalee glanced up to find Faeleen watching her with her wide hazel eyes. She shifted her attention to the mirror behind her friend.

She didn't recognize the face staring back at her.

It'd worked.

Again.

Emmalee breathed out a sigh of relief.

Her normally dark brown, almost black, wavy hair had changed to an auburn shade. It reached halfway down her back and was nothing but frizzy curls. Her dark eyes were light green now, with a glint of blue around the pupils. Her nose had shrunk and now curved to the left, and freckles spilled over the bridge of her nose and onto her cheeks. The shape of her face had changed, the spell having made it rounder. She could barely see her own cheekbones.

When she glanced down at the rest of her body, she found curves she'd not had before, and when she glanced at Faeleen, she had to look up.

Emmalee let out a mix between a cough and a laugh.

"I can't remember the last time I was this short." Emmalee twisted a strand of the red hair around her finger. "I hope the clothes still fit," she said, glancing at the servant's uniforms on the table.

"We ought to check," Faeleen said, grabbing the one closest to her. "Let's change."

Emmalee's uniform was a bit loose, especially around her neck and upper arms. It was also too long. But there was no easy way to change it besides bunching it at the waist and hoping it wouldn't draw too much attention. If that was the only thing that went wrong, the night would be a success.

EMMALEE LOWERED HERSELF down from the tree where she'd stashed her bag with her rune pen, canteen, and other clothes and belongings. She didn't want to risk taking them into the castle and losing them—especially the rune pen—let alone being caught with them.

Faeleen was watching the castle from the hill on which they stood. Lights flickered in the street as people made their way to the castle gates. Well, the upper-class folk were moving that way since they had been invited.

"Ready?" Emmalee asked, standing beside Faeleen.

"Let's go bring them home," Faeleen said.

The welcome banquet would serve as an excellent distraction, though Emmalee wasn't a fool. She hated the king, but she had to give him credit where it was due—the man could plan. Emmalee fully expected plenty of security during the festivities, especially with the visitors from Jerr Pinn. However, the guards would be looking for Emmalee Estrada, not Andria Potts, the name she'd created while planning. And they certainly wouldn't expect Emmalee to have help.

As they made their way toward the servants' entrance, keeping their hoods up and heads down, Emmalee ran over the plan multiple times to calm herself down. The closer they got to the castle, the more other servants joined them. The real servants didn't seem to pay them any heed. No doubt the king—or rather whoever had planned the ball, because she doubted the king had stooped so low—had requested extra servants for the ball. It was a perfect cover for two unassuming women to sneak into the castle.

It was the row of eight guards at the gate that worried her though, and she stayed in line with Faeleen and the servants as they waited to be let in one by one.

"Name?" a young guard with a monotonous voice asked her when she got to the front. The guards around him scrutinized her carefully, their expressions stern.

"Andria," Emmalee said, offering the guard a smile.

He didn't seem impressed. "Last name?"

"Potts," she said, trying not to notice the fact that the guard next to him was now looking at her. Her heartbeat sped up, and she kept her face as neutral as she could while holding back a swell of dark magic.

"I haven't seen you before," the guard said, pressing his lips into a fine line as he crossed his arms.

"My sister asked me to come be an extra hand for the festivities. I typically work in the lower town with the baker. Not the really good one in the center of town, but the mediocre one that's closer to the blacksmith. But don't tell him I said that because—"

"Don't care. Next," he said, rolling his eyes as he waved her in.

Emmalee hid a smirk as she fell into step behind the servant who had been checked by the guard across from hers. Faeleen joined her a second later, and the two disappeared into the castle halls.

The two women had tested out a few different stories until they'd agreed that more pointless information was a safer option than short answers that might lead to more questioning.

Emmalee and Faeleen followed a group of servants, who left their cloaks in a small room with only two doors—one leading in and one leading out.

Pots and pans clinked together and voices hollered over one another as Emmalee removed her cloak and laid it next to the others. According to the floor plans she'd studied, they were about to enter the kitchen.

It was chaos.

Servants skittered about, some carrying trays of food, other trays of goblets filled to the brim with various colored liquids. The room was hot, and while there were plenty of smells, the one that stood out the most came from the three roasted pigs sitting on the biggest counter.

The sheer amount of food passing by Emmalee made her stomach growl. They had eaten before leaving for the castle, but the aromas around her made it feel like she hadn't eaten in days.

When a servant bumped into her from behind, Emmalee reminded herself that she was not there to gawk at the delicious-looking food; she was there to get Evangeline and Ariella out. With an air of confidence, Emmalee walked to where an older woman was handing trays to a line of servants. Faeleen followed. The older woman didn't look twice at them before handing them both a tray and sending them off after the other servants.

However, as soon as Emmalee left the kitchen and entered a hallway, she paused, resting the tray, which held two plates piled with food, on a small table.

"It's that hallway, right?" Emmalee whispered to Faeleen, nodding in the opposite direction of where the other servants were walking.

"I think—"

"Everything all right?" a young servant asked them, raising an eyebrow when he stopped in front of them.

"Yes," Emmalee said, offering a smile. "I just have something in my shoe." She leaned over and waited until the servant moved on and there was a lull in servants coming out of the kitchen behind her before straightening.

With a glance both ways down the hallway, Emmalee followed the map in her head, checking around corners before fully stepping out. Faeleen was never more than a few steps behind her. However, after a few turns, Emmalee nearly ran straight into a pair of guards roaming the hallways.

"What are you two doing down here?" the tallest of the two asked, peering down at them.

"We were told to take these to the guards standing post at the dungeon," Emmalee said, offering a small curtsy.

"Really?" the other guard asked, cocking his head to the side as he watched Faeleen curtsy too. "It's a bit early for dinner, don't you think?"

Emmalee put the sweetest smile she could on her lips. "That's what I said, but the kitchen is in a state of chaos, and they figured it'd be easier to get the food out all at once, even to those posted."

"Hmm," the taller one said, and Emmalee froze when he reached forward and pulled a chicken leg from one of the plates. "All right, then. Carry on," he said, taking a bite as he and the other guard walked away.

Blinking a few times, Emmalee waited until her heart stopped racing before continuing. Faeleen remained quiet beside her.

A woman carrying a black cloak nodded to her as she passed. She didn't even look twice at the women.

The dungeon entrance was right where the servant had said it would be. But when Emmalee got closer, something wasn't right. The two guards—whom she had fully intended to knock unconscious with her magic—were already slumped over near the stairs leading down. A tray of food similar to the one she carried lay on the floor, and the contents were spread across the ground as if they'd been dropped.

"Em?" Faeleen said, worry evident in her voice.

Emmalee held a finger up to her mouth, quieting her friend as she glanced at the empty corridor. "Leave them here," she said before leaving her tray of food near one of the guards. She nudged him with her boot, but he didn't react. When the other guard snored, Emmalee nearly jumped out of her skin.

"What's going on?" Faeleen whispered, placing her tray by Emmalee's.

Shaking her head, Emmalee didn't respond. She had no idea, and she didn't like the unease rising in her stomach. Emmalee started down the winding staircase. The farther she went, the darker it got and the worse the smell was.

The stairs ended, opening into a hallway on both sides of them with cells on either side of the long hall. Emmalee turned her head in either direction, squinting to see if she could find Evangeline or Ariella right away. But it was impossible.

"Do we split up?" Faeleen asked, and Emmalee quickly shook her head.

"Too risky if we're caught. Come on." Sighing, Emmalee took the right hallway first, but the cells were filled with unfamiliar faces. All the prisoners on that side were male, and Emmalee quickly moved to the left branch.

As they walked along the cells, Emmalee peered through the bars, trying to discern which ones held her friends. Emmalee was concentrating so much that when a hoarse voice whispered to her, she jumped.

"Who are you looking for?" a woman to her left rasped, gripping the metal bars separating them with both hands. She was much older than Emmalee, and a ratty dress hung limp around her thin frame.

"Two blond women. One with white-blond hair and the other with long straight hair," Emmalee replied, turning to face her.

"The second one isn't here. They took her a few days ago. The white-blond one, she's gone too. So is her friend," the woman said in a lilting voice.

"What do you mean 'gone'?" Faeleen asked, ice dripping from her voice as she stepped up to the cell with Emmalee.

"Left a few minutes ago." She grinned at her, though there was nothing but madness in her eyes. "Escaped," she hissed.

Chapter 45

LENORA

Lenora's posture remained perfect—not because she sat at a table elevated from the rest of the company alongside her husband and the visiting guests from Jerr Pinn, but because Merla had not yet returned. Butch sat next to her on her left, though his attention was on Lord Aric and some of the other leaders of Jerr Pinn, who sat on his left. If it had been any other banquet, any other night, any other festivity, Lenora would've ignored the crowd. She would've waited silently.

But somewhere in the castle, her handmaid was risking her life because she'd been ordered. Lenora finished the rest of the sweet liquid in her goblet, and a servant appeared almost as if by magic to refill it for the third time. She wished it were something stronger, but Helena had reminded her to stay away from anything fermented.

"Thirsty?" Akina said, a joking air filling her words.

Forcing a smile onto her lips, Lenora nodded. "Very."

Lord Aric and Lady Layanna's daughter, Akina, was plain, though her outfit sparkled with the pure number of jewels on it. The gown probably weighed half as much as the twenty-year-old herself. Typically, the wife of whatever dignitary was visiting sat on the other side of Lenora, but with only sixteen out of twenty-one representatives of the Jerr Pinn oligarchy present, the seating chart had been cast aside. Akina had apparently requested to be placed next to Lenora when Layanna requested to sit next to her husband on the other side of Butch.

Akina had managed to strike up a few conversations with Lenora despite her distracted mind. Every thirty seconds—or at least it felt that way—Lenora would scan the crowd of people all sitting at smaller tables laid in rows.

Kaylene stood at the side of the room, and Lenora met her handmaid's gaze. There was a frown on her fair features, and Lenora's stomach twisted. The corset hiding her baby bump felt tighter than usual, and Lenora tried to calm her racing heart and, in turn, her air-depraved lungs.

"May I ask you a question, Your Majesty?" Akina asked, and Lenora nodded, though she didn't look at the girl, too focused on the doors at the back of the throne room hall. From the platform where she sat with the other dignitaries—a platform on which the two thrones typically sat—she had a clear view over all the tables.

"Go on," Lenora said when the young woman didn't ask right away. After another second of silence, Lenora finally glanced sideways.

Akina shocked her when it appeared she was almost fighting back tears. "What is it?"

The young woman cleared her throat, her hand rising to wipe away any moisture before anyone could notice. "Your marriage was arranged, correct?"

Lenora nodded.

"How did you react when you were told you had to marry your husband, a complete stranger?"

Lenora's mouth felt dry, and her throat tightened. The crown was heavy on her head, the band of her dress too restricting.

"I was . . . surprised," Lenora finally managed to say, lowering her voice. Next to her, Butch was engrossed in his conversation with Akina's father. That didn't mean he wasn't listening though.

Lenora kept her voice at a low volume as she continued. "I wasn't ready, in my mind, to get married. Not to a stranger."

Akina's lips tightened, and she nodded. "I understand."

Lenora placed her hand on the young woman's, softening her expression. "It's difficult, but it's doable. Is he a stranger?"

"Yes."

"When?"

"A few months. I'll have to move away from everyone to go, and . . . and I'm terrified." Akina's voice was soft, and beneath Lenora's hand, she trembled.

No wonder the young woman had been eager to sit next to her.

There was nothing, at least in Lenora's opinion, that she could say to make the situation better for Akina. She would marry the stranger just as Lenora had married Butch.

"It wasn't easy," Lenora said after a pause. "But . . ." She cast a glance at her husband, catching his twinkling eye for a second before a soft smile crossed her lips. A moment later, Butch's hand rested on her thigh beneath the table. He was definitely listening. "But at least for me, things have gotten better." Lenora turned her attention back to Akina, covering Butch's hand with her own.

Akina's gaze flicked between Lenora and Butch before she gave a small nod. "I just think I'll be lonely."

"Do you have any handmaids? Is that . . . I mean, is there anyone who might travel with you, keep you company?" Lenora wasn't sure what customs Jerr Pinn did or didn't have when it came to servanthood.

Her mind wandered as Akina answered. The thought of her handmaids had her scanning the elaborately decorated throne room.

Merla still hadn't arrived.

The typical lanterns that were kept throughout the castle had been switched out for intricately detailed metalwork, which cast a lovely glow throughout the room. In order not to clash with the floor-to-ceiling maroon curtains that hung at the back of the room near where the thrones typically sat, the servants had brilliantly tied maroon into the color scheme for the festivities.

Amidst other decorations on the tables were flowers in white, maroon, and bright yellow. Throughout the room, wonderful scents filled the air as a seemingly never-ending stream of servants came in with trays of food. Three roasted pigs were brought out, which had Lenora's stomach turning—she preferred poultry. Thankfully, Kaylene had seen to Lenora's eating habits, making sure her plate held only her favorites—not that she had eaten much.

"Thank you for your advice, Your Majesty," Akina said, pulling her hand out from under Lenora's.

It hadn't even occurred to her that she had still been holding the girl's hand, having been distracted once more by the crowd.

"Of course." Lenora inclined her head as she took another sip from her refilled goblet. When the girl didn't speak right away, Lenora was left to fill the absence of conversation with the memories of getting ready for the festivities, or rather making sure Merla and Kaylene knew exactly what their roles were during the banquet.

Merla had been braiding Lenora's hair up, working it around the crown. It was more extravagant than she normally wore it, but maybe it just felt that way as she anxiously waited in the chair for Merla to finish.

"And you've placed the clothing outside?" Lenora had asked Kaylene, who was fixing a few loose threads on the inside sleeve of the dress they'd made for the queen to wear during the festivities. It was a beautiful dress made from dark blue fabrics imported from Jerr Pinn. Her handmaids had suggested using the fabric as yet another way to welcome the guests and show the camaraderie between Phildeterre and Jerr Pinn. It had not gone unnoticed.

"I did," Kaylene replied, nodding.

"And you have the sleeping draft from August, right?" Lenora asked Merla, who nodded because she had seven pins clamped between her lips. "All right," Lenora said, refraining from nodding even though it was her initial response. "Make sure you're not the one to deliver the tray because the guards will recognize you. Send a servant. And take a cloak from my closet—maybe the plain black one. Hide your face from the other prisoners."

"I will," Merla had said, sticking the last pin into Lenora's hair. She'd adjusted a few but otherwise seemed content with her work. "I'll return to the banquet when I'm done."

As Lenora scanned the crowd below the raised dais, Merla still had not appeared through the doors. Lenora lifted her chin, catching Kaylene's attention again. As long as Lenora had known her, Kaylene had had a tendency to rock back and forth on her heels and toes when she was nervous. As she stood against the wall next to some of the Jerr Pinn guests, she bounced up and down.

The desire to tap her foot as she watched Kaylene's nervous behavior increased, but Lenora pressed her heels into the floor to keep from doing it. Few, if any, of the attendees would pay attention to those along the side of the room, but if the queen of Phildeterre started to act nervously, they would certainly notice.

And then the fear she'd been trying to drown in her goblet slipped in when she caught the eye of Marshal Thorne, who stood near the door. He offered her a respectful smile, nodding his head. But she couldn't stop her mind from leading to a question she'd been trying to avoid. What if she was found out? What would her husband do if—when he realized that his prized prisoner had escaped under his nose—he found out that his wife, the woman growing his child, had planned it all?

Lenora licked her dry lips, pulling at the front of her dress when it constricted her again.

"I suppose it's time," her husband said, startling her when he leaned over and whispered into her ear.

She turned to him, raising an eyebrow. "For?"

"Time for me to address the crowd." He offered her a smile, though a frown replaced it for a second. "What's wrong?"

Lenora forced her lips to curve upward, bowing her head. "Nothing's wrong. I'm sure they're eager to hear from you," she said, reaching for her glass for what felt like the hundredth time. She abruptly ended their conversation by sipping from her goblet, returning her gaze to the throng below them.

Butch's chair scratched along the floor as he stood. The clamor in the room died down in just a few seconds, and not for the first time, Lenora was impressed with the control her husband had over crowds. Though he bore no magic, he had power over people.

"Gentlemen, ladies"—he glanced down at Lenora—"and visiting friends, thank you for joining us tonight to celebrate the arrival of our dear allies from Jerr Pinn. With this ball, we officially welcome you to Phildeterre."

Lenora switched her gaze from her husband to the crowd. With all their faces turned upward toward him, it was as if he had enchanted them. His captivated audience listened silently, and only a few of them whispered while he spoke.

Movement at the back of the room caught Lenora's eye, and she nearly choked. A sigh of relief slipped from her lips when Merla came through the door. However, she didn't get far before Marshal Thorne stepped out and stopped her. Lenora's heart thudded as she watched the interaction, no longer listening to the benevolent words her husband spoke. Instead, her entire focus was on the marshal and her handmaid. They whispered back and forth a few times before he nodded to her and she continued along the wall, stopping next to Kaylene.

Lenora quickly moved her gaze from her handmaids, once again scanning the room in an effort to look nonchalant. On the inside, however, a terrible mixture of panic and relief sent tingles throughout her body. Merla was back, and by the looks of it, everything must've gone well. But what if it hadn't?

After several more seconds of watching the crowd, Lenora decided it was safe to look back at her handmaids without drawing attention, especially as her husband finished his speech and the crowd went back to their own discussions.

Merla was talking to Kaylene, her focus on the younger handmaid. However, Kaylene was watching the queen, and she directed Merla's gaze to Lenora's. With a simple nod, Merla doubled the amount of relief within Lenora.

"He's good with the people," Akina said, and without having to worry about Merla or the plan, Lenora allowed herself to relax and take a bite of a roll on her plate.

"His father practically trained him from the day he was born," Lenora said after she finished her bite. "Have you had a chance to visit the portrait hall on the third floor since you arrived?"

Lenora continued the small talk, finding it easier and easier to connect with the young woman with both her handmaids standing next to the wall. Time went by quicker than before. Laughter sprouted down below, and the room felt brighter, though nothing about the lanterns had changed.

Before she knew it, Butch stood next to her and offered her his hand. "I believe it is time for us to entertain this crowd with a dance, my queen."

Lenora took his hand, a pleasant surge of warmth traveling from his touch through her body. They made their way around the table and down the stairs until they stood in the center of the throne room. Every eye rested on them. Lenora tensed.

Her father watched them with narrowed eyes, a drink in his hand and a sneer on his lips. She hadn't seen him since her husband had asked Marshal Thorne to escort him out of the throne room after the arrival of the delegates. She'd almost—*almost*—forgotten he was there.

"Eyes on me," Butch whispered into her ear, leaning forward. "Eyes on me."

Music rippled through the air as Lenora stared up at her husband's face. He placed a hand on her waist and held her hand in his. With a confident touch, he guided her effortlessly into the dance. Butch led, and Lenora followed. Despite his broad frame and warrior's build, he was graceful.

With each passing second, Lenora relaxed into the rhythm—relaxed into him. The colors around them blurred as they spun and swayed. She kept her gaze on Butch's deep brown eyes.

As they danced, Butch smiled at her. His voice came out a low murmur meant only for her. "I believe I made a serious mistake this evening that I must apologize for."

Lenora frowned. "What?"

He leaned closer. "I haven't told you how absolutely breathtaking you look."

Her cheeks warmed, and she dropped his gaze for a second.

"Eyes on me, Lenora," he said, amusement in his voice. When he recaptured her gaze, he grinned. "Stunning."

A shiver ran down Lenora's spine at his words, her heart fluttering in a way it hadn't done in years. Not since—

"I heard you talking to Aric's daughter." Butch's words pulled Lenora back as he spun her out and into his arms. "It wasn't easy at the beginning, was it?"

Lenora's stomach twisted at the concerned look that flashed in her husband's eyes. "No, but that doesn't mean we haven't been trying. And we've been through a lot."

"Too much," he whispered, his brow creasing.

She had no doubt his mind had gone to the same place hers had, especially when his gaze dropped to the hidden bump in her dress.

"Things will get better. They already have," Lenora said, hoping her voice sounded more confident than she felt.

As the music drew to a close, Butch spun her one last time before pulling her close. He placed a soft kiss on her hand, their eyes locked, and for a moment it seemed as though everyone else in the room had vanished. The applause from the onlookers was a distant sound, one Lenora hardly registered as she stared into her husband's eyes.

Butch released her and, with a nod to the crowd, led her back to the raised dais where their table awaited. He helped her up the steps, his hand lingering on hers. When they reached their seats, he pulled her chair out for her, sliding it in as she sat down.

The orchestra began to play a new song, and couples danced in the center of the room between the tables. The room became a sea of shifting colors and motion. Lenora watched the dancers with a serene smile, her heart beating a little faster with excitement.

"Excuse my interruption, Your Majesty, but I need a word." Marshal Thorne's sudden appearance behind Butch startled Lenora, and she couldn't help a quick glance at her handmaids. They were whispering to each other, and Kaylene had a frantic look on her face. Lenora returned her attention to her husband.

"Of course." Butch nodded, his jaw tightening. Every ounce of softness he'd shown her during their dance had already disappeared. "If you'll excuse me," he said to Lenora and the delegates around them.

Butch stepped back with Marshal Thorne, who leaned forward and whispered into the king's ear. Lenora's good mood ended as soon as Butch's face darkened and he straightened. He nodded once to Marshal Thorne.

"I must see to something, but I'm sure my wife will be better company than I am. I'll return shortly," Butch said to the Jerr Pinn leaders, apologizing before following Marshal Thorne back behind the tables.

After noticing several extra guards waiting at the entrance to the doors, Lenora stood, trying to follow her husband and the marshal.

"Where are you going?" she asked, glancing between the two men.

Butch's jaw clenched, and he shook his head. "I need you to stay here. Keep them entertained." He nodded toward where Lord Aric and his wife were talking with some of their companions. "I must see to something."

"But what's—"

She froze when he stepped up and leaned forward, hiding his face from the rest of the room as he whispered into her ear.

"Stay here, Lenora." His voice was tight, unyielding, and when he pulled away and looked at her, his gaze was hard.

Lenora narrowed her eyes at him as she raised her chin. "All right."

Before she returned to her seat, she forced her face into a compliant and pleasant mask. Meanwhile, nothing but panic circulated through her veins.

Chapter 46

Evangeline saw the first guard too late. She and Odette had followed the map all the way to where they were supposed to leave through the servants' corridor, ducking around pillars and into inset doorways at any sign of people. And it had worked.

Until they reached a narrow hallway of rooms. At first glance, the hallway was empty. Evangeline's heart was already racing—it was supposed to be the last corridor. The door at the end of the hall opened to the outside. She picked up her pace, glancing over her shoulder to make sure Odette was keeping up. She was.

Halfway down the hallway, Evangeline skidded to a stop, her panicked gaze on the door to freedom as it opened from the outside. Her hands trembled as she sprinted to the nearest door, trying the handle.

Locked.

"Go, go, go," Evangeline said, her voice a hoarse whisper. She pointed back the way they had come, and they both turned around.

"Stop there," a loud voice called, echoing through the hallway. A breeze of fresh air blew in through the door, and Evangeline's stomach tightened. So close. They'd been so close.

Evangeline sprinted down the hallway away from the door, glancing over her shoulder at not one but two guards pursuing them. She pushed her muscles harder than they'd gone in months. Her chest burned, and a cramp formed in her side. But she wasn't concerned for herself.

Odette had started in front of her but was losing speed. By the time they made it to the end of the hallway, the older woman was lagging several feet behind Evangeline.

"I can't keep running," Odette panted as Evangeline tugged her down a new hallway—one they had not been down.

"You need to find a place to hide," Evangeline said, checking over her shoulder. "Take this and throw it into the first fire you see," she said, shoving the letter the handmaid had given her to give to Emmalee. If she was caught with it, she risked getting the people who'd helped her in trouble. It wasn't like the envelope was hard to spot in her tunic. "The map too," she said, handing over the other parchment. The guards had not yet made it to the end of the hallway. "There," Evangeline said, pointing to a door. "Try it. I'll lead them away and buy you as much time as I can."

Before Odette could argue, Evangeline pushed her toward the door and started running down the hallway again. She only hoped Odette had gotten the door opened and closed behind her before the guards entered the hallway. Their thundering footsteps pounded behind her, and she didn't dare check to see how close they were—not when she was trying to navigate unknown territory.

Every corridor looked the same. Had she been somewhere on the route from the dungeon to the king's office, she might have been able to tell where she was. But from the stone bricks to the intricate tapestries blurring past her, she was lost.

"Stop!" one of the guards behind her hollered, and as she turned the corner into another hallway, she risked a glance. They had gained several feet.

Evangeline yelped when she ran straight into another set of guards, struggling as they restrained her arms. They'd been waiting around the corner, probably alerted by the other guard's call.

"Let me go," she spat, trying to wriggle out of their firm grasp.

Just as her magic began to swell, it disappeared. They cuffed her hands behind her back.

"Where's the other one?" one of the guards who'd been pursuing her asked as he and his partner caught up.

Evangeline couldn't help but let out a breath of relief. Odette had remained hidden. Though disappointment and fear pressed down on her, she could at least breathe easier knowing her friend hadn't been caught. At least not yet.

The guard who'd asked the question stepped up in front of her. With a man on either side of her gripping her upper arms tightly, she had nowhere to go.

"Where is she?" the guard demanded, glaring down at her. He wore a red collar different than the other three.

Evangeline clamped her jaw shut, refusing to look directly at him. She gasped when he struck her with the back of his hand, her head snapping to the side. Her skin stung and began to throb after a few seconds. Evangeline sucked in a breath of air when the captain reached forward and gripped her by the throat, yanking her head toward him. His hand pinched her airway, making it difficult to think of anything but trying to get a breath of air.

"Tell me where the other prisoner is, or so help me I'll—"

"Captain Malkim," one of the guards said, interrupting the man with the red collar. "The king needs to know about this."

The captain released Evangeline. She choked, sucking in air through her bruised windpipe. He glanced around at the other guards, clearing his throat.

"In there," he said, nodding to a door near them. "You two and I will wait with her until the king can step away from the banquet. Commander, you go find others to search for the other prisoner and send word to the king about the escape."

The guard who'd been with the captain saluted before departing around a corner. Evangeline glared at Malkim, returning to her resolve of silence. She would not speak. She hadn't given up Emmalee, and she would not give up Odette.

"Move," one of the guards next to her said as they pulled her toward the door the Malkim was unlocking.

Inside the room was a study similar to the one Thorne had taken her to, and just as before, Evangeline's gaze went straight to the bookshelves along one wall. The room was reversed from the previous one, with the books along the left side of the room and the sitting area on the right. A window let in the first moonbeams of the night, leaving the horizon colored in bright white light.

Captain Malkim stepped in front of Evangeline, blocking her view of the window. "We will find her, the other prisoner."

Evangeline ignored him. Her cheek still throbbed from when he'd hit her, and she wanted nothing more than to retaliate. But restrained as she was, the only thing she could do was infuriate him with her silence. That, at least, held some satisfaction.

"How did you escape?" He lifted his chin, staring down his crooked nose at her. While he was not shouting at her as he had in the hallway, his even tone was almost more intimidating. A fiery look crouched behind his eyes, like he was ready to snap her neck should she blink at him in the wrong way.

She hated that the thought even crossed her mind, but she couldn't help but think that an interrogation with the king was almost preferable in that moment. At least he kept his hands to himself—or to his unfortunate desk.

"Speak!" the captain shouted, and she tensed her muscles to keep from flinching.

Breathe. She needed to breathe. Her stepfather had screamed at her before. So had the king. And others. She just needed to focus on something else. Something—

She could do nothing to stop him when he snatched her by the back of her hair, drawing a knife and tilting her head back. With a few steps, he backed her against the wall. Air slammed out of her chest at the impact. The guards at her sides disappeared, apparently more than willing to let go and watch whatever horrible show their captain wanted to display.

Evangeline winced at the bite of the blade on her neck but continued to give what she hoped was a defiant look even as fear filtered through her entire body.

"Tell me where the other prisoner is. Tell me now or I'll cut you, you little—"

"Do it and your king will see you hanged," Evangeline growled through gritted teeth, keeping her voice low. She had not wanted to speak, but something about the bloodthirsty look in the man's eye made her question whether he'd actually slit her throat.

"What makes you think you're so special? Hmm?" He shook her, letting her head slam back against the wall. The blade dug into her neck, and fire followed.

Evangeline blinked rapidly, trying to keep tears at bay from the pain radiating in her skull. With her hands cuffed behind her back, she could do nothing but clench them into useless fists.

For a second longer, he held the knife against her skin, pressing in just enough to draw blood. He seemed to recognize the threat behind her words, but instead of retreating, he snarled at her.

"You're not special. You're a criminal." He replaced the blade at her throat with his hand, squeezing until her eyes bulged. "Tell me how you escaped the cell." Malkim trailed the tip of his blade along her cheek, not pushing hard enough to cut—not yet at least.

"I'd rather . . . die," Evangeline croaked, lifting onto her tiptoes to try to release the pressure of his hand around her neck. It stung, reaffirming the notion that his blade had broken skin when he'd pressed it against her throat.

Blackness crept in around her vision, but despite the room blurring, she held the captain's glare. When her head began to feel fuzzy like the outside of a peach, he released her, shoving her to the ground.

Evangeline gasped when her shoulder and then her head hit the floor. She sucked in air, curling her knees up to her chest. Out of the corner of her eye, the captain slipped his knife back into his belt.

He sneered down at her but didn't say anything else.

Evangeline let her head roll back on the floor, closing her eyes for one moment in the hope that the lack of light and color might lessen the throbbing in her head. It didn't. And it only made her feel more vulnerable, what with the three guards in the room watching her.

Malkim began pacing back and forth in front of the unlit fireplace.

Eventually the room filled with silence. Minutes passed by. Evangeline sat up, leaning against the wall and pulling her knees up. The two guards who had been holding her now stood on either side of the door. Their purpose was clear. A message. There was no way out unless it was straight into an unmarked grave.

Malkim and both guards straightened when a knock resounded on the door.

"Enter," Malkim said, and at the same time a wicked smile crossed over his lips, Evangeline's heart dropped.

Two more guards filed in with Odette between them. "She was hiding near one of the servants' corridors, sir," the guard on the right said.

"No," Evangeline whispered, her gaze meeting Odette's. The older woman seemed exhausted, defeated. And it was all Evangeline's fault. She'd forced her friend to come with her, and now her life was in danger. Fear flooded through Evangeline, and not for the first time, she felt on the verge of tears.

"Well done," Malkim said. He nodded to the side, and the guards followed his nonverbal order to move Odette farther into the room. "Now, how about you tell me how the two of you escaped?" He directed his attention to Odette, and Evangeline tensed on the floor. Had Odette gotten rid of the parchments? It didn't appear like she still had them on her person. But if she was caught with them . . .

Odette met Evangeline's gaze again before the captain stepped between them.

Evangeline held her breath. She knew she could take the interrogations, but she had no clue how her friend would hold under pressure.

Especially from the violent captain.

Chapter 47

BUTCH

Butch kept stride with Silas as his friend led him down the hallways and away from the banquet.

"How?" Butch asked again, knowing Silas had about as much knowledge of the escape as he did. Butch kept his hands clenched as fists at his sides.

"Like I said, my best guess is we were so concerned with keeping Estrada out that we lost sight of keeping her in," Silas said, his voice tight. "This way."

Butch followed him down one of the lesser-traveled hallways—at least lesser traveled by him. He did, however, realize how close they were to one of the exits out of the castle. The prisoner had gotten so close. If she had escaped . . .

"Your Majesty," a guard outside a doorway said, saluting in respect. "They're inside."

Butch barely acknowledged him before barging through the door.

"How did this happen?" Butch asked, directing his question at the second-highest-ranking guard in the room.

Captain Malkim, one of Silas's best, saluted him before responding. "I've been trying to get the answer to that question in your absence, Your Majesty."

"And?"

"Neither will speak," he said, glaring at Estrada's friend. She sat on the floor, and despite an angry red mark on her cheek, a trickle of crimson trailing down from her temple, and a smear of blood on her neck, she held a defiant look in her eye as she returned the captain's glare.

Butch turned his attention to the other woman who had escaped. She was older, and he vaguely remembered her from a trial over a year prior. "How did you escape?" he asked her, hoping she'd be more willing to talk than Estrada's companion.

Silence pervaded the room. Butch's blood boiled.

"Return this one to her cell. I'll deal with her later."

"No!" Estrada's friend said, her eyes wide. "Don't." She struggled to her feet, her hands chained behind her back. At her movement, two guards grabbed her upper arms, one on either side.

The older woman caught Butch off guard when she nodded her head in respect to him. It was the last thing he'd expected after declaring her a prisoner once more. But a memory returned, and he understood why.

He'd spared her.

And she knew it.

When the older woman was gone, Butch addressed the remaining guards in the room. "Captain, you and the others wait outside while Marshal Thorne and I speak with the prisoner."

"Of course, Your Majesty," the captain said, saluting.

Butch nodded to each guard as they left. When the door shut, Butch took a second to regain control over his facial expressions before turning to the prisoner.

"Tell me how you got out of your cell," he said, clasping both hands behind his back. He hid the relief he felt at the prisoner's bound wrists. At least with the magic-dampening cuffs, the worst she could do was headbutt him.

The woman lifted her chin, glaring at him. She did not speak.

"Someone must've let you out, right?"

Nothing.

"Was it a guard?"

Not a word.

Butch rubbed his brow, thinking of the whole host of people in the throne room. They'd comment on his absence soon. He glanced at Silas, who was frowning at the prisoner.

"What is it?" Butch asked, waiting for a second for his friend to realize he was speaking to him.

Silas nodded toward the prisoner. "She's bleeding."

The blood on her temple continued to creep down the side of her face, and the smudge of crimson on her neck had darkened along a line that ran horizontally across her thin neck. Drops of blood had started to leak down her skin. They didn't seem like serious injuries, but Butch could still understand Silas's curiosity.

"What happened?" the king asked, expecting there to be silence again.

She flicked her glare from Silas back to the king. Silence.

Silas straightened next to him. "Did one of the guards . . . ?"

The prisoner pinched her lips together again, and the king sighed. A headache was starting to form, and he took his crown off his head to run a hand through his hair. His formal crown had always been a bit tight, and he'd been wearing it for several hours because of the festivities.

"You're not going to tell me who freed you, are you?" he muttered.

"You're learning, Your Majesty," she said, her voice too cheery.

"All right, then. In that case, you—"

A guard barged through the door, interrupting Butch. "Apologies, Your Majesty, but we need to get you somewhere safe."

"What's happened?" Butch asked, returning his crown to his head. His heart beat faster. If something had happened while he was gone . . . If Lenora was in trouble . . .

"A body. An officer, Your Majesty."

"Who?" Silas and Butch asked at the same time.

"Don't know, but we need to get you somewhere safe."

Butch glanced at Silas, whose features darkened. Before Butch could respond, Silas turned to him. "I want you in a safe room."

Butch opened his mouth to remind his friend who ruled the country, then closed it. Instead, he nodded. "She'll come with me," he said, nodding to the prisoner. "I'll continue to question her."

"Absolutely not," Silas said, shaking his head. "She's—"

"Bound by cuffs. She's not a threat right now." Butch glared at the prisoner before turning his back on her and stepping closer to Silas. He lowered his voice when he spoke next. "Get Lenora somewhere safe first. Do you understand? And the delegates."

Silas nodded, already backing toward the door. He turned to the guard who'd entered. "Take His Majesty and this prisoner to the nearest safe room and lock it down. Remain outside and do not, under any circumstance, open the door until I or another marshal is present," Silas ordered, drawing his sword as he approached the door. "Understood?"

"Yes, sir," the guard said, saluting. Silas didn't return it, his attention on Butch as he paused in the doorway.

"Don't do anything stupid, Your Majesty."

Butch almost laughed. Almost. "You too, Marshal." He nodded, watching as his friend left. "Where was the body found?" he asked the guard, who gripped the prisoner by one arm and pulled her toward the bookshelves on the left.

"The lowest floor near the dungeon, Your Majesty," the guard said, pulling a hidden lever disguised as a bookend. The bookshelf farthest on the left swung open, revealing a hidden tunnel.

A thought crossed the king's mind, and he stopped following for a second. His attention fell on the prisoner.

"Your Majesty?" the guard said, his voice rising. "Is something the matter?"

"Walk," Butch said, clenching his fists. The prisoner, who had been staring into the dark passage, turned to look back at him with wide eyes. "I said"—he pushed her by the small of her back—"*walk*."

Anger already pumped through his veins.

An officer had been killed on the same floor as the dungeon entrance.

Had the prisoner killed him?

By the time they reached a safe room three rooms down, Butch was vibrating with anger. If she had killed one of his men in her desperate attempt to escape, he was going to find out, and he wasn't going to take her infuriating silence as an answer.

"Thank you," Butch said as the guard opened the safe room door for him. There were several safe rooms throughout the castle, built into walls long before his grandfather's reign. Ironically, they were secured with runes, though his grandfather, King Kylian, had made sure that the runes were hidden from sight, triggered by mechanics Butch himself did not quite understand.

The rooms were soundproof from the inside and protected, for the most part, from magic on the outside. However, they weren't the largest rooms. The one they'd stopped at only held a cot, a dresser, a lantern, and a small box with medical supplies.

"I'm sure this will all be sorted soon, Your Majesty." The guard uttered an apology as he lit the only lantern in the room and closed the entrance—a wall of bricks—behind him.

The moment the bricks sealed, Butch turned to the prisoner. With a single move, he freed his sword from its sheath and held it beneath her chin.

"Did you kill him?" Butch snarled, and the woman frowned at him.

"What?" the prisoner asked, raising an eyebrow. "Of course not."

"Don't lie to me," he said, taking a step toward her. She didn't retreat, but she did glance down at his blade.

"I'm not lying." Her voice was even. "I didn't kill your man." She narrowed her eyes at him. "I was too busy trying to get out of this awful place."

"How?"

She rolled her eyes, and after a glance at the cot next to her, she sat down. Sat down.

While he held a sword to her throat.

Butch couldn't think of another person who would have the audacity to ignore his threat to their life and sit down—without his permission no less.

His hand tensed around the hilt of his sword before he forced himself to take a deep breath. A moment later, he returned the sword to its sheath. She clearly knew as well as he did that he wasn't going to kill her—at least not in the safe room.

To his surprise, he believed her when she said she hadn't killed the officer. He wasn't sure why, but he knew she was telling the truth.

"Who helped you escape?"

The prisoner chuckled, then winced as she moved her neck. Though it did not appear to be a deep cut, he was sure it stung. And it was still bleeding.

Sighing, he crossed the room and removed the box of bandages and healing supplies from the top of the dresser. "Here," he said, putting it on the cot.

"What do you expect me to do with that?" she asked, raising that infuriating eyebrow again.

"You're hurt."

"I'm aware."

"There are bandages in there and—"

She rolled her eyes, moving her arms so the chains binding her hands behind her rattled.

"Oh, right," he said, rubbing the side of his face. "I guess I'll . . ." His words faded off. Butch picked up one of the folded cloths and took a step toward her.

"Don't," she said, leaning back from him. The prisoner shook her head. "I'm fine."

He lowered his hand, frowning as he tossed the cloth back into the box, which he put back on the dresser. "All right, then." He glanced around the room, and finding nowhere else to sit, he leaned against the opposite wall from the cot.

As the room filled with silence, his thoughts transitioned from the safe room and the prisoner to his wife and unborn child. Butch hoped Silas was taking them to their own safe room, hoped that the other delegates and the rest of those celebrating were unharmed. Sighing, he removed his crown, placed it on the dresser, and leaned forward to rub the back of his neck. No matter what was happening outside those walls, there was nothing he could do about it from inside the safe room.

And by the glare the prisoner was giving him, he had an agonizingly long wait ahead of him.

Chapter 48

EMMALEE

E mmalee and Faeleen ascended the winding staircase from the dungeon, their steps echoing softly in the dimly lit corridor. If what the prisoner had said was correct, there was a chance they could still find Evangeline—at least, that was her hope.

But Ariella . . .

Another broken piece of her shattered heart cracked, and she clenched her hands into fists to keep her emotions from surfacing. They wouldn't help her focus. She needed to find Evangeline and she needed to get Faeleen out safely. Then she could fall apart at losing Ariella.

Losing Ariella.

Because she was gone.

"This wasn't supposed to happen," Faeleen whispered, her voice edged with panic. "If she's not here . . . If they already took her away—"

"Focus, Fae. We need to get somewhere less conspicuous. Then we can figure out what to do next." Emmalee forced a calm expression, though her heart pounded in her chest.

As they reached the top of the dungeon staircase, they found the unconscious guards still slumped against the floor. The sight was a small relief, but Emmalee's mind still raced.

The castle was large, too large for Emmalee to search without some sort of system in place. Maybe she could think of a spell to help with—

"What happened here?" a male voice called. A royal guard sprinted toward where the two men were still slumped over.

"I don't know, sir," Emmalee said, willing her voice to sound innocent. She glanced at Faeleen, silently pleading for her to play along. "I went down to check if something had happened. I found—" She stopped in the middle of her sentence when she noticed the royal-blue collar circling his neck. In fact, the longer she looked at him, the more familiar he appeared.

The man was a mountain, all muscle and height. And the look he was giving her, as if she were something he'd stepped in and was trying to remove from his boot . . .

The marshal from Shongbay.

Levick. That was what the guard, Stoll, had said.

Marshal Levick.

The man who'd been in charge of the guards who'd raided Shongbay and killed her husband and daughter.

Emmalee saw red.

"What did you find?" he asked, standing back up after examining the nearest incapacitated guard.

"Nothing," Emmalee said, her voice dipping low. It came out smooth as she tilted her head, a sneer on her lips. With a quick scan of the empty hallway, Emmalee flicked her wrist and sent a wisp of dark magic toward the man.

Within a second, he collapsed to the floor, as unconscious as his comrades.

"Em, what are—"

"Help me get him into that linen closet." Emmalee pointed to a door down the hall. "We'll question him to find out what happened."

"It's not part of the plan," Faeleen argued even as she helped Emmalee drag the enormous man.

"Fae, he was in Shongbay. He was there when . . ." Emmalee struggled to swallow at the thought of her husband and daughter. "Besides, he's a marshal. Apart from asking the king, he's more likely than anyone to know what happened to Ari."

Faeleen didn't argue after that.

They maneuvered Levick's unconscious body into the linen closet, the cramped space barely accommodating his size. They both grunted when they dropped his trunk-like arms. Emmalee leaned over, holding herself up by her knees as she caught her breath.

As they stood in silence, Faeleen's face filled with fear and confusion. "Now what?"

"Let's remove his weapons." Emmalee helped Faeleen, taking the marshal's sword and a knife strapped to his belt before standing back.

"How long will he be unconscious?"

Before Emmalee could answer, Levick stirred. His eyes fluttered open, and he groaned as he tried to sit.

Faeleen moved before he was fully alert, lunging at him.

"Where's my sister? What did you do to her?"

Levick's eyes widened, and then he scowled. He shoved Faeleen back. "Get off me, you little—"

"Tell me!" Faeleen hissed, slashing at his face with her claws. He caught her wrist despite her speed and saved himself from what would've been extremely deep gauges. Instead, the pointed talons barely grazed his cheek.

Before he could hurt Faeleen, Emmalee extended her hand and sent her magic to restrain him. He struggled but couldn't move. Apparently, that satisfied Faeleen's bloodlust for the time being.

It was enough to see the blood drain from Levick's face as realization must've seeped in.

"You . . . You're Estrada. But how . . . ?"

"Appearance-changing rune." Emmalee waved away his unspoken question. "The woman who was brought back from the Black Forest, the one with long blond hair and teal eyes," Emmalee said, keeping her voice as level as she could. "Where is she?"

Marshal Levick narrowed his eyes at Emmalee. "How do you know about her?"

"She's my sister," Faeleen snapped. "Where is she?" She still knelt next to Levick, too close for Emmalee's comfort. But as long as her magic held him still, Faeleen wasn't in any danger.

"She was executed not long ago," Levick said, glaring at Faeleen. But his confidence only lasted until he turned his attention to Emmalee.

With the temperature dropping low enough in the room for Emmalee to see her own breath, she didn't have to glance down to know that dark magic was radiating off her in waves.

"Executed." The word tasted sour in her mouth. "He killed her?"

Faeleen seemed frozen in place. And then everything came crashing down. Faeleen screamed, agony lacing her voice as she leapt at the marshal's throat.

"No, wait!" Emmalee dropped her grip on Levick to stop Faeleen. "We need to ask—"

Emmalee blinked. In one swift motion, Levick drew a hidden dagger and buried it deep into Faeleen's side. She cried out, slamming against the wall as Levick pushed her off him.

"Fae!" Emmalee screamed, but before she could rush to her friend's side, Levick moved.

He shifted to his knees, bloody knife still in hand.

"You," Emmalee hissed, her dark magic swirling in her veins. "You've taken everything from me."

"What do you—" Levick's eyes widened.

Emmalee choked. The sight of Faeleen bleeding out behind him, coupled with the confirmed loss of Ariella and the memory of her murdered family, fueled Emmalee's rage.

"Guards!" he shouted a second before Emmalee let her magic surge.

Dark tendrils of magic wrapped around Levick. He struggled, his eyes filled with terror as he swung at them with his knife. His *useless* knife.

"You were there when your men murdered my husband, my daughter." Emmalee stood above him as he writhed on the floor. "I remember you."

"No, please . . ." He wheezed out. "I-I h-have . . . wife . . . Please don't."

Emmalee almost stopped at his words.

He had a family.

One she'd likely destroy if she killed him.

But she'd had a family once too.

And because of him, they were gone.

Emmalee squeezed her fists, unleashing all her magic as it strangled the marshal. His body convulsed and fell limp.

Lifeless.

Breathing heavily, Emmalee dropped to her knees beside Faeleen, who was slumped against the wall, pale and shivering. Faeleen covered her side with her hand, but blood continued to ooze out between her fingers.

"No, no, no," Emmalee mumbled, pulling down a pile of washcloths from the shelf above her. "This wasn't supposed to happen," she whispered. "We need to get you out of the castle. There's an infirmary. Remember? We'll go there, and . . . I'll go. It's not far." Emmalee couldn't make sense of the words pouring from her mouth.

Faeleen moaned as Emmalee pressed a folded washcloth against her wound. "Ari's d-dead. She's d-dead," Faeleen whimpered.

"I know, Fae, I know. I'm so sorry." Emmalee wiped infuriating tears from her eyes. They were causing everything around her to blur. It wasn't the time to cry. She needed to get Faeleen out of the castle. She needed to find out what had happened to Evangeline. She needed to mourn Ariella.

Faeleen's breathing continued to grow shallower and shallower. Her eyes fluttered shut, and panic gripped Emmalee around the throat.

"Stay awake, Fae. Open your eyes." Emmalee raised a hand to cup Faeleen's face only to realize the washcloth she'd been holding had already soaked through with blood, leaving her hand stained and trailing blood onto Fae's pale skin.

"No, Fae," Emmalee pleaded, choking on tears and half sobs. "Open your eyes, Fae, p-please." Her magic swirled uncontrollably, responding to her grief and anger.

There had to be a way to heal her. There had to be a spell. A rune. Something.

But she hadn't brought her rune pen, and even if she had, she wouldn't know what to do.

And her magic . . . She hadn't learned any healing spells.

Why hadn't she learned any healing spells?

Emmalee pressed her forehead against Faeleen's, closing her eyes as tears fell down her cheeks.

"I . . . miss . . . my s-sister. Em . . . I d-don't w-want to d-die." Faeleen's voice was weak, and she seemed to choke on the words. "I-I'm s-scared."

Emmalee pressed a kiss to Faeleen's forehead. After all the years Ariella and Faeleen had protected her, Emmalee had failed them both.

"I'm right here, Fae," she whispered, squeezing Faeleen's hand. "Right here."

"C-cold." Faeleen shivered.

The temperature had stayed frigid in the room, and Emmalee shuddered when she realized she was the one still doing it. Her magic twisted and writhed in a massive storm in the small linen closet, throwing clean sheets and towels every which way.

"I'm sorry, Fae," Emmalee whispered, cowering against her friend. "I'm so sorry."

Her magic exploded outward in a violent tumult.

And when the storm subsided, Faeleen was gone.

Emmalee cradled her lifeless body, rocking her back and forth as she cried silent tears.

"I'll make them pay," Emmalee vowed as she pressed another kiss to Faeleen's forehead. "For you, for Ari, for Anwell and Hazel, for everyone. They will pay. *He* will pay."

She knew she was wasting time, but it felt like utter betrayal to leave Faeleen behind in the closet. And to leave her with the body of the marshal . . .

Emmalee gritted her teeth.

That wouldn't do.

Faeleen deserved better.

Levick did not.

She wanted the king to know. Wanted him to fear her. She'd made it into his castle without his knowledge. Had killed his marshal. And he would be next if she had anything to say about it.

Emmalee scooted away from Faeleen, gently laying her head on a pile of towels that had fallen in her magic storm.

With less care, she grabbed a linen sheet and Levick's knife. Using his blood, she wrote her message with her finger, staining the fabric crimson. When she was done writing, Emmalee stuck her head out of the small storage room, making sure the hallway was clear before she stepped out.

Somehow, it was still empty.

Not bothering to waste energy lifting Levick with her hands, she focused on dragging him out with her magic. And when she was finished, he sat propped against a wall with the message in blood pinned to his chest with his own knife.

"Hey!" a voice cried from the other end of the corridor. "You there, what's—stop!"

Emmalee ran. And as she sprinted down corridor after corridor, she released the last of her tears.

Anwell and Hazel were gone.

Ariella and Faeleen were gone.

Evangeline was missing.

Emmalee bit back a sob. Her ears were ringing, and she made blind turns until her lungs were on fire.

She couldn't remember what floor she was on, having gone up and down several servants' stairs. The sound of footsteps following her had stopped, and she wasn't sure how long she'd been running when she heard a cacophony of voices. People filed out into the hallway, striding towards large doors that let in a fresh breeze from outside. The front exit. Freedom. And with her disguise rune still active, it was her chance to escape the nightmare of the castle.

It was just a matter of getting out the doors unnoticed.

Slipping into the crowd was too easy. The exit was within reach.

And that's when her wrist started to itch.

Chapter 49

SILAS

Silas's voice cut through the din of the crowd. "The king sends his apologies, but for reasons I cannot disclose, the welcome ceremony is being cut short. Please make your way toward the entrance hall."

Captain Malkim stood near him, giving him a slight nod. Silas stepped away from the raised dais.

"The queen?" Silas asked, glancing behind him.

"Already in a safe room with some of the delegates. And I have a few of my commanders rounding up the rest of the Jerr Pinn guests and escorting them to other safe rooms."

"Good." Silas nodded, his attention on the crowd slowly leaking out of the throne room. "Get the rest of these guests out safely. I want boundaries put up. Look for anyone trying to sneak away. Anyone suspicious is to be held for questioning. Understood?"

"Yes, sir." Malkim saluted and jogged down the steps.

Silas followed behind him, his eyes constantly scanning the crowd. His men were working hard to move the guests out of the castle, calming the more frantic ones with gentle yet firm words.

He neared the exit to the throne room, and as he opened his mouth to bark out more orders, something—or rather someone—caught his eye.

A woman was moving through the crowd, and he blinked as her appearance shifted before his eyes. For a split second, she was short with curly bright auburn hair, but the longer he looked, her hair shortened, straightening out and darkening.

She grew several inches taller. She looked down as if she was realizing the change in her appearance at the same time. The woman had paused in the stream of people who were moving toward the main entrance. She looked back.

Silas took a step forward, his eyes widening.

The sketchbook.

He'd seen this moment before.

It was her.

Estrada.

And when her dark eyes met his, Silas's heart pounded in his chest. He pushed through the crowd, ignoring the protests of the guests he jostled. He opened his mouth to call out, to warn his guards, but the guests . . . He'd start a panic. It'd be chaos. All the easier for her to escape. If he could just get to her quickly enough, maybe she wouldn't hurt anyone else.

He just had to be fast enough.

"Move!" Silas snapped, and several people skittered out of his way. "I said move!"

Estrada's mouth curled up into a sneer as she took a step backward.

She was going to leave.

As she raised her hands, a dark mist began to swirl around her. Silas's eyes widened when he realized what she was doing.

"No!" Silas shouted, lunging forward. "Stop her!" Silas yelled, his voice barely audible as the entrance hall descended into chaos.

The mist thickened, spreading rapidly, shrouding the room in inky tendrils. Shouts and screams filled the air as guests and guards stumbled and collided in their desperate attempts to flee. The dark fog clung to his skin, cold and suffocating. It seemed to have a mind of its own, coiling around him, slowing his progress. He pushed through it, eyes fixed on Estrada's retreating figure.

But she was already too far away, disappearing into the darkness she'd created.

With a final defiant glance back at him, Estrada raised her arms, and the mist surged outward, forcing everyone back. Silas stumbled but kept his footing. By the time he regained his balance, she was gone.

The mist, however, continued to grow denser. Silas faltered when he nearly tripped on a woman who'd fallen. He helped her to her feet, guiding her toward the nearest wall.

"Wait here, and help others," he said before entering the fray again.

His men shouted orders, trying to maintain some semblance of control, but it was useless. The guests were in a frenzy, and Estrada had used it to her advantage.

"Marshal Thorne," Captain Orin called, and Silas turned to the sound of his voice.

"Here!" Silas shouted, and it wasn't until he was a foot away that he found the captain. "Estrada escaped," Silas growled. "It's too late to close the gates, but I want you to send out seven commanders and nine of their officers each into Cyanthia and the Black Forest. I want her found!"

"Yes, sir." Orin saluted and started hollering at his men.

As the mist began to dissipate, Silas cursed under his breath and then louder as he stomped back toward the throne room.

He'd seen her.

Had only been a short distance from her.

And once again, she'd slipped through his fingers.

"Marshal Thorne?" a guard called from behind him.

Silas took a deep breath, and forcing his anger into the chasms of his mind, he shifted his face to a granite expression. "Estrada was here, and I want to know exactly what parts of the castle she was in."

"Sir?" the guard said, confusion on his face.

"Estrada," Silas spat. "I want information." When the guard didn't move, Silas glared at him. "Go!"

Silas stormed down the corridors, the scowl on his face making guests and guards alike scurry out of his rampaging path. It wasn't until he was back in the empty throne room that he released the reins on his anger. With a shout of frustration, he turned and swung his fist down on the nearest thing, which happened to be one of the thick wooden tables. Pain ricocheted up his arm from his hand, and he grimaced.

"Marshal Thorne, we have something," a guard, one of Levick's commanders, said in a wavering voice.

"Speak, then," Silas barked with his back to the man. He shook out his hand to test if it was broken. It wasn't—at least not from what he could tell.

"Another body was found in a linen closet near where Marshal Levick was found."

"Levick's dead?" Silas's chest tightened.

"Yes, sir." The guard seemed surprised Silas didn't know. "It was his body that was found earlier."

Silas rubbed his jaw, then gave a brief nod. He'd process the marshal's death later, when he didn't have to manage the chaos in the castle.

"The other body—is it one of ours?" Silas's gut twisted. If Estrada had managed to kill another one of his men . . .

"A woman, sir."

Silas straightened, turning to face the guard. "Take me to her." He noted the other guards filtering into the room. "What are you all doing here? Double the number of men at every entrance and exit. I want search parties in the streets. Estrada was here." Silas pointed to the floor, his eyes narrowed. "I want her found. Move!"

Silas gestured for the guard who'd spoken to lead him to the other body. As he walked, his mind wandered down paths it had no right to travel. When one of his men had told him that Evie had escaped her cell, the panic that had coursed through him had been unmatched. What if he lost her? Silas clenched his jaw.

And when he'd seen her bruising face and the blood seeping into the collar of her tunic, his fury had clawed at him for release.

Why? He didn't understand. She was a prisoner. She'd tried to escape. And yet the sight of her injures had turned his gut as much as when she'd collapsed in Butch's office from the infection in her wrists—the infection he'd let go unnoticed.

He balled his hands into fists at his sides as he walked behind the guard. Conflicting emotions churned inside him. If Butch was injured while Estrada was present in the castle, he would never forgive himself.

"The body's in here," the guard said, opening a door to a linen closet.

Silas halted when he saw her body lying in a crumpled bloody heap at the back of the room.

He swore.

Chapter 50

EVANGELINE

Evangeline leaned her head back against the wall, staring at the ceiling of the safe room as she had in her cell for months. She hadn't spoken since the king had moved across the room, eventually sliding down the wall to sit on the floor. It had been amusing to her when she'd taken the cot and seen the confusion in his eyes, even if he'd been holding a sword to her throat at the time. And while proper customs and manners dictated she give up her seat, she refused.

Her head throbbed, and her neck and cheek stung. But none of it compared to the way her body had ached when she'd gotten sick from the cuffs. And to be wearing them again left her body trembling even as her mind told her she wouldn't get sick from just a few hours.

Evangeline ventured a glance at Butch only to find him staring at her with an intense gaze, which he'd been doing since they'd fallen silent. It made her stomach turn, and she looked away again.

"She killed him, didn't she?" he finally asked after what felt like twenty minutes of silence. "Estrada."

Evangeline frowned at the ceiling before turning it on him. Silence would be so much easier. However, she'd already shattered that option. Maybe she could do more if she could make him see reason. If that was even possible . . .

"Emmalee wouldn't be that foolish. She'd never enter this place," Evangeline said, narrowing her eyes.

Butch tilted his head, adjusting his legs so they were straight in front of him. "I think you're wrong."

"And I think you're inept." She shrugged, staring back at the ceiling. Evangeline could feel him watching her, but she closed her eyes, keeping them closed until he spoke again.

"You don't think she'd try to come after you?"

"No," Evangeline said, tasting the bitterness of the lie on her tongue. She didn't need or want the king to know that one of her biggest concerns was her friend doing something irrational to get her out and getting caught in doing so. It would negate the sacrifice Evangeline had made in the woods however many months ago. But Ariella's words floated back to her. She'd said Emmalee was trying to save her. If she was in the castle tonight . . .

"She's killed others," Butch continued, his voice even despite the subject matter.

Evangeline remained emotionless. She didn't want to believe that Emmalee had killed anyone, but she could still remember the look of determination in her friend's eyes after Evangeline had rescued her from the boulder field. The look had been deadly.

"And you haven't?"

"I'm the king."

"So, you get a free pass. Got it." Evangeline rolled her eyes. Even with her sharp tone on the outside, her heart ached on the inside. Her mind went to Ariella again. He'd killed her, likely without a second thought. She narrowed her eyes at him. "You killed Em's family," Evangeline spat, tilting her chin down to glare at him. "I'm not saying she's right, but neither are you."

"Her magic is—"

"Natural. It was handed down to her just like everyone else. Just like me."

Butch bristled at her words. "It's corrupt."

"And murdering a two-year-old girl isn't? Your logic is twisted, Butch. The sooner you realize that, the sooner you'll become the king we all thought you'd be."

His face darkened, and she shifted farther back on the cot when he stood. With her arms chained behind her, there wasn't much she could do to protect herself should he attack. Captain Malkim had proven that.

"It'd be wise of you to think before you speak," he said, his voice a low growl. "I am your king, and I deserve respect."

Evangeline's heart raced, not because she was nervous, but because he had spoken words she'd heard before—from her stepfather. She stood too, glowering at him.

"Respect, *Your Majesty*, is earned. It's not a right." Her gaze flicked down to his hand, which wavered by a knife handle on his belt.

A vein in his forehead bulged, and he turned the color of an eggplant the longer she held his glare.

"And you should know better than most the positive side to magic," Evangeline added when he didn't say anything.

"What do you mean?" he asked, his voice still gruff, though it appeared by his rising eyebrow that some of his anger had shifted to curiosity.

"The magic that sent you flying twenty feet off the top of the hill in the boulder field is the same magic that saved your life when you were about to be killed in a glorified ditch." She hadn't thought the confession through before it'd already slipped out from between her lips.

It took Butch a second before he responded. "I'd almost forgotten."

Evangeline scoffed. "Of course you have. Quick to forget the positive, yet you cling to the negatives."

He shot her a glare, then rolled his shoulders back and seemed to relax a moment later. Butch ran his fingers through his hair before smoothing down his short beard. "I suppose I owe you a thank-you."

She snorted, shaking her head. "I didn't remind you for your gratitude." Evangeline sat back down.

"Why?"

"Why say it, or—"

"Why save me if you so clearly despise every aspect of my person?" He leaned against the wall.

Evangeline snorted, unable to keep a small grin from crossing her lips. "It was an accident. I didn't want to see anyone else get hurt. You were disguised; I didn't know you were . . . *you*. I only realized after I'd saved your life."

Butch nodded, his intense stare resting on her once more. "If you had known, would you have done the same?"

She didn't answer right away. It was a question she'd asked herself afterward, and she had been unsure then too. "Would you keep someone who has done nothing but possess magic as a prisoner in your dungeon?"

"How does that—wait, *you* attacked me. That's—"

"I'm not talking about me. I know what I did; I protected my friend. But Odette hasn't done anything, yet you've kept her as a prisoner for over a year."

"Odette? The woman who tried to escape with you?"

Evangeline nodded, sitting straighter. "You've held her prisoner despite the trial being inconclusive. You can't expect—"

"It was conclusive."

"What?"

"She may have told you it was inconclusive, but she was convicted. Your friend has magic, and—"

"You punished her for it."

"I *spared* her. My council wanted her dead. I saved her life. Put off her execution. She was grateful, as you should be."

Evangeline shook her head. "But she said—"

"Not everyone is as proud of their heritage as you and Estrada," Butch muttered, his voice filled with bitterness.

She tensed. "I never said anything about being proud. But I am not ashamed, nor should she be."

Butch picked up his crown, which he'd discarded early into their stay in the safe room. He ran his fingers over the jewels, a scowl on his face as he stared at it. When he eventually looked up at her again, it was gone.

"You're fond of her."

"Odette?"

He nodded. It felt like a trap. They'd used Faeleen against Ariella. If he was planning to do the same with Odette . . .

"Why?" Evangeline asked, her jaw set.

Silence returned for a few more moments as he continued to feel the crown while keeping eye contact with her. "Let's make a deal," he drawled. "I will spare Odette the punishment owed her for breaking out of the dungeon if you work with Silas and me to find Estrada."

Evangeline was already shaking her head before he'd finished. "No."

"Are you sure?" He raised an eyebrow, his voice a silky tone that left Evangeline feeling like she'd been wrapped in a spider's web.

"Yes."

"The punishment is death." His tone flattened, and his face darkened. "Really? You want to condemn your friend to death?"

Evangeline struggled to swallow, her chest tightening as though all the air had left the room. Odette was going to be put to death because Evangeline had been too stubborn. Because she'd forced the handmaid to let Odette escape with her. She'd all but condemned Odette to death herself.

It was exactly what she'd expected. He was trying to use Odette against her. And the person who would lose most would eventually be Emmalee if the king had his way.

But she'd already failed Odette not once but twice—first in the alley when she was initially arrested, and now with the failed escape attempt . . .

Evangeline rose to her feet, using her shoulder to move a piece of hair that had stuck to the side of her face. "If I help you, it will be on my terms."

Maybe there was a way to save Odette and Emmalee.

A double cross to the king. Once Odette was safe—

"Which are?" he asked, his voice a little too eager.

Evangeline bit her lip. She had to be careful, think through the demands. They had to be worth the chance that she might accidentally get Emmalee in trouble. But if she wasn't in a cell, maybe she could be more help to her friend. Evangeline lifted her chin. "If I help you, Odette goes free with no record of her wrongs kept."

"Done."

"*And* you and your council will instate a new law that gives a fair trial to everyone, whether they have magic or not. No more killing first and asking questions never."

The king balked at her words, the muscles around his shoulders and neck tensing. "That's outrageous."

"It's the only way I'll help. Show me you're willing to change, Butch," Evangeline said, her voice matter-of-fact. And while she intended to help them find Emmalee, her mind was already coming up with ways in which to turn on the agreement and escape with her friend. But those thoughts were cut short when Butch shook his head.

"Absolutely not."

"Fine. Then kill me now," Evangeline said, nodding toward his belt where his sword and knife rested. "Prove to me that you're no different from your father and his father before him."

The king followed her line of sight, and he rested his hand on the hilt of his sword. For a second, Evangeline questioned whether she had taken a step too far. His brow furrowed, and he closed his eyes. She could tell from the look of concentration that he was trying to control himself.

"You ask too much," he said, his voice low. When he looked back at her, his gaze felt heavy.

"Then that's on you."

Chapter 51

LENORA

Lenora paced inside her room, waiting for Merla and Kaylene to enter. It was the morning after the disastrous festivities, which had ended with her and quite a few of the delegates from Jerr Pinn being ushered into a safe room and kept there for what felt like hours. Her husband had not joined them.

It was only when Marshal Thorne had come to let them out of the safe room that Lenora found out her husband had been taken to a different one and that he was all right. Merla and Kaylene had stayed with Lenora throughout the time in the safe room.

Lord Aric and the others from Jerr Pinn who'd been with her had asked her questions, none of which she'd been able to answer.

Even more frustrating, not a single guard cared to answer her own questions. She was the queen, for goodness' sake. Thankfully, the guards had taken them to one of the larger safe rooms. She couldn't imagine spending the hour or longer in one of the smaller rooms with only one cot and little else.

The genial small talk had tapered off after half an hour, allowing Lenora to slip into a bout of worry. Worry that something had gone wrong with the escape plan. Worry that it would somehow be traced back to her. Worry that her husband had somehow gotten caught up in it. If he had gotten hurt . . . Lenora couldn't bear the thought.

Now, as Lenora continued to stride back and forth across her room, she wrung her hands. She could still hear the urgency in Marshal Thorne's voice as he told her to meet the group of guards outside the throne room. He had only begun to address the rest of the crowd as Lenora and the delegates reached the exit.

A knock on her door had Lenora pausing. "Enter," she said, her voice not as strong as she'd hoped it to be.

Kaylene and Merla came in, the latter with a tray for breakfast on her hip.

"Good morning, Your Majesty," Merla said, placing the tray on a table near the door. "How are you feeling this morning?"

"Close the door," Lenora said, the words coming out quieter and quicker than she had anticipated.

When they were alone in the room, Kaylene poured Lenora a cup of tea and joined Lenora and Merla near the window.

"Did you find out what happened last night?" Lenora asked, accepting the cup from her friend. She switched her attention from one handmaid to the other. The two women exchanged glances, both of their expressions saddening.

"She was caught," Merla eventually said. "Both of them were."

"Both?" Lenora asked, her mind racing. There was only supposed to be one jailbreak.

"She insisted that the woman in the cell next to hers be released as well, otherwise she wouldn't leave."

Lenora didn't comment, knowing Merla had made the same decision she would've if their roles had been reversed. "What happened?"

"From what I heard, she didn't even make it out of the castle," Merla said.

"And is she—"

"She's back in the dungeon." Merla didn't let Lenora finish her question before answering it. "She'll probably be executed, but the guards seem to think, with the delegates still visiting, the king will put it off. They are quite magic friendly."

"I heard they're adding extra security to the dungeon until he makes a decision," Kaylene added.

With each bit of bad news, Lenora's stomach twisted more. "So, they ended the welcome ball because of the jailbreak?"

Merla shook her head. "Marshal Levick was found dead. Murdered by the sound of it."

Lenora raised her hand to her chest, her eyes widening. "What? Who killed him?"

"No one would say," Kaylene said. "Apparently, someone with dark magic was in the entrance hall. Sent the guests into a panic."

After several seconds, Lenora whispered, "Estrada was . . ."

"I don't know," Merla said, patting Lenora's arm. "But they haven't found anything that connects you. You're safe, Your Majesty."

"The note—"

"I don't know what she did with it, but no one has mentioned anything," Merla answered. "What I *do* know, though, is that many of the female guests from Jerr Pinn, including Lady Layanna and Lady Akina, are expecting you for midafternoon tea. Should I tell them you'll be joining them soon?"

Lenora sighed, glancing down at the teacup she already held in her hands. She had no desire to sit around and waste time with worthless small talk or to be pestered with questions she couldn't answer about the previous night's events. However, she was sure that her husband would have Marshal Thorne investigating the prisoner's escape. So, hoping to remove suspicion from herself, Lenora agreed.

The thought of Marshal Thorne reminded Lenora of a question she had wanted to ask Merla since the banquet.

"Why did Thorne stop you when you came back into the throne room?"

Merla's brow furrowed. "He wanted to know where I had been."

Lenora struggled to swallow. "What did you tell him?"

"That I was having my monthly cycle and needed to refresh," she said, a glint in her eyes.

Lenora choked on her laughter. "Good. That's good." Lenora took a breath as relief flowed through her. It was short and believable and had likely prevented further questions. The perfect lie.

"Send word to the female guests from Jerr Pinn. I'll eat breakfast now, then prepare to join them for tea," Lenora said, sipping from the cup.

"Shall I stay?" Kaylene asked as Merla curtsied and left.

"Yes."

By the time Lenora finished breakfast and joined the others in the small family room in the west wing on the second floor, some of her nerves she'd collected from the night before had begun to fade.

But even as she sat down across from Akina, who was reclining on a chaise longue, Lenora had to fight the urge to send Kaylene or Merla back down to the dungeon to check on the prisoner. She knew it was too much of a risk, especially with the heightened security. But she wanted more answers.

"Quite a night, wasn't it?" Akina asked, grinning at her. "I would say you've certainly outdone yourself when it comes to entertainment."

"Akina," her mother scolded from a nearby armchair.

"It's all right," Lenora said, forcing a smile onto her lips. "I agree. Though I wouldn't say it was planned. I would've preferred a normal night. But I'm glad you were entertained, Akina."

"Have you received any more news on what occurred?" Lady Layanna asked, lifting a teacup to her lips. She sipped from it and placed it down on the side table before folding her hands in her lap.

Lenora thanked a servant as she poured some tea and handed her the cup. "Unfortunately, I haven't had a chance to speak with my husband yet. I'm just as much in the dark as you."

"Oh, I doubt that," Akina said, a smirk on her lips. "I'm sure the royal guards are more willing to speak to you than they were to any of us."

"I wish that were the case," Lenora said, noting how the truth tasted sweeter in her mouth than the lies. "They won't speak unless my husband gives them the freedom to do so."

"That's . . . unusual. You're their queen, are you not?"

"I—"

"And where is the king this morning?" another woman asked.

The question caught Lenora off guard. "I assumed he was meeting with the male delegates. Is he not?"

Lady Layanna shook her head. "Not without me he's not." She nodded to a few of the other women in the room. "We are representatives for the country just as much as our husbands and male counterparts. If your husband is only meeting with the men, then he is only meeting with half of our leadership. I do hope that's not the case." Lady Layanna's tone held a bite.

Lenora frowned, sipping her tea, which was hotter than she preferred. Her husband, though terrible at planning ceremonies, was typically very hospitable and wholly focused on guests. Something wasn't right.

"You don't think it's something serious, do you?" Akina asked when Lenora glanced at her.

"I'm sure it's nothing. He's likely following up with whatever happened last night. Nothing to worry about." Lenora nodded her head.

"You're sure?" another woman asked, raising an eyebrow.

311

Instead of responding—she couldn't trust her voice not to betray her—Lenora smiled and sipped the tea.

Akina looked like she was going to continue to push, but to Lenora's relief, someone knocked on the door. Kaylene answered it, stepping back when Marshal Thorne entered the room.

"I apologize for interrupting," he said, bowing to Lenora and inclining his head toward the other women. "The king would like a word with you, Your Majesty," he said, and the smile on his face looked as forced as Lenora's felt.

"Of course," she said, rising to her feet. "If you'll excuse me, ladies."

The other women nodded to her as she left the room. Kaylene followed her out.

When the door closed, Lenora paused, as did Marshal Thorne.

"What happened last night, Silas?" Lenora asked, all air of formality vanishing from her voice. She rarely called the marshal by his given name but hadn't been able to stop it before it slipped from her lips.

Marshal Thorne's eyes widened for a moment before he glanced at Kaylene. He returned his steady gaze to Lenora. "The king has asked that I escort you to him." He kept going even though Lenora opened her mouth to start arguing. "He has some things he would like to discuss with you."

Without allowing for any retort, Marshal Thorne turned on his heels and started down the hallway. Instead of trying to convince Marshal Thorne to talk, Lenora began to plan how she would speak with her husband.

She had learned over the years that he did not respond well to accusations—even subtle ones—and she had a list she could unleash on him: he had abandoned her in the middle of a banquet; he had left her with unanswered questions for hours; and he had all but forgotten his kingly and host duties toward the delegates, leaving her with the weight of the responsibility. She knew it would not land well. Instead, she began prioritizing which questions she would ask first.

By the time they reached her husband's study and Marshal Thorne knocked on the door, she felt better prepared. However, that was only until Marshal Thorne informed Kaylene that Butch wished to speak to Lenora alone. Once again, the desire to argue filled Lenora, but she pinched her lips shut and walked through the door he was holding open instead.

"Good morning, or I suppose we're nearing afternoon," Butch said, rising from his desk. His eyes held dark circles beneath them, and the smile he offered her was weak. But he still stepped out from behind the desk to kiss her hand. "How are you?"

"If I'm honest, I'm quite shaken," Lenora said, pulling her hand out of his. It was a true statement, but it had to do more with the failed rescue attempt than being trapped in a safe room with the delegates.

However, since her husband was none the wiser, he must've assumed it was the latter.

"I know, and I'm sorry it's taken me this long to meet with you. I've been in meetings all night," he said, running a hand through his blond hair. "Something happened during the banquet, and—"

"What? No one will tell me anything," Lenora said, taking a seat across from the desk he leaned against. It wasn't entirely true. Her handmaids had passed on quite a bit of information, but she wanted to hear it from Butch.

He pressed his tongue into his cheek, glaring at the wall over her. With a sigh, he shook his head. "Two prisoners escaped from the dungeon."

Lenora raised her eyebrows, doing what she could to feign surprise. "How? I didn't think that was possible."

"I didn't either. And . . ." His voice died out, and he rubbed his face with both hands. "Marshal Levick is dead."

Lenora froze. She had almost forgotten, having been too focused on her own involvement in the prisoner's escape. "Dead?"

Butch nodded, biting his bottom lip. "He was found near the dungeon."

She could barely find the strength in her voice to ask the question gnawing at the back of her mind. Was she the reason the marshal was dead? "Did the prisoners . . . ?"

"No," Butch said, his voice lower. "There was a message addressed to me and traces of dark magic."

"Estrada," Lenora whispered, her gaze lowering to the floor before her. Her mind swirled. She had hardly considered that the woman who had captured her many months earlier would reappear in her life—let alone in the castle.

"I'm sorry, Lenora. I tried to do everything I could to secure this place. But she slipped in unnoticed and killed Marshal Levick."

"Did she free the prisoners?" Lenora asked, raising her gaze back to her husband's face. Though he did not seem to suspect her, she was slowly devising a plan to make sure things stayed that way.

His shoulders slumped under what seemed like an enormous weight. "Not directly. At least, that's what the men are telling me. And when I spoke to one of the prisoners, it didn't seem like she was aware of Estrada's presence in the castle."

"She? Which prisoners escaped?" Lenora asked, tilting her head.

Butch scratched his jaw a few times, grimacing before he actually answered. "They didn't escape. They tried." He pushed his hair back. "The one you saw in the infirmary and one of the prisoners she's apparently gotten attached to."

"And you've already spoken to them?"

"I have."

Lenora straightened out the skirt of her dress, folding her hands in her lap when she was finished. "And you can't get either to tell you what happened?"

"No."

More relief spread through Lenora, and she hid it by lowering her gaze back down to the floor. Not only had Estrada's friend not talked, she also clearly hadn't given up the letter that would've exposed Lenora fully.

Maybe it's only a matter of time, Lenora thought, her panic rising again. If the prisoners talked, not only was she herself at risk, but Merla and Kaylene had willingly helped her as well.

"I have increased the security within the castle again, but I felt it was only right to tell you about Estrada. I wanted you to hear it from me." Butch met her gaze when she glanced up. "I doubt she'll try to rescue her friend again right away, but I have no doubt that the prisoner is still high up on her list of priorities."

Lenora nodded, finding no need to respond. Besides, her mind was already departing to the thoughts and feelings she'd experienced during her time with Estrada. Fear at first. A desire to see her handmaids again. And then the one she had not been expecting: freedom. Not physically, of course, since she had been abducted and held as bait, but emotionally. No pressure to behave in a certain way. No royal duties to fulfill. No one to please but herself.

"I must meet with some of the delegates to apologize for my absence, but if you need anything from me—" His sentence cut off as Lenora rose to her feet.

"Lady Layanna was asking when you were planning to meet with the rest of them. You know she and some of the other women are leaders in Jerr Pinn, right?"

Butch nodded. "I'm aware. I'm supposed to meet with all of them and my council after lunch to discuss the proposed trade agreements."

"Oh . . . Well, good luck, then." She inclined her head, though some small part of her had hoped he might invite her to join the conversation with the delegates after hearing that women were just as much leaders as the men. She tried not to let the disappointment show on her face.

"Lenora," he said, his voice more serious than before. "These things I've told you have been in confidence. Do not share them with anyone else, especially our visitors. We don't need the whole world to know how easily an enemy slipped into the castle unknown."

Chapter 52

SILAS

Silas descended the dismally lit steps to the dungeon, the flickering torches casting long shadows against the stone walls. He strode through the dungeon corridor, heading in the opposite direction from where Evie's cell had previously been. Under his direct order, Evie and the other prisoner she'd escaped with had been separated and were now on opposite sides of the dungeon. His footsteps echoed off the walls, and any whispers from prisoners died off as he passed.

When he got to her cell, he watched her for a moment. She sat at the back of the cell, staring at names past prisoners had somehow carved into the stone.

Her cell was farthest from the stairs, and none of the cells around her held other prisoners.

"What do you want, *Silas*?" She wrinkled her nose as she said his name. His first name. When had she learned his first name?

The sound of it on her lips disrupted his thoughts for longer than he cared to admit.

She still hadn't looked at him, so he waited to respond until she did. He held up the small medical kit and the lantern.

"Don't want you getting another infection."

"Why didn't you send Helena or Dianna?"

"They're busy." And they were, the last time he'd checked. Several guests had been injured in the stampede Estrada had caused. "I wanted to make sure you were all right."

When Silas entered the cell, she shifted, putting her back against the wall with her legs curled under her. Silas stepped toward her after the door closed behind him. He took a deep breath, nearly choking on the sour smells of the dungeon.

Silas knelt next to her, placing the box of supplies and the lantern beside him.

"Let me see," Silas ordered, his gaze already locked on the column of her neck. The way it moved when she swallowed. The way her crimson blood had stained a dark brown. The cut marring her perfect pale skin.

Evie didn't move, and when Silas's gaze traveled back to her face, he caught her watching him.

"Who did this to you?" he asked, his voice low.

She remained silent, her gaze fixed on his face. A dark bruise covered her cheek, and before he knew what he was doing, he was reaching across the space and cupping her chin in his hand. With a gentle tug, he positioned her face to see the bruise better.

Fire flared in his gut. One of his men had done this. He was sure of it.

"Tell me who hurt you," he said, his patience wearing thin. But the anger wasn't for her. No. He needed to know which of his men had laid a hand on Evie, and then he would give a very, *very* clear reminder that she was off-limits.

Evie leaned back, pulling her face from his hand. When she looked up at him, her eyes were filled with a mixture of confusion and what he'd come to recognize as fear and her infuriating obstinance. "It doesn't matter," she muttered.

"It matters to me," he replied, his voice firmer.

"Why do you care?"

"I—" Silas's words caught, and he cleared his throat. "It's my responsibility to make sure my men behave like men, not boys. Tell me, Evie, so I can make this right."

She regarded him for a moment longer before lowering her chin and dropping her gaze to her lap. "Malkim."

Fates. The captain was one of his best. And yet he'd crossed a line. A surge of irritation flooded through Silas, and he clenched his hands into fists to distract himself. He took another breath, forcing his anger to remain under control, for his emotions to remain composed.

"Thank you," he said, the words snipped. He opened the small medical kit and took out a clean damp cloth. "I'm going to take care of that cut now," he said softly, leaning closer. "Is that all right?"

Evie held his gaze for a moment before nodding once. She didn't resist as he moved closer, gently lifting her chin with his thumb. His fingers brushed against her soft skin as he cleaned the wound on her neck. She must've been holding her breath. He was.

Silas's entire focus rested on Evie. The way she gazed up at him with her round brown eyes. The way she didn't flinch from his touch, even as he cleaned away the dry blood. The way she let out a soft sigh when his fingers stroked the skin just below her ear.

As he finished bandaging her neck, their eyes met again. The rest of the dungeon seemed to melt away as her gaze dropped to his mouth, then shifted back up to his eyes. For a second, neither of them moved. He leaned over her, inches from her face. The heat of her body mingled with his, and Silas's hand lingered on her cheek. Her breath danced over his skin. The urge to lean in and close the distance overwhelmed him, but he held back.

Evie was the first to break the spell, her gaze dropping to the floor as he pulled away and sat back on his heels. Silas's mind raced. He'd never been so enraptured by a woman before, and it unnerved him.

Trying to hide his shaking hands, he packed up the medical kit and grabbed the lantern in his other hand.

He stood abruptly. His movements were jerky and uncoordinated.

"I should go," he said, his voice gruff. "I need to . . . have a *word* with one of my captains."

Evie looked up at him, and something in her gaze mirrored the confusion he felt inside.

Silas turned and left the cell, the door clanging behind him. He ascended the stairs without realizing it, his thoughts fully captured by the woman he'd left below. He paused for a moment at the top to collect himself.

He had to get her out of his head. She was dangerous, not just because of the things he'd seen in the sketchbook, but because of the spell she'd somehow cast over him. No one else besides Butch had been able to hold such power over him.

She was dangerous all right.

SILAS STOOD IN the center of the training room. He'd long since lost his jacket and rolled up his sleeves. His muscles were tense, coiled like a spring ready to release.

He'd called Captain Malkim there for a reason, and he intended to make his point clear. The door creaked open, and Malkim stepped in, his eyes scanning the room before settling on Silas.

"Sir," Malkim said, his tone respectful but wary as he saluted. "You wanted to speak with me?"

Silas returned the salute, then nodded toward the barrel of practice weapons. "Choose."

Malkim hesitated for a moment before choosing a stave and moving to the opposite end of the mat.

"Do you know why you're here?" Silas asked, circling Malkim like a lion prowling around its prey.

The captain tightened his grip on the stave. "I believe so, sir."

Silas didn't wait for further explanation. He lunged forward, the stave slicing through the air. Malkim barely had time to react, raising his own weapon to block the strike. The impact sent a jolt through Silas's arm, but he was already moving back before the sensation ended.

"You laid a hand on the prisoner," Silas said, his voice cold. "And a knife."

Malkim struggled to maintain his stance as Silas pressed forward with a series of rapid, precise attacks. "I—"

"You had no authority to do so." Silas caught Malkim in the stomach with the stave, and he doubled over.

"I know, sir. I lost control."

"Lost control?" Silas spat, his mind flashing images of the cut on Evie's throat. The bruise on her cheek. The blood on her temple. "You think that's an excuse?"

Malkim staggered back. "No, sir. It's not."

Silas ordered him to stand up, and Malkim returned to a fighting stance. "You are one of my captains, Malkim."

"I know."

"You should know better."

The clash of wood echoed through the training room. Malkim's breaths came in ragged gasps as he tried to keep up with Silas's relentless pace.

"I regret it, sir," Malkim said, his voice strained. "I let my anger get the better of me. It won't happen again."

319

Silas paused for a moment, his staff hovering in the air. Wasn't he letting his anger get the best of him? Yes. Yes, he was. His anger, his strange need to protect Evie, pushed him forward. He struck again, this time knocking Malkim's stave out of his hand and sending him to the ground.

"If it does," Silas said, standing over Malkim and directing the tip of his staff at Malkim's face, "you will be relieved of your duty." Silas's chest heaved with exertion. "Do I make myself clear?"

Malkim nodded, wiping sweat from his brow. "Yes, sir. Crystal."

Silas took a step back, lowering his staff. "Get up," he ordered.

Malkim scrambled to his feet, his movements clearly meant to hide any stiffness or pain.

Silas looked his captain up and down. He nodded, finally allowing some of his anger to dissipate. He'd made his point, and by the genuine sincerity scrawled on Malkim's face, he truly was sorry. Still, though, the man had hit Evie.

"Pick it up," Silas said, nodding toward Malkim's abandoned practice weapon. "We go again until you win."

Chapter 53

BUTCH

Butch sat at the head of the long council table, his eyes bloodshot from lack of sleep. Tense silence filled the room, which held more chairs than normal. Apart from his council members, all sixteen of the delegates from Jerr Pinn sat around the table, making it feel smaller than normal. Lord Aric and Lady Layanna sat closest to him.

His council members had just finished presenting the proposal for trade agreements, and in the silence that followed, Butch felt the last of his patience fading away.

He needed sleep.

He needed to write a consolation letter for Levick's wife.

He needed an answer from Jerr Pinn.

He needed to get the prisoner's words from the night before out of his head.

He needed Estrada's head on a spike.

"You need to clarify something for us, Your Majesty," Lord Aric said, stirring Butch from his thoughts.

"Please, go on," Butch said, shifting in his seat so as to face Lord Aric better.

"This search for the sorceress named Emmalee Estrada. How much of your resources have you poured into it?"

Butch refrained from rubbing his temples. He'd known it was a mistake to inform the delegates of Estrada and her interruption of the welcome ball.

"Might I ask what this has to do with trading before I answer?" Butch asked, scratching the scruff on his chin.

"As you know, we do not support your war on magic," one of the other delegates said. By the man's violet eyes, Butch had a feeling the man had some percentage of dryad blood in his veins. Of course he didn't support the war.

"I'm aware," Butch said, inclining his head.

"We cannot overlook the hostility toward those with magic, like Estrada, whom you persecute," another delegate added.

Butch clenched his jaw, his fingers drumming on the table. "This war my grandfather started began in order to restore peace to the country," he said, trying to keep his voice calm. "Estrada is a prime example of the destruction King Kylian sought to end. She has caused untold damage, not to mention she abducted my own wife."

Lady Layanna leaned forward, her eyes narrowing. "We are aware of what took place, Your Majesty. And while we do not condone the woman's actions and threats against the queen, neither can we condone your continued approach to condemn all magic users indiscriminately. This is not justice, Your Majesty. This is persecution of an entire people group."

Butch opened his mouth to argue, but the blasted prisoner's words from the safe room echoed in his mind.

He took a deep breath, his gaze meeting Lady Layanna's. "I understand your concerns," he said slowly, each word measured. "I would like to think that creating a trade agreement between our two countries would be a step in the right direction, considering Jerr Pinn's stance on magic. Wouldn't you agree?"

A man with silver eyes and pointed ears spoke next. "It would if we could assure our people they would be safe entering Phildeterre. However, we can't."

"We could—"

"The hostility in this country is not just in this castle—it's spread to your people." The man spoke over Councilman Clive, who tried to argue. "Can you promise us, Your Majesty, that if I, an elf, entered your marketplaces, ears showing and all, I would not be accosted by some magic-hating civilian?"

"In other words, Your Majesty," Lady Layanna said in a taut voice, "can you assure us that your people are willing to change?"

Butch glanced at his council members. He could think of several of them who would not change even if it meant giving up their position on the council.

"What if I could show you we are moving in the right direction?" Butch asked, avoiding the question in a way he hoped would go unnoticed.

"It's the only way I'll help. Show me you're willing to change, Butch."

"Go on," one of the delegates said as Butch took a deep breath.

If this worked . . .

"I'm in the process of making a new law that will give a fair trial to everyone, whether they have magic or not." The words left Butch's mouth before he could process them.

The room fell silent, and his council members regarded him with wide eyes and slack jaws.

Lord Aric raised an eyebrow, clearly intrigued. "A fair trial? Is that not something magic folk already receive?"

"Not according to my grandfather. But it's something I intend to change."

Some of his council members exchanged panicked whispers, and Councilman Macaw was trying to get Butch's attention at the end of the table without making any noise.

Lady Layanna whispered into her husband's ear, a stern expression on her face. The other delegates whispered amongst themselves.

"That is certainly a significant step, King Butch. But words alone are not enough. We need to see action," Lord Aric finally said

Butch nodded. "Of course. I understand. But this is a step toward change, is it not?" The words tasted sour in his mouth. He didn't like the new law idea, not a bit. But if it won the Jerr Pinn delegation and Estrada's friend to his side, he could find it in himself to stomach it.

The other delegates murmured amongst themselves for several long seconds. Lord Aric and Lady Layanna exchanged a glance, a silent communication clearly passing between them.

Finally, Lord Aric spoke. "We appreciate your willingness to take this step, Your Majesty." The "but" was evident even before Lord Aric continued. "But we cannot commit to signing the treaty until we see significant change implemented and succeeding."

A pang of frustration flashed through Butch, and he gritted his teeth as he forced his mouth into a pleasant smile. "I understand your position," he said, even as his stomach and the hope he carried plummeted off a cliff. "Jerr Pinn's neutrality is respected, of course, and I hope you all will reconsider once you see our progress."

Lady Layanna stood, and many others followed suit as she kept her steady gaze on Butch. "We will be watching closely, Your Majesty. Show us that your words are not empty promises."

The delegates rose and began to file out of the room. Butch watched them go as exhaustion weighed down on his eyelids.

His council members stayed behind, much to his chagrin.

"What was that?"

"A law you're to put into effect as soon as possible," Butch said, rubbing his brows as he responded to Councilman Clive. "That, and a waste of my time, apparently."

"It was foolishness, boy," Councilman Macaw snapped.

A second later, Butch was on his feet, his hands braced on the table as he glared daggers at his father's councilmen.

"Listen to me carefully, men. I am trying to pull Phildeterre out from possible destruction. If that means making nice with the magic-loving Southerners, then so be it. I don't like it either. But you will pass that law, and you will be respectful to our guests. We need allies outside of ourselves." He turned his ire on Councilman Macaw. "And if I hear a word of dissent, I will have your position stripped from you before you can beg for mercy. Is that understood, councilmen?" The words tasted of acid, and Butch made sure to hold each and every one of their glares before slamming both hands down on the table. "I *said*. Is. That. Understood?"

"Yes, sire."

"Of course, Your Majesty."

"Yes."

The mutterings of his ignorant council echoed in his ears as he stormed out of his council room.

That was *not* how that meeting was supposed to go.

He needed a drink.

Maybe a bath.

And definitely a nap.

Chapter 54

EVANGELINE

Evangeline sat on the cold stone floor of her new cell, staring at the wall next to her. The worst part wasn't the cold or the darkness—it was the isolation. She missed Odette desperately. The separation gnawed at her like rats on bones, making every moment feel like an eternity. The worry for her friend and what the king might do to her after their failed escape attempt never left. It was a never-ending cloud pressing down on her until she couldn't breathe.

She wrapped her arms around her knees. What if Emmalee had been foolish enough to try infiltrating the castle? The thought sent a shiver down her spine. Emmalee was brave, but her bravery seemed to stroll hand in hand with recklessness as soon as her emotions got the best of her, especially when Emmalee thought she had planned everything. And if she'd gotten hurt. Or arrested . . .

The dam broke. Evangeline buried her face in her hands and sobbed, the sound echoing off the stone walls. Every negative thought crashed down on her at once.

It seemed like she cried for hours, and when the sun rose, shining a tiny ray of light through the window high above her, Evangeline realized it *had* been hours. She'd cried through the whole night.

Evangeline wiped her cheeks, wincing when she pressed too hard on the bruised one.

That shifted her mind to another place she didn't want to go. To Silas kneeling beside her, a breath away. To the intoxicating sensation of his fingers brushing her skin. To the heat that'd flooded her stomach at his touch on her chin, forcing her to look at him. To those beautiful crystal eyes that seemed to see right through her to her core.

She tried to banish the thoughts. She had no desire to think of Thorne—of Silas—with, well, desire. But some tiny voice in the back of her mind told her resistance was futile. He wasn't just attractive—he was also kind, and he genuinely seemed to care. She'd witnessed the fury in his face when she'd finally told him who'd hurt her. He'd been . . . protective . . . of her.

To distract herself, Evangeline turned to the wall and scanned the names that'd been carved there. She'd tried to read them earlier, but the moonlight hadn't been bright enough. Instead, she'd traced the ridges with her fingers. There had to be hundreds of names scrawled in different handwriting.

She crawled closer. How many of the people who'd sat where she sat had gotten out alive? Again, she lifted a finger and traced the names as she read them.

Her breath caught.

Wren Shry.

Her father's name. His handwriting.

"How?" she whispered, following the sharp lines.

A shiver ran down her spine. Her father's name, here, in this awful place. Had he not abandoned her and her mother, leaving them alone and her mother desperate for support, even if it came from a wicked man? Had he been imprisoned in this cell before he'd left his family? Or had he been arrested after he'd disappeared that night so many years ago?

Evangeline traced his name, her fingers brushing against the cold rough wall. Had he actually left the prison, or . . . ?

She choked at the terrible new thought. Had he died there, alone and forgotten? What if he had?

She trembled as guilt flooded through her. What if, after all the years she'd spent trying to forget the man she thought abandoned them, hating him for leaving her vulnerable to Jonathan Dipthy's abuse, her father had been trapped and praying for the day he'd be reunited with his family? What if he'd sat there, thinking of them? Longing for his wife? Missing his daughter? What if he'd died there, knowing he'd never see them again? Evangeline's throat tightened at the thought.

Her eyes filled with tears again, but this time for a different reason. This time she cried for a little girl in a bookshop who believed her father when he said he loved her, right before he snuck out the back of the shop and left her life

326

forever. Wren Shry, the man who'd left her and her mother to fend for themselves. The man who'd all but pushed her mother into the arms of Jonathan Dipthy, the stepfather who'd abused her until she left home at twenty-one.

Evangeline had tried to forget her father. Had tried to erase him from her memory. But seeing his name in his handwriting brought all the pain of her childhood tumbling back.

What if she'd been wrong?

Evangeline slumped against the wall, her body shaking with silent sobs.

She cried for the father who'd left and never returned. She cried for the childhood she'd been robbed of. She cried for a mother who'd lost herself when her husband abandoned her.

Evangeline's shoulders shook with the force of her crying as she remembered the nights she'd fallen asleep with tears wetting her pillows. Nights when she'd wondered what she'd done wrong to make him leave them.

She wondered why she'd been so unlovable.

Maybe he'd sat there with nothing but love in his heart, hoping his family missed him.

Maybe he hadn't failed her.

Maybe she'd failed her father.

Evangeline cried until she fell asleep in a little pool of sunlight.

PART FOUR

Chapter 55

BUTCH

Butch sat down in his chair with a grunt, rubbing his temples as he tried to stave off the exhaustion threatening to overwhelm him. It was all he could do to keep his growing headache at bay. He hadn't slept in what felt like days, the constant stream of issues demanding his attention and leaving him perpetually on edge.

The Jerr Pinn delegates had departed the day before, and their refusal to sign the trade agreements still stung. His father would've been outraged. Probably would've done something to start a war with the southern country. Butch couldn't be bothered.

And now, to add insult to injury, his walking abscess of a father-in-law continued to stay on the second floor and was even more obnoxious after somehow discovering his daughter was pregnant. Butch had inquired about Puck's estate in Cyanthia and whether its renovations were finished. Taking that as an impertinent insult, Puck had droned on and on about his right to be there as Lenora's father until Butch could've sworn his ears were bleeding. He'd agreed, if only to shut the man up. As long as he stayed far, *far* away from Lenora and Butch, his meddlesome presence could be allowed. Even if the thought of Puck grated on Butch's already-frayed nerves.

Butch took a deep breath, attempting to calm down.

If his father hadn't made the infuriating deal with Puck, allowing him a constant presence in the court, he wouldn't have to deal with the man. Butch stopped himself from going down that trail. If his father hadn't made the deal, he wouldn't be married to Lenora. At least some good had come from his father and Puck's meddling.

A small grin crossed his lips. Yes, Lenora was certainly worth the headache Puck gave him. And more.

If he hadn't been about to meet with the prisoner to discuss a deal, he would've gone to the royal apothecary's lab to see if August could whip him up something to help ease the pounding in his skull. The headaches, and sometimes migraines, had been consistent since the night Estrada had intruded within his home and killed Levick.

There hadn't been any more news after Butch had been informed about the other body, apparently the sister of the woman he'd beheaded earlier in the month, and the confirmation that dark magic had been the instrument of Levick's death. As far as Silas had worked out, Ariella's sister, Faeleen, had entered the castle with Estrada on the night of the welcome ball. The two had likely been looking to rescue Estrada's friend and Faeleen's sister. Things had gone wrong, and somehow, Estrada had walked out of the castle and her friends hadn't.

His crown lay abandoned on his desk, and he was standing at one of the wide windows when someone knocked at the door.

"Are you ready?" Silas asked after he'd entered and closed the door behind him.

"I'd dance naked through the streets if I thought it would help me avoid this conversation," Butch muttered as he joined Silas, sitting across from him at his desk. Butch leaned his elbows on the surface, rubbing his face with both hands.

"Now that would be nightmare fuel."

Butch snorted. "As if I don't have enough."

Silas's gaze turned serious. "You've seen how stubborn this woman is. Are you sure she'll agree to this deal?"

"You'd know better than me, considering how much you two have chatted." Butch didn't attempt to hide the bitterness he still felt toward the subject. Silas stiffened but said nothing. Butch sighed. "I've already started the council members on the new law. They're fighting me tooth and nail, but they'll do it."

"Did you threaten their jobs?"

Butch grunted.

"Good. 'Bout time." Silas leaned back in the chair across from the desk. "Those arrogant half-wits needed a rude awakening."

"Oh, I was plenty rude." Butch leaned his chin on one hand. "And as long as she holds up her end of the bargain, it'll be worth it, even if it was only because it impressed some of the Jerr Pinn delegates." Butch sighed, leaning back. "The problem is, I don't trust her to follow through. And it feels wrong, being manipulated into this."

Silas shifted across from him, fidgeting with a wrinkle in his trousers.

"What?" Butch asked, his voice carrying the skepticism he was feeling.

"There's already a law that says those *suspected* of doing magic will receive a trial. This new law is just widening that scope to all magic folk, putting them on a more even field—a fairer field." Silas's voice remained even, but his eyes flicked downward for a second. When he glanced back up, whatever had him hesitating was gone. "Besides, I'm sure it'll satisfy the prisoner."

Butch nodded, though it wasn't in agreement. It was because he wasn't listening. For some reason unbeknownst to him, a question he'd been meaning to ask his friend wormed its way into his head and out through his lips before he could stop it.

"Has she told you her name?"

"Excuse me?" Silas asked, his brow creasing.

"Estrada's friend. What's her name?"

Silas shrugged. "Have you asked her since she started talking to you?"

"No."

"I suppose you should, especially if we're going to work with her."

"I guess it's time, then." Butch scratched the back of his head, and Silas nodded.

"I'll go get her."

"And her friend, Odette Hallenbeck." Butch was surprised how quickly the other woman's name had returned to the front of his mind. The two men stood. "I'll wait here." Butch ran his fingers through his hair before placing the crown back on top of his head. Even if it was only for a few minutes, it always felt good to take the crown off.

"I'll be back."

The rotten feeling growing in Butch's stomach since he'd first made the decision to take the prisoner's deal was swallowing every positive emotion that dared reveal itself until the only thing he could feel by the time he sat back down behind his desk was an overwhelming sense of dread.

Even if he kept his side of the bargain and Estrada's friend got what she wanted, there was no assurance that she would keep her word. There was no way to know that she would help him find Estrada.

Butch pinched the bridge of his nose. For the first time in a while, the room felt like his father's office instead of his own. It was almost as if he could feel his father's disappointment—his fury even—that his only son would be making deals with a person with magic. His father would've thought it inconceivable. Irresponsible. Idiotic.

When a knock on the door resounded, Butch dragged himself out of his thoughts. Taking a few short breaths, he straightened his crown and called for them to enter.

"Your Majesty." The prisoner he'd spared bowed her head toward him, but Estrada's friend retained her regular glare.

"Sit down," Silas said, pulling a chair from the side of the room and placing it next to the one in front of the king's desk.

When both women were sitting and the door to the office was closed once more, Butch leaned forward on his desk. It did not escape his notice that both women were wearing magic-dampening cuffs.

"I know we've already been through this, but I'm going to ask again. What happened on the night you two escaped from your cells?"

Neither spoke, nor did they make eye contact with him. Estrada's friend stared defiantly at the map behind him while Odette kept her gaze fixed on the floor.

"Who let you out?"

Silence.

Butch exhaled, his stomach already twisting, and he clenched his hands into fists behind his back. But with a deep breath, he released his firm grip.

"All right," he muttered, straightening.

He turned his gaze on Estrada's friend and waited until she flicked her attention to him. The bruise on her cheek continued to fade, and for a second, he frowned. According to Silas, Captain Malkim had been on temporary leave since the day after the welcome ceremony. While the king was grateful to the captain for apprehending the escaped prisoners, he agreed with Silas that the man's actions after catching the two women was unacceptable and a misrepresentation of the men in the royal guard.

Besides, the results of Captain Malkim's way of interrogation had proved an important point—Estrada's friend would not be broken by mistreatment or cruelty.

333

"Odette Hallenbeck," Butch said, watching as the older woman's eyes widened at the mention of her name. "You are free to leave. All charges made against you as well as all judgements are wiped clean and will not be held against you any longer."

"Wh—" Odette glanced from Butch to Estrada's friend. "Free?" she asked, her voice breathless. "How?"

Instead of answering her question, Butch nodded to Silas, having already discussed how the conversation would go. His friend stepped forward, ushering Odette to her feet and undoing the cuffs on her wrists.

"Come with me," Silas said, gesturing toward the door.

Estrada's friend watched silently, her gaze flicking to Butch every couple seconds. Something flashed in her eyes—it almost looked like appreciation.

Silas escorted Odette out of the room, and Estrada's friend craned her neck to see her leave. When they were gone, Butch waited for the prisoner to turn her attention back to him.

"How do I know you're not just taking her out to execute her?" she asked before she'd taken her eyes off the closed door.

Butch had anticipated the question, and he rounded his desk, motioning for her to stand. "I'll show you," he said, nodding toward the door.

Though hesitant, the prisoner rose to her feet and walked in front of him toward the door, which he opened for her. He led her to a balcony that overlooked the castle courtyard—one on which he'd given many speeches. The double doors let in fresh air, and Butch waited for her to join him outside.

But when he looked at her, she stood with her eyes closed, her chest expanding with what appeared to be an extremely deep breath. It struck him. This had to be the first time she had stepped foot outside in nearly six months. A soft smile crossed her lips, and he stared at her as a breeze lifted a strand of hair off her cheek.

He was still staring when she opened her eyes. Any sign of relief in her vanished, and she tensed again at the sight of him.

"Come watch," he said, clearing his throat as he held the door open for her.

It would take a few more minutes before Silas walked out the main doors with Odette, but it was the perfect place to watch from. And he couldn't stop a little scrap of hope from sticking—maybe, if she saw her friend released in good faith, Estrada's friend would be even more compliant.

"I haven't forgotten," she said, though she was concentrating on the ground below them when she spoke.

"Forgotten?" he asked, keeping his voice steady.

"The deal."

"I've freed your friend of all charges against her, and," he said, nodding toward two figures—a male and female—as they crossed the courtyard, "I'm letting her go."

"Which is only the first part of the agreement."

Butch tried to keep his voice pleasant, though all he wanted to do was glare at her. "Your agreement. Not mine."

"Well," she said, turning to face him. "It's my help you need."

"I don't need you," he said, anger clipping his words as his gaze narrowed. It was a lie, but her stubbornness continued to bring out the annoyance he was trying so desperately to repress.

"Then send me back to my cell." She kept her own glare on him, not backing down. "Or you could show that you have some sort of compassion for *all* of your subjects and make an inclusive law for the benefit of people with magic."

He was sure that if her wrists weren't bound, she would've crossed her arms over her chest—it seemed like something she'd do.

Butch opened his mouth to respond but closed it instead when he caught sight of Silas escorting Odette out of the courtyard. It had not been for nothing, and neither was putting into action a law with which he didn't agree.

It had all been for a reason.

And as much as he hated to admit it, he did need her—at least until he found Estrada.

And besides, the legislation seemed to have interested the dignitaries from Jerr Pinn. Maybe with a bit more convincing, the trade agreements could be signed.

No. None of this was for nothing. He just had to keep reminding himself of the fact.

Butch forced a pleasant smile onto his face—one he used when he had to be polite because of his station, not because he wanted to. "I've already put such a law into motion. Discussed it with my council and the delegates from Jerr Pinn."

The shock his words gave her was evident on her face, though she was clearly trying to hide it by glaring at him.

"I don't believe you," she said, glancing once more at the courtyard, though Silas and her friend were no longer in sight.

Butch wanted to point out that her believing him was not part of her agreement, but he refrained. "It's true."

"What will this law state?" she asked, raising an eyebrow.

"Those with magic may no longer be executed without a fair trial, just like those without magic."

She frowned but didn't respond. Butch waited for her to speak, not wanting to explain that while he had proposed the idea, it would likely not take effect for quite a while since his council would surely continue to fight him on it.

When she still hadn't spoken, Butch cleared his throat. "I've satisfied your demands, and now it's a question of whether you're one to keep your word."

"I am." She spoke right away, as if the mere suggestion that she would cheat him was completely absurd and insulting.

"Good," he said, equally as sharp. "Then you'll assist us in tracking Estrada down."

She clenched her jaw but nodded. "And we'll see if you're true to your word."

He frowned. "Meaning?"

"If what you say is the truth, then should you find Emmalee, you must bring her in for a fair trial."

As challenging as it was to keep a glare from darkening his face, he somehow managed. He had no intention of giving Estrada a fair trial. With all she'd done, he'd already decided how the ruling of her trial would end.

Guilty. She was guilty.

But he didn't tell Estrada's friend that.

He nodded, changing the subject instead of answering her question directly. "If we are to work together, you ought to tell me your name."

She shook her head. "No."

"Why?"

"There's power in a name."

He didn't question it. He was too tired to argue. "Then what do you want me to call you?"

Estrada's friend frowned, cocking her head as she stared at the ground. When she looked up at him, she smirked.

"Lia."

Chapter 56

EVANGELINE

"**W**here are we going?" Evangeline asked Silas, following him up a flight of stairs. They were in a part of the castle she'd never been to, and she'd tried to keep track of what floor they were on. Her best guess was the second floor.

Silas didn't answer her question despite the fact that it was the third time she'd asked it. The only questions he'd answered were those regarding Odette, and even then only with a sharp nod of his head.

Yes, he'd really let her go.

No, she wouldn't be followed home, or wherever she ended up going.

Yes, she'd been grateful.

No, Evangeline couldn't go see Odette.

"Have you forgotten how to speak or something?" Evangeline asked, speeding to walk next to him. She was by no means short, but he was tall enough that her normal stride was insufficient.

A servant frowned at Evangeline when they passed, her gaze flicking between the marshal and—if Evangeline had to guess the servant's thoughts—a very filthy bound woman. And by the way she stared, it was clear they made an unusual sight for the upper floors. No surprise there.

"In," Silas said, stopping at a door and unlocking it with one of the keys on his belt.

"Oh, it speaks," Evangeline grumbled, giving a suspicious look toward the room.

"You asked. I answered. We're going in."

Evangeline pinched her lips into a thin line, glancing back over her shoulder at the servant, but she had disappeared into one of the many other rooms littering the corridor.

Silas held the door open for her, and when she didn't move, he pressed her forward with his hand on her lower back.

It was a bedroom, nicer than any she'd ever had. A bed twice the size of the ones she'd left behind in her various apartments sat against the wall on her left with bedding that didn't look like it would rub off skin like sandpaper. On either side of the bed were small tables, both with unlit lanterns on top. Across from the bed on the opposite side of the room was an empty desk with a chair, to the right of which sat a hip-high wardrobe. A mirror hung over it.

A wide window with a seat in front of it faced her when she entered the room, letting in rays from the late-afternoon sun. It warmed her face, and she held back a soft grin as she turned back to Silas.

He was watching her from in front of the closed door.

"Why are we here?" Evangeline asked, adding as much skepticism to her voice as she could.

Silas took a step toward her, and she retreated one in response. He held up his hands, holding the keys to her cuffs between his pointer finger and thumb.

Evangeline kept her eyes on him as he undid the cuffs before reattaching the key and the restraints to his belt as he stepped back. He copied her stance, crossing his arms over his chest.

"The king thought you should be moved from the dungeon since you've agreed to help find Estrada."

A multitude of emotions flooded through Evangeline at the same time she felt her magic emerge, what with the lack of magic-dampening metal. She clenched her hands into fists, hiding them beneath her folded arms.

"Meaning?"

"This is your new room." He nodded toward the window, something like amusement crossing his face when she couldn't hide her reaction.

"My . . . room . . ." Her voice faded as she glanced back at her surroundings. It was more than she could've ever afforded outside the castle.

Silas shifted, and Evangeline returned her gaze to him, though her mind was still trying to process the idea of sleeping in the large bed or spending hours writing at the desk. She hadn't written in a journal in, well, she didn't know how long.

"But since it doesn't have the same magic-dampening effect as the dungeon, you'll have to wear this." Silas held up a small circle that looked similar to the cuffs he had just removed. It had a latch on one side, and he motioned for her to hold out her wrist.

She didn't.

Evangeline took a step back again, shaking her head.

"Last time you made me wear something like that for a long time, I nearly died. It took weeks for the infection to go away. Look." She held out her wrists for him to see, but not close enough for him to reach without first advancing toward her—and she was ready to move away if he did. "There are still scars."

Silas's jaw tightened at the sight of the warped skin around her wrists, but he lifted his chin. "This isn't as tight or heavy as the ones that did that. And I had the blacksmith smooth out the inside, so it isn't as likely to cut you." He held out his hand, not moving toward her. "You have to wear it."

Evangeline shook her head again, but he didn't move, nor did he try to force it onto her. He waited for her to come to him. Her eyes were fixed on the cuff in his hand. Inside, her light magic swelled, rebelling against the hesitation in her resolve.

"Evie," he said in a soft voice, and she glanced up at his face when he said her name. Every time he said it, her stomach nose-dived off a cliff. "It's for your own safety."

"How?" Evangeline asked, her brows knitting together. "How is taking my magic away for my own benefit?"

Silas lowered the hand with the cuff, and Evangeline's eyes tracked it as he placed it on the dresser. "Few others in the castle know of what you can do."

"So?"

He tilted his head down as he put his hands on his hips. "The king has great patience, but there are those here who don't." Silas paused, raising his gaze to meet hers. "There are still those who would kill you if they knew."

"Kill me?" She tried not to let the trickle of fear filling her reach her face, but she couldn't stop it from leaking into her voice. Maybe it was safer in the dungeon.

Silas nodded. "At the first sign of your magic."

Evangeline sighed, glancing from the marshal to the cuff. After a moment of silence, she spoke. "It requires a key?"

"Yes," he said, holding up a small key looped around his belt with a thin silver chain. "This key. Since the cuff was specially made, there's only one as of right now."

Evangeline ran her thumb over the scars on her left wrist. They had begun to fade, but she had a feeling they'd always be there—faintly hidden on her skin, a reminder of the weakness she'd felt while sick.

"I don't . . . I don't want to. What if I—"

"I won't let what happened before happen again." Silas cut her off, shaking his head. "If you get the slightest irritation, I'll take it off, and we'll figure out something else. I promise."

Evangeline closed her eyes and lowered her head. The more she thought about hiding her magic away, the more it fought her. She was trembling trying to keep it from showing.

"I . . . I can't," she whispered, her voice barely audible. When she opened her eyes, the walls started to close in, and she clutched at her chest as her lungs forgot to work.

Silas stepped closer, his tone gentle. "Evie, breathe. It's going to be all right."

Her breathing quickened, her chest tightening as memories of the dungeon flooded back. The darkness. The pain. The infection that had nearly killed her. Even with the window shining bright light on her, she couldn't feel the warmth. She was trapped. Helpless.

Evangeline's magic flared in response. A light flashed, emanating from her glowing skin.

Silas didn't flinch. "Look at me," he said softly, stepping even closer, though he didn't touch her. "Just focus on me. Breathe with me, okay?"

Tears blurred her vision as she tried to look at Silas. "I—"

"In," he instructed, taking a slow deep breath. "Out."

She shook her head. How was she supposed to breathe when there was no air?

"In," Silas repeated, standing directly in front of her. He waited for her to copy this time. "Out."

Her breaths were shallow and erratic.

"Again." His voice remained steady and calm. "In, good. Now out."

With each breath, she kept her eyes locked on his. They were an anchor in the ocean of anxiety trying to drown her. Evangeline managed a deeper breath, the air filling her lungs more than it had moments earlier.

"That's it," Silas encouraged. "Keep going. Good girl, you're doing great."

He continued to breathe with her. Each lungful grew steadier, even if the sickly panic still clung to her insides. Slowly, the tightness in her chest began to ease. Evangeline's hands still trembled where they clutched her chest.

"I'm right here," he said, his brow furrowing. "I won't let it hurt you. It's to keep everyone safe, you included."

That logic still seemed a little twisted to Evangeline. But what if the other option was going back to the dungeon? She started to panic again before taking several slow breaths.

"You'll remove it if it hurts?" she whispered, scanning his face for any trace of deceit.

"I promise," Silas said firmly.

Evangeline struggled to swallow. With the back of her hand, she brushed the moisture from her cheeks.

Before she could overthink it, she held out her left wrist, her eyes pinched closed. In a few seconds, the cold metal clamped over her wrist. It stole the air out of her lungs, and she cringed.

Breathe. She needed to breathe. The warmth she'd felt from her magic disappeared the second the lock clicked.

"Thank you," he said, stepping back as she opened her eyes.

"Don't lose the key," she mumbled, twisting the cuff so the lock rested on the top of her wrist where the skin was tougher. He was right though: it was more comfortable than the cuffs that had given her the infection.

Silas nodded. However, his gaze had drifted down from her face and lingered on her neck. The cut Captain Malkim had given her had started to heal, scabbing over and itching. And she assumed the bruise on her cheek had shifted to a sickly green.

"I spoke with him," Silas said, clearing his throat. "Malkim. He understands what he did was wrong. He apologized."

"You *spoke* with him? What'd you say?"

Silas rolled his lips inward as he tilted his head to the side, his gaze dropping to the floor before her feet. "It was less speaking, I suppose, and more . . . training." A tinge of amusement colored his voice, as if it was an inside joke she'd missed. "Either way, I doubt he will bother you again. And he won't be posted at your door. Ever."

"Good," Evangeline said, nodding once. Inside, though, her mind went wild. Silas had gotten an apology out of one of his captains for her.

Silas straightened his collar, which was marked with royal blue to show his rank. "I'll send for a servant to draw you a bath. There's a set of fresh clothes there," he said, pointing to the end of the bed. "I'll return later to show you where you can and cannot venture in the castle. You'll need to be escorted by a guard wherever you go, and there will be at least one posted outside your door at all times."

Evangeline had crossed the room and was examining the clothes. They were plain, but at least they weren't disgusting like the ones she was wearing.

"Do you have any questions for me?" Silas asked when she turned to face him again.

"Plenty," she said, crossing her arms over her chest. "None that matter now."

"All right." He inclined his head, and without another word, he left.

EVANGELINE BRUSHED HER fingers through her wet hair. The bath had been wonderful despite the fact that the water had been cold. The room still felt luxurious compared to the stone floor and damp, musty dungeon air.

A smile had lingered on her face since Silas had left. Odette was free. Evangeline had seen her walk out of the courtyard with her own eyes, and while she didn't trust the king as far as she could shoot him in a catapult, she had more faith that Silas would see her friend out of the castle safely, even if he wouldn't allow her to go see Odette.

And then there was the fact that if the king was telling the truth about the law he'd started, the magic folk in Phildeterre would be one step closer to being treated as equals, though that still seemed to be eons away.

The edge of the cuff Silas had put on her wrist caught in her hair, and she glared at it, the positive emotions she'd been dwelling on vanishing in seconds. It may not have been as heavy as the double cuffs, but it still fulfilled its job. Even as she sat on the window seat, a draft blew in through the cracks along the seal of the window, and Evangeline shivered, wishing the cuff weren't there so her magic could warm her.

Someone shifted outside her door, and Evangeline tensed. While she had gotten used to the sound of people moving about the dungeon, it unnerved her to know that a guard was just waiting for her to make some sort of escape attempt. She wouldn't—not yet at least.

With a sigh, Evangeline leaned her head back against the wall. What she wouldn't give for a good book, especially with the afternoon light shining down on her. The window seat would make the perfect reading nook if only she had something to read. She pondered what her chances were of convincing Silas to let her borrow a book or two from the king's extensive collection.

As if summoned by her thought about him, Silas knocked on the door and entered only after she opened it.

"Ready?" he asked, hovering just inside the room near the young guard.

Evangeline nodded, twisting her hair back so it would stay out of her face for a little while. It'd grown out several inches since she'd been arrested, and it annoyed her to no end. If she could chop it off to be at her jawline again, she would. But she doubted Silas or any of the guards would allow her to borrow any sort of sharp object.

Evangeline followed him out into the hallway, eyeing the guard the same way he watched her—with wariness.

"This is the second floor. If the king and queen are hosting any guests, they will typically reside on this floor," Silas said, gesturing forward. He took longer strides than her, but she wasn't about to speed up just to keep pace with him. After a few seconds, he slowed down for her, and she couldn't hide her smug grin.

"Is anyone residing here now?" Evangeline asked, noticing that all the doors, which were identical to hers, were closed.

Silas's expression soured. "One person. But if you're wise, you'll stay far, *far* away from him. He's . . ." Silas paused, clearly searching for an appropriate descriptor. "He's vexing, to say the least. He's in the opposite wing." Silas waited for her to catch up when she fell behind, entranced by an intricate tapestry of the Glass Fields. She'd never been that far north, but she'd read about it and seen many paintings and depictions of the area.

"So, I have the whole wing to myself?" Evangeline asked, finally drawing her eyes from the artwork to glance at Silas.

"For now." Silas gestured for her to follow him.

Evangeline twisted the magic-dampening bracelet around her wrist as she took in the hallway. In all the times she'd been escorted from the dungeon to the king's office, she'd rarely admired the decorated corridors of the Cyanthian castle—she'd been too busy putting on her quietly stubborn resolve.

"This is the nearest sitting room," Silas said, pausing at a door. He opened it, and Evangeline passed through. "You're welcome to use it as long as you're—"

"Attached at the hip to a guard. I know," Evangeline said, her attention on the chain of bookshelves on the left wall. The layout of the room was almost identical to the one the guards had taken her and Odette to the night they'd tried to escape. "Am I allowed to bring any of the books back to my room?" she asked, already scanning the titles lining the nearest shelf.

"Yes. Just bring them back when you finish." Silas stayed by the door, and when she glanced over her shoulder at him, he was watching her with his careful gaze.

"What?" she asked, turning toward him and crossing her arms over her chest. "Why are you staring at me?"

"No reason," he said, though a slight grin crossed his lips. "If you're finished . . ." He gestured toward the door.

She was anything but finished; however, with his assurance that she'd be allowed to return, Evangeline made a note of where the sitting room was in relation to her room as she followed Silas down the hall again.

He continued the tour, directing her attention to where the wing her room was located in met the opposite wing. "You're to stay on your side of the floor, understood?"

Evangeline nodded.

"And unless you're told to meet with the king in his office, you must stay on this floor."

"Okay," Evangeline said, peering around him at the grand staircase leading down to the first floor in one direction and up to the third in the other. "What's on the third floor?"

"It doesn't concern you," Silas said, his voice clipped.

Evangeline frowned but didn't argue as he took her back in the direction of her room, though it was through a different set of hallways.

"I'm still coming for you."

Gasping, Evangeline spun around, clutching a hand to her chest when Emmalee's voice spoke as clearly as if she'd been standing a foot away. But the hallway behind Evangeline was empty.

"What?" Silas asked, and when she glanced back, his hand was on the hilt of his sword.

She blinked a few times, trying to calm her heart as she tried to come up with what she could tell the marshal. "I-I thought I saw a rat," she said, pointing at the floor just behind her. She had no fears of the rodents—especially after

344

her time in the dungeon—but it was the best she could come up with since her mind was still racing after hearing her best friend speak to her. Had she been doing it all along and the amount of magic-dampening metal in the cells had kept her from hearing it? Was this the first time Emmalee had tried to contact her? Evangeline's heartbeat thundered in her ears.

"A rat?" Silas raised an eyebrow, his stance relaxing.

"Could've been a mouse," Evangeline said, tucking a strand of hair behind her ear before lowering her hand back to her side. She needed to calm down. Breathe. Her body was trembling, but she tried to hide it by straightening her posture.

Silas didn't say anything else, and she didn't want to give him any chance to doubt her, so she continued down the hallway without another word. He took the lead with only a few strides.

But while he rambled off various other rooms that she might have some interest in, the only thing Evangeline could focus on besides the back of his head was Emmalee's voice.

Emmalee was still coming for her. Evangeline rubbed the palm of her left hand with her thumb. She needed to stall the king's search for Emmalee until either she or her friend could come up with a plan to get her out of the castle.

"This is the record hall, though I doubt you'll have any need to go in there," Silas said, gesturing to a set of double doors and snapping Evangeline out of her thoughts.

"What kind of records?" Evangeline's ears perked up. Would they have records of her father?

"Any and all records. It's quite extensive." Silas answered her question while watching her with a wary expression. "As I said, it's doubtful you'll need to go in there."

"Of course," Evangeline said, pasting a small smile onto her face. "What about food? Does a new room mean an improvement in that department too? I'm hungry."

It was as if she hadn't asked about the record hall as Silas smirked and continued the tour. He was focused on pointing out a few of the gardens through the windows when Evangeline glanced over her shoulder, marking the location of the record hall in her memory.

Unlike what the marshal had said, she had a very, *very* strong feeling she'd return to that room. And hopefully soon.

Chapter 57

EMMALEE

Emmalee paced the small cluttered room, her hands trembling as she glanced around at the chaos surrounding her.

She had stayed on the outskirts of Cyanthia even though she knew it held a considerable risk remaining that close to the enemies trying to find her. But she'd managed to find a small house that had been abandoned near the very edge of the lower town. Plenty of people in Cyanthia wore cloaks, and as long as she kept her hair back and out of sight beneath her hood—she'd taken to braiding it into two braids—she could blend in fairly well with the rest of the citizens.

It was the nicest place she'd been in since she'd left her home over a year and a half earlier. Well, it had been before she'd gotten there.

It was smaller than the tiny house in which she'd been raised but was better furnished and less worn down. The house held one bedroom at the back, and judging by the small stack of books on magic shoved haphazardly into a hole in the floor, which had been covered by a rug, the people who'd inhabited the house must've either fled for their lives when they were found to have magic or had been executed.

The location also allowed her to stay more up-to-date on the news circulating around her and the king.

King Butch must've figured she'd return to the place she'd been hiding before. He had sent out wave after wave of guards in the days after the welcome banquet. However, he'd sent most of them into the Black Forest. And while he kept Cyanthia under heavy guard, she was less likely to be noticed with the ratio of people to guards. It was, after all, one of the largest cities in Phildeterre.

Instead, she hid right beneath his nose.

The once-tidy house on the edge of Cyanthia was now in shambles, and it'd only been a few weeks since the tragedy at the castle. Papers were strewn across the floor, books were open and discarded, and the faint smell of molding food lingered in the air. She hadn't bothered to clean in days, her desperation eclipsing any semblance of normalcy.

Ari and Faeleen were gone.

Not gone.

Dead.

Because of her.

The weight of their loss bore down on her like a fallen tree trunk, crushing her body beneath it. She had failed them both, just as she'd failed to rescue Evangeline.

The thought of Evangeline still trapped in the castle wore at her nerves, and each day that passed without her best friend made the pain sharper and more unbearable.

Emmalee caught a glimpse of herself in the mirror. Her dark hair had lost its sheen and remained tangled and unkempt. Dark circles underlined her eyes. Her clothes were wrinkled and stained. She felt like a wraith, a complete shadow of herself.

Tears welled in her eyes, threatening to spill over, but she blinked them back. With a sniffle, she turned from the mirror.

All she wanted to do was curl up on the bed in the back room and go to sleep.

Her thoughts spiraled further. What if she lost Evangeline too? She was the last person in Emmalee's life, and if she were to remain lost to her forever . . .

Emmalee slumped down on the couch, her hands covering her face.

"You can't give up, darling. She still needs you." Anwell's voice echoed in her thoughts, and she squeezed her eyes shut, wanting nothing more than to feel his warm hand on her shoulder.

Emmalee held back tears as she thought of Evangeline. She'd sent a message to her a few days after the ball, hoping, as she had the times she'd sent messages before, that it would reach her friend. But there was no way to tell. Still though, Emmalee held out her hand, letting her magic take another message to Evangeline. One she herself needed to hear.

"You are not alone."

Chapter 58

EVANGELINE

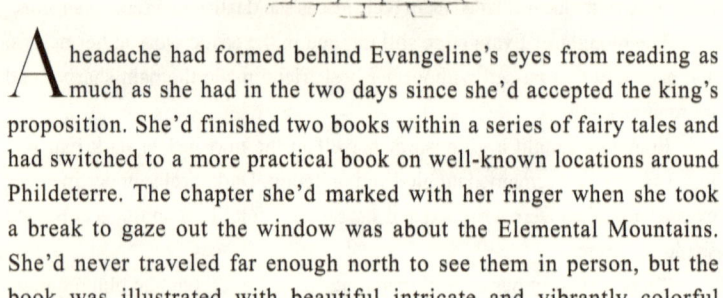

A headache had formed behind Evangeline's eyes from reading as much as she had in the two days since she'd accepted the king's proposition. She'd finished two books within a series of fairy tales and had switched to a more practical book on well-known locations around Phildeterre. The chapter she'd marked with her finger when she took a break to gaze out the window was about the Elemental Mountains. She'd never traveled far enough north to see them in person, but the book was illustrated with beautiful intricate and vibrantly colorful drawings of the locations.

The page she'd paused on included a drawing of one of the tallest peaks. There were apparently a labyrinth of caves within many of the mountains, formed thousands upon thousands of years earlier when there had been volcanic activity. Evangeline wasn't surprised though, because her father had told her stories of the mountains.

"It's where the dragons once lived. A safe place to raise baby dragons away from hunters," he'd said as he held her on his lap. They'd been reading a book with illustrated drawings of different species of dragons and wyverns when Evangeline asked why she'd never seen one.

Evangeline sighed, closing her eyes. She'd blocked the memory for the longest time. Thanks to the name etched into her cell, many such memories had floated to the forefront of her mind in recent days.

She opened her eyes again but no longer felt like reading.

As Evangeline stared out the window from the seat next to it, she felt the familiar pull she'd experienced many times—the desire to go see the very things about which she'd been reading. The Cyanthian castle was too far from the Glass Fields, so even if her window had been pointed north, which it wasn't, she wouldn't have been able to see past the roof of the Black Forest.

Evangeline marked the book with a ribbon she'd found at the back of one of the drawers in the desk—she'd never commit the sin of folding the page to mark her spot. She placed the book next to her and leaned her head back against the wall, pulling her knees up to her chest. While the room was exceedingly more comfortable than the cell—a horse's stall would be more comfortable, in fact—it held the same purpose: imprisonment.

The guard outside her door knocked, and she glanced over her shoulder.

"Yes?" It didn't matter if she answered or not; they'd enter without her permission. But it still gave her the feeling of control to respond, and she would not give it up.

The door opened, and Silas walked in.

"The king and I would like to have a word, if you're not busy," he said, bowing his head in a brief nod.

Swinging her legs over the edge of the window seat, Evangeline snorted. "What could I possibly be busy with?" She raised an eyebrow, standing.

The waistband of the trousers left for her was a little large. It likely would've fit if she hadn't spent months wasting away in a cell. She pulled the waistband up, fixing the flowing tunic she'd tucked in when it twisted. The sleeves of the tunic were obnoxious, but her own clothes had been past the point of being saved. She'd lost so much weight while in her cell and the infirmary that the rags had hung on her like she was, in fact, a coatrack instead of a woman. She'd made do with the borrowed clothing by rolling the sleeves up past her elbows. The only clothing she'd kept were her boots, which she slipped on before following Silas out of the room.

"Have you been finding your way around well enough?" Silas asked, and Evangeline tried to hold back a sigh as soon as the small talk began.

It wasn't that she hated shallow conversations—her sister, Linetta, abhorred them—but she was not in the mood, especially with the headache from reading lingering in her temples and the thoughts of her father pulling her into what was most assuredly a downward spiral.

349

"I have a guard with me every time I leave my room, so it doesn't particularly matter if I remember which halls are which, does it?" Evangeline countered, crossing her arms over her chest as she walked.

"Hmm." He snorted. "Fair point, I suppose."

Evangeline was thankful when he didn't ask more pointless questions. The walk to the king's office was shorter from her new room than from the dungeon, and she made note of the record hall as they passed.

When they entered, Butch stood next to his window, his hands in his pockets with his sleeves rolled partially up his arms—like Evangeline's.

"Well, I almost didn't recognize you," Butch said, pulling one of his hands out to gesture toward the chair in front of his desk.

"That's because I'm clean," Evangeline muttered as she rounded the chair and sat down.

Silas moved toward the window when the king sat down across from her at his desk. It was a small shift, but Evangeline noticed Silas's change in position. When she'd been interrogated every other time, the marshal had either stood behind the king or near the door. Not only had his position in the room changed, but he did not stand at attention. Instead, he leaned against the wall and crossed his arms.

"Your new accommodations are—"

"Fine," Evangeline said, cutting the king off as she turned her attention from Silas to Butch. "What did you want to discuss? As I mentioned before, I have no idea where Emmalee is since I've been here for . . ." Evangeline frowned as her words trailed off.

"A little over seven months," Butch finished when she could not.

Had it really been that long? Evangeline lowered her gaze to the floor in front of the desk, fidgeting with the cuff around her wrist. She thought of those who knew her; how many already thought she was dead?

"I understand what you're saying." Butch's voice was straightforward with little emotion beneath it. "So, I thought we might discuss something else. The night you tried to escape—"

"I'm not telling you—"

"Nor would I expect you to," Butch interrupted, holding up his hand to silence her. "And I'm not about to waste my time and patience asking. I would like to discuss what you know about Estrada's cunning entrance within the castle walls that night."

Evangeline scoffed. "I told you already, she isn't foolish enough to try—"

"She did," he said, cocking his head to the side.

"And she got out too. I saw her leave," Silas added.

"I want to know how she got in." Butch's voice was flat.

Frowning, Evangeline glanced at Silas, whose nod confirmed the king's statement. He clenched his jaw, his body turning to granite. Whatever had happened, he was clearly still angry about it.

"Emmalee was really here?"

"Looking for you, I'd assume. And another prisoner, as she was not alone."

Evangeline tensed. Someone else? Who would—

Faeleen. Evangeline's stomach dropped. She must've come for her sister. She tried to keep her face from revealing the emotions roiling inside her.

"The two of them apparently got sidetracked when my marshal caught them."

"Your man who died?" Evangeline straightened. "You think—"

"Yes." Butch nodded. "And I don't just think. I know."

Evangeline's heart raced, and she lifted her chin when her throat struggled to swallow. But her pride refused to let her show the conflict of emotions in her head.

"How?"

"How did she enter? Or how—"

"How do you know it was her?" Evangeline clarified as she shifted in her seat. Even though it was slight, she could hear the waver in her own voice. "What evidence do you . . ." Her voice trailed off when the king stood.

Butch reached down onto his desk and picked up a linen with dried blood and held it out for her to see.

Her stomach dropped at the sight, not because of the blood, but at the words written with it, all of which were in Emmalee's neat handwriting.

A little bit of justice for the blood you and your men have spilled. For Ari & Fae and for Anwell & Hazel. Evangeline read under her breath, her hands tightening into fists in her lap. She'd even signed it with her initials.

Foolish girl.

Foolish, foolish girl.

And Faeleen. She was dead too?

The blood drained from Evangeline's face as the room swayed around her. She felt sick. Reaching out, she clutched the arms of the chair, clinging to them as a lifeline.

The night in the boulder field, Evangeline had seen the royal guards lying, unmoving, at the bottom of the hill. But it had been self-defense, hadn't it? Maybe the marshal's death had been a matter of self-defense too. But the words. The note Emmalee had left behind . . .

"You're surprised," Butch said, returning the cloth to his desk. "Ariella and Faeleen are the two Pumarians. And the other two are referring to her—"

"Yes." The word came out breathy from between her lips. "Her husband and daughter." Evangeline's gaze had followed the bloodied message to the desk, and when she glanced up, Butch was watching her with a neutral expression painted across his face. "But why would she kill your man?"

Butch glanced at Silas, who nodded back. The king cleared his throat, crossing his hands behind his back and puffing his chest out as he spoke. "We think Marshal Levick caught Estrada and her friend, Faeleen, when they were looking for you, and Levick tried to prevent their escape. Also, my marshal was in Shongbay the day Estrada's family died. He was—"

"You mean the day *you* killed them," Evangeline said, lifting her chin. As shaken up as she was from finding out what Emmalee had done, she would not let the king escape the blame owed him.

"Marshal Levick was in charge of the raid," Butch said, barely acknowledging her interruption besides narrowing his eyes at her. "He was convinced that Estrada would come after him because of his role. She did."

"And he wasn't the first," Silas added, straightening from where he leaned against the wall. He waited for a nod of approval from his king before he continued. "Estrada has killed other guards before. Tortured others, leaving them incapable of anything except lying in beds in near-vegetative states."

Evangeline wanted to respond, to say she didn't believe them. But she couldn't. Her tongue—or rather her head—wouldn't let her. Because she *did* believe them even though she didn't want to.

Neither the king nor the marshal spoke, and the silence swallowed the room. Evangeline tried to reconcile the memories she had of her best friend, who had brought her cakes when her stepfather wasn't home, with the woman who tortured and murdered royal guards. The effort resulted in a splitting headache, and Evangeline raised her hands to massage her temples.

Eventually, the king cleared his throat again. "I know this might be a bit overwhelming to hear. But Estrada isn't as innocent as you make her out to be."

Evangeline bit her tongue hard enough that the shock of pain kept her from making a retort. It wouldn't be worth it. They had the note from Emmalee in her handwriting. That alone unsettled Evangeline. She kept her eyes downcast, her mind failing to do anything but replay the words Emmalee had spoken to her after the boulder field.

She'd wanted Butch to suffer from his injuries, perhaps die from them.

Butch's voice pulled her from memories as dark as the Black Forest. "How do you think she got into the castle?"

Evangeline shook her head, closing her eyes as she rested her head in one hand, leaning to the side of the chair. "I don't know. Like you said, I haven't seen her since that night in the boulder field. I don't know what—I don't know how she—I just . . . I don't know." Evangeline frowned as her headache grew, encasing the entire right side of her head in throbbing pain.

"How would you have done it?" Butch's question caught Evangeline off guard, and she furrowed her brow at him.

"What?"

"How would you try to enter the castle unnoticed?" Butch shrugged as he sat back down, leaning back against his chair. He crossed his arms over his chest.

"That's a stupid question," Evangeline muttered. When the king glared at her, she rolled her eyes. "I mean, I wouldn't. If you hadn't noticed, I *don't* want to be here. And Em wouldn't either."

"You have magic," the king said, all but ignoring her response. "How would you use it?"

Evangeline scoffed, shifting in her seat. "What does this have to do with—"

"Answer the question," Silas said, though his voice didn't sound as demanding as the king's would've saying the same thing.

After a glance in the marshal's direction, Evangeline bit the inside of her cheek. "I don't know." She held up a hand to silence the men before they interrupted her. "I mean, I've had my magic since I turned twenty-one. And while it's strong, Em's is . . . different."

"What do you mean?" the king asked, sitting up. There was an edge to his voice.

"In the minutes following her magic manifesting, I saw her do things I had never dreamt of attempting."

"You mean burning my guards within an inch of their lives?" Butch's tone darkened at the same time as his face.

"Yes," Evangeline said, not intimidated in the least by his shift.

"Wait," Silas said, stepping forward. "Estrada didn't have magic before then?" He sent a quick glance toward Butch, who frowned.

"No." Evangeline directed the words toward the king.

Without an explanation, Butch nodded toward Silas, who clearly understood some unspoken command.

"Let's go," Silas said, approaching Evangeline.

"What do you mean?" Evangeline asked, rising to her feet as she glanced between the two men.

"We're done here for now." He led her to the door, holding it open for her.

Evangeline stopped in the doorway, turning to face the king. "You didn't know Emmalee didn't have magic before you killed her family?" She ignored Silas when he tried to usher her out of the room. "You took her loved ones and any chance she had for a normal life when you sent those men to raid Shongbay, and you didn't know?"

"Come on," Silas said, pulling her by the wrist, but she easily slipped it from his grip.

The king stood but did not speak. His gaze remained steady on her, darkening as she continued.

"This war has made enemies where there were simply people trying to live their lives. Innocents. You and your ancestors have stomped on the anthills for years, and now they're coming out. My guess? Emmalee won't be the last." With that, she spun on her heels and walked away.

Chapter 59

LENORA

Lenora noticed the face in the upper window when she was in the gardens with Merla. The second-floor guest rooms were rarely occupied, especially in the wing of the castle they walked along. They hadn't been filled since the delegates from Jerr Pinn had left nearly two months prior. At first, she had thought it was a maid tidying one of the rooms, but she recognized the blond hair, even as the woman stood and departed from the window seat.

"Did you see that?" she asked Merla, pointing toward the window, which was now empty.

Merla peered up to where Lenora pointed, the basket of tulip bulbs in her hands tipping. "See what?"

Lenora frowned, glancing back to the window before scanning the rest on that floor for any trace of movement. "I thought I saw . . ." She took a deep breath, then let it out slowly. What, or rather who, had she seen?

Estrada's friend?

Why would she be on the second floor?

She'd been caught trying to escape the dungeon.

"My lady?" Merla's voice drew Lenora's attention once more. Her handmaid had paused and was watching her with a creased brow. "Is everything all right?"

Lenora nodded, clearing her throat. "Everything's fine. I just thought I saw someone in the window up—"

"Your Majesty, apologies." A group of royal guards, six in total, came around the corner.

Lenora froze at the sight of them. Had her husband figured out her role in the prisoners' escape? Her pulse raced, and a bout of lightheadedness overtook her.

"His Majesty sent us. He has requested that, should you desire to be outside the castle, you be accompanied by six guards at least."

Lenora frowned. "He said that?"

"Yes, Your Majesty," the man at the front said, giving a slight bow. "You are free to continue with—" He glanced at Merla, who held the basket of bulbs and was piercing him with a glare. "With whatever you were doing."

"Don't you think this is a bit excessive?" Lenora asked the guard who'd done all the speaking. "I mean, I'm within the castle gates."

"It's not my place to have an opinion. We are simply following the king's directions to speak with you."

"Of course," Lenora said, gracing them with a small smile while a trail of annoyance clawed its way through her. She knew why her husband had made the order. She had been abducted and was carrying his child. But six guards while she was still within the castle perimeter?

Lenora glanced up at the window, a thought already filling her mind. "Well, I'm sorry you all went through so much trouble. I was just getting a bit cold, as it turns out. Merla, would you return those bulbs to the greenhouse for me please?"

Merla raised an eyebrow, but she did not question the queen's true motives as Lenora departed, striding toward the nearest entrance. The guards fell into step behind her, and two raced ahead to open the doors.

"Thank you," she said, nodding to them. "Does my husband require me to be followed into the garderobe as well?"

She could've sworn the guard nearest her blushed.

"Of course not," he mumbled, offering her a salute before she turned and left them at the door.

As she walked down the hall alone, she tried to calm her frustration. If she altered her way of thinking, it was almost sweet. It showed Butch was thinking of her, that he cared about her safety.

But it still felt as though the castle walls had gotten that much closer, that much more suffocating.

She hadn't told the guards a full lie. Her hands were cold as she removed her gardening gloves. But then again, they were always cold.

Lenora was halfway to one of the staircases leading to the second floor when Kaylene stopped her.

"Your Majesty, I was just coming to join you in the gardens." Kaylene's smile faltered for a second. "Is everything all right?"

Lenora wasn't sure what had given her away, whether it had been some hint of confusion in her eyes or perhaps the way she had been striding faster than her typical pace. Either way, she forced her face to relax, softening her gaze as she smiled at her handmaid.

"Everything's fine. Apparently, I'm to be followed by six guards if I step a toe outside." Maybe she hadn't fully convinced herself that her husband's command was endearing quite yet, if her bitter tone had anything to say about it. "It's all right though. I was getting a bit chilled anyway," Lenora said, holding up the gardening gloves she'd just removed. Before Kaylene could speak, Lenora continued. "I completely forgot to return these to the greenhouse. Would it be too much to ask you to take them there for me?"

"Of course not, my lady."

Lenora smiled. "Thank you very much." Lenora nodded to her before continuing in the direction she'd been moving.

Before she could be stopped by anyone else, Lenora scurried up the stairs to the second floor. She turned to the left at the top of the stairs and followed the hallway. The last thing she wanted to do was run into her father, who was residing in the opposite wing. He supposedly spent most of his time in the upper town of Cyanthia, hobnobbing with the upper class. As long as he stayed away from her, her sanity might remain intact.

The wings were almost exactly the same, except mirrored, and she tried to keep her orientation toward the direction of the gardens. If she could remember which side of the castle they'd been on from where she stood, she'd find the room she was looking for faster.

But she didn't need to worry about the orientation of the gardens or the direction the rooms were facing. She knew she'd found the room when she turned down a hallway and only one of the doors had a guard posted outside.

"Your Majesty," the guard, a young man with freckles, said, saluting as she approached him.

Unlike the pace she'd been traveling at before, Lenora slowed down, lifting her chin and striding with confidence.

"Afternoon. What are you doing here?" Lenora said, placing a gentle smile on her lips.

The guard straightened his shoulders, but his brow creased. "I'm afraid I can't say, Your Majesty."

"Why not?" Lenora asked, guessing the man's response before he spoke it.

"The king has—"

"Never mind," Lenora said, whisking his words away with a flick of her hand. "I was simply stretching my legs. It was a bit cold outside." While her curiosity wanted her to pressure the royal guard into telling her what was going on, she had already confirmed that her husband didn't suspect her of having anything to do with the escape during the banquet, and she didn't want to shift any attention to herself.

"Your Majesty," the guard said, saluting once more as she continued down the hallway.

Catching a fistful of her skirt in her hand, Lenora quickened her pace as soon as she was around a corner and out of sight of the guard. Her mind raced, trying to comprehend why the king had moved Estrada's friend up to the second floor—if it even was who she thought it was. Did the move have to do with the prisoner breaking out? Or maybe it was because Estrada had broken into the castle.

Lenora paused in the middle of the corridor.

The mere thought of Estrada brought with it a ghost of the feeling she'd had while abducted: freedom. Freedom from the stone walls surrounding her and from the pressures of royal life. Lenora frowned as she resumed walking, though at a slower pace. Her mind could not comprehend why she felt relieved at the thought of a woman who had stolen her away from what was familiar.

Her brow remained furrowed until she reached her own quarters on the third floor. Tossing her cloak onto the edge of her dressing table, Lenora sat down in front of her mirror.

She wanted answers about the prisoner, yet she knew a typical guard either wouldn't know or, if they did, wouldn't tell her out of loyalty to her husband. What she needed was someone who knew what had happened who was more likely to speak to her. Someone like . . .

"MARSHAL THORNE?" Lenora rapped on the door the servant had directed her to for a third time. The servant had said they'd seen him entering the room not more than an hour earlier, but maybe they'd been mistaken. Maybe he was—

"Your Majesty? What's wrong?" Marshal Thorne opened the door, sleep still clinging to the side of his face where faint lines were etched into his skin from his pillow. He wore a light tunic and a pair of trousers, both of which were in such a disheveled state that she could only guess he'd thrown them on when he'd heard her knocking.

"Nothing. I didn't realize you were sleeping. I apologize for waking you." Lenora glanced over her shoulder, and Marshal Thorne followed her gaze.

"It's no matter. Why are you here?"

"I'd like a word with you."

"Here?"

"Inside, perhaps?" she said, nodding toward his room. She knew it would look inappropriate to anyone passing, but the hall remained empty.

As if he realized the same thing, he checked the corridor once more. A moment later, Marshal Thorne stepped back, holding the door wider for her to enter.

"What did you need to discuss so urgently that you came all the way here?" Marshal Thorne asked, his body language stiff as he put good distance between them. Well, as much distance as he could in the small room.

Her bathing room was at least twice as large as his entire bedroom. In some way, it reminded her of the simplicity of her room in the tiny house where Estrada had taken her.

Lenora shoved the thought away, clearing her throat. "I need you to be honest with me, Marshal."

"Of course, Your Majesty." He frowned. "About what?"

"What happened to the prisoner who was in the infirmary after she tried to escape?"

Marshal Thorne bristled. "How did you know she tried to escape?"

Keeping a calm façade, Lenora responded, "Butch told me the day after the welcome ball. He wanted me to know from him." It was both true and the perfect excuse for asking. "But what he didn't tell me was what he did with her. I'm worried about her. She was so sickly in the infirmary, and—"

"She's a prisoner, Your Majesty. With all due respect, she shouldn't be a concern of yours."

"But she is," Lenora countered. "And I'd like some indication that she's okay. That my husband didn't . . ." She took a deep breath. "That my husband didn't secretly execute her out of frustration for her escape attempt."

Marshal Thorne regarded her, crossing his arms over his broad chest. His bright eyes held a flicker of irritation.

"I assure you, Your Majesty, she is alive," he said, his tone clipped. "But her fate is not your concern."

"Where is she? What condition is she in?"

"That information is confidential. For your safety, it's best if you just drop this. She's a criminal."

Frustration boiled within Lenora. She took a step closer, her voice rising. "I'm not asking to befriend her, Marshal. I'm asking after her well-being. I saw how ill she was, and I can't stop thinking about her." And she also needed to know where the woman had hidden the incriminating letter she'd had Merla pass on for the prisoner to give Estrada.

Marshal Thorne's jaw clenched, his eyes narrowing. "I can't divulge anything more."

She wanted to push harder. Wanted answers. But she knew she was walking a fine line.

"Fine," she snapped. "Then I suppose we're done here."

She turned to leave, the room swaying as she spun. The walls swirled into a dizzying blur. She'd only taken a few steps when the dizziness intensified and her vision darkened at the edges.

"Your Majesty!" Marshal Thorne's voice sounded distant.

Lenora swayed, reaching out for support that wasn't there. The world tilted. As if she were watching it outside of her body, she saw herself fall, her legs giving way beneath her. Somewhere in the back of her mind, she recognized it was a mirror she was looking at just as strong arms caught her, preventing her from hitting the floor.

Darkness swallowed her whole.

Chapter 60

SILAS

Silas reacted before he realized what was happening. He'd noticed the color draining from Lenora's face, but she'd started to swoon before he could tell her to sit down. Not that she would've listened.

He scooped the unconscious queen into his arms, mind racing. With his jaw set, he kicked open his door, startling a servant nearby.

"Inform the king immediately," he ordered, already moving down the corridor. "Tell him the queen has fainted and is in the infirmary."

The servant nodded, sprinting past him in the opposite direction.

The queen felt light in his arms, and he did his best not to jostle her. Silas's heart pounded in his chest. Was he responsible? She'd been in his room; what would Butch think? Did this have to do with her pregnancy?

When he reached the infirmary, Helena already stood by the door, speaking with a guard.

"Helena." Silas's voice broke as the older woman looked at him with wide eyes.

"Inside, now," she ordered. "Does Butch know?"

Silas nodded, following her to the nearest bed, where he laid Lenora down gently. "Yes, I sent word. She was fine, and then she fainted." He stepped back, running a hand through his hair, trying to steady his nerves.

"Dianna!" Helena shouted, and the younger physician entered the room.

Silas moved out of their way, watching as they scurried around the bed, checking the queen's vitals.

A few minutes later, Butch burst into the room, his face a mask of panic. "Where is she?" he boomed, his frantic gaze finding Silas. "What happened?"

Silas nodded toward the bed, where Helena and Dianna were wiping Lenora's forehead with a damp cloth. Before Butch could storm over and disrupt the two women's care, Silas intercepted him, placing a firm hand on his shoulder.

"Silas," Butch seethed, his glare scalding.

"She's in good hands. She fainted. I brought her straight here." Silas let go of Butch, slightly concerned he might lose his hand if it remained on his friend's shoulder any longer.

Butch's eyes were wild as he looked from Lenora to Silas. "Why was she with you?"

Nodding toward the infirmary door, Silas beckoned Butch out into the hallway. Once the door closed, Silas took a deep breath.

"She came to my room asking about the prisoner. She wanted to know where she was and whether she was still alive after she tried to escape."

Butch frowned. "What did you say?"

"That she was alive and that she shouldn't be Her Majesty's concern." Silas glanced at the door behind Butch. "She seemed upset, and when she turned to leave, she collapsed."

"Has Helena said anything? Is the baby—" Butch stopped speaking when Silas shook his head.

"Helena hasn't said anything. I can ask if—"

"No. Thank you for bringing her here. You may leave." The dismissal felt sharp, like a cut from a knife. Butch's jaw clenched as he nodded to Silas before turning on his heel and reentering the infirmary.

The door slammed shut in Silas's face.

He tried to justify it. His friend was worried, and rightly so. And the queen had come to him instead of her husband for answers. And there was a lot of stress on Butch's plate.

Silas's feet carried him aimlessly as he walked through the castle. He'd finally been able to fall asleep in a nap before the queen had woken him at his door. But now . . . He doubted he could fall back asleep now.

When he stopped outside a familiar door with a guard standing beside it, he paused. Taking another deep breath, he raised his hand and knocked.

The sound of footsteps approached from the other side of the door, and Silas straightened.

Silas met Evie's gaze. "I . . . I'm sorry. I don't . . . I didn't . . . I shouldn't be bothering you." The words tumbled out of his mouth before he could stop them. He turned to leave.

"Silas." Her voice made him pause. "What is it?"

"Would you like to go for a walk?"

Chapter 61

EVANGELINE

He looked like a lost puppy on the side of the road with his big round eyes and a sense of turmoil flickering within them. What else was she going to do? Tell him to get lost?

Besides, a walk sounded divine after being stuck inside her room all day. "Absolutely," she said, already returning to her room to put on her boots.

He followed her without an invitation, lingering by the doorway as she sat on the edge of her bed.

She hadn't seen him for a while, at least two weeks. She had just assumed the king had been busy, and that likely meant his marshal had been too. But maybe something else had happened.

Silas remained quiet as she unlaced the first boot. His gaze roamed over her room, and he kept his hands in his pockets. He wore a light tunic and a pair of trousers instead of his royal guard uniform. His hair was disheveled on one side, as if he'd been sleeping. And the heaviness behind his bright eyes . . .

"Has the room been all right?" Silas asked just as Evangeline realized she'd been staring at him.

Evangeline raised an eyebrow. "As far as prison cells go, it's a little bright and warm. Not enough rats. The view of the stone walls barricading me from freedom are particularly riveting."

When she glanced at him out of the corner of her eye, he was regarding her, probably to see if she was teasing or not.

"It's good, Silas. Better than the dark hole I was in before."

He nodded, pressing his lips together. "Good."

She started with the second boot as Silas wandered in farther. "Romance?" Silas asked, holding up a book she'd started earlier that day.

"Are you judging?" Evangeline asked, her cheeks heating as she pulled on the other boot.

"A bit." He glanced sidelong at her before smirking and opening to the middle. "Shall I?" he asked, clearing his throat.

Evangeline's eyes widened, and she glanced at her doorway, where the other guard still stood at attention.

"Silas," she said, her tone warning.

That was apparently the only encouragement he needed before he started reading aloud in a dramatic voice.

" 'His eyes bored into hers, burning her like twin blazing stars.' " Silas moved out of Evangeline's way, sprinting to the opposite side of her bed as she tried to reclaim the book.

"Stop, Silas! Stop!" Evangeline couldn't keep the grin spreading across her lips.

He did not listen. He read louder. " 'Olivette heated in an instant, catching on fire from within. Passion danced between them, unspoken yet palpable in the dim candlelight of her bedroom. He prowled toward her like a hungry lion ready to devour her whole. With just one touch—' " Silas grunted as Evangeline smacked him in the face with a well-aimed pillow.

"Give it back."

Silas raised an eyebrow, skimming the rest of the page. His eyes widened, and he shut the book with one hand. "Well, you certainly have an interesting taste in books."

"At least I read," she muttered, snatching the book from his outstretched hand.

"I read." He smirked. "Lots and lots of reports. Not nearly as . . ." He paused, clearly searching for a word.

"Interesting?"

"Thought-provoking."

"Ha. Ha." She rolled her eyes as she tossed the book onto the bed. "You say that, but I bet you're going to find this book and read the rest of it when no one is watching."

"Don't give me any ideas." Silas nodded toward the door. "Shall we?" He offered his arm, and she hesitated. It seemed, well, formal. He must've noticed her hesitation. "You don't have to. I just thought . . . Actually, I don't know what I was thinking. I—"

He stopped talking when Evangeline took his arm.

"Thank you," she said, a strange warmth—not from her magic— spreading in her stomach.

As they left the room, he waved off the guard posted outside her door. The guard, Benji, who was kinder than some of the others, nodded and stepped back, allowing them to walk down the corridor unescorted.

They moved through the castle in silence.

"I thought we might wander the gardens. Would you like—"

"Yes," Evangeline said, maybe a little too eagerly. "Sorry," she amended. "It's just . . . I haven't been outside much, and I've been longing to. I didn't know who to ask though."

"Me. Ask me," he said, a soft smile crossing his lips as his gaze trailed over her face.

"Can we?" She glanced toward a window. "Go outside, I mean."

"Of course." He led her down a flight of stairs and to a beautiful set of double doors.

As soon as they opened, Evangeline inhaled deeply, savoring the fresh air and the scent of blooming flowers. Her grip tightened on Silas's arm. She had only been outside once since she'd been imprisoned— when the king had proven he'd released Odette—and that moment had been too short.

Silas walked beside her, silent as she took in the vegetation around them. Evangeline didn't recognize most of the beautiful plants, but when they rounded a corner, she did recognize some of the herbs.

Lavender, chamomile, valerian.

A plan began to form in her mind, and not knowing the next time she'd have the opportunity, she decided to act.

"This place is beautiful," she said, her voice soft with awe.

Silas nodded. "I'm glad you like it."

"Do you mind if I pick a bouquet for my room?" She paused in the middle of the path.

"Of course not," he said, releasing her arm.

Evangeline thanked him. She began to pick a few sprigs of lavender, adding other herbs from a list written in her mind to the makeshift bouquet.

Silas stood behind her, his shadow eclipsing her body as she knelt on the path. But he remained silent.

Evangeline continued to pick herbs and plants she recognized, her hands moving deftly. In case her shadow was knowledgeable in the art of mixing drafts, Evangeline mixed a few useless plants into her bouquet.

"There," she said, a satisfied smile on her lips. "What do you think?" she asked, holding it out for him to examine.

"Lovely," he said, and she glanced up to find him staring not at the blooms in her hands but at her face.

Evangeline couldn't look away, captured completely in his relentless gaze. His burning gaze. Her skin tingled, and she lowered her bouquet as she stepped closer to him.

He, in turn, took another step toward her.

"Thank you for this," she murmured, and his gaze dropped to her lips. "For letting me see the garden."

When he met her eyes again, his were sad. "Of course, Evie."

"I should get these in water. Do you think I could borrow a vase?" she asked, stepping away and tucking her chin. Evangeline busied herself with moving a few of the plants around in the bouquet.

"Whatever you need, it's yours."

Except freedom, she silently thought as she took Silas's arm and walked back into her giant stony prison.

Chapter 62

BUTCH

Butch was nearly asleep in the chair next to Lenora's bed in her chambers when she stirred. He'd been sitting vigil since Helena had cleared her and the baby and allowed her to be moved to the comfort of her room.

"Butch?" she said, her voice soft.

"How do you feel?" Butch asked, shifting so he sat closer to the bed. He reached for her hand, holding it gently in his.

"I . . . I'm okay. What happened?"

"You fainted," he replied, watching her for a reaction. She gave none. "Silas brought you to the infirmary."

Butch wondered if she would confirm Silas's story. He trusted his friend with his life, yet he wanted to hear the words from his wife's lips.

"Right. I must've forgotten to drink enough water this morning," she said, rubbing her forehead with gentle fingers. She tensed, her hand dropping to her stomach. "Is the baby—"

"Healthy," Butch said, nodding.

Relief flooded through her pale face. "Good. Very good."

"Are you sure you're feeling all right?" He wanted to make sure before he brought up her presence in his marshal's bedroom.

"Yes, I'm fine," she insisted, sitting straighter. "It was just a fainting spell."

Butch scratched his jaw, letting her hand go as he lowered his head. When he looked back at her, she regarded him with a careful gaze.

"I have something you should know, Lenora," he said, watching the way she perked.

"That sounds ominous."

"Estrada's friend—the prisoner you saw in the infirmary—I've moved her to the second floor, the opposite wing from your father." He waited.

"Why would you do that?" Her voice was breathy.

"The matter of why doesn't concern you, but I thought you should know. You ought to avoid the area. I have it guarded, but I want you to remain safely away from her."

"She'll be guarded all the time?" Lenora asked, and while her voice continued to remain skeptical, her facial expressions were neutral.

Butch nodded. "If she leaves her room, she will be accompanied by a guard, though according to Silas, she's really only left to get books from the study near her room." He had hoped his mention of Silas would encourage her to open up about her conversation with his friend.

It didn't.

"Are you sure it's wise? I mean, it can't be more difficult to break out of a guest room than a cell. Aren't you afraid of her trying to escape again?"

"I'm not."

"You're not?"

"I'm not. She . . ." He paused, wrinkling his nose before deciding to be honest with his wife. Maybe his honesty would convince her to be honest. "She has made a deal with me. In return for her cooperation, I have met two of her demands."

"She wanted to be moved to the second floor?"

Butch paused. He hadn't considered the fact that he'd moved Lia willingly. He cleared his throat. "Um, no. I released her friend, who'd been a prisoner for nearly two years, and . . . and I'm in the process of creating a new law she, um, suggested."

Lenora's features hardened. "You're implementing a law dictated by a prisoner?"

Bristling, Butch gave a short nod.

"I see." The two words came out snipped.

"I'm sure this news is surprising to you," he said, choosing each word carefully.

"It is."

"Right." Butch pressed his hand to his mouth, nodding a few times. "Well, I have a question for you before I go."

"Yes?"

"Where were you when you fainted?"

Lenora's gaze flicked to his, her pupils dilating as her eyes widened. "Why?"

"Because Silas was the one who brought you to the infirmary, not Merla or Kaylene."

She picked at her nails nervously, her hands resting in her lap. "I . . . I was in Silas's room. I wanted to ask him about the prisoner. He refused to tell me anything, and—"

"Why didn't you come to me?" Butch clenched one of his hands to channel his annoyance. It didn't work. He kept his voice even as he spoke. "I would've told you."

"Would you? Or would you have told me that it was none of my business? That it didn't concern me? You hardly speak to me about things that matter to you. Why should I ask you questions you'll brush off and refuse to answer?" she asked as soon as he'd finished. Her voice was filled with as much anger as he felt. "You're busy all the time. You haven't given me any reason to believe that you would be completely transparent about what you're doing for every hour of the day. You can't honestly believe that—"

"So, you try to undermine me by going to my men for information? To my best friend? In his bedroom? Do you not see how that looks?" He raised his voice, his arm flinging out to gesture to the door. "Do you want the servants talking? You're pregnant with our child, Lenora. You can't just sneak off to guards' rooms!"

"It's Silas! What were we going to do?" Lenora shot back, her cheeks flushing. She knotted her hands into the bed sheets, twisting them relentlessly. "Don't you trust him? Don't you trust me?"

"I could ask the same of you!" he retorted, shaking his head as he ran his fingers through his hair. "Is it so hard to believe that I keep things from you to protect you?" Butch's voice rose in volume, easily overpowering hers. "And then you go behind my back?"

"Of course I did," she snapped. "Because I knew you'd be a temperamental mess if I said that I'd been to the second floor to figure out why I saw Estrada's friend in one of the guest rooms."

Butch's ears buzzed, and he went rigid.

"You what?" His voice was a low growl, and when she didn't respond, he leaned forward, invading her space. "Lenora, what did you do?"

"I just told you," she said, though her voice was weaker than before, as if she'd realized she'd said something she should've kept quiet. "I saw her, and I went to check the second floor."

"How?" Hearing the harshness in his voice, Butch cleared his throat and repeated the question at a lower volume. "How did you see her? Where?"

Lenora gestured toward the window, through which the drizzling rain was visible. "I was outside with Merla in the garden. I recognized her from the infirmary." She crossed her arms over her chest. "But when I went to go figure out what was happening, the royal guard posted outside her door would tell me nothing, so I spoke with someone more likely to tell me."

"You should've come to me," Butch said, softening his tone even more, but she only added more venom to hers.

"You should've been honest with me from the start." Lenora narrowed her eyes at him. "And you should've let that poor girl go a long time ago."

"That's none of your—" He stopped himself, but the damage was already done.

"Exactly," she said, dropping his gaze as she glared at her hands. "You should go. I'm sure you've got kingly business I wouldn't understand to take care of."

"Lenora, don't—"

"Just go, Butch."

He stood, his body reluctant to move without fixing things. But Lenora had turned onto her side, facing opposite him.

"I'm having Helena and Dianna check on you every other hour for the next three days. I want you to stay here, in this room, until Helena can confirm that you're all right."

She watched him from the bed as he made his way to her door. "But—"

"No," he interrupted, his eyes hard. "This isn't up for debate. I can't risk anything happening to you or our child."

"You're punishing me?"

Butch shook his head, his hand on the doorknob. "I'm protecting you."

Chapter 63

EVANGELINE

I t'd been nearly a month and a half since Evangeline had taken the king's deal, and she was going stir-crazy. To keep herself from going completely mad, she'd started planning how she would slip into the record hall.

After seeing her father's name in the cell, she'd decided she needed to know what had happened to him. She needed to know if he'd died there. Maybe she'd never know if he'd desired to get back to her and her mother, but at least she could find some closure. Guilt still filled her every time she considered how long she'd resented him for abandoning her and her mother, especially since it might not have been by choice. Likely all she would find, though, was that he'd just been executed like the many other magic folk who'd gone through the dungeon in Cyanthia.

Because it had to be her father who had magic.

Her mother certainly never had it.

Evangeline paced her room, her mind racing. After having the magic-dampening bracelet for over a month, she'd already developed the habit of spinning it around and around her wrist, which she did as she paced.

She'd timed her trips to the study nearest the record hall to learn when the record keeper locked up. She'd noted the kind woman, who had smiled at Evangeline and her guard as she'd passed, and, more importantly, where the woman stored the key. Evangeline knew at some point she'd have to use the skills Emmalee had taught her as a child and pickpocket, but she could only do that when she was truly ready. The key would certainly be missed, and she'd only have one shot with the limited ingredients she'd collected—which she kept hidden away in her room—for the sleeping draft.

A knock on the door had her pausing mid-step. Shaking her head, she crossed the room, pulling the door open. Benji nodded to her, then stepped back so Silas could enter her room.

"He wants to speak with you," Silas said, and without needing him to clarify, Evangeline sighed.

"I'll get my boots," she mumbled.

As Silas took her to the king's office from her room on the second floor, Evangeline laid out more of the first floor, having already covered her wing of the second floor multiple times. She stored the layout away in the back of her mind should she need it later. She had shut down Silas's small talk as soon as they'd entered the hallway, ignoring his question about the books she'd been reading over the last week.

The truth was, while she had been reading, she hadn't actually been *reading*. Most of the time, her brain had skimmed words and phrases, but none of it remained after several seconds of staring at the pages. Her mind lived elsewhere, lingering on her father, on whether Odette was somewhere safe, on Linetta, and, of course, on Emmalee.

Not an hour earlier, she'd heard a third magical message from her friend, another promise that she hadn't given up on her. How many messages had Emmalee sent her that had been blocked by the magic-dampening metal in the cell over the nearly seven months she'd been in the dungeon?

As she walked beside Silas, she twisted the bracelet, which was preventing her from reaching out to Emmalee—not that she would know how. Emmalee had never taught her the spell.

Since Silas had been the one to lock the bracelet onto her wrist, her frustration and annoyance had quickly turned from the metal cuff to him as soon as he'd knocked on her door.

Hence the silent treatment.

The last thing she wanted to do was speak to the king, and part of her wished she could return to her vow of silence. At least she was consistent then. But now the king expected her to speak.

She clenched her teeth as she entered Butch's office.

"Welcome back. Sit down," Butch said, already seated at his own desk.

He didn't need to tell her. She was already halfway to the chair, and the order had her muscles tightening, desiring to revolt against his command.

Butch regarded Evangeline for a long moment—long enough for her to notice the dark circles under his eyes. "What can you tell me about Estrada before her powers manifested?"

Evangeline returned her right hand to the bracelet on her opposite wrist. Something about the way the king cocked his head with an expectant expression on his face made Evangeline's insides squirm. Telling them about Emmalee's past seemed wrong, like she would be betraying her friend's trust. What if she accidentally said something that would help the king? She didn't actually want to give the king any arrows to fire at her best friend. Then again, maybe talking about Emmalee could be a beneficial thing. Maybe it would help them see her in a good light.

"Why?"

"Not a 'why' kind of question." The king placed a fake smile on his lips, shrugging. "What do you know?"

Evangeline considered her words before they even made it to her lips, and many she held back. "She grew up on the streets of Cyanthia. She eventually became a teacher before she was married. She's very clever and loves learning. She wanted all her students to develop a love for it as well. Many did—at least the ones I met."

"And before that? Where are her parents?"

"Don't know. She was orphaned at a young age." Evangeline answered truthfully, and she wondered how much of it Butch already knew from Ariella, how much of it he was waiting for her to confirm.

Butch frowned, but he didn't pester her. "How did you meet?"

Evangeline opened her mouth, but before she could answer, someone knocked on the door.

"We'll return to this subject in a minute. Enter," Butch said, standing.

Turning in her chair, Evangeline widened her eyes when the Mongoose walked in. She hadn't seen the guard for months and had nearly managed to wipe her mind of the awful way he'd treated her when she'd been in the dungeon.

The same vehemence he'd possessed before burned through her at his glare, but the angry wrinkled skin crawling up his arms and the left side of his neck all the way up his skull, which he'd shaved, distracted her.

"Commander Stoll, we're currently in the middle of something," Silas said, his brow furrowing.

Stoll's glare didn't break from Evangeline as he nodded. "I'll be quick." He pointed to his face, sneering at Evangeline. "A gift from your friend," he growled in a dark voice as he crossed by her toward where Silas stood. He saluted first to the king, then to Silas.

"Can this wait, Commander Stoll?" Butch inclined his head toward the guard, but he, too, wore a frown.

The Mongoose was not in a royal guard uniform and instead wore a simple tunic and trousers. His eyes flared with barely controlled anger. "No, it cannot wait. I've waited long enough. I want my position back. I'm ready. I want to return to my duties to hunt down the she-devil who tortured me." Stoll's face wrinkled, the damaged skin puckering as he scowled at Evangeline. "I'll make her talk."

Silas's expression hardened as he straightened his posture. It looked like he grew several inches with the single motion. "That's out of the question."

Evangeline forced herself to breathe, meeting Stoll's glare with an indifferent expression. She didn't want to let on how much his anger scared her. People were unpredictable when they were angry.

"Has she talked?" Stoll snapped, glancing toward Butch.

"Marshal Thorne and I have things well under control, Commander. I suggest you return home and continue to recover." Butch's tone didn't leave room for argument.

Except Stoll didn't get the message.

"That's outrageous! I've recovered. I want out. I want to find that little—"

"Commander, that's enough," Silas ordered.

"And strangle her until she's blue in the face. Until her lungs give out." Stoll took a step toward Evangeline, who felt lightheaded and scrambled to her feet. But before he could advance any farther, Silas was between them.

"I said *enough*," Silas growled, his hand resting on the hilt of his sword.

"You're protecting her?" Stoll scoffed, and from around Silas's rigid back, Evangeline watched as he took a step away from them, almost as if Silas had struck him with his words. "She's the enemy."

"Stoll," Butch said, his voice low but not nearly as threatening as Silas's had been. "Your physical recovery, while a miracle, is one thing, but your temperament is another. You will not be reinstated until we're certain you're capable of fulfilling every aspect of your role."

The Mongoose's face twisted in rage, a sight Evangeline knew she'd have nightmares about for weeks. "That sorceress tortured me for hours. She set me on fire! I want her bones crunching beneath my boots. I want her crying out for mercy because I've destroyed everything she loves."

Butch lifted his chin. "You're proving my point. I cannot have my men distracted, and that includes by rage. I want Estrada to face justice. Revenge is a completely different beast, and I won't have it run rampant amidst my guards. Is that clear?"

Evangeline's pulse quickened at the mention of her best friend's name. At the moment, the king's justice sounded far better than the horrors Stoll wanted to see done to Emmalee. Though, Evangeline reminded herself, justice would likely still see Emmalee executed.

Stoll sputtered for a second, shaking his head. "She kidnapped the queen! She murdered my brother! Corwinn is dead because of her." Stoll turned his livid gaze on Evangeline. "And she's still alive because of her."

Willing herself to stay calm, Evangeline met Stoll's glare with one of her own. She clenched her hands at her sides, fighting the tremor that threatened to rise.

He moved faster than a man his size should've been capable of. One second Silas stood between them, and the next Stoll's hands were around her neck and he'd slammed her into the wall behind her. Evangeline clawed at his hands, her eyes widening as she tried and failed to breathe.

As quickly as he'd grabbed her, he was gone, yanked away by two strong sets of arms.

"Get your hands off her!" Silas roared as he and Butch wrestled Stoll across the room.

Evangeline choked, sucking in air as her hand instinctively went to her throat. It hadn't been more than a few seconds, but the room had already started to darken. She bent over, breathing down deep lungfuls as Silas held Stoll's arms behind his back.

Butch crossed the room back to Evangeline and placed a hand on her shoulder. "Get behind my desk," he ordered, and with a push, he put the large piece of furniture between her and Stoll. A second later he was storming across the office. Butch flung the office door open. "You two, get in here and help Marshal Thorne."

Evangeline leaned on his desk, shaking as she watched two guards rush into the office, their eyes wide.

"Your friend is evil. Magic is evil, and everyone who practices it deserves what's coming for them." Stoll fought against Silas to no avail.

Silas, his face set in grim determination, quickly gave orders. "Get him out of here. Out of the castle."

"So, this is how it is, then?" Stoll bellowed, trying to shake off the two men who took his arms. "You're going to protect the sorceress and her friend while I'm left to rot?" Stoll's eyes flared with hatred. "Some protector king you are."

"That's it! You're leaving. Get him out. Now!" Silas barked. The guards continued to drag Stoll away, and Silas met her eyes for a moment before looking to Butch, who stood in front of his desk like a guard dog. "You'll be all right if I go make sure he's—"

"Yes. Go." Butch gave a brief nod. When the door slammed behind Silas, Butch's shoulders dropped, and he spun on his heels. "Are you all right?"

She wasn't sure why, but the only thing that escaped her mouth was a hysterical laugh followed by what was probably a sob. She fought desperately to keep from crying, though her eyes brimmed with tears. Evangeline bit her lip, begging her body to stay composed for a little longer.

Butch's expression softened slightly, though his manner remained as formal as ever. "He's gone. I'll make sure he stays away."

Evangeline nodded, wiping her eyes with the back of her hand. "Thank you. I-I didn't expect him to—"

"Neither did I." Butch's gaze was steady as he regarded her. "He's a danger to everyone, including himself." He tapped the desk with two fingers and then nodded to the chair she typically sat in. "You should sit."

There was no reason to argue.

Her mind raced. Every part of her wanted to believe everything Stoll had said about Emmalee was slander and that her friend wasn't capable of such horrible things, yet a small voice in her head reminded her of the fire Emmalee had created when her magic had first manifested. And the damaged skin on Stoll's face and hands was burned into the back of her mind. Emmalee hadn't been able to control her magic then. But now . . .

She was still trying to process what had just happened when Butch spoke again, taking his seat at his desk.

"I almost thought you'd gone silent on me again," Butch said, leaning back in his chair. "I was worried."

Evangeline forced herself to focus, pushing through her shaken state. "It's too late for that," she muttered, taking a deep breath as she wiped the remaining moisture from her eyes. Though her heart rate still felt elevated, she was able to breathe deeply.

"Do you see it?" Butch asked after a moment of silence. His postured shifted back to something more regal, more . . . distant. "My perspective of Estrada? After seeing what she did to the commander?"

Evangeline scowled at him. Of course he'd focus on making Emmalee the enemy again after one of his men had just attacked her.

"Why? Should I?"

"Excuse me?" Butch raised an eyebrow, scratching his jaw.

"You still refuse to see her from mine. Hardly seems fair."

"Life's not fair." He leaned back in his chair, his unwavering gaze on her.

"Clearly," she muttered. Evangeline glanced out the window near Butch's desk. Would Silas return? She preferred he be in the room as a buffer. Neither of the two times she'd been alone with the king had been pleasant, to say the least.

"Your opinion on Estrada hasn't changed in the slightest, then?" Butch asked, drawing her attention back to him.

"Has yours?" she retorted.

"Yes," he said, surprising her. He leaned forward, resting his elbows on the desk and his chin in his hand. "I find her even more of a threat now than I did yesterday. In fact, my desire to see her apprehended and charged for every drop of blood she's shed grows every day."

Evangeline's lips tightened into a thin line. "Funny," she said, cocking her head as she rose to her feet. "I feel the same way about you."

Before she lost her courage, Evangeline turned toward the door just as it opened and Silas reentered.

"It's taken care of. He's—" Silas frowned, his gaze flicking between Evangeline and Butch. "Is everything all right?"

"Perfect," she snapped. "I'm done here," she said, pushing past him and out into the hallway.

She made it five steps before Silas slammed the office door and caught her around the upper arm.

"What was that?" he asked, his voice low. "What did I miss?"

"It doesn't matter. He won't change." Evangeline yanked her arm out of his hand, stepping back.

"He just helped save your life," Silas argued, gesturing back toward the office. "He's shown you mercy every day you wake up and haven't been executed. And that's how you treat him?"

"Yes. Because no one else will stand up to him."

"Stoll just did, and look how it turned out for him."

Evangeline ignored Silas's comment, crossing her arms over her chest as she glared at him. "Just because he's king doesn't mean everything that man says is law."

"Actually, it kind of does," Silas said, keeping up with her easily when she started down the hallway. "And you have to respect him."

She stopped, snorting as she rolled her eyes. "He said the same thing."

"When?"

"When I got locked in one of the safe rooms with him. And you know what I told him? Respect is earned, Silas, not freely given. That manipulative boy with a crown is hardly a man worthy of an ounce of my respect." She kept walking, then turned around and paused when Silas didn't continue with her.

He stood in the middle of the hallway, his head lowered. A furrow creased his forehead.

She frowned at him. "What?" she asked after several seconds of silence.

Silas looked up at her with his intelligent azure eyes. "I suppose you think the same of me?"

Some of the air left Evangeline's chest, though she tried to hide it. "What do you mean?" she asked, but she knew exactly what he had meant; asking the question just gave her more time to come up with a response, which was proving a more difficult task than her heart wished it to be.

"Do you respect me?"

She had not expected him to rephrase it in such a blunt manner, and it was as if he had sucked the rest of the air out of her lungs with the question.

What did she think of Silas? Her mind sped as it raced to piece together fragments of thoughts and opinions. None of them made sense though. Not the way her stomach warmed when he was near. Or the way her heart seemed to triple in speed when he said her name. The way she dreamt of him kneeling before her. Looking up at her with his beautiful eyes. Running his fingers along her skin. His lips . . .

Evangeline cleared her throat.

379

She didn't hate him as much as she did the other guards; that much had been clear when the Mongoose had entered the office. There were worse men out there. And she knew he had refrained from giving her the punishment her words had deserved. If anyone had shown her mercy, it had been him.

Yet he continued to stand by the side of a man who was hunting down her best friend. Not only that, but it was clear his loyalty wouldn't waver. He would continue fulfilling orders that put not only Emmalee but others with magic in a position of unfair persecution.

Evangeline cast a glance over her shoulder, hating the silence of the empty hallway. Sighing, she lowered her arms to her sides. "You've been kinder to me than most," she said, and Silas's posture straightened in front of her. "But I find it difficult, if not impossible, to give any respect to someone who would so blindly follow the orders of a man who unjustly persecutes innocent people based solely on the way they were born." How she had strung together a coherent sentence with the manic state her mind was in baffled Evangeline.

Silas opened his mouth as if he was about to respond, then closed it, tightening his lips into a thin line. "I see." He said nothing else, instead gesturing toward the corridor. They walked the rest of the way to her room in complete silence.

And while that shouldn't have bothered her, Evangeline felt something writhing in her stomach, like a pit of snakes, coiling and slithering about her insides. She pushed away the thought that it was guilt. Why should she be guilty? She had spoken the truth.

It wasn't until she caught a glimpse of the dejected look in his eyes that the guilt started to make sense. She waited until he closed her door, leaving her alone in her room, before she let her shoulders sag.

He felt like her only ally in the entire castle, as strange as it was to think of him in that way.

And she had hurt him with her words.

Evangeline rubbed her hand over her brow, sighing as she sat down on the side of the bed. A covered tray rested on her bedside table, but she didn't feel hungry despite the rumble in her stomach. She did, however, go to it because she knew it would have a cup of water. Her throat hurt from Stoll's assault. She doubted the water was cold, but it would likely help ease a bit of the ache, not to mention the dryness. She took her first sip, then paused, the cup hovering in her hand just below her face.

Something white was stuck to the bottom of her cup, the corner of it just peeking off to the side so she could see it.

Glancing behind her toward the door, Evangeline sat down on the edge of her bed. She slid the piece of parchment off the bottom of her cup, wiping it against her trousers before unfolding the soggy paper. The ink had smeared, but the handwriting was familiar—it was the same handwriting that had nearly helped her escape the castle. On it were written four words: *To Rule a Kingdom.*

Chapter 64

BUTCH

Butch sat at the head of the council table, his gaze moving from one council member to the next as they argued over his new law, which would give all magic folk a fair trial. As with every council meeting since the delegates had left and he'd foolishly spat out the law without first consulting his council, the conversation had devolved into heated debates. Voices rose to higher and higher volumes. Butch pinched the bridge of his nose.

"Your Majesty," Councilman Clive said, his tone exasperated. "If it's not obvious, this law is already causing problems."

"How?" Butch drawled, rubbing his temple. "It's not even in place yet."

"It undermines the very fabric of our justice system," Councilman Macaw said.

Butch resisted the urge to roll his eyes. "The fabric of our justice system, as you so strangely put it, is already frayed. This law isn't going to make the old thing worse."

"His Majesty is right," Councilman Paulin, one of the kinder and more reasonable council members, said. "This law would ensure a chance at justice for all, not just those without magic."

"We know what the law will do, Paulin," Councilman Macaw snapped. "We're saying it goes against everything the last two generations have worked toward."

"It's a necessary step toward a fairer system!" someone else shouted.

"It's going to be impossible to implement," someone else argued.

"People will resist."

"Not everyone."

"Yes everyone."

"Says who?"

"That's enough," Butch bellowed, slamming his hand down on the table. Every head turned toward him. "Arguing is going to get us nowhere. As you have all pointed out, we need to discuss implementation of this law, because"—he glared at Councilman Macaw, who matched the glare—"it *will* be implemented whether we all like it or not."

A knock on the door interrupted him.

"Enter," he called, and a servant with an apprehensive look on his face crossed the room to Butch.

"Your Majesty," he said in a low voice. "Lord Puck requests an audience with you."

Nodding toward the table of unhappy upper-class men, Butch said, "I'm a bit busy at the moment."

"He's trying to get to the third floor, Your Majesty. He demands to see Her Majesty." The servant averted his gaze when Butch's face twisted in anger.

"Of course he is." Butch stood, nodding to the servant. "Very well." He would almost prefer staying in the den of vipers arguing over the new law than dealing with his father-in-law, but he knew Lenora would be distraught if her father showed up to her chambers unexpected.

"Gentlemen, you better return tomorrow with a plan to implement this law smoothly. We'll adjourn for now. If you'll excuse me."

He left the council chamber, the echoes of the arguments still ringing in his ears.

"In here, Your Majesty," the servant said, indicating a door to a study on the second floor with two guards posted outside. "Good luck."

Butch almost smiled, nodding to the bold servant, who clearly knew a thing or two about the demon behind the door. He should've warned his staff better.

"Your Majesty," Puck crooned as soon as Butch walked through the door. The older man was already on his feet. "I'd like to discuss why you've decided to keep me from my daughter."

"You mean my wife?" Butch challenged, sticking his hands into his pockets. He rolled his shoulders back, lifting his chin in an attempt to look every bit the king. His father and Puck may have been . . . friends—could it be called friendship if neither of them truly respected the other?—but that did not mean Butch had to kiss up to the oily man.

"Yes, Lenora, *my* daughter. I ought to be allowed to visit her whenever I so choose."

Butch forced a smile. "As you've somehow been made aware, *my* wife is currently with child. *My* child. If she does not wish to see you, that is her prerogative."

"She needs her father, especially in her . . . condition."

"Her 'condition' is pregnancy. As far as I know, that does not require your attention or your . . . company." Butch inhaled before he spoke the last word, looking Puck up and down with an expression he hoped read as distaste.

Puck's face twisted with frustration before he masked it with a concerned smile. "Of course, *Your Majesty*. I only have her best interests at heart."

"Sure you do, Puck." Butch clenched his jaw. "But I won't allow you this freedom—not without her explicit permission. Lenora makes her own decisions."

"Is that wise?"

"Yes," Butch said without hesitation. Whether he believed it or not, he trusted his wife far more than the manipulative ex-king before him. No doubt the man wanted some sort of return to power since Butch's father had united the five kingdoms of Phildeterre and taken the ultimate throne. And no doubt the man would try to use his wife to do so.

"Well then." Puck offered him an appraising look. "How about you go tell my daughter to invite me to dine with her."

Butch bit the inside of his cheek, shaking his head in awe at his father-in-law's audacity. "If she wishes to see you, I'll make sure to tell you myself."

With that, he left Puck standing in the study alone. Butch made quick work of the last staircase to the third floor, heading straight toward the queen's chambers. They had not spoken since their argument over the prisoner several days earlier, and with Puck breathing down his neck, it seemed like an appropriate time to get his relationship with his wife back on track—for her sake as well as his own.

As he approached her door, he took a deep breath, straightening his collar and running his fingers through his hair. It couldn't be that bad—at least, he hoped it wouldn't be. With a determined expression, he steeled himself for the impending conversation.

He knocked, and in a matter of seconds, Kaylene opened the door.

"Your Majesty." She curtsied, opening the door wider for him.

"I need a word with her alone, if you don't mind," Butch said, his gaze switching from Kaylene to Merla, who stood behind Lenora at her vanity. Whether the handmaid had been braiding or undoing a braid from Lenora's hair, he couldn't tell. Either way, Merla also curtsied and followed Kaylene out of the room without a word.

"Butch," his wife said, her voice strained. She met his gaze in the mirror as he crossed the room to stand behind her.

"Lenora," he said, trying to read her expression to see if she was still upset with him. It was hard to tell.

Tension kept her posture straight, her shoulders rigid. Her hands clenched in her lap. Her hair fell down her back in a cascade of black silk, and it was then that he noticed she only wore a thin dressing gown. Butch drew his attention back to her face, meeting her dark eyes.

"I want to apologize for the way I spoke to you after you woke up from fainting," Butch said before he lost his courage. "I shouldn't have spoken so harshly. I'm sorry." His eyes fixed on her reflection, unable to move from her porcelain features.

Lenora's gaze remained on the mirror too, not turning to face him directly. "Thank you for apologizing. I . . . I'm sorry as well. I know I should've gone to you."

"Thank you," he murmured, his voice low as he took a step closer to her. "I spoke with Puck just now," he said, watching as she turned to stone. "He interrupted my meeting with the council to demand to see you on his terms."

Lenora's eyes widened, but before she could turn to face him, he stepped forward until her back pressed against his front. He swept her hair off the back of her neck, letting his fingers brush over her soft skin. She inhaled but did not flinch away.

"I told him you get to decide if you see him, not the other way around." He watched her in the mirror as her gaze followed his hand, which trailed from the back of her neck across her shoulder and down her arm. She shivered. He smirked. "You are his queen, after all," he said in a low voice.

At that, she smiled. "I am, aren't I?"

"And mine."

"And yours," she whispered, her breath hitching as he bent down and pressed a kiss to her neck, just below her ear.

"I'm sorry," he whispered against her skin, relishing the way she melted into him. "For everything."

Lenora closed her eyes, one of her hands trailing up to run her fingers through the back of his hair. At her touch, his knees nearly gave out on him. He hadn't realized how much he'd missed it, even in the last few days. Her nails gently scratched his head as he pressed more kisses to the column of her neck.

"I know," she said, her voice breathy and intoxicating. "I know."

"And I've missed you," Butch said, suppressing a groan as she tilted her head to the side, giving him more access to her skin. He accepted it by trailing kisses until she stopped him, turning his head to face her.

She pressed a kiss to his lips, lingering there as a smile curved her lips.

"Prove it."

Chapter 65

LENORA

Lenora lay nestled in Butch's arms, her heartbeat slowing down as his comforting presence lulled her into a deep sleep. As she drifted off, her mind slipped into a dream.

She stood in a lush meadow similar to one she remembered near her father's castle in the Black Forest. The sky stretched above her, painted in all the beautiful shades of twilight. The scent of wildflowers filled the air, and a gentle breeze rustled through the grass.

Lenora walked barefoot, the soft earth cool beneath her feet. In the distance, a figure stood beneath a large willow tree.

Her heart quickened as his features became clearer and clearer: his silver eyes first, then the short chestnut hair that fell in waves around his face, and his pointed ears.

Leo.

He wore a simple tunic and breeches, just as he had every other time she'd seen him.

And the warm smile on his face . . . It felt like home.

"You found me," he said, holding out a hand. "I thought you'd gotten lost, my sweet bloom."

Lenora took his hand. "Where did you go?" she asked, letting him pull her into a hug. She barely reached his armpits.

"Away."

"Why?" She looked up at him, her eyes scanning his face for answers.

His smile faded, replaced by a look of sorrow. "I had to," he said, pressing a soft kiss to her forehead.

"But we were supposed to be together. You promised."

Leo's grip on her tightened even as he started to fade before her eyes.

"I'm sorry, Nora."

"I needed you," she cried. She tried to hold on to him. "I need you now."

She reached out as he stepped back, but her hand passed through him like mist. Panic surged through her.

"No! Don't leave me again!"

He was already gone by the time Lenora collapsed to her knees, sobs racking her body. The meadow darkened.

She was alone.

At least, she thought she was.

From the shadows surrounding her, though, a figure emerged. The darkness bent to her will, bowing to her as she crossed to Lenora.

"What are you doing here?" Lenora asked, wiping her cheeks with the backs of her hands.

"I'm here for you." Estrada held out her hand, but Lenora hesitated.

"What do you want from me?"

"I think, Lenora, you desire something I can give you." Her voice was serene and calm. Gentle, even.

Lenora's eyes shot open, and she froze in her husband's arms. His calming breaths on the back of her neck reassured her she hadn't woken him, which came as a relief. There wasn't a single part of the dream that she could tell her husband.

Not a single part.

Chapter 66

Evangeline sat on the edge of her bed, gaze fixed on the tray of food still resting on her side table. Outside her window, the sun had already set. She tightened her fingers on the small cup with a mixture she'd painstakingly made with rudimentary instruments and ingredients. Even without proper equipment, she knew she'd done what she could. Her past employer, Elthia, would've been proud of her apothecary skills. Well, maybe not if she knew what Evangeline was using it for.

Evangeline pinched her lips together.

Her father's name carved into solid stone flashed across her mind.

It was time.

Carefully, she poured the sleeping draft into the soup, ensuring the liquid was mixed in and undetectable. If this didn't work, there was no backup plan. She'd have to start from scratch. Figure out another way to get answers.

Her heart pounded in her chest as she carried the tray over to the door and knocked.

It had felt strange the first few times she'd knocked from the inside of the room, but the first time she hadn't, she'd been held at sword point until she'd explained in a frantic voice that she was finished with her book and wanted a new one. So, she rapped her knuckles against the door, waiting for the guard she knew was there to respond.

He didn't.

Risking a sword to the eye, Evangeline peeked her head out.

"Excuse me," she said, her voice deliberately soft, unassuming. "I don't have much of an appetite tonight. I'm not sure if you've eaten already, but would you like some? It seems a shame to let it go to waste."

The guard raised an eyebrow and then shrugged. "Sure, why not?" He took the tray, nodding his thanks. Then he began to eat.

Evangeline offered him a small smile before closing the door, silently praying the draft would take effect soon.

Minutes felt like hours. Evangeline paced back and forth in her room, twisting the bracelet on her left wrist around and around and around.

When it seemed like she'd waited long enough for something to have happened, she carefully opened the door. Evangeline let out a relieved breath and slipped out of the room at the sight of the guard slumped against the floor in a deep sleep.

It didn't take long to navigate the corridors, and she kept to the shadows, her steps light and swift. When she reached the record hall, she crossed her fingers, hoping she wasn't too late.

If she'd timed it right . . .

The record keeper stepped out of the room, closing the door and locking it behind her. Evangeline tucked away her smile as she counted the seconds. The woman turned to walk down the hallway toward where Evangeline hid around the corner. Evangeline held her breath, and when the footsteps were close enough, she rounded the corner.

"Oh, I'm so sorry!" Evangeline exclaimed as she stumbled into the woman. As she helped the woman steady herself, Evangeline deftly slipped the key from the record keeper's belt.

"Oh, no, dear. Don't worry. I'm all right," the woman said with a smile as Evangeline fussed over her. "Have a good evening," she said, patting Evangeline on the shoulder as she continued down the hall.

Evangeline watched her disappear around a corner before grinning down at the silver key in her hand. Checking over her shoulder, Evangeline slipped the key into the lock. Her hands remained steady as she opened the door and then closed it behind her. Feeling around in the low light, Evangeline finally found a lantern and a match. She lit it.

The sight that greeted her made her pause. An overwhelming weight fell onto her chest. She couldn't breathe.

Rows upon rows of records stretched out before her, towering shelves filled with books that seemed to reach to the ceiling, two stories high. The sheer volume of information had her lungs failing to function and her heart working twice as hard. She had no idea where to begin, had not planned for so many records.

Taking a deep breath, she steadied herself against the nearest shelf. The records of prisoners had to be somewhere in the vast archive before her. It was just a matter of figuring out what sort of system the record keeper used to organize the documents. That would be simple enough.

She hoped.

Evangeline had grown up in a bookshop, after all.

How hard could it be?

Really hard, as it turned out.

Evangeline started with the nearest shelf, scanning the titles and labels on the spines of the books and ledgers. Her gaze darted from one title to the next, searching for a pattern. She pulled out a few volumes before replacing them.

Frustration mounted with each second that passed.

She couldn't understand what order the records were stored in. It wasn't alphabetical—not by title, at least. And not by subject.

Evangeline let out an annoyed sound as she wrinkled her nose and gazed around. She'd barely made it a few rows in, and it already felt like time was running away without her.

She didn't know how long the sleeping draft would last on the guard posted outside her room. If she returned after it'd worn out, that would raise questions, and she'd certainly be caught.

Her desperation grew, and Evangeline moved faster from shelf to shelf, her thighs burning from squatting to read the titles on the lowest shelves and then rising to read the ones on the highest. Evangeline tilted her head as she walked down the aisles until her neck felt as though it might be permanently sideways.

The task seemed impossible the more she thought about it.

"Come on," she whispered to herself, wholly focused on the records in front of her. "Where are you?"

She flipped through another ledger, using the light of the lantern propped on the shelf to skim the page.

There had to be a record somewhere in the room with her father's name in it. Something that could tell her what'd become of him after he'd abandoned her. Something to make the risky endeavor of sneaking into the record hall worth it.

The dim light from the single lantern cast long shadows across the hall, making the towering shelves seem even more imposing. Evangeline shivered. The room was cold, biting through her thin tunic to her skin beneath.

"Ugh, come on," she said, louder this time as frustration filled her voice. "Where is it?"

"Looking for something?"

Evangeline spun around, her heart leaping into her throat.

The Mongoose stood a few feet away, a smug grin on his face. The burn scars on his face and neck seemed even more ominous in the harsh light from the lantern.

"You shouldn't be in here," he said in a singsong voice, taking a step toward her. She retreated a step in return.

"Did you follow me?" she asked, her voice cracking.

"Not quite, little mouse." Stoll tilted his head, a predatory grin crossing his face. "I went to your room first, and when I found your room empty, I decided I'd have to try another night."

Evangeline's body thrummed with energy, though she wasn't sure whether it was urging her to stay and fight or flee for her life. "Try what?"

"To kill you."

Flee.

Definitely flee.

But he'd gotten closer again. She retreated a step, moving deeper into the shadows and away from her lantern.

"You went to my room to kill me?" she asked, stalling as her mind tried to work out an escape plan. She wasn't that far from the exit. She could outrun him.

Maybe.

But maybe not.

"Emmalee Estrada murdered my little brother in that boulder field. He was all I had left. And now I'll take you from her." Stoll sneered at her, his teeth eerily bright in the light.

"It won't bring your brother back," Evangeline said, gauging the distance to the end of the aisle as she continued to back up.

"You think I don't know that?" Stoll growled. "But it's a start."

Before Evangeline could react, Stoll lunged at her. She moved to the side just as he tackled her to the floor, his shoulder ramming into her rib cage as he wrapped his arms around her.

The air whooshed out of her lungs when her back hit the ground. Stunned, she lay still for a second, urging her breathing to return. But he managed to straddle her, pinning her to the ground with one large hand around her neck and the other holding her left hand against the cold floor. With only one free hand, Evangeline scratched at his skin.

"Please, Stoll," she begged, choking as his fist tightened around her throat. Her eyes widened.

With the lantern lighting him from the back, all she could make out in his silhouette were the ghostly whites of his eyes and his teeth displayed in an animalistic grin.

He leaned closer, pressing more of his weight onto the hands holding her down. But a thought formed somewhere in the back of Evangeline's mind, even as the lack of oxygen started to affect her vision.

Just a little closer, and—

Evangeline raked her nails down the side of Stoll's face when he got too close. He swore, howling in pain as he released her to cover his face.

She didn't hesitate. With a buck of her hips, she dislodged him, distracted as he was, and squirmed away. In seconds, she made it to her feet and sucked in air as she ran down the aisle.

Evangeline turned the corner, her gaze darting around frantically, searching for any means of escape. The rows of records seemed endless. But she couldn't stop—not when angry footsteps pounded nearby.

Maybe that was an advantage.

He'd managed to sneak up on her originally because she'd been so distracted, but in theory, she could be quieter.

It went against every instinct, but Evangeline stopped running. Her lungs thanked her for it, but her heart pounded its revolt.

She held her breath, begging her poor lungs to hold out a little longer as she tiptoed down an aisle. If she could sneak to the front, she might be able to—

"Little mouse, where'd you go?" Stoll's voice filled the room, originating somewhere to her right. The sound of it made her tremble.

She let out a little of the air trapped in her chest, taking a small step forward.

The board creaked.

"I hear you," he crooned.

Evangeline's gaze snapped behind her. Still empty. She let out more air, turning back to face forward.

And screamed.

Stoll loomed in front of her, a giant hulking shadow blocking the direction she'd planned to go.

He reached out faster than she expected, gripping her by the arm and slamming her into the nearest bookshelf. He gripped her neck again, this time with both hands.

It was twice as effective, and in no time, blackness swarmed her sight.

"Found you," he muttered, his breath rotten.

With no other plan, Evangeline did what she'd done before in similar situations when her stepfather had used her in his schemes: She kicked between his legs. Hard.

He dropped.

She ran.

Stoll cursed behind her, shouting awful things at her. She didn't stop. Wouldn't stop. Not again.

Evangeline turned down another aisle, praying it would lead to the exit. Instead, she ran smack into a solid wall.

The wall grew arms and steadied her.

"Silas," she gasped, staring up into familiar blue eyes. "Help," she managed to whisper before her legs gave out on her.

He caught her, gripping her by both arms. "Where?" Silas asked, his voice calm.

Evangeline didn't have time to respond before thunderous footsteps pounded in their direction.

"Stand down, Kendrick," Silas said, moving Evangeline until he stood in front of her. Thankfully, her legs had decided to function again. "That's an order, Commander."

"This witch deserves to die. She and Estrada. They're the same."

Silas drew his sword, the steel catching any glimmer of light. "I said stand down." Silas's voice dropped to a growl.

Evangeline stumbled backward when Stoll charged Silas, his own sword drawn in a flash. The sharp clash of metal filled the air as Silas parried Stoll's attack.

"Run, Evie," Silas ordered, not looking at her as he blocked another blow from Stoll. "Go!" he barked.

Hesitating for a moment, Evangeline watched as Stoll shoved Silas up against a bookshelf. The impact shook the two-story shelf, and the thing teetered.

"Evie!" Silas shouted. "Get out of—" Silas didn't finish, instead hissing in pain.

She started to run as soon as she noticed Silas gripping his side. Stoll gripped Silas by his head, slamming it into the shelf. The Mongoose fixed her with his venomous glare. Dropping his sword, he started toward her.

She ran.

Her arms pumped at her side.

It wasn't enough.

Stoll grabbed her hair, yanking her to a stop and pinning her to the stone wall. Her skull smacked against the stone, and stars twinkled in her vision.

He used both his hands to secure her as she struggled to look past him, hoping she'd see Silas. But no. Stoll had cornered her again. Alone. Again. She couldn't breathe. With one hand in her hair and his other trying to catch her wrists as she tried over and over to land a hit, Stoll held control. She grunted as he gave up on securing her hands and instead punched her in the stomach, then kneed her in the same place.

With his hand yanking her head up, she couldn't bend over when the pain in her stomach tried to pull her down.

"You are scum," he whispered into her ear. "You deserve death. My brother didn't."

"Please," Evangeline panted, but she cringed when he slapped her across the cheek.

"Begging won't save you. Nothing will."

"Release her, Stoll," Silas gasped, his breathing labored but his voice still commanding.

Stoll spun around to face Silas, using Evangeline as a barrier between them. With one hand still tearing hair out of the back of her head and the other one wrapped around her throat, he backed away, dragging her with him.

"I'm walking out of here, Thorne," Stoll called.

"No, you're not." Silas held his sword with his right hand while his left covered the right side of his torso. Darkness bled between his fingers, staining his shirt. "You're under arrest."

"For what?"

"Attacking someone under the protection of His Majesty, the king."

Stoll barked out a laugh, then yanked hard on Evangeline's hair until her neck was exposed. "She's a prisoner. A rat."

"She's not . . . She's . . . Let her go, Kendrick."

Stoll spat to the side, and Evangeline whimpered as he dragged her back another few steps. Silas followed, keeping the same distance between them. "What kind of marshal chooses this"—he shook Evangeline—"over his own man?"

"Stoll, I'm warning you—"

"You're a traitor, you know. She has magic, Silas! And she's friends with that . . . with that . . . sorceress!"

Evangeline's wide eyes found Silas's, and a second later, he returned his icy glare to the man slowly dragging her toward the exit.

"This woman is important. Very, *very* important. If you kill her, you'll ruin things bigger than you or me. If you kill her—"

"*When* I kill her, I'll be doing the world a favor. And getting justice for Corwinn. For my brother."

Evangeline narrowly avoided Silas's outstretched sword, catching herself on her hands and knees when Stoll shoved her toward Silas. She hit the ground hard and turned in time to see Stoll disappearing out the record hall door.

Silas swore, taking several steps in the direction Stoll had gone before stopping and turning to look at her.

Evangeline pushed herself to her feet, using the wall for support.

She didn't know what she was doing until she'd already wrapped her arms around Silas's waist in a tight hug.

He hissed, pushing her away, and replaced his hand over his side.

"He caught me with the tip of his sword," Silas explained, leaning against the wall.

"I'm so sorry," Evangeline said, raising her shaking hand to cover her mouth.

"I'm fine," he said, though it came out more as a grunt than anything. "Get the lantern. I need . . . I need to get . . . get men looking f-for him." Silas started to slide down the wall, but Evangeline caught him. He was heavy, way heavier than she could hold without some help.

"Silas, I need you to help me," she rasped, her throat still sore from the two times Stoll had nearly choked her to death.

With just enough assistance from Silas, Evangeline managed to maneuver him to the front of the record hall. "Stay here," she said before running back to the lantern, which still glowed where she'd left it. By the time she returned to Silas, lantern in hand, he'd propped himself up against a table and was using his hand to ball his shirt against his side.

He stood there bare chested, watching her approach.

"To staunch the bleeding," he muttered.

Evangeline nodded, her tongue suddenly refusing to work as she stared at the chiseled lines of his chest. The broad muscles spanning across his back and shoulders. A tattoo of a tree reaching with its roots down to the waistband of his pants and growing all the way up the left side of his torso to where branches spread over his shoulder and across his chest. The branches crisscrossed over his bicep, and as she brought the lantern closer, the details of tiny flowers came into focus.

"Evie," he gasped, snapping her out of her daze. "If you don't mind . . ." He held out his arm, gesturing for her to get closer.

"Right, sorry," she said, blowing out the lantern and leaving it on the table. She took her position next to him and gritted her teeth as he leaned his weight on her.

Together, they walked out of the record hall.

And Evangeline couldn't stop her mind from wandering to the pure relief that had filled her the moment Silas had stepped in.

The moment his arms had wrapped around her.

The moment he'd saved her life.

Chapter 67

SILAS

Silas's side was on fire, and the worst part was that he had no desire to go to the infirmary. Despite a raging storm of dizziness threatening to topple him over—a bloody souvenir from Stoll striking his head—he refused to leave Evie's side until she was safe in her room.

Even when they came across two of his men on patrol.

It was at that point he started to regret removing his shirt to staunch the blood flow coming from the wound on his side.

"Marshal, what is going—is that blood? Get Helena," Commander Volmar barked to the man next to him. The other guard had not taken two steps when Silas stopped him.

"No," Silas said, leaning heavily on Evie's shoulders as the hall tilted. "Kendrick Stoll is somewhere in the castle. I want him f-found." He winced as he readjusted his grip on his side. "He is under arrest. Is that understood, Commander?"

Commander Volmar looked at him with wide eyes before glancing at Evie beside him.

"Please, Benji," she said in a small voice.

At her words, the commander stood a bit taller.

Silas narrowed his eyes at "Benji," waiting for him to respond. Some part of Silas knew his reaction came from a spot of jealousy, but he shoved the thought away.

"Spread the word about Stoll," Commander Volmar finally said to the other guard, who saluted both Volmar and Silas before running off. "Sir, you're injured."

"Really?" Silas said, sarcasm slipping from his lips as he grimaced. "I hadn't noticed."

Apparently, Evie was not amused by Silas's retort. "Stoll cut his side, and it's b—"

"Bring a medkit to her room," Silas interrupted. "I'm escorting her there to make sure Stoll doesn't try anything else."

"I'll bring a kit, but do you want me to alert Helena? If the cut is deep—"

"I'm fine. Medkit, *Benji*. Five minutes." Silas dismissed him with a flick of his wrist, moving toward the nearest staircase and dragging Evie with him.

"That was rude," Evie muttered under her breath. "He was only trying to help."

Silas clenched his jaw but said nothing as he realized his mistake in choosing the servants' staircase. It may have been closer, but it was narrow and winding. Walking side by side with the beautiful human crutch next to him wouldn't work.

"I'll go first," he said, gripping the wall for support.

It took more concentration than he would've liked, and by the time he got to the top, his head spun, and he had to press his temple against the cold stone until it stopped.

Problem was, it didn't stop.

"Silas?" Evie said, her voice gentle as she placed a hand on his forearm. "Are you—I mean, can I help?"

He was grateful she hadn't asked if he was okay. "Yes, here." Silas held up his arm, gesturing for her to resume her spot next to him. He'd be lying if he said he didn't enjoy her warmth as she pressed against his bare skin.

They walked slowly down the hall of the second floor. Silas's side throbbed, and his vision blurred intermittently from the blow to his head. The corridor seemed endless, like something from a nightmare.

"Did you do that?" Silas asked when they rounded a corner and he saw the guard who was supposed to be posted at her door slumped on the floor.

"I think there are more concerning things at the moment," she mumbled under her breath.

"He's not dead, is he?"

That made her pause, and she squirmed under his weight so she could glare up at him. "Do you really think I'm capable of cold-blooded murder?"

He refrained from pointing out that her friend was.

"No. So, he's sleeping? How'd you manage that?"

"Doesn't your side hurt or something?" she countered, tugging him forward and opening the door with her free hand.

Silas rolled his eyes. "You're impossible."

"I'll take that as a compliment." She guided him inside her room and helped him sit on the edge of the bed. A second later, she went back to close the door.

Silas closed his eyes for a moment when the room swayed.

"Why won't you go to the infirmary?" Evie asked, her voice traveling past him, and when he opened his eyes, she'd disappeared into the small bathing room attached to her bedroom.

"Wasn't sure if he'd try again. Didn't want to risk it," Silas responded as Evie came back into the room with some clean cloths and a bowl of water.

"He said he came to my room first but found I wasn't here. He . . ." Evie pressed her lips together, a frown tugging at her forehead. "He said he came to kill me."

"Pretty sure he made that clear." Silas ground his teeth together, scowling at nothing in particular.

"Hold still," Evie instructed as she knelt on the floor beside him.

"Yes, ma'am," Silas murmured, hissing in pain a second later when she pulled his blood-soaked shirt from his side. The touch of her fingers on his skin sent shivers down his spine, and she chided him when he trembled.

He couldn't take his eyes off her. Not when she dipped a cloth into the water. Not when she raised it to his side. Not when the determined look on her face turned to something like concern.

"This looks bad, but I think the bleeding is slowing," she said, finally looking up after a minute. "Are you sure you don't want to go to—"

"I've had worse. Trust me." He caught and held her gaze, and even when she looked down, scanning his bare chest and the lines of the tattoo trailing along his skin, he watched her.

In that moment, he would've given anything, paid anything, to know what was going on in her mind.

Did she notice how close they were? Did she feel the way his breath hitched every time their skin touched? Did she realize that his heart beat faster when she was near?

"What?" Evie asked, drawing his gaze from where it'd dropped to her mouth, trailing along the lines of her lips. "Silas?"

How was it possible that his name coming out of her mouth set his body on fire? More than the pain in his side. More than the flames in the lanterns around the room. More than the blazing inferno he'd gone into to save the very man who'd tried to kill her.

One word, his name, spoken by Evie, and he couldn't breathe. The only thing he could think about was how his name would taste when she spoke it against his lips.

"Silas? What's wrong?"

He blinked.

Stoll must've hit him harder on the head than he'd thought.

"I'm fine. I think . . . I think I may have a concussion." His voice came out raspy.

And he was still staring at her mouth.

"What?" Evie said, her voice rising in alarm.

"Stoll slammed my head against a shelf."

"Right," she said, standing and bending over him.

Silas held his breath as she cupped his cheeks, turning his face to the side as she examined his head. "Oh no, it's been bleeding too. Why didn't you say something?" she scolded, leaning over him to grab the cloth she'd been using on his side. Evie continued to cup his cheek with one hand as she dabbed the cut on his head with the other. He stared up at her, watching the way she bit her bottom lip in concentration.

Did she know how maddening her mouth was? When she was speaking. When she was silent. When she was standing close enough for him to smell the soap on her skin.

His chest tightened.

Evie tilted his head, angling it for a better view of the wound on his skull. The world swayed. Before he knew what he was doing, he lifted his hands to steady himself, grasping her hips as though she were an anchor.

She tensed, her brown eyes focusing on his face.

Evie's gaze dropped to his mouth. Silas's heartbeat quickened. Her soft hand on his cheek brushed along his jaw, and he let out a low groan. When she let her thumb trail over his bottom lip, he nearly melted, sinking into her touch. Evie dropped the cloth, letting her hands stray along the back of his neck with her nails. The sensation sent goose bumps up and down his arms.

His hands clenched around her waist, pulling her closer. Closer.

"What are you doing?" Evie whispered, her voice breathy as she tilted her head and blinked down at him. She flicked her gaze from his eyes to his mouth, the same thing Silas was doing to her.

The distance between them closed inch by inch.

"Tell me to stop," he whispered, only a few inches from those lovely lips. "Tell me this is a terrible idea." His side burned as he tilted his head back farther. "Tell me—"

"Stop talking," she breathed, stepping closer until she stood between his legs, her hands moving to either side of his neck. She stroked his jaw lightly with both thumbs.

"Evie," he murmured, near enough to feel her breath tickle his face.

"Silas."

There it was, that fire she so effortlessly created within him.

"Can I—"

"Please," she whispered, the word a desperate, needy thing.

How was it that she wanted to kiss him as much as he wanted to kiss her? She leaned down.

A breath away.

A knock at the door had Silas's body tensing and Evie scrambling out of his grasp, leaving him cold and frustrated.

"What?" Silas barked, ready to rip the head off of whoever walked through the door.

Commander Volmar saluted as soon as he entered. "I brought the medkit."

Before Silas could shout at him to get out, Evie crossed the room, a smile on her face. Despite the tension from the moment they'd shared and the abrupt ending to it, she looked composed. Kind. Beautiful. Kissable.

Silas scowled at his commander as Evie took the medical kit and thanked him.

"The officer outside. Is he—"

"He's fine," Silas said, rolling his eyes.

"What happened to him?"

Evie's eyes were wide when she glanced over her shoulder at Silas. An idea formed in Silas's mind, and he opened his mouth before he could think it through.

"Stoll came here looking for her." Silas nodded toward Evie. "The guard is unconscious. He'll be fine." None of it was a lie, technically. Stoll *had* come to Evie's room in search of her. And the guard outside her room *was* unconscious and would be fine.

"Good." Volmar glanced at Evie and then the medkit in her hands. "Can I help with—"

"No," Silas said, his tone curt. "I'm fine. Get out."

Evie shot him a warning glare before turning back to Volmar. "Thank you for bringing this, Benji."

"Of course, miss." He sent a cautious look over her head to Silas, who returned it by mouthing "get out" with a scowl on his face. "If there isn't anything else, I'll go join the search for Stoll."

"Find him, Commander," Silas shouted even as Volmar left the room.

Evie turned back to Silas, her expression taut. "Why do you insist on being rude to him?" she asked, bringing the medical kit to him on the bed.

"I don't know. Why do you like him so much?"

"He's one of the only guards who's been kind to me." She answered the question without looking at him, but something in the sad tone of her voice made his stomach twist in an uncomfortable way. He hadn't considered that maybe the guards weren't kind to her. With Stoll's attack, it shouldn't have been such a surprise. And Malkim had hurt her too.

"I'm sorry," Silas said, placing a hand on her arm to get her attention. "I should've realized sooner that my men were . . . well, acting foolishly."

Evie shook her head, shrugging out from his grip. "I'm a prisoner. It makes sense they wouldn't like me."

Silas opened his mouth to argue, then slammed it shut to keep from crying out when she pressed a cloth dipped in what smelled like vinegar to his side. It burned, and he dug his fingers into her duvet to distract himself.

"Can you lean back for me?" she asked, waiting as he adjusted himself until he was propped up on his arms, legs still hanging off the edge of the bed. Evie began placing bandages along the cut on his side, and once again, Silas watched her.

However, whatever spell had been over them earlier had been broken the moment "Benji" had knocked on the door. Silas wrinkled his nose.

Evie worked with deft and precise fingers, and soon enough, she finished securing the bandages with a wrap around his torso.

When she sat back on her heels and looked up at him, Silas's breath caught. She looked perfect despite the flyaways in her hair, the bruises forming on her cheek and neck, and the blood from his own wounds staining her skin and tunic. Absolutely jaw-dropping.

403

"How did you know I'd be in the record hall?" she asked, her voice soft but insistent.

His stomach lurched. Silas hesitated, his mind racing for an answer that wouldn't reveal too much. He couldn't tell her about the dreams. The nightmares. Instead of replying, he countered, "What were you doing in there in the first place?"

Evie frowned, clearly displeased with his evasion. "That's not an answer."

"And neither"—he grimaced as he stood from the bed—"was that."

"Silas."

"Evie?" He lifted an eyebrow, scanning the room and noting the bloody mess they'd made. Silas sighed. "I'll send someone to clean up." He swayed a little, steadying himself against one of the posts of the bed.

Evie's eyes flickered with concern, but she didn't move from the floor.

"I'm going to go make sure someone *awake* is posted outside your room. Do me a favor and stop putting my men to sleep."

"Silas, you didn't—"

"Good night, Evie," he said over his shoulder.

His mind continued to race as he made his way through the castle after setting one of the kinder guards up at her door.

He needed to find Stoll.

A draft from a window made him shiver.

First, though, he needed a shirt.

Chapter 68

BUTCH

He stood with his hands twisting in his tunic, still too large for him, looking up with blurry eyes at the door of his father's office. His small hand trembled as he reached for the doorknob. The heavy wooden door creaked open, revealing his father sitting behind the massive desk, his face a stone-cold mask of disapproval.

"Son," his father's voice boomed. Butch flinched. "Come here."

Butch stepped inside, his heart a pounding fleet of drums in his chest. The dreary walls of the room seemed to close in around him until the room was too small. He approached the desk, his legs shaking, and stood before his father.

King Valryn towered over him even while seated.

"Do you know what I learned this morning?" his father growled, rising to his feet. His shadow loomed over Butch. "Speak, boy!" His hand lashed out before Butch could react, striking him across the face.

Butch whimpered, his bottom lip trembling. "I-I don't know."

"Don't lie to me."

"I-I'm n-not. I d-don't know." Butch balled his tiny hands into fists at his sides, staring up at his father with what he hoped was an appropriate expression.

"I heard you and that servant boy were caught sneaking out through the servants' entrance when you were supposed to be watching the guards train."

Butch trembled. "I . . . I . . ."

"You . . . You . . ." his father mocked. "Speak like a prince, boy! Not a bumbling fool from the lower town."

"I-I'm sorry." Butch's eyes drew moisture, and he clenched his jaw as he avoided his father's eye.

A mistake.

His father leaned over him, taking Butch's jaw in his hand and jerking it upward until Butch's gaze met his father's crippling one.

"Tears are for women and weak men. Are you going to be either of those?" His fingers dug into Butch's cheeks.

"N-no." Butch bit back the traitorous tears.

"No, what?" His father's low voice gripped Butch's trembling heart.

"No, s-sir."

His father's eyes bored into him, and a second later, he grabbed Butch by the collar. "You're weak," he spat, dragging him closer. "Just like your good-for-nothing mother. Stay away from that servant boy."

The room spun as his father shoved him backward until Butch fell and hit his head on a nearby chair. When he blinked a few times, another person appeared in the room.

Puck leaned against the wall with a cruel smirk on his face.

"A disappointment through and through, it would seem," Puck sneered. "I suppose I'm to blame for ever thinking you'd be good enough for Lenora. And your poor child. A pathetic man makes for a pathetic father, and you, Your Majesty, are the king of fools. Your child is doomed."

Butch lurched to his feet, moving to swing at Puck for his insults. His fist connected with his father-in-law's jaw. His head snapped to the side, but when he swiveled his head to look back at Butch, his face held a bloody sneer.

"That's right, hit me. Show me how much you resemble your father."

Butch punched him again.

"Good, son. That's how we teach a lesson, isn't it?"

Butch's knuckles were bleeding by the time he pulled back for a third swing. Or maybe it was Puck's blood.

"This. This is the kind of father you will be," Puck shouted, his face a bloody mess. He spat a crimson glob to the side, still smiling maniacally. "Your child will have more scars than you if you keep this up. Come on, son. Give me another one."

The office twisted around him, morphing into dark stone walls. Somewhere in the distance, chains clinked and prisoners moaned.

A small figure huddled in the corner of the cell. The child looked up at him, eyes wide with fear. He didn't know how, but he knew the child, recognized it as his own.

Butch wanted to throw up at the look the child gave him—trembling and terrified, looking at him with the same fear he'd once had for his father. Butch tried to speak, to comfort the child, but his voice came out as a harsh, commanding roar.

"Worthless! Absolutely worthless!" he heard himself shout, the words sharp and echoing in the dungeon.

The child flinched, tears streaming down ruddy cheeks. Butch's heart broke at the sight.

He heard his voice again, biting and cold, a whisper of his father behind his words.

"Tears are for the weak. The pathetic. So cry. Show me who you really are, child! A weak, pathetic little mistake."

Butch choked. He longed to reach out, was desperate to take back the words, to offer comfort. But his hands were stained with blood, and the child recoiled from his touch.

Jolting awake, Butch pressed his hands to his face. The room was dark, the only sound his ragged breathing. He sat up, running a trembling hand through hair slicked with sweat. He shoved the covers off, needing air.

Stumbling to his balcony, Butch lifted the latch and swung the doors open. He took a deep breath. Cool air filled his lungs, and he shivered.

The night felt eerily still, especially with dark clouds blocking most of the light from the three moons.

He leaned on the railing, letting the chill of the night air calm his racing thoughts. The nightmare kept its claws wedged deep within him, and with a sigh, he knew he wouldn't find rest again—at least not for a while.

After a few more minutes, Butch went back inside, pulled on a shirt, trousers, and his boots, and left his chambers. His steps were quiet in the dimly lit corridors, and his feet followed a familiar path to the training rooms without much help needed from his mind.

As he entered the hallway containing the multiple training rooms, someone grunted from the one closest to him. Butch peered through the crack where the door had been left open, and a small smile crossed his lips.

"Sleep is for the weak, right?" Butch said, leaning against the doorframe.

Silas looked up from where he'd been practicing a series of slow, deliberate exercises.

"Apparently," he said, straightening from his fighting stance. Silas wasn't wearing a shirt, and a bandage wrapped around his midsection.

Butch frowned at it, removing his own shirt and tossing it to the side of the room. "Does that mean I have to go easy on you?"

Silas bit his cheek, glancing down at the bandage. "That one doesn't, but my concussion does."

"How'd you manage that?" Butch asked, his back to his friend as he riffled through the weapon options. He chose a longsword, swinging it around a few times to check the balance. As with all the training weapons, the blades had been dulled. But he knew from experience they left pretty nice welts if wielded well.

"Commander Stoll. He attacked the prisoner. I managed to stop him, but not before he left a few love marks."

"Should you be exerting yourself down here? When did this happen?"

"I'm fine. And it happened a couple nights ago." Silas dropped back into his stance, and they began to circle each other.

"Why didn't you tell me?" Butch raised an eyebrow. "Is it because it was her?" Though he'd done his best to forgive Silas for hiding the fact that the prisoner had spoken to him long before she'd ever uttered a word to Butch, a small remnant of bitterness resided within him.

"No. I've just been busy between overseeing training for the recruits and managing Levick's men, not to mention responding to the other marshals. There's just been . . . a lot, I suppose. And now I have half a mind to hunt Stoll down myself and arrest him." Silas muttered the last part under his breath as he readied his weapon.

"Why did Stoll attack her this time?" Butch asked, striking first. He remembered the way the commander had tried to strangle Lia in his office, the clear hatred he had for her written in bold letters across his scarred face.

"I don't know. To finish the job, maybe. He clearly said he blames Estrada for his brother's death, and I think he believes killing her best friend will somehow make things even." Silas grunted, parrying a blow.

Butch scoffed. "That's not how it works."

"Obviously," Silas said, wincing as Butch forced him to bend out of the way. "Is Lia all right?"

"Lia?"

Butch lifted an eyebrow. "What do *you* call her?"

Silas avoided the question by dodging Butch's attack and landing his own blow to Butch's knee. It wasn't hard, but the loss still stung.

"Lia's fine. A little banged up, but she's strong."

"She'd have to be to go up against a commander in my royal guard one-on-one and get away alive," Butch muttered as he reset. "I assume you have men looking for Stoll."

"I've already sent out two groups. He was one of my commanders in charge of surveillance and reconnaissance though, so I have a feeling he's not going to be the easiest person to find. He's got connections most of us don't know about." Silas stepped forward, raising his sword. "But I'm handling it." The terse words did not go unnoticed.

"You're being careful though, right?" Butch asked as Silas made the first move.

"Of course. I have my men—"

"I mean with Lia, or whatever you call her when I'm not around." Butch cut off Silas's argument with a parry and a strike Silas narrowly avoided. "She can't be trusted. She's still Estrada's friend."

"I'm aware."

"You're clearly besotted with her, which I don't understand in the slightest. It could be a trick."

"I know."

"And it's playing with fire." Butch swatted Silas's attack away.

Silas's jaw clenched. "I'm aware."

"Just because she's attractive doesn't mean you can—"

"I said I'm aware, Butch," Silas snapped, managing for the second time to land a hit, this time on Butch's shoulder. It would certainly leave a mark. By the tense tone of voice, Butch had a feeling Silas had meant it to.

"You're sure you can handle her without getting burned?"

Silas waved off the question, clearly done with the subject as he moved across the mat. "Why are you down here anyway?" he asked.

"Couldn't sleep, just like you, I'd wager."

"Brother," Silas said in a warning tone of voice.

"I've been thinking about fatherhood," Butch said, surprised at the words that came out of his own mouth. He hadn't expected to speak with such candor. But if he could trust anyone, it was the little servant boy his father had loved to hate. "I had a dream, or a nightmare, really." Butch moved to the center of the mat for another round, but Silas shook his head after checking the bandage on his side.

"I'd better stop," he said, gesturing toward one of the practice dummies on the side of the room with his sword. "What was the nightmare about?" Silas put his practice weapon away as Butch stepped in front of the hay-filled pell.

"My father teaching me a lesson," Butch ground out as he swung, striking the dummy in the torso and then on the opposite side of its neck. "And then Puck was there."

Silas groaned from where he leaned against a nearby wall. "He'll make anything a nightmare. Even reality."

Butch couldn't stop the grin on his lips at Silas's comment.

"Truer words, brother," Butch said, running through training combinations he knew by heart. For some reason, though, he didn't convey the third part of his dream—at least not in detail. "I suppose I am concerned I'll be like them."

Silas was silent long enough that Butch paused to look at him.

"You're not him. Or Puck." He must've been waiting for Butch to meet his eye. "You see where they've made mistakes, and each day I've witnessed you fight hard to not fall into the same traps."

Butch scoffed, turning back to the abused pell. Hay fell out of open cuts despite the dulled weapon. "I may be more like them than you realize, Silas."

"You're not. The prisoner, Lia—she's proof of that. If your father were alive, he'd—"

"Have my head for the things I've done since his death," Butch finished, striking the dummy with what would've been a killing blow. He'd be lying if he said he hadn't pictured his father standing before him instead of the training pell.

"I'm not going to convince you, am I?" Silas gave an exasperated sigh.

Butch smiled, leaning on the sword as he turned to look at his oldest friend. "Not tonight."

Silas bit his cheek, then nodded. "Well then, get to work. You've gotten sloppy since you started sitting around all day on that overglorified chair."

"And you've gotten bossy since you switched out the red collar for a blue one."

"Because you *begged* me to."

"I did not."

"You were on your knees and everything."

Butch let out a loud laugh, the sound filling the room. For the first time since he'd woken from the suffocating nightmare, he felt as though he could breathe again.

Chapter 69

EVANGELINE

Evangeline's stomach dropped. She tightened her grip on the arms of the chair, where she sat across from Butch's desk in his office.

"Of course, Your Majesty," Silas said, saluting before he turned to leave the room. His crystal gaze caught hers, and he gave her what was likely meant to be a reassuring nod. Instead, the idea of him leaving her alone in the office with the king made her skin tighten, her pulse racing.

As soon as the door closed, Evangeline flicked her gaze back to the king. Butch stood at the window, a frown etched into his brow. Evangeline hadn't heard the order Butch had whispered to Silas, but whatever it was had to do with what Butch was watching outside the window.

Evangeline cleared her throat.

Butch's gaze remained fixed outside, his jaw clenched. A long moment passed before he finally turned his attention to her. "Did you think of something useful you can tell me about Estrada?"

She bristled. "That depends," Evangeline said, her eyes narrowing at him. "Are you done looking at your reflection in the window?"

His expression darkened. "Watch your tone. Remember to whom you speak."

"Oh, I remember," Evangeline said, scrunching her nose. "My jailor. A murderer. And a—"

"Enough!" he shouted, slamming his hand down on the side of his desk. "You forget your place."

"And you forget that I'm not afraid of you," she shot back, meeting his glare with defiance of her own. She stood, her hands on her hips. "You summoned me in here to question me, and yet all you've been doing is staring out that window and brooding."

His eyes flashed with anger, and for a moment, she thought he might lash out. She braced herself. Instead, though, he took a step closer, glaring down his nose at her.

"You have no idea the pressure on my shoulders right now."

Evangeline scoffed. "I sure don't. But I can tell you that demanding answers from me only to ignore me when I'm right in front of you is a waste of our time."

"Oh, and what would you rather be doing? Am I interrupting some important part of your day?" His tone was harsh. Demeaning. Butch's gaze latched on to hers as he stepped closer until they were a foot apart. "You go where I tell you when I tell you because I hold your life in my hand."

Evangeline pressed her lips together, a blatant threat on her tongue. The only reason the roles weren't reversed was because of the wretched bracelet on her wrist. However, pointing that out might get her a one-way trip to the executioner's platform.

Besides, she'd never act on it.

"No witty retort?" he goaded, his rich brown eyes ready to burn a hole through her head.

Evangeline opened her mouth to respond, leaning closer with a scathing comment on the tip of her tongue, but the office door flew open and the queen stormed in.

Chapter 70

LENORA

Lenora froze in the doorway to Butch's office.

It'd been a good day, as far as the pregnancy went. She'd been getting headaches periodically, and her hands and feet had swollen a bit, but it wasn't anything she couldn't handle. And when she'd woken and noticed the sun bright and high in the sky, she'd decided to go out into the garden on the fresh fall day. She hadn't even had a throbbing headache yet.

Not until Marshal Thorne came out to interrupt her time in the garden and scold her for not having the required six guards around her. She'd practically been able to hear her husband's voice coming out of the marshal's mouth as he repeated what was undoubtedly the king's reprimand.

But only a small headache had started. And more importantly, the marshal had unintentionally stoked a fire within her. Instead of taking out her frustration for her husband's overprotection on his best friend, Lenora had stormed into Butch's office, only to find him nose to nose with another woman.

The headache tripled, and the room swayed.

"Lenora," Butch said in greeting, the only hint of his surprise a slight widening of his eyes.

"What is this?" she demanded, gesturing toward the woman.

No, not just any woman.

Estrada's friend.

The prisoner.

She was prettier up close, probably because she wasn't lying half dead on an infirmary bed or distorted through a second-story window. The woman had medium-length white-blond hair, which she'd pulled into a half-up ponytail with a strip of yellow ribbon that fluttered as she turned to face Lenora. Her round brown eyes widened as her gaze met Lenora's. Though pale, likely from her time in the dungeon, her skin held a dainty blush over her cheeks and the bridge of her nose, where a spattering of light freckles rested. The woman wore a white tunic with a leather corset around her thin waist and a pair of dark brown trousers clearly too large for her, because a belt cinched a little too much fabric around her middle. The knee-high boots looked worn and weathered and, out of everything she wore, seemed to be the only thing that fit her properly. Despite the ill-fitting clothing, she was not short like Lenora, standing three to four inches taller.

Which put her three or four inches closer to Lenora's husband's face.

The room tipped again, and Lenora leaned against the wall. "Butch?" she asked, trying to force sharpness into her voice, but it came out weaker than she'd hoped.

The headache swelled, and Lenora gripped her head.

"Sit," Butch said, crossing the room in a few swift strides to guide her into the chair in front of his desk.

But as soon as she let go of the wall, up became down and left became right.

Butch caught her as all the light disappeared from the room.

WHEN LENORA WOKE, she was in her own bed and the curtains were closed, leaving the room quite dark. The familiar scent of lavender and chamomile filled her nose, and she shifted rather uncomfortably to breathe better; the baby was taking up more than its fair share of her abdomen.

Movement beside her caught her attention, and Lenora startled at the sight of Helena sitting next to her, a concerned expression on her lined face.

"What happened?" Lenora murmured, running a hand over her stomach.

"You fainted again, Your Majesty," Helena said gently, leaning forward to brush a strand of hair out of Lenora's face. "Is it true you've still been vomiting and have had persistent headaches?"

415

Lenora nodded. No doubt Helena had spoken to Merla and Kaylene to learn the details of her pregnancy.

"Why didn't you come to me?" Helena asked, a mixture of concern and exasperation crossing her face as she furrowed her brow.

"I-I didn't think anything of it."

Helena sighed. "Have you had any other problems? I noticed your feet are swollen."

"Um . . ." Lenora scratched her cheek. "Well, when I have the headaches, sometimes I see flashes of light in the corner of my eye, like a migraine. And every once in a while, my vision goes blurry. There's a pain below my ribs sometimes too, but I thought it might just be the baby taking up more room and pushing on things." Worry began to creep in as Helena's expression grew grave. "What is it? Is something wrong with the baby?" Lenora's grip on her blanket tightened. Her heart raced, and the sickening memories of her past failed pregnancies filtered into her mind.

If something was wrong . . .

If she'd failed again . . .

"I'm not positive, but some of these things could be a sign of a sickness some women develop during pregnancy." Helena rested a reassuring hand on Lenora's leg. "If it is this sickness, there are a couple things we can do to keep it from progressing, starting with staying off your feet and resting as much as possible. But I'm afraid the only true 'cure,' so to speak, is to deliver the baby."

"So, I have to stay in bed until the baby comes?"

"It depends if you have this sickness. I'll contact one of my friends. She's a midwife and will have greater insight than me. I'll arrange a meeting, if you'd like."

Lenora nodded.

"In the meantime, I need to go inform your husband about this. He asked me for an update when you awoke."

"Thank you, Helena," Lenora said, nodding as the physician left her alone in her room.

If fear was a monster, it was sitting on her chest, claws gnarled and twisted into her body, snarling over her.

Chapter 71

BUTCH

Butch's nerves made him feel sick as he climbed the last few stairs to the third floor. After his wife had fainted in his office, he'd sent Lia away and carried Lenora to her room, deciding to have Helena come to Lenora rather than the other way around.

And when Helena had told him the news that Lenora might be sick, he hadn't been able to think of anything but his wife.

The basket in his hand felt foreign as he lifted his free hand to knock.

Merla answered the door, curtsying as soon as she saw him. "Your Majesty," she said, stepping back and opening the door.

"Evening, Merla." He nodded to her and then to his wife's other handmaid. "Kaylene. Would you mind helping me set this up?" He offered Merla the basket containing the picnic the cook had prepared for him at his request.

"Of course," Merla said, taking the basket.

Butch crossed the room to Lenora, who watched him with a guarded expression.

"May I?" he asked, gesturing to a place on the bed next to her.

Regarding him for a moment longer, she finally gave a small nod.

"We need to talk," he said, taking a deep breath before he leaned back against the headboard. "When you walked into my office earlier this morning, I was questioning the prisoner about Estrada. We were arguing right before you came in."

Lenora remained silent, looking straight ahead instead of at him.

"I'm not sure what you thought was happening, but I can assure you, neither of us wanted to be in that room together." He reached for her hand and considered it a small success when she didn't pull away. "I'm sorry if I hurt you in some way."

"It wasn't seeing you together that . . . Well, that didn't help. But I was mad, Butch," she said, finally looking at him. Her eyes were sad. Dull, even. "I was upset you sent Marshal Thorne outside after me."

"I just wanted you to be—"

"Safe, I know. But you're suffocating me. I'm under enough stress as it is without having forty guards around me when I pee!" She gave an exasperated sigh, closing her eyes as she leaned her head back against the headboard. "I just need air to breathe." A second later, a small smile crossed her lips. "It's hard enough with this child playing squeeze the lungs every hour of every day." When she cracked one eye open to look at him, her smile grew. "I just need you to understand that while I appreciate how much you care, I also need to be able to have some freedoms."

Butch squeezed her hand. "I understand, and I'm sorry. I just . . . I'm worried. About you. About the baby. And now with what Helena said—"

"I know," she said, her voice solemn again as every hint of amusement vanished from her face. "I'm scared too. Scared I'll lose another one."

They were silent for a while, watching as Merla and Kaylene set up the picnic on the small table. When they were finished, Butch helped Lenora over to the chaise longue, sitting next to her. After a little while, their small talk shifted to a topic Butch had been avoiding as much as possible.

"It's been a little over four months since he arrived, and he's already got nearly the entire upper town in an uproar," Butch said in a low voice, his eyes narrowing at nothing as he sipped from his glass. "I have half a mind to send him back home now, only a few months out from when the baby is due to arrive."

"He'd be livid," Lenora said, a very kissable smirk on her lips.

"Good." Butch clinked his glass against hers, downing the rest of his wine while she sipped on her water. "Would serve him right for riling up the upper class about the 'injustices' of the war on them. As if they're the ones on the front lines of battle, paying the price with their lives, or in the slums, wondering where their next meal is coming from," Butch muttered.

Lenora was silent, her face drawn by the time he finished ranting. "I could . . . I mean, maybe he would listen to me."

Butch held back a scoff. "Lenora, has he ever listened to you?"

"No, but like you said, I am his queen now."

Chuckling softly, Butch leaned forward and pecked her on the forehead. "You certainly are. And—" He sighed, sitting straighter and pulling her closer by the hip. "If you want to meet with him, I'll arrange it."

BUTCH REGRETTED ARRANGING the dinner with his father-in-law from the moment Puck waltzed into the room several days later already drunk.

"It's about time my only daughter invited me to dinner," he said, brandishing a half-empty bottle of some sort of ale. His eyes were bloodshot, and his steps wobbled as he approached.

Lenora had been in bed since Helena had confirmed with the midwife that she did have the sickness Helena had suspected. Butch had made sure to visit her every day, even if it was only for an hour.

But today he'd spent most of the day with her. He'd read to her, told her stories from his childhood that involved getting into trouble with Silas, and napped with her when they'd both gotten tired in the middle of the day.

Besides relieving herself, she'd hardly moved.

But now she stood next to Butch, her hand nearly shattering his in a bone-breaking grip. Unsurprisingly, she'd reached for his hand as soon as her father had made his presence known by pounding on her door.

Butch gave her a reassuring squeeze before greeting his father-in-law.

"Please sit, Puck," Butch said, gesturing toward the sitting area.

"Is there a reason we're meeting in my daughter's chambers and not a proper dining room?" Puck asked, glancing around with his nose wrinkled.

"I'm sick," Lenora said, taking a seat next to Butch.

"So that's why you're lying around like an invalid while he lets the country fall apart."

Butch nearly choked on his drink.

"Father!" Lenora said, casting a wide-eyed look first at her father, then at Butch. She likely expected him to explode.

Oh, how he wanted to explode.

Very few had the audacity to speak so rudely in front of him.

Instead, Butch clenched his jaw and remained silent.

A glint of cockiness flashed over Puck's face. "What?" he asked innocently before nodding to Butch. "Even he knows it."

"That's enough," Butch growled.

"Now, if I were king—"

"The world itself would burn," Butch said, waving over the servants to begin serving food. "Shall we?" He was all too eager to start eating. It would mean a greater chance that Puck's mouth would be full, rendering him unable to speak.

As Butch shot daggers at his father-in-law over the table, he wondered if he'd get in trouble for carving out Puck's tongue and hanging it as a trophy in his office.

He smirked at the thought.

"So, you're sick now, huh?" Puck said, eyebrow raised as he looked at Lenora.

She seemed to wilt next to Butch as her father turned his ire on her.

"Yes, I—"

"Probably because you took so long to get pregnant. I told you you should've started on that sooner. Now look at what you've done." He gestured toward her stomach and then her bed with the end of his fork.

Lenora's voice wavered, but she held her ground before Butch could step in. "I'm doing everything I can. The physician said the only real cure is delivering the baby, and I can't do that for several more weeks."

Puck didn't respond verbally—thank goodness for chicken—but he did give his daughter an unimpressed glower.

"If I may, Puck," Butch said through gritted teeth. "My court is out for the next month. You may no longer be king of Haysinlin, but you still have land and people you're in charge of. What do they do while you're gone? Celebrate?" Butch raised an eyebrow, covering his small smile with his goblet.

Butch's father-in-law's fork paused midway to his mouth. "The men I left in charge are more than capable." Puck's eyes narrowed at Butch. "And I'm here to ensure my daughter isn't being neglected."

Lenora choked next to Butch, and he cast her a sideways glance to make sure she was all right before returning his ire to Puck.

"Then you're in luck. My wife and unborn child are receiving the best care."

Puck scoffed, waving the fork dismissively. "Care? Keeping her sequestered in her room like some delicate flower? That's not care. She needs to be stronger. Needs to grow a backbone."

Lenora shook her head. "I'm supposed to stay in bed and rest."

"Rest," Puck repeated, rolling his eyes. "You were always too soft. Always needing to be coddled and pampered. I bet if you were stronger, you wouldn't be in this position."

Butch stood abruptly, the chair scraping loudly against the floor. "Out," he barked, pointing to the door. When Puck didn't move, Butch stomped around the table, grasped him by the arm, and dragged him out of the room.

"Release me," Puck hissed, and Butch did, but only once they were in the hallway with the door shut.

Butch took a deep breath, trying to calm his nerves before he did something stupid.

Like shove his father-in-law against the nearest wall.

Which he did a second later.

"Listen to me carefully," he whispered, his voice icy. "Lenora is now queen. Has been since you and my father played matchmaker. She is *my wife* and *your queen*. And not just queen of Cyanthia or Haysinlin. Lenora Maudit is queen of Phildeterre. That woman in there is far more important than you will ever be." Butch tightened his grip on the lapels of Puck's jacket as he pressed him harder against the wall. "If I ever hear you utter another word against her or one meant to hurt her like that again, I will make you regret it until the day you join my father wherever he's burning."

Puck, face flushed with anger and no doubt too much alcohol, glared at Butch. "You're threatening me? I'm her father, boy."

"You're a bully, Puck. And a lousy drunkard at that." He shoved Puck, then let him go, taking several steps back in case Puck decided to get violent. A memory of the nightmare he'd had earlier in the month flashed in his mind, and he pictured Puck standing with his face bloodied.

Butch clenched his fists.

Taking a deep breath again, Butch rolled his shoulders back, letting his face fall into an indifferent mask.

"You've tormented her enough. She allowed you to stay because her heart is bigger than mine. And you repay her by making her feel small and insignificant." Butch lifted his chin. "If you can't treat her with the respect she's earned, then you're not welcome here."

Puck opened his mouth to respond, but Butch held up a hand, silencing him.

"Get your things and get out of my and my wife's home. I want you gone by tomorrow at midday." Butch leveled him with a glare his father had used on him many, *many* times. "Now get out of my sight."

"Fine," Puck spat. "But this isn't over. I'm still a part of your court."

Butch didn't bother responding. He turned on his heel and reentered Lenora's chambers, shutting the door firmly behind him.

Chapter 72

EMMALEE

She'd been seen. It'd been a stupid little gust of wind that'd managed to knock her hood off her head. She'd been gathering information about the king's movements, trying to learn more by eavesdropping on drunk guards at pubs. It'd worked, at least a little. She'd learned when the delegates from Jerr Pinn had left. She'd heard that the trade agreements had fallen through. She'd learned that there'd been a prison break on the night of the welcome ball—Evangeline's, she knew—and it'd failed. And she'd learned that the king continued to search for her in the Black Forest.

But she continued to push her luck every time she left the house.

And when her hood fell back and revealed her outside the most recent pub, a man had only seen her for a second before the damage was done.

She'd used her magic to knock him unconscious as he'd opened his mouth to call out, and then she'd returned to her home in Cyanthia, gathered what she could carry, and left.

Emmalee stood at the edge of the field where the tiny house she, Ariella, and Faeleen had grown up in sat. Her gaze scanned the familiar surroundings. It remained untouched, unnoticed by the king and his men despite its close proximity to the edge of Cyanthia.

Memories of her childhood with Ariella and Faeleen flooded her mind: Working in the small garden out back for food to fill their empty stomachs. Making trip after trip to the nearby stream to refill the barrel of water outside the house. Playing hide-and seek in the surrounding trees.

The sisters' deaths weighed heavier on Emmalee in the small field than they had directly after the failed rescue attempt over five months earlier. But after being seen, the tiny house felt like the only home she could return to, even if it felt emptier than it had when she'd come after the deaths of her husband and daughter.

Emmalee approached the tiny house, and when she pushed the door open and stepped inside, the silence struck her. The air hung thick with the scent of the dried herbs and flowers she'd left behind.

Emmalee missed Evangeline with an ache that grew stronger each day. She sat at the small table with room only for two. The last time she'd sat there, the queen had been sleeping in the second bedroom. Emmalee's brow furrowed when she realized she even missed Lenora's company.

How strange.

She'd been alone for five months, and it felt like a lifetime.

Focusing, Emmalee drew on her magic. She needed to feel connected to somebody, to someone who cared about her.

Well, cared more than just to see her dead, as plenty of people did.

Her magic formed droplets of darkness in the palm of her hand. She murmured her message to Evangeline.

"I miss you."

As tears welled in her eyes, she released the message, watching her magic slip away, vanishing out of the house as it hopefully found its way to her best friend.

Chapter 73

LENORA

Lenora was sure she was dying as she lay back against her pillows. With the curtains pulled closed, the room stayed dark except for the lanterns and the fire in the fireplace. The only sounds were the occasional rustle of Helena's robes or the murmur of whispered voices as she, Lenora's handmaids, a midwife, and a few female servants spoke.

Her sickness had worsened over the weeks, and the headaches, vision problems, and pain had become almost unbearable.

Thankfully, either Helena or Dianna was present during most hours of the day. They monitored her closely, checking to make sure both she and the baby remained healthy. And at least once a day, sometimes twice, Butch came to see her. The dark circles beneath his eyes did not go unnoticed by her, but she was sure she looked worse. Sometimes he read to her. Other times they simply talked. Every once in a while he would lie next to her as she rested on her side, and he'd rub her back.

Three days earlier, Helena had suggested they try to induce labor. She'd made it to thirty-seven weeks, and the sooner she had the child, the sooner the symptoms of the sickness would go away. At least, that was what the midwife had assured her.

Lenora had dutifully taken the prescribed doses of blue cohosh root, cotton root bark, and black cohosh root without complaint. She drank red raspberry leaf tea and held still as the midwife applied uncomfortable pressure to specific points.

Nothing seemed to be working—until the midwife suggested a rather unpleasant-sounding treatment.

Lenora felt exposed as the midwife sat on the opposite side of the bed, lifting Lenora's chemise. A minute later, Lenora gasped in pain as the woman proceeded to do exactly what she'd told Lenora she was going to do.

"I apologize, Your Majesty. I know it's not comfortable."

Understatement.

Certainly the most significant understatement to have ever been uttered.

The midwife continued for a moment, and then the pressure released. A warm sensation spread between her legs, followed by a rush of fluid.

Lenora's eyes widened, and she gasped. "Was that—"

"Yes." The midwife gave her a small smile. "Congratulations, Your Majesty. It's time to have a baby," the midwife said as a sharp cramp swelled in Lenora's lower abdomen.

Chapter 74

BUTCH

B utch paced the length of the hallway, his footsteps echoing off the stone walls as he grumbled under his breath. Every so often, he would pause and strain to hear any sound from behind the heavy wooden door that barred him from Lenora's room. His heart raced each time he heard her cries of pain. The sounds sucked him back to a memory he'd give anything to forget.

She'd been so pale when they'd finally let him in to see her. And the blood . . . He'd seen his fair share of blood, but the amount pooling on her bed, between her legs, on Helena's and the midwife's hands as they'd tried to stop Lenora's bleeding . . .

Butch felt the urge to punch a wall, and he clenched his hand in his pocket.

They'd kicked him out, just like they had before, as soon as she'd gone into active labor.

The women had been firm despite the fact that he was the king.

"It is not the place for a man."

"She's my wife, Helena," he'd pleaded. "My place is by her side."

Helena had narrowed her eyes at him but had gotten distracted when another contraction had Lenora moaning on the bed. "Please go, Your Majesty. We'll let you know as soon as she's finished."

Now, as he paced back and forth, he regretted being obedient. He should've been in there. Decorum could go straight into the fireplace for all he cared.

He tried to occupy his mind with something—*anything*—else. With every cry, every muffled moan, his heart clenched and his panic mounted.

When he couldn't take it anymore, he summoned the nearest servant. "Find Marshal Thorne," he ordered as he ran his hands through his hair. "Tell him I need him at once."

The minutes stretched into what felt like hours, and just as he thought he might break down the door, the sounds behind it shifted. Lenora's cries ceased.

His stomach plummeted.

"No," he whispered, his hand already on the doorknob. "No, no, no. Not again." He flung the door open and nearly collapsed at the sight of the midwife pressing a baby to Lenora's bare chest.

"Your Majesty," Helena said, the first to notice Butch standing slack-jawed in the doorway. "Come in," she said, motioning for him to shut the door.

Lenora had tears in her eyes as she looked down at the small, slightly purple child on her chest.

"Rub the baby's back until we hear crying, dear," the midwife said, her focus on Butch's wife and child. "We need to hear those lungs clear."

Butch's steps toward the bed faltered when a loud wailing filled the room.

"He's a loud one," the midwife said with a wide smile.

"He?" Butch breathed the word.

A son.

He had a son.

Butch's gaze crashed into Lenora's at the same time she looked at him.

"Come," she whispered. Silent tears streamed down her cheeks, and as he crawled onto the bed next to her, she looked at him with a joy Butch had never seen before.

Butch pressed a long kiss to Lenora's temple, murmuring into her ear how strong she was, how proud he was of her. All the while, he stared at his son.

He was so small. A thin layer of dark hair covered his head, and his eyes were squeezed shut as he cried.

"Do you want to hold him?" Lenora asked.

"Yes," Butch said without hesitation. "Should I—do I keep my shirt on?" He glanced from Helena to the midwife.

"That's your choice, Your Majesty. I haven't cleaned him yet, but—"

Butch was already untying the top of his tunic and had it off before the woman could finish speaking.

Lenora smiled before gently passing the baby to him.

428

His son's tiny body felt impossibly fragile, and Butch's heart swelled with an emotion so powerful it stole his breath away. He carefully brought the baby close to his bare chest.

"He's beautiful," Butch whispered, his voice breaking. "Perfect." When he looked at his wife, she was beaming at him, her eyes shining with more tears. "Thank you."

Butch choked, unable to find the words to express what he felt. He held his son close.

His son.

"A name. We need a name," he said, realizing that he and Lenora had somehow not discussed the topic beforehand.

Lenora nodded. "I have one, but if you don't like it . . ." Her words trailed off.

"What is it?" he asked, watching as she leaned over to stroke the top of the little boy's head.

"Dio, short for Diomedes."

"Diomedes," Butch repeated, a smile crossing over his lips. "Diomedes Maudit."

"You like it?" Lenora asked, peering up at him with her large dark eyes.

Gently, and without jostling the baby, Butch leaned over and pressed a soft, sweet kiss to her lips.

"I love it."

Chapter 75

EVANGELINE

Evangeline walked beside Silas, trying to pay attention to anything besides the way their hands brushed every couple seconds.

She hadn't seen him more than once or twice since Stoll had attacked her in the record hall over a month earlier.

"I haven't found him," Silas said, his voice low. He kept his focus straight ahead instead of looking at her, and Evangeline questioned what emotions he was trying to hide by avoiding her eyes. "I'm sorry."

"I appreciate you trying," Evangeline said, pausing as they reached the double doors to the garden. After weeks of sitting either in her room or in the study reading or walking around and around in circles on the second floor until Benji requested they stop, Evangeline had jumped at Silas's request to take a walk in the gardens.

"I'll find him," Silas said as he finally looked down at her. He tucked his hands into his pockets, his face downcast.

Evangeline took a step closer to him until only a foot separated them. "I know you will. I'm not worried, Silas."

That wasn't entirely true.

She'd woken on multiple occasions with the residual image of Stoll choking her imprinted on the backs of her eyelids. But she wasn't about to tell him that. He looked tired enough as it was.

"Is everything all right?" Evangeline asked. "Besides Stoll still being missing, I mean. You look . . . I don't know. Off."

"Haven't been sleeping well. And there's a lot going on with—"

"Marshal Thorne!" a servant called, sprinting down the hall toward them.

Silas took a protective step in front of Evangeline, blocking her with his broad shoulders. "What's happened?"

"The king requests your presence immediately," the servant said, panting.

"His office?" Silas asked, his voice taut.

Evangeline peeked around Silas's arm, watching as the servant shook his head.

"No, he's—" The servant stopped talking when his gaze landed on Evangeline. "Um, I . . . I shouldn't . . ."

"Where is the king?" Silas's voice held an edge.

"He's outside Her Majesty's room." The servant was still regarding Evangeline with a suspicious look when Silas bristled next to her.

"It's happening?"

The servant nodded.

"Finally," Silas whispered. He spun around to face her, and whatever was happening, it had created a wide grin over Silas's lips. "I'm sorry, but I have to go."

Evangeline frowned, then nodded. "Of course."

"I promise I'll come see you later," he said, already following the servant down the hallway.

It wasn't until she was alone in the corridor that she realized the blatant mistake he'd made.

She was *alone*.

Outside her room.

Evangeline glanced at the double doors leading out to the garden. It'd be so easy to slip out, and maybe she could find a way to the castle gates. Her heart thumped in her chest as she flicked her gaze from the two doors to the hallway in front of her.

It could be her only chance to escape.

She took a tentative step toward the doors.

Silas's bright eyes flashed in her mind. And the longer she stood there, hand raised as if she was about to open the doors, she remembered the moments in her room after Stoll's attack.

Silas's strong tanned body, warm beneath her skin.

His breath on her thumb as she traced his lips.

The feeling of his hair slipping through her fingers.

He'd promised to come to her later.

What if she wasn't there?

Despite everything, she'd grown fond of his company. Craved it, even.

And what if she was caught?

What if she wasn't?

What if, somewhere out there, Stoll was waiting for her?

What if she wasn't caught but Butch blamed Silas? What would happen to him?

When had she started to care?

The weight of all the what-ifs settled onto her, and with a frustrated sigh, Evangeline turned away from the garden doors. She made her way to the second floor. Instead of going back to her room, she sequestered herself in the study. But as she took her favorite seat near the window, annoyance at her choice started to bubble within her.

When had she grown so comfortable in her prison?

When had the castle become a gilded cage?

She'd missed her opportunity, and what if it never came again?

And all for what?

Silas?

He was the entire reason she was a prisoner in the first place.

Evangeline groaned, rubbing her face with her hands. She could try to go back down to the first floor and make an escape. It would look more suspicious to go now.

She leaned back in the chair, letting her eyes close for a second before sighing and pushing herself up. Wandering to the window, she peered out. It was already getting dark, the sun having set behind the horizon. The sky was a mix of deep blues and purples, the last traces of daylight clinging to the edges of the clouds.

The ground below was still, and for a moment, the peaceful scene calmed her restless thoughts.

Something caught her eye. A silhouette moved, partially hidden by the shadows of trees. Evangeline's heart skipped a beat.

She squinted, trying to make out more details, but the person remained indistinct, shrouded in encroaching darkness.

Her pulse quickened.

The person had stopped moving and stood still, nearly indistinguishable.

It almost looked like . . .

Evangeline stepped back from the window, pressing her back firmly into the bookshelf nearby.

It had looked like the person was watching her.

Whatever—or rather whoever—it was, she didn't like the idea of being seen.

Evangeline left the study and returned to her room, where she explained to the guard on duty why she was alone. He seemed skeptical until Evangeline said he could ask Marshal Thorne to confirm her story as soon as he saw him. Once she was in her room, she strode straight to the window and promptly closed the curtains.

Maybe the person hadn't been watching her.

Maybe it hadn't been there at all and she'd just imagined it.

But whatever the case, Evangeline didn't stop shivering until she was shoulder deep in a hot bath.

PART FIVE

Chapter 76

LENORA

Lenora couldn't imagine life without Dio. Even just a few days after giving birth, she could hardly remember what life had been before him. She cradled Dio in her arms, marveling at his tiny features. His eyelids fluttered in his sleep, and she beamed down at him. Love swelled in her heart.

Helena had been up to check on her and Dio multiple times, and Merla and Kaylene brought her whatever she needed, but for the first time in a while, she was alone with her baby.

Settling back against the pillows propping her up in bed, Lenora gently reached over and picked up a pen and a small pad of parchment that Kaylene had brought her before Lenora had sent her away.

Lenora glanced down at her sleeping boy in one arm, and with a bit of finagling, she managed to prop the notebook up on a pillow.

She began to write.

My darling Dio,

I don't know if I knew what true love was until I held your tiny body in my arms. You are everything I'd hoped you'd be and more. I find myself staring at your sweet face, dreaming of the man you will be someday.

You are my miracle, my son, and my heart. Each moment I spend with you is a blessing. As your mother, I will do all I can to protect you and guide you as you grow.

She paused, her eyes misting over as she reread the words—words she wished she'd heard growing up.

Lenora glanced at Dio, her heart squeezing as she thought of how much one tiny person had changed her world in the seconds after she'd first held him against her chest.

A soft knock on the door had her putting aside the half-finished letter and scooting farther up on the bed.

"Is he sleeping?" Butch whispered as he closed the door gently. His expression softened as his gaze landed on the sleeping baby in her arms.

"Yes," Lenora said, nodding as she patted the spot on the bed next to her.

Her husband took the invitation, slipping his boots off before crawling onto the bed. "May I?" Butch asked, holding out his arms as he flicked his gaze from Dio to her.

Lenora smiled. She handed the sleeping prince to his father. Something in her heart melted bit by bit every time she watched Butch hold their son. He brushed his finger along Dio's cheek with a reverent touch.

"Perfect," Butch whispered, leaning back against the headboard. "Absolutely perfect."

Resting against her husband's shoulder, Lenora breathed in his warm scent. They sat in silence for a while, watching Dio sleep. She marveled at the gentle way Butch cradled their son. She'd seen him be tender before, to her especially, but this was something different, a side of him she hadn't yet seen.

A side she *needed* to see.

It was a stark contrast to the fierce protector and controlling king she knew him to be.

As she nestled closer to him, Lenora's eyes widened.

Was she falling in love with her husband?

The thought thrilled her at the same time it scared her.

The last time she'd fallen in love with someone, Leo had left her suddenly and without so much as a goodbye.

Lenora turned her head to look up at Butch. He met her gaze, his brow furrowing.

"What's wrong?" he asked, voice still low so as not to wake Dio. "Lenora?" he prompted when she didn't respond right away.

"I . . . I'm scared."

Butch stiffened. "Of what? What happened?"

"I think—" She bit her lip, staring at his mouth in an attempt to avoid his probing gaze. "I think I'm in love with you."

Butch's expression softened instantly. With one hand, he reached over and cupped her cheek, his thumb gently brushing away a stray tear she hadn't noticed. "Lenora, why are you scared?"

"Because . . . what if . . . what if you leave me too?" The words came out as a faint whisper, her voice trembling. She leaned into his touch, closing her eyes. She didn't want to see his expression.

"Look at me, Lenora." Butch's voice was a caress, luring her eyes open. "I know you've been hurt in the past. I won't pretend to know what happened. But you have to know, I'm not going to leave you. Ever. You're my wife. We may have been strangers when we married, but we aren't now." His thumb trailed along her bottom lip, his gaze following close behind.

Heat pooled in her stomach despite the aches and pains of a healing body.

Lenora kissed his thumb, relishing the small grunt it elicited from her husband. "I wasn't sure it was possible."

Butch smirked. "To love me?"

"Butch." She shook her head, pausing when Dio shifted in Butch's arms. But he stayed asleep, and she continued. "No. To find love in an arranged marriage."

"I can attest," he said, checking Dio once more before leaning down to press his lips to hers. "It is very, *very* possible." He kissed her again.

He loved her.

Her husband loved her.

Lenora let Butch kiss her until they woke the baby. But after calling in one of the nursemaids, who took Dio away, she let her husband kiss her again.

And again.

And again.

Chapter 77

EVANGELINE

Evangeline frowned, reading the four words on the secret message she'd received many weeks earlier over and over again. *To Rule a Kingdom.* It was as short as the other notes but not nearly as useful. She had been using it as a bookmark in the books she'd borrowed from the study. Evangeline read the four-word message often, especially when the book she'd chosen was too slow.

However, she'd finished her current book and was in need of a new one. Evangeline had taken the message out to stare at it. Maybe the message had ended up on her meal tray by mistake.

Sighing, Evangeline put the paper on the side of her bed and, grabbing the finished book, crossed the room to the door.

Evangeline knocked once to avoid startling the guard on the other side before opening the door.

"Benji," she said, greeting the young commander with a grin. "I'm glad it's you standing out here. The other guard—"

"Sisco?" Benji suggested, his gaze dropping to the book in her arm. He stepped aside, falling into step behind her as she led the way to the study.

"Maybe. Anyway, he keeps questioning why I want to go to the study. As if it's not obvious." Evangeline slowed down until Benji was forced to walk next to her. She hated when he followed like a shadow, much preferring to match her step to his.

"Probably Sisco. I don't think he knows what a book is," Benji offered, a grin on his freckled face.

Yep, Benji was definitely her favorite.

He was taller than her by a few inches and had bright red hair that would likely form beautiful curls if he'd let it grow out. Instead, though, he kept it short like the rest of the guards.

"At least you know what a book is." Evangeline handed him the one she'd finished, and he turned it over as they walked, skimming the back.

"What is this, romance?"

Evangeline nodded, taking it back from him. "It wasn't my favorite, but still entertaining."

"My wife reads those kinds of books all the time."

"I think your wife and I would be good friends, then," Evangeline said with a wide grin.

"I don't get those kinds of stories though."

Evangeline shrugged. "They're a nice break from reality." She frowned before hiding it with a smirk. "I bet you benefit from them too." She raised an eyebrow, chuckling when the tops of Benji's ears turned bright pink.

"Um, uh . . ." He cleared his throat, scratching behind his head as they came to a stop in front of the study door. "Well, I mean—"

"I'm just picking on you, Benji." She glanced at the door. "Are you staying out here, or do you want to come in?"

"Definitely out here," he said, relief in his voice as he held the door open for her. "Have fun with your, um, stories."

Evangeline winked at him. "Oh, I will."

With the finished book in hand, Evangeline approached the bookshelves. After a few seconds of scanning the titles, Evangeline found the spot from which she'd taken the book in the first place. She put it back into its home before scanning the titles next to it to see if any caught her eye. None did.

The process of finding another book to read took longer than she'd thought it would. She'd been reading so much that it was hard to find something interesting. It didn't help that her mind could not decide if it wanted something true or fictitious to devour.

The romance book had been fun, especially to tease Benji with, but she wanted something different, something more . . . exciting.

Something that would whisk her away from her comfy prison cell into another world.

Evangeline's gaze rested on a crimson book near the bottom of the bookshelf. The golden script along the spine was fancy enough that it took her longer to read the title, and she read it twice just to be sure it said what she thought it did.

To Rule a Kingdom.

Glancing over her shoulder toward the door Benji had propped open, she let out a quiet breath at the sight of Benji's back. He wasn't paying attention. Evangeline squatted down. Maybe it was the bright crimson that'd caught her eye, or maybe the elegant writing. Or maybe it was the fact that the book had been pushed in so it was no longer flush with its brothers and sisters.

Either way, the title had cemented Evangeline's curiosity, and with a gentle tug, she freed the book from its place. She had read the title correctly, and the thought of the slip of paper back in her room had her checking the doorway again as she struggled to swallow.

Had the note been intentional? It'd been in the same script as the notes in the dungeon . . .

Evangeline flipped the cover open. The title on the inside was written in the same font as the spine, though it was easier to read on the white paper with black ink than on the cover.

Evangeline took a few pages in her fingers, flipping through them until she froze. A piece of parchment slipped out from somewhere within the middle of the book.

The appearance of the parchment left Evangeline's heartbeat quickening, and nervous energy spread through her fingers as she pushed the parchment back between the pages of the book. If the paper was what she thought it was—another message—she needed to be within the safety of her room before reading it.

But she didn't leave right away. While she had every intention of reading what was scrawled on the parchment, the book held little interest to her. She had no desire to rule any kingdom, so she stayed several minutes longer until she carried another two books on top of the one with the parchment.

"Find something interesting?" Benji asked when she emerged with her stack of books.

"Let's hope, otherwise we're coming back."

After she got to her room and thanked Benji, Evangeline closed the door and went over to the window seat. She placed the two books she intended to read next to her as she sat down with *To Rule a Kingdom* still in her hands. Taking out the parchment, she discarded the book next to the other two.

Unlike the secret message from earlier, the parchment was full-size, which was likely the reason it had been hidden within a book rather than a food tray.

It was, in fact, a message, though its long format was more like a letter. Evangeline squinted at the handwriting—same as all the messages before—and it did not take long before Evangeline's guess at the identity of the sender was confirmed.

I suppose I shouldn't be surprised you've managed to find this message. You are, after all, friends with a very intelligent and cunning woman, whom I shall not mention for both of our safety.

I was disheartened to find that your departure from the castle had not gone as smoothly as planned. It has, however, worked in our favor because correspondence should, in theory, be easier.

Evangeline paused, wrinkling her nose. It would've been easier if she'd thought to search for a book in the study. She felt stupid. It'd been obvious after she'd found the book that the four-word message had been a title. Evangeline rolled her eyes and went back to reading the letter.

It is not too much to assume that you know at this point who I am. But if it is not clear, I spent some time with your friend, though not by my will. You might be surprised to know that I do not resent her as my husband does. I do not even hate her because she allowed me to experience something I had forgotten the feeling of: freedom.

I want you to experience that too.

When your friend stole me away from my duties here, I felt as though I could breathe for the first time in years. That is not to say I did not miss my friends. I did. But to be free from the duties tied to me . . . It was a gift.

I owe your friend a debt for giving me this gift, even if it was not permanent. I believe that by helping you leave, I might repay her.

However, I do not as yet have a plan. Until I decide the best time to move, I will contact you only if I hear of information that is pertinent to you. Otherwise, I will keep our communications to a minimum for your sake and mine.

It ended so abruptly that Evangeline wondered if she was missing another page. The parchment rustled as she turned it over to check the back side. It was blank.

For the next few minutes, she read the letter over again. Her mind spun at the idea that the queen was trying to help her once more despite the failure of the last escape attempt. Evangeline glanced out the window, staring out over the gardens below. Her thoughts drifted when she was unable to draw any new conclusions from the letter.

Someone was watching her.

Evangeline bristled when her full attention turned to the man in the gardens staring directly at her. It was hard to make out any details, especially since he wore a hat and a scarf covered the lower half of his face. But the position of his body and the angle his head was craned at made it clear that it was her window at which he was staring. He stood as still as the statue of an elegantly dressed woman next to him.

An image of the Mongoose charging through the record hall after her flashed through her mind, and she stumbled back from the window.

Whether or not it was him, she didn't like the feeling slithering through her at the thought of being watched.

Especially if it was him.

If it was Stoll, how had he gotten onto the castle grounds? Silas had assured her that he had men looking for the rogue commander.

The hair on the back of Evangeline's neck stood on end, and she tucked the letter back into the book, picking all three up and moving to her bed. But even minutes after she'd left the window seat, an uncomfortable chill crept up her spine and throughout her extremities.

Evangeline startled and clasped her chest when someone knocked on her door. Tucking a strand of hair behind her ear, she took a deep breath before allowing the person to enter.

"Are you all right?" Silas asked, frowning as he closed the door behind him.

Evidently, the deep breath had not removed the apparent look of fear from Evangeline's face. "I'm fine. I just—" She couldn't stop herself from glancing over her shoulder toward the window. She cleared her throat, straightening her shoulders. "Does the king need to see me?"

"What happened?" Silas ignored her question. He crossed the room to the window, peering out before turning his gaze to Evangeline.

"Nothing," Evangeline said too quickly. "It was nothing." She bit her bottom lip, aware of how terribly she was lying.

"Evie." Silas's gaze flicked over her face, lingering for a longer period of time on her mouth.

Evangeline closed her eyes for a brief second, collecting her thoughts before she joined him next to the window. The man who'd been watching her was gone. For some reason, that sent even more of an unpleasant sensation through her body than knowing where he was.

"I was reading here, and when I looked out, someone was watching me." She nodded toward the garden, and Silas's gaze followed her gesture.

"Down there?"

"Near the statue."

Silas leaned forward, resting his hand on the wall and craning his neck. When he stood straight again, his lips were pressed together.

"When was this?"

"A few minutes ago. Right before you came in."

"Huh," Silas muttered. "Do you think it was him?"

"Couldn't tell," Evangeline said, wrapping her arms around herself. "He wasn't dressed like a guard."

"And his face. You didn't recognize it?"

"I couldn't see it. He had a hat and scarf on." Evangeline's gaze kept flicking from Silas to the garden. "He just stood there, staring at me."

Silas regarded her with attentive eyes. "I'll have someone investigate." He took a step back from the window, nodding toward the door. "Come on. Let's go for a walk."

Evangeline cast one last glance at the gardens before following Silas out of her room.

Silas sent Benji to check the gardens before catching up to her in the hallway where she waited for him. He didn't lead her down to the first floor; instead, they wandered around the second floor. "I know I never explained why I ran off a couple weeks ago."

"You said the king and queen had something important going on," Evangeline recalled, thinking of Silas's explanation the day after he'd left her alone standing by the garden doors.

"They did, and I'm sure you'll hear this soon enough, so it doesn't matter if I tell you. That day, the queen was in labor. She gave birth to a son, and Butch needed me for . . . support," Silas said, pausing. He grinned at her with a genuine smile.

"That's so exciting!" Evangeline squeezed his forearm before she realized what she was doing. She quickly dropped her hand and his gaze. "I'm sure Lenora is overjoyed."

"They both are," Silas agreed.

Evangeline glanced up to find him studying her face. She opened her mouth to say something, then recognized the door behind him.

The record hall.

She must've been too obvious, because a second later, Silas turned to look.

"You never told me why you were in there."

"You're right," Evangeline said, continuing to walk past the room even though she felt the familiar pull to go find answers to twenty-year-old questions tug at her.

"Evie, why—"

"Didn't we come to an agreement that night? I won't tell you why I was in there, and you won't tell me how you *knew* I was in there. Or have you changed your mind?" She didn't glance at him as he caught up and easily matched her pace.

"I haven't, but Evie—" He tugged at her arm, turning her to face him. "Just promise me it doesn't have to do with harming the king or his family."

Evangeline frowned. "Of course not." She pulled her arm from his grasp. "Believe it or not, I don't have ill intentions toward Butch. And I certainly don't have it out for the queen and her new son." Not when she was clearly still trying to help Evangeline reunite with Emmalee. "I thought we were past that."

"My job is to protect him, and—"

"I haven't once tried to hurt him or anyone else since you brought me here. Do you—" She paused, biting her bottom lip. "Do you really despise magic folk so deeply?"

Silas's eyes widened, and he took a step back as if she'd slapped him. "I never . . . I have never once said I hate those with magic. Not once."

"But I'm still the enemy." Evangeline didn't phrase it as a question.

Silas remained silent for a moment, his gaze dropping to the ground. When he finally spoke, his voice was softer, almost pained. "You're not my enemy, Evie. But my duty is to the king, to protect him and his family. That's what I've lived my life doing and what I will do until the day I die. I swore an oath."

"And me? Am I the one you're protecting him from? Am I a threat in your eyes?" Evangeline crossed her arms.

He met her gaze with such an intensity that it stole the breath from her lungs. "No. You're . . . You're much more than that. Butch is . . . He's my king, and I'll always prioritize his safety. It's not about you being a threat. It's about my loyalty to him."

Evangeline remained silent.

Silas took a step closer, his hand reaching out as if to touch her but stopping short. A second later, he cleared his throat and shoved both hands into his pockets. "Honestly, I . . . I care about what happens to you. I care *about* you." He let out a dark chuckle. "More than I should, probably. It—" He sighed, running a hand over the back of his neck. "It complicates things, to say the least."

It became difficult to swallow as Evangeline processed his words. In the same moment her heart wanted to skip a beat, it also twisted with the implications. She wasn't trustworthy to him, and for some reason, that mattered.

"You care about me, but you can't trust me. Is that it?"

"Yes. I mean no. I just—"

Evangeline held up a hand, stopping him. "Don't. I understand." She held up the magic-dampening bracelet on her wrist. "I'm still a prisoner. Thanks for the reminder." Lowering her hand, she dropped his gaze and scowled at the floor. "I'm done with the walk for today. Take me back to my fancy cell please."

"Evie, I—"

Knowing exactly where she was, Evangeline strode off in the direction of her room.

Silas didn't fight her.

Somehow, that hurt most of all.

Chapter 78

SILAS

Silas paced his quarters, frustration mounting with each pass by his door. His search for Stoll had been as fruitless as the country-wide search for Estrada. Any leads he received evaporated into thin air, and each dead end felt like a personal failure.

He'd done everything he could to hide the worry that'd consumed him when Evie had mentioned that she thought someone was watching her through her window several days earlier.

If she got hurt again because Silas had failed to catch Stoll . . .

An image flashed through his mind of a nightmare he'd had a few times.

Evie bleeding on the study floor, terror in her beautiful brown eyes.

Silas blinked, rubbing his face until the image dissipated.

Though he'd warned the guards he'd put into rotation outside her door about Stoll, he questioned whether it was enough and whether there were any that might sympathize with him. Plenty of people hated Estrada, and those who knew Evie was connected continued to grow despite his best efforts.

And why couldn't he keep his thoughts from clinging to her?

Despite the fact that she was still technically a prisoner, he found himself spending more and more and *more* time with her.

But she could still be a threat to Butch.

Silas ran a hand through his hair, turning on his heel to pace back in the other direction.

She could be the reason his best friend ended up dead, and yet every single part of him longed to be near her. To draw her close. To . . .

His resolve cracked.

The next moment, he threw open his door and stalked out. On the way to the second floor, Silas intercepted a servant no doubt heading toward Evie's door—no one else was residing there since Butch had finally sent his obnoxious father-in-law home.

"I'll take that to her," he said, startling the servant girl. "Sorry." He offered her a smile, taking the tray from her hands. "I was heading in that direction anyway." When she gave him a confused look, he clarified. "This is for the woman on this floor, right?"

The servant girl nodded.

"Then I'll make sure it gets to her. Thank you." He waited until she was gone before continuing down the hall.

"Commander Volmar," Silas said, holding the tray with one hand to return the salute offered him.

"Marshal Thorne," his guard responded with a smile. "What'd you do to get kicked down to food delivery?"

"I asked nicely," Silas replied. He knocked on Evie's door and entered, closing the door before she had a chance to respond.

Evie looked up from the window seat, her eyes wide.

"Silas? What are you doing here?" Wariness filled her voice, and he couldn't stop the pang of guilt that ricocheted through his chest at the thought of how their last conversation had ended. She didn't seem to be shutting him out, which was a good sign, but he knew he'd hurt her with his words.

He set the tray down on the small dresser, then shoved his hands into his pockets as he leaned against the wall. "I thought I'd join you for dinner, unless you'd prefer *Benji's* company." He raised an eyebrow, watching her roll her eyes.

"If Benji's not available, I suppose you'll do for company," she retorted with a smirk, sticking a piece of parchment into the book she'd been reading. "What's the occasion?"

"No occasion. Just passing by." He moved the tray to the window seat next to her before pulling over the chair from the nearby desk.

"Just passing by? On the empty second floor?" Evie raised an eyebrow, scanning his face. "Uh-huh, sure."

Silas shrugged. "Maybe I wanted good company."

"Uh-huh." She reached for the cup on the tray. "Well, I'm not going to argue against food and conversation. I never would've thought it possible, but I think I'm tired of reading." She sipped the water before returning it to the tray with a small grin. "And I grew up in a bookshop, so—" At the personal admission, her gaze darted up to meet his. "I mean, I—"

"A bookshop, huh? Sounds fun." Silas leaned back in the chair, threading his fingers together behind his head. He didn't miss how her attention flicked to his arms. He smirked.

"Yes, but I didn't mean to say . . . I shouldn't . . ."

"Then you don't have to. Though," he said, tilting his head to the side as his gaze roamed over her, "I would like to know what you did before you came here."

She narrowed her eyes at him for a moment, chewing on a piece of chicken. "You mean before you arrested me?" she asked with a pointed tone.

"If you'll tell me, yes."

Evie pushed some of the green beans around on her plate, her attention somewhere just past his head. "I worked for a doctor as an apothecary, though I never finished my apprenticeship."

"Really? In that village where I found you?"

"You mean the *warded* one?" After a brief pause, during which she briefly narrowed her eyes at him, she nodded. Evie's brows creased. "I'm still at a loss for how you got through the wards."

Silas gave her a smug grin before shrugging again. "I won't tell you that, but it does seem only fair that I tell you something personal."

"It does, doesn't it?" She continued to eat her meal slowly, watching him with her guarded eyes.

He gestured toward her. "What would you like to know?"

"Anything?"

"No, but if I can answer it, I will."

"Why do you care so much for Butch?" The skepticism in her voice was obvious, but Silas ignored it as he let a wide grin cross his face.

"Easy. He's my brother."

Evie's eyebrows rose. "You mean you're—"

"A prince?" Silas let out a laugh at her bewildered expression. "Far from it. But when my parents left me here at the castle as a young boy, Butch and I became friends—closer than friends. We became brothers, though not by blood, obviously." Silas tried to hide the tightening in his chest with another chuckle, though to his ears, it sounded forced.

He and Butch were certainly not related by blood, and if his friend knew about what ran through Silas's blood, he—

"So, you grew up here, then?" Evie's voice thankfully pulled him out of the series of thoughts that lurked, ever present, in a dark corner of his mind.

"Yep. I think I know this castle just about as well as the king."

Evie dropped his gaze, focusing on the plate next to her as the conversation lulled.

"What drew you to being an apothecary?" he asked after several seconds of silence.

"My mother," Evie said in a soft voice. She continued to avoid his gaze, and he sat straighter, resting his chin on his hands.

"She was an apothecary too?"

Evie shook her head. She took a deep breath, a sigh slipping from her lips before she finally looked up at him through her lashes. When she did, the grief in her eyes punched him in the gut.

"She got sick. I started reading all the books in the shop, trying to find a remedy. In the end, she . . . she died."

Before he knew what he was doing, Silas moved the tray of food to the chair he'd been occupying and took the seat next to her. He placed a hand on her knee, waiting to see if she'd tense or move away. She didn't.

"I'm sorry for your loss. Were you close?"

Evie nodded. "When my father left, she was all I had. Then she remarried, and . . ." Evie's words died off as she shook her head. "Let's just say my stepfather isn't a nice guy."

Silas's jaw clenched. A sudden urge to find the man who clearly had hurt Evie—though he didn't know how—and make him apologize by whatever means necessary filled Silas.

"My mother passed, but I kept studying to become an apothecary. I figured it was my way out of the house." She scoffed. "When my magic manifested on my twenty-first birthday, I decided it was time to leave. I met a woman who agreed to take me on as an apprentice, and I fell in love with it. I got to help people, and . . . This is going to sound strange, but I like the puzzle of putting together the right amount of each ingredient. Making each draft potent enough to work, but not too much that it affects some other part of the body. There's a balance that I enjoy searching for."

A strand of hair fell from behind her ear as she inclined her head, and Silas refrained from reaching over and pushing it back.

"When I . . . After you . . ." She fished for words, her attention on her hands in her lap. "After the gully, I knew I couldn't go back."

Silas shook his head. "I didn't know who you were."

"Stoll did," Evie said, her voice firm as her expression shifted to one of distaste. "He'd just recently arrested Odette, and I was there when it happened. And I . . ." Evie bit her lip. "I ran into him again in the forest right before the gully. For all I knew, he'd told you about me."

"He didn't. At least not that I remember."

Evie shrugged. "Well, either way, I went to go pack my things and saw my employer being questioned by guards. I knew I had to run, so I did."

"Where'd you go?" Silas prompted when she stopped talking.

"The only place I felt safe."

Realization bloomed through Silas, and he nodded slowly. "Estrada."

Evie closed her eyes, and for a second, he thought she might cry. "She's my sister in the same way Butch is your brother. Silas, she's hurting. She's lonely. And I know she's done horrible things, but—"

"You love her still."

"Yes," Evie said, tears filling her eyes. "And I'm scared I'll be the reason she's caught and killed. I-I d-don't want that t-to h-happen. That's w-why I l-led you away f-from her that ni-night." Evie covered her face with her hands, leaning forward until her elbows rested on her knees.

Silas removed his hand from her leg, moving it to her back. He didn't know why he was rubbing comforting circles. He wanted Estrada arrested. He wanted her to pay for her crimes.

But for the first time since he'd arrested Evie, he understood.

If the roles were reversed, if Butch were the one who'd lost everything and had lashed out, wouldn't Silas do everything he could to protect him?

Yes.

Anything.

He'd die for Butch.

And sitting with Evie, he understood.

Over a year ago, Evie had exchanged her freedom and was willing to lay down her life for Estrada. And her mindset remained the same.

Not because she was brave, though she clearly was.

Not because she was stubborn, though it seemed to be her most dominant trait.

Not even because she loved Estrada, though that was obvious in the tears she shed for her friend.

No, Evie had given up everything because she truly believed Estrada was worthy of saving, that she could change.

And what if she was right?

"Come here," Silas said in a soft voice. With a gentle tug, he pulled Evie onto his lap, where she buried her face in his chest. He wrapped both arms around her, pressing light kisses to the top of her head.

They stayed like that until Evie's gasping breaths turned to hiccups. And not long after that, she fell asleep in his arms.

Chapter 79

LENORA

Lenora stood in a lovely field, surrounded by the trees of the Black Forest. It was a familiar place she hadn't seen in what felt like a lifetime. The old tiny house sat in the center of the field, spangled in the golden glow of the afternoon sun. She blinked. The warmth of the sun bathed her skin, and the rich scent of earth filled her lungs as she breathed deeply. Leaves rustled in a light breeze.

She wasn't alone.

Kneeling in the garden behind the tiny house, Estrada worked at the soil. As if she sensed Lenora watching her, Estrada looked up and smiled a warm genuine smile that reached her eyes.

"Are you going to join me?" Estrada asked, her voice carried through the wind.

Lenora took a step forward. Then hesitated. Hadn't she tried to escape this little sanctuary? Why? It was more beautiful than anything she'd ever seen. And peaceful. And . . . freeing.

At the thought, Lenora crossed to the garden and knelt next to Estrada. They worked side by side, their hands moving in sync as they tended to the plants. It felt normal. Easy. Perfect.

Lenora woke with a start, her heart pounding in her chest. The dream lingered. The emotions it stirred were fresh and vivid as she glanced around the dark room.

She was alone.

The fire had gone out, and the room felt chilly.

Pulling the covers higher up until they covered the lower half of her face, Lenora stared at the canopy over her bed.

Why did she continue to have dreams about Estrada? More than that, why did she prefer them to reality?

She thought back to the dream, to the peacefulness. The warmth.

As she lay there, her thoughts drifted to the letter she had tried to pass on to Estrada through the prisoner. She wondered what had happened to it. Wondered if the prisoner had read it.

Those pained words. The ones no one around her seemed to understand. Even her husband, who'd lost the same children she had.

But Estrada had understood.

She'd lost a child. A daughter.

More than anything, Lenora wanted a friend who could sympathize. A friend who wouldn't look at her with pity but with understanding. Despite the love and care she'd received from her husband, especially since things had begun to change between them, and even with her sweet friends doting on her and Dio, she felt alone.

Utterly and completely alone.

And she had a feeling Estrada probably felt the same way.

Chapter 80

E vangeline sat across from the king's desk, hyperfocused on the way Silas's jacket pulled tight along his strong arms when he leaned against the wall. The same arms that had held her close as she'd cried herself to sleep several nights earlier.

Her mind kept drifting back to that night, as if it'd stuck an anchor there, one she was incapable of removing. The warmth of his embrace, the comfort in his steady breaths, the solace in the small circles he'd rubbed into her back—it all lingered in the forefront of her mind.

Especially as she stared at him in the king's office.

Butch's voice cut through her reverie. "Lia, are you listening?"

She snapped her attention back to the king, knowing from the heat in her face that her cheeks were flushed. "Yes, or . . . no. What'd you say?"

He narrowed his eyes. "I've asked you several times now if Estrada has any connections up north."

"Not that I know of," Evangeline said, blinking. Thoughts of Silas still tangled her mind. "She said she's lonely, so I doubt she's been in contact with anyone else."

The room fell silent.

"Excuse me?" Butch finally said, his voice low. "When exactly did she say this?"

Evangeline opened her mouth, but nothing came out as she realized her mistake.

"Has she spoken to you since you've been here?" Butch leaned forward at his desk, his commanding stare burning a hole through her.

"I—no, I mean . . . I haven't seen her since—"

"When did she tell you she was lonely?"

Evangeline opened and closed her mouth, searching for a way to make up for the secret she'd revealed. She could lie, but glancing at Silas, who was studying her closely, she had a feeling he'd point it out right away.

"Lia," Butch growled, "how has Estrada spoken to you?"

With a sigh, Evangeline closed her eyes. "Magic. She's been sending me messages. I can't respond." Evangeline twisted the bracelet on her left wrist. "I wouldn't know how even if I could."

The king didn't respond, a look of consideration passing over his face before he nodded. "What does she say in these messages?"

"She's just trying to make me feel less alone," Evangeline said quickly, hoping her words might downplay the significance.

"What *exactly* has she said?" Butch asked, continuing to pin her with his harsh gaze.

"That she misses me. That I'm not alone. That she hasn't forgotten me." Evangeline refused to repeat the ones that would truly put Emmalee at risk. The messages that said they'd be together again. That Emmalee hadn't given up on her. That Emmalee was trying to figure out a way to get to her. That when Evangeline was free, they'd get justice.

"How does the magic of these messages work?" Butch asked.

Evangeline shook her head. "I don't know. I never learned."

He gave her a skeptical look but didn't continue down that line of questioning. "How frequently does she send these messages?"

"It's not consistent."

"Has she mentioned anything that would indicate where she is?"

"No," Evangeline said without hesitation. And even if Emmalee had, that certainly wouldn't be something she'd convey to the king.

"Have you—" Before Butch could finish his question, a knock on the door interrupted him. "Enter." He didn't sound happy, but a mask of indifference covered his face. "Yes?"

"Her Majesty and His Highness are waiting for you to share a meal."

Butch's stern demeanor softened at the mention of his family. He nodded to the servant before turning his attention back to Evangeline. "This

456

conversation isn't over, Lia. We'll continue later. And if Estrada sends you another message, I expect you to tell me right away."

He didn't wait for her to respond before waving her away. Silas joined her at the door.

"I'll escort you back to your room," he said, and her stomach twisted.

The last thing she wanted after possibly revealing something the king could actually use was to continue the conversation with the king's best friend.

Despite that, she nodded.

It didn't take long for Silas to begin his own line of questioning. "How long?"

"How long what?" she asked, trying to sound casual, but her voice came out strained. She should've just stuck to being silent.

"You know what I'm asking." When she shook her head, he gave an exasperated sigh. "How long have you been receiving Estrada's messages?"

Evangeline walked faster, as if that might help her evade his questions. To her chagrin, he easily matched her pace.

"Evie," he said, tugging on her arm to pull her to a stop. "Talk to me."

"I think I've done enough talking today. And maybe forever." She wriggled out of his grasp, not that he made it difficult. He released her without much fuss. "Emmalee sends me comforting messages, and I can't respond. That about sums it up. There's nothing else to say."

Silas stuck his hands into his pockets as he regarded her. They'd stopped at the top of the second-floor stairs, and anyone walking by would be able to overhear their conversation. Silas seemed to recognize that when he greeted a few servants wandering past with baskets of laundry on their hips. He nodded once.

"All right," he said matter-of-factly. He gestured for her to continue down the hallway. He didn't ask any more questions as he dropped her off at her room, saluting to the guard already posted there.

Evangeline was disappointed to see it wasn't Benji.

Without another word, Evangeline disappeared into her room. She closed the door firmly behind her, leaning against it as her heart pounded. She'd said too much.

Even if the king didn't find anything against Emmalee in the words she'd spilled in his office, there would be more opportunities to make mistakes.

And for Emmalee's sake, that wasn't something she could afford to do.

Chapter 81

BUTCH

Butch shared a quiet meal with Lenora, the rays from the sun leaking in through the window beside them. His son slept peacefully in a bassinet across the room, attended by a nursemaid. Butch kept gazing toward his son, marveling at his tiny features. His black hair had already thickened, and while he resembled Lenora in that way, Butch liked to think his son had his eyes.

It was like every time Butch regarded his son, emotions fought for supremacy within him. Love. Protectiveness. And a fierce determination to create a safe, magic-free world for him.

As Butch turned back to Lenora, she gave him a soft smile, her eyes twinkling. "Beautiful, isn't he?"

"He is," Butch agreed, nodding his head in approval. "Just like his mother." He took a sip from his glass, giving her an appraising look. "I'm quite lucky."

She blushed.

He loved it.

"How have you been feeling since his birth?" Butch asked. He'd spent the night with her a few times since his son's birth nearly two and a half months earlier, but not as much as before. "Have all of the symptoms of your sickness gone away?"

Lenora nodded. "I'm well."

"And you've been sleeping well?"

She dropped his gaze. "A few vivid dreams here and there, but overall, it's been . . . fine."

"What kind of dreams?"

She didn't respond right away. "Dreams of her."

Butch froze. "Her?"

"Estrada."

"What?" he asked, sitting straighter. "What kind of dreams?"

"In them, I'm with her again." Lenora's voice was soft.

His heart sank. She'd been having nightmares, but he hadn't realized they'd been about her time as bait. "Lenora, I'm sorry."

She glanced at him with wide eyes. "It's not your fault. They aren't bad, really. Just . . . frequent."

"No," he said, reaching across the table to hold her hand. "I'm sorry she used you to get to me."

Lenora squeezed his hand. "It worked out. I needed to see you'd come for me."

"Of course," he said, bringing her hand up to his lips and brushing a soft kiss against her knuckles. "I was so worried about you. What she was doing to you. Whether you were lonely." Butch paused, his brow furrowing.

The conversation with Lia earlier flickered through his mind.

"Butch? What is it?"

"I think . . . I think I have an idea."

"What kind of idea?"

He looked at her with a grin that spread over his lips, growing wider second by second. "One that will catch Estrada."

"What?" Lenora pulled her hand from his grasp, her eyes widening. "What are you going to do?"

Butch pinched his lips shut, shaking his head. "I don't know yet. Not fully. I . . . I need to test some things first."

"What do you mean?"

He regarded her for a second before he decided to explain to her the messages Estrada had been sending the prisoner. How it showed that she clearly still valued her friend highly. That her willingness to break into his castle, despite how difficult and dangerous that had to have been, showed how much she was willing to risk.

"The problem lies in the fact that this castle is defended from the outside well, but it's too easy to escape. I need a location where escape is near impossible. Somewhere like . . ." His voice trailed off as a chill ran down his spine. "I think I need to speak with some of my men. Would you excuse me?"

He left his wife and son in the small family room, his mind already racing.

If this worked, he might just succeed in protecting his family and his country.

Chapter 82

LENORA

Lenora's head reeled. The look in her husband's eye when he realized he might have a plan to capture Estrada had been absolutely predatory. Her stomach had filled with dread instantly.

Estrada had showed her a peculiar kind of kindness. Had sympathized with her. She'd even catered the way she'd prepared meals to suit Lenora's preferences. That was something even the castle cooks didn't do.

She couldn't let her husband hurt Estrada.

Lenora tensed on her seat, and Merla, who'd been brushing her hair, noticed.

"Is something the matter, Your Majesty?"

"I'm just a bit tired." She gave a small smile to Merla and then to Kaylene through the mirror. "I'd like some time alone."

The handmaids exchanged glances, then nodded. They curtsied before leaving her alone in her chambers.

She couldn't warn Estrada—not when she didn't know where she was.

But there was someone she could tell.

And with that thought in mind, Lenora sat down at her writing desk.

She began to write.

Chapter 83

SILAS

Silas stood in the study once again, the familiar weight of the sword heavy in his scarred hands. His heart pounded as he approached her. Her brown eyes locked onto his, wide with fear. He couldn't stop his hand, couldn't prevent the blade from plunging into her stomach. Her scream echoed in his ears as he ripped it out. She clutched her abdomen, sliding down the bookshelf and leaving a trail of blood. She was dying, and all he did was stand above her.

Silas sat straight up, vaulting off his bed in the darkness. He ran his hands through his hair, over his face, around the back of his neck. His heart raced. He was panting.

The nightmare haunted him every time he closed his eyes.

He'd killed her over and over by now, and somehow, it only got worse.

He needed to see her. Needed to feel her breath on his skin, the beat of her heart in her chest. See her whole and well.

Dressing quickly, he left his room, taking the steps to the second floor two at a time.

The guard posted outside her door snapped to attention as he approached.

"Sir?" the guard asked when Silas didn't return his salute.

"Take the rest of the night off," Silas ordered, his voice gruff.

"Sir, I—"

"Did I stutter, Officer?"

The guard hesitated for a moment before saluting a second time and walking away. Silas waited until the guard was out of sight before knocking.

When she didn't answer right away, he slammed his flat hand against the door three times. And continued to do so over and over again until a very disgruntled-looking Evie opened the door.

She wore only a light chemise, her hair in frizzy white-blond waves around her face. Her right cheek was pinker than the other, as if she'd been sleeping on her side. And her intoxicating mouth . . .

"Silas, what—" She stopped talking when he stepped forward, catching her by the waist and backing her into the room.

"Silas . . ." His name slipped out from between her perfect lips and wound around and around his heart.

With one hand on her cheek, the other pressing her into him, he kissed her.

She gasped against his mouth, her eyes widening in surprise before they fluttered shut.

When he finally pulled away, staring down into her flushed face, his heart melted. She was smiling.

"Hi," she whispered, her gaze flicking from his mouth to his eyes and back down again.

"Hi," he replied.

"Would you like to explain why—"

"No," he muttered, shaking his head as he tucked a flyaway strand of hair behind her ear. "No, I wouldn't."

Evie bit her lip. "Okay." She focused all her attention on his mouth. "What would you like to do instead?"

"This."

The fracturing dam of self-control within him burst. Silas kicked the door behind him shut, spinning around with her until he pressed her against the wall. She gasped, lifting her chin to stare up at him.

Silas collected both her hands in one of his and pinned them above her head. He used his free hand to trace the pad of his thumb over her soft lips, across her jaw, and down her neck. She shivered.

Her dilated gaze found his. "Kiss me, Silas."

His grip on her hands tightened. "Say that again."

"Kiss me." Her voice was breathy.

"My name," he said, his lips pressed to the sensitive skin just below her ear. "Say it."

"Silas," she sighed, arching into him as he kissed along her neck. "Please."

He grinned against her jaw. "You set me on fire every time you say my name. Did you know that?" His free hand traveled along the opposite side of her neck until he cupped her face again.

"Silas," she whispered.

"Evie." He loved the way she seemed to melt just as much when he said her name.

"Evangeline," she said, her voice small. "It's actually Evangeline."

"Beautiful," he whispered, leaning down to press another kiss to her lips. When she lifted up to try to make it last, he chuckled. "You want me to kiss you, Evangeline?"

She let out a partial moan as he leaned down just far enough to brush his lips against hers as he spoke.

"As you wish."

Fire spread through his body, heating him from the inside as they connected once more.

In a matter of seconds, her lips parted, allowing him to deepen the kiss. It grew hungrier, more desperate. Silas's hand moved from her cheek to tangle in her hair. His other hand dropped hers, trailing down her side until he pulled her closer by the waist. Evangeline's hands draped over his shoulders, one making its way up to stroke through the back of his hair.

Silas poured every pent-up emotion, every concern for her safety, every moment of confusion, every second of longing into her mouth. She bit his bottom lip. He groaned, eliciting a smile from her.

The taste of her, the feel of her, was everything he'd been denying himself.

And he needed more.

"Why do you haunt my dreams, Evangeline?" he said against her lips. "Why can't I stay away?"

She responded by kissing the corner of his mouth, his jaw, his neck. Silas let out another low groan, pressing against her hip from where she'd come off the wall.

"Why, Evie?"

"I don't know," she whispered, chest heaving as she ran a hand down his cheek. "But I feel the same."

He kissed her again, his movements more controlled this time, though no less passionate. Her warmth radiated through the thin fabric of her chemise as his hands roamed up and down her back.

Evangeline responded with equal fervor, her fingers threading through his hair.

It wasn't until he'd kissed her lips swollen and they were breathing too heavily to continue that they broke apart.

"I think," he murmured, his forehead resting against hers as he closed his eyes. "I think I've wanted to do that for a long time."

"Really?"

He kissed her forehead, pulling her into a hug he wished could last forever. She was safe. Wasn't bleeding out. It'd been a nightmare, nothing more.

"Really."

Chapter 84

BUTCH

I t'd worked. Butch's small-scale test had worked. It'd taken two weeks by his count to get the information to spread, but in the end, Estrada had fallen for the bait and confirmed his theory.

The pieces of a puzzle he'd been working on for over a year were finally falling into place. Butch leaned back in his chair, a small grin on his face. His plan would succeed, and now it was only a matter of putting every domino into place so they were ready to fall when he wanted them to.

The only part of his plan that he was unsure about was the location. Not that he didn't have one. It was the location itself he didn't like.

Loathed, actually.

Château Lavfor.

The name alone made his skin crawl.

That wretched place continued to torment him even after he'd shut it down and would torture him again as he prepared to use it in his plan against Estrada.

The monstrosities his father had committed in that dark place flickered through Butch's memory. They may have had magic, but his father's victims hadn't deserved the experiments and misdeeds done to them.

Butch had been forced to participate, his hands stained with blood he'd never wanted to spill.

A memory pierced through his thoughts, one he'd long since locked away. The terrified purple eyes of a young female dryad, no older than he was at twelve. Her screams tore through the sterile hallways as he followed his father's orders. The blood that'd coated his skin, beneath his nails. The tears that'd streamed down her face as she begged for him to stop.

The same tears falling down his face as he'd tried and failed to escape the château, only to be returned to the horrible rooms by his father's men. His punishment had been longer hours there, sometimes overnight.

Butch's stomach churned at the thought of returning. It was necessary though. Lavfor, as demented as it was, created a nearly perfect cage: easy to break into, near impossible to escape.

He knew.

He'd tried.

And failed.

Again and again and—

A knock at the door yanked Butch out of his dark memories. "Enter," he called, shifting in his chair.

Silas walked in looking exhausted. Dark circles framed his eyes, and his shoulders sagged.

"Brother," Butch greeted, gesturing for him to sit. "You look like—"

"I know. Sleep has been a bit fickle lately." Silas rubbed the back of his neck, wincing. But when he straightened, some of his fatigue vanished. "You requested to see me? Are Lenora and Diomedes all right?"

"Yes, thank you," Butch said, his voice tighter than necessary. The truth was, he hadn't seen either in quite a while, too busy with his council's final pushback against the new law about to pass, as well as sending more men north to deal with a new wave of rebels fighting in the battles, and, of course, his plan.

"I've been working on a plan to catch Estrada."

Silas's eyes widened. "Really? Since when?"

Butch ignored the question, diving instead into detail about the small-scale test that had succeeded.

"That's . . . Wow. That's brilliant, brother." Silas sat back in the chair, rubbing the side of his jaw. "But what makes you think she'll fall for the bait?"

"Well, we both know she's not heartless."

"She's killed my men. Your guards."

Butch clenched his jaw, nodding. "Oh, I haven't forgotten." He tapped his finger against his wedding ring. "And never will. But no one is completely evil."

A curious look crossed Silas's face. "How do you mean?"

"Evil is a corruption of good. For evil to exist, there must first be good." Butch shrugged.

"Even Estrada? After everything?"

"Yes. She's corrupt and a murderer, but she clearly loved her family and loves her friend. Lia said herself that Estrada has sent her messages. She hasn't forgotten about her or abandoned her. She's just waiting for the right time to strike."

"And if you control when that time is, then—"

"I strike first." Butch smirked. "Exactly."

Chapter 85

EMMALEE

Emmalee had spent the last several months in the tiny house, biding her time. And while it'd been a refuge, it also often felt like the walls were closing in on her.

Once a week, she ventured into Cyanthia with the help of the disguise rune. She'd learned through experimentation—one of which had left her with obnoxious green hair for a week and a half—that a week between uses seemed to be pretty safe. At least the green hair had shifted back to her dark brown. The routine of going into town had allowed her to gather valuable information and, of course, supplies. Especially when the royal guards got drunk and loose-lipped at the pubs. Drunkards were much easier to slip coin purses from anyway, and the information made it more than worth her while. They rarely noticed her in the corner, disguised by magic, nursing a drink and listening to their overtly loud conversations.

In fact, a few weeks ago, they'd foolishly spilled the king's quiet order to bring in people from Shongbay who knew her for questioning. They'd even mentioned names, though some of them had been indiscernible because of the slurring. But Emmalee had been able to warn Anwell's old assistant and a few others, advising them to go into hiding before the guards could reach them. It was a small victory, and seeing the kindness and appreciation in her late husband's assistant's eyes had made the trip worth it, even if she had cried herself to sleep after returning to Shongbay.

A different kind of energy filled the air in the Cyanthia lower town as Emmalee stuck to the less traveled streets and alleyways. The usual hum and noise of the marketplace was overshadowed by grumbling and whispered complaints. Emmalee moved through the crowd, keeping her hood drawn despite her shifted appearance. She listened to snippets of conversation as she made her way to the pub.

". . . the road . . ."

". . . whole week . . ."

". . . utterly ridiculous . . ."

Despite her curiosity, she continued to the pub without asking questions.

The raucous noise when she got inside had Emmalee wishing she were back in the tiny house. Unfortunately, staying in the quiet house was not an option. She'd run out of material to research, and none of it felt like she was getting any closer to rescuing Evangeline from the castle.

No news made it to her abode unless she was the one to go out to get it. She had checked the hub of the outer town where any pertinent information was posted on the bulletin boards at the center of the square. However, the only thing that had caught her eye were the posters of her that had been there for ages, the parchment weathered and torn.

It was strange to see her face glaring back at her. She had never been the type to stand in front of the mirror for long periods of time, nor could she remember such harshness behind her eyes, which glared at the passersby, who did not pay the poster, or the woman in front of it, any heed.

The disguise rune had lengthened her hair, lightening it several shades. Instead of tying it back like she normally would've, she let it flow down her shoulders. She must've been several inches taller as well because she could see over most of the heads of the people around her in the pub.

There were several pubs within Cyanthia, but she had chosen the one closest to the castle knowing it would cater to the royal guards more than the ones in the lower towns.

Five men dressed in royal guard garb sat along the counter nearest to the server—a wiry old man who moved as if his joints were bound together with metal. Most of the other patrons sat scattered around the room at various tables or in huddled groups, likely muttering about whatever the people outside were discussing.

Depending on the disguise rune to protect her, Emmalee boldly approached the counter, taking the only open stool at the end.

"I'll be right with you," the man behind the counter said, his head jerking down in a nod to acknowledge her.

Emmalee offered a smile, nodding back. Her attention was on the guards though, some of whom had glanced in her direction as she'd sat down. All too easily, she eavesdropped on their conversation while she stared at the wall opposite her.

"Cavanaugh said they mainly ran into issues with locals who had business down here." The guard closest to her was speaking, and with his back turned to her, Emmalee's ears strained to hear each word he spoke. "I get it though. I'd be upset too. It's their livelihood."

"Especially since it's for a whole week," another added from down the counter.

"Right," the one in the middle said. "I don't understand why it has to take that long. It's one person and not even a quarter of a day's ride to Lavfor from here."

The man closest to Emmalee grunted, shrugging his shoulders. "You know why the king's doing it. Extending the time means that she won't know exactly when to strike. He's worried the sorceress is planning something. But, I mean, she's only one person. She can't be watching all the roads all the time. In my opinion, the king's a bit paranoid."

Emmalee's posture straightened at the mention of the king, but before she could hear anything else, the server stepped in front of her and drew her attention away from the conversation next to her.

"What can I get for you?" he asked, a grin on his wrinkled face.

"Uh . . ." Emmalee hesitated, her mind racing. She wanted her thoughts to remain clear, so with a small smile of her own, she replied, "Water for now."

"All right. Let me know if you'd like anything else," he said, filling a glass with water and passing it to her over the counter.

Emmalee nodded, but her attention was already back on the guards. Her gaze, though, remained fixed on the reflections of the men in the bottles lining the shelves across from her.

"That's because you weren't there that night," the man closest to her growled, though she wasn't sure which guard he was upset with until the seemingly youngest of the group responded.

"So I've never met Estrada in person." The mention of her name had Emmalee tensing as the guard in the middle continued. "I was the top of my training group. I could take her."

The other four men exploded with laughter, and Emmalee forced her mouth to remain relaxed instead of curling up into a smile.

"You'd be dead in seconds if you met Estrada," one of them said, amusement still tingeing his voice.

"I second that," another added. "I don't care if you were elected as the king's marshal when you came out of your mother's womb. That woman is dangerous. She killed Levick, you know."

"So what? He was good at fighting, but he wasn't the brightest. And you're saying that you'd all run if you saw her?" the guard in the middle challenged.

"No. But I'm not naïve enough to claim that I could take her." The guard next to Emmalee shifted after he spoke, leaning his elbow on the counter. "I saw her in the boulder field that night. Sent me flying like I was nothing more than a bug. She's dangerous. That much dark magic . . ." His words trailed off.

"Sounds like you're scared of her," the man in the middle said.

"A little fear is good for you."

"Danby's right," the guard at the very end of the counter said, agreeing with the man—Danby, apparently—who sat next to Emmalee. "I'm supposed to guard the road north to Lavfor when the prisoner is moved, and I'm embracing the nerves. If I see Estrada, I'm not running, but I'm definitely not going to challenge her to a duel one-on-one."

"She wouldn't waste her time on you anyway," Danby replied, straightening next to Emmalee. "If what the king said is true, her focus would be too much on the woman. As someone who'd be in her way, you'd be flung against a tree before you knew what was happening. Trust me, I know from experience." He rubbed his shoulder.

Emmalee's hands tightened around the glass of water, and she took a few deep breaths when the coolness of her magic slipped through her veins like ice in a mountain stream. *Evangeline.* Her mind focused even more on their words, trying to piece together useful information that would help her save her friend.

"As obnoxious as it is for the people who use the direct roads between Lavfor and Cyanthia, it was pretty wise of the king to shut them down and block them off. At least that way we can keep a better eye out for her," the guard at the end said.

"That's assuming she even knows what the king is trying to do," another one responded.

"I don't see why His Majesty doesn't just keep her here," the guard in the middle muttered as he took a swig from his glass.

Emmalee struggled to swallow. If they were moving Evangeline, it was the perfect time to try to rescue her. She wouldn't have to deal with the magic-dampening cell or trying to get into the heavily guarded Cyanthian castle again. And even if the king did get Evangeline to Lavfor, it couldn't be as difficult to get into as the castle.

She tried to listen to when they were planning to move Evangeline, but the guards were shifting their conversation to less useful topics.

Still, she stayed for another twenty minutes, listening to them go on and on about the new schedules that had gone out the day previous. Their conversation drifted to the weapons each would choose to fight a dragon, and it was around that time that Emmalee decided to leave.

However, she didn't go far. Instead of going back to her house, Emmalee waited outside, sitting on a bench, until the guards filed out of the pub. Danby and the guard he'd been sitting next to came out first. They headed straight to the castle, and she watched them go. An hour later, the man who'd been sitting at the end of the counter came out, also heading toward the castle looming in the distance.

When the guard who'd been next to him came out later, Emmalee almost lost hope. But just as she was getting ready to go back to her house—the sun had long since sunk behind the horizon, which meant the nightly patrols would begin soon—the guard who'd sat at the center of the five men came stumbling out of the pub.

She couldn't have planned it better. Rising to her feet, Emmalee followed the man as he went through an alley to the left of the pub, using the wall to steady himself. The castle was in the opposite direction, and when she glanced behind her, Emmalee let a small smile reach her lips. No one seemed to have noticed her slip into the alleyway.

The guard had stopped partway down near a barrel, which he leaned against.

Emmalee cleared her throat, pasting a wide grin onto her face when the man startled and turned to face her. "I'm sorry, sir," she said in her most pleasant voice. "I didn't mean to frighten you."

"You din't," he slurred. The guard had light brown hair cut short to his scalp. He appeared unstable enough to fall over at any second, and his gaze traveled up and down Emmalee's disguised form multiple times. "Wha' d'you want?"

"Do you know when the roads to Lavfor are going to be closed?"

He raised an eyebrow, leaning to the side as he peered down the alleyway behind her. "Why?"

"I'm from there. I'm supposed to return for my sister's wedding soon, but I'm not sure how to get there without the main roads. I was hoping you could tell me when they're supposed to close so I can prepare ahead of time."

The guard's expression pinched, and he shook his head. "Not supp'sed to talk 'bout it." His words slurred together. "Private stuff."

"Oh, I'm sorry," she said, taking a step back. "I just didn't want to miss my sister's big day." She forced innocence and sadness into her voice and face. "I won't bother you any longer." Emmalee turned away but only had to take one step before the man did exactly as she thought he would.

"Hold on," he said, his boot scratching the cobblestone street as he stepped toward her. "I din't mean t'be rude."

Emmalee turned back to him, tucking a piece of the long hair the disguise rune had given her behind her ear. She looked at him through her eyelashes, blinking slowly with wide eyes.

"It's all right. I was just . . . I was just hoping for some answers." She spoke in a hushed voice, twirling the end of her hair around her fingers.

"I understand. It's all a bit excessive, if you ask me," he muttered.

"Oh?"

"All we're doin' is moving one person to Lavfor. It doesn't need t'be a big deal. But the king . . ." His words fell away when his unfocused eyes landed on Emmalee. "Never mind. Jus' know that the road'll close in two weeks for a week." He blinked a few times, his eyes fixed on her face. "You probably shouldn't be walkin' 'round this late. I can take you to the nearest inn, and—"

"I'm sure I can find one," Emmalee said, a smile returning to her face. "Thank you, sir."

Before he could say or do anything, Emmalee turned on her heels and left the alley. She had the confirmation she needed to start making a plan. Hopefully two weeks would be enough time.

The king was moving Evangeline to Château Lavfor—which, to her knowledge, was a smaller, less protected castle. She had work to do.

Chapter 86

BUTCH

Butch stood in his office, packing the last of his things for his journey to Lavfor. He wasn't sure what all he needed, but since there was no telling when Estrada would strike, he was bringing a bit of work. It also would, he hoped, serve as a distraction from the horrible memories that would inevitably try to strangle him to death.

He'd already said goodbye to Lenora, who seemed worried for him, staring at him with an anxious gaze and pleading with him to reconsider. He'd kissed her softly, assuring her he'd be careful.

Butch paused next to his desk when a knock sounded at the door. "Enter," he called, fastening the last buckle on his travel bag.

Silas stepped into the room, his expression serious. "I have a request."

Butch raised an eyebrow. "Go on."

"I'd like to remain here in Cyanthia, if I may. To keep an eye on the prisoner."

Frowning, Butch leaned against his desk. "Keep an eye on her why? If it's because you don't wish to return to Lavfor—"

"It's not that," Silas said, shaking his head.

"You don't think Estrada's fallen for the ruse?"

"It's not that either. But if there's even a slight chance she hasn't, wouldn't you prefer I keep your best bait?" Silas stuck his hands into his pockets. "Besides, I'd like to stay back to protect Lenora and Diomedes as well. Just in case. You know I'd lay down my life for all three of you."

"I'm aware." Butch regarded his friend for a long moment before nodding. "It's a good idea. I'm sure you'll keep them safe."

A brief silence hung between them. Butch broke it by stepping forward and clapping a hand on Silas's shoulder. "If all goes well, I'll rid the world of Estrada and we can go back to whatever normal was nearly two years ago."

Silas offered him a small smile. "Just come back in one piece."

"I plan on it, brother."

THE RIDE TO Lavfor was swift—swifter than Butch had thought it would be. No wonder some of his men had been complaining about the extensiveness of his plan. But it had to seem extensive. That was the point. He had needed a reason for his men to talk about it, for word to spread throughout Cyanthia—and hopefully the rest of Phildeterre—as to the plans he had to move Estrada's friend to a new location.

The more people talked, the more likely it was that Estrada would try to interfere with the plans. And that was what he wanted, what he was depending on.

It'd worked in Shongbay. The people he'd sent his guards to question had disappeared before his men had arrived. He had to hope it was because of her. He'd done his research on the people Anwell Estrada had associated with. To his surprise, there was more information readily available about Estrada's husband—information he probably could've used to interrogate Lia had he thought about it.

Too late now.

The plan had already begun.

It was no secret that the château in Lavfor was less secure—at least from the outside—and less traveled to. Most people knew he'd shut it down. It served as the perfect bit of gossip. The news that the king might be reopening the horrifying château spread like a deadly disease, at least according to his guards in the nearby villages and towns.

Few people knew the extent to which his father had gone to make Lavfor an unassuming château from the outside and an inescapable nightmare from the inside. Despite the rocky relationship with the Dark King, he had somehow arranged for metal to be shipped from the Dark—a world parallel to their own reached only through portals, all but one of which had been destroyed. Butch knew his father must've paid the Dark King very well for his resources. It would've taken years—maybe even generations—to have the same amount of metal mined from the Elemental Mountains. The magic-dampening metal was present but quite rare; it was much more bountiful in the Dark.

His father had used the metal to create the cells in the dungeon, as well as half of the experimentation rooms. Weapons, chains, and instruments of torture had all been formed from the metal and were abandoned when Butch had shut Lavfor down.

From the outside, though, the château seemed innocent.

Butch stood before Lavfor, taking in the sight of the three-story building that had haunted his dreams for years. Its stone façade, weathered even in the last five years, was covered in creeping vines that snaked their way up the walls. The overgrown courtyard gate—barred to prevent intruders—creaked as it opened. Many an execution had been held in the space, now with the appearance of a forgotten garden.

A satisfied smirk crossed Butch's lips. He liked the idea that his father's horrible creation was slowly being reclaimed by nature and weeds.

It was hard to believe that such a tranquil-looking place had been the site of so much suffering.

The château's windows were dark and empty, like hollow eyes staring out into the world with a malevolent gaze. Butch's stomach churned. His father had been a master at cruelty, and Lavfor had been his masterpiece.

Taking a deep breath, Butch steeled himself and jogged up the steps, Silas's best men following behind and around him. He clenched his hands into fists, releasing them with a sigh before he walked through the front doors.

"Let's get this place ready, shall we?" Butch asked, his nose wrinkling at the stale smell filling the air. He turned to the five captains Silas had recommended. "I want men patrolling the roads as well as the château. If Estrada even begins to think of this as a trick, she won't show." Butch glanced around the entranceway.

"Yes, Your Majesty," Captain Malkim said, saluting. Butch was surprised Silas had sent him, considering how annoyed his friend had been when the captain had abused Lia. But Silas had said the man had apologized, and Butch trusted Silas's judgment.

"Estrada's made it clear that she's cunning. If we mess up any one part of this plan, she'll know. The only ones who know that the prisoner is still in Cyanthia are you five and Marshal Thorne." He paused, snorting. "And my wife."

"The queen knows?" Captain Malkim raised a bushy eyebrow. "Why?"

Bristled by his question, Butch cleared his throat. "Because I'm married to her, and I answer her questions when she brings them to me. Now, make sure those on the perimeter are on the lookout for anyone who is not a royal guard."

"Yes, Your Majesty." Captain Malkim nodded and saluted. Turning on his heels, he departed down the hallway just as a pair of patrolling guards rounded the corner on the opposite side.

Butch nodded to each in turn. A small grin crossed his lips.

This could work.

It had to work.

However, his good mood started to drain out of him the farther he ventured into the château. He hadn't walked the halls since he'd shut the place down officially.

For many of his summers, from ages nine to fifteen, Butch had been sent to Château Lavfor by King Valryn for "extra training," as his father had referred to it. What had once been a safe haven where members of the royal family could get away from the hustle and bustle of life in Cyanthia had been turned into a place to study those with magic—or rather torture them until their corpses could be studied.

The rooms he passed, which were now empty, had once been filled with tables and equipment used to discover ways to combat magic—to eradicate it without eliminating over half the population of the country. Butch shoved his hands into his pockets, pulling his gaze down to the floor beneath him instead of the room that held a particularly gruesome memory of a young woman who'd been part fae. Many faces from those summers had haunted his dreams for years, and even though many had been dead when he'd been forced to stand in during an examination, he had seen too many live examinations as well.

Butch coughed to cover the silent screams echoing through his mind.

He'd had the château emptied of all its horrors, yet the memories remained.

Somehow, Butch ended up in the same place he had when he was a child looking for a place to hide from the miserable sights around every corner: a linen closet. Checking over his shoulder and confirming that the hallway was empty, Butch reached for the knob. It was strange how familiar it felt in his hand.

The door creaked as he pulled it open. The air inside was musty, likely because it hadn't been opened in many years. The space felt smaller than it once had, even when he was a fifteen-year-old boy already growing into his body.

In the past, Butch had closed the door tightly behind him, but he left the door open, using the light from the window at the end of the hall to show the scratches near the bottom of the wall. Tally marks. Each visit he'd been forced to stay there marked by a separate scratch. Crouching down, Butch sighed, running his fingers along the rough surface. A prisoner in his father's house.

How many hours had he spent hiding in there?

Footsteps sounded from a nearby hallway. Butch shot to his feet, closing the door to his safe haven before anyone could ask him what he was doing. He brushed off the knees of his trousers, which had gotten dusty from the floor of the closet.

"Your Majesty." A guard saluted as soon as he came around the corner. "We've prepared a study for you."

"Excellent. Lead the way."

Chapter 87

EMMALEE

Emmalee crouched high in the tree, her eyes fixed on the silhouette of Château Lavfor. She hadn't known much about the place, besides what Ariella and Faeleen had told her about it being a bloody death sentence for magic folk when it was still open. But with the talk of the towns being that the king might be reopening Lavfor, Emmalee had gleaned that it was bad. Really, *really* bad.

The fact that the king was moving Evangeline there did not bode well for her friend's lifespan, by the sound of it.

That, along with the fact that she hadn't had time to figure out the layout of the interior, meant it was even more vital she save Evangeline before her friend was forced to step a single foot through the giant doors.

The château itself wasn't nearly as large as the castle in Cyanthia, and though it'd clearly seen better days, it didn't look like the torture castle many people had called it.

Unassuming.

Just like her.

She almost smiled.

Emmalee had been watching the rotation of guards for hours, noting their patterns and weaknesses. But until she was about ready to move to a new tree for a different vantage point, there'd been no sign of a prisoner transfer.

A carriage rattled down one of the roads leading to the château gates, and Emmalee grinned. She was ready, knew each spell she'd use.

And she was about to enact the first one when a sound from a different road caught her attention.

Another carriage.

A few seconds later, a third. All coming from different roads, all with their own caravan of guards both on and off horseback.

Emmalee's heart sank at the sight. There was no way to tell which one held her friend. She could maybe send her magic to see for her, but even the closest carriage seemed a bit too far for that particular spell.

She ground her teeth, glaring at the carriages as they rolled up to the large iron gates.

The king had outplayed her.

Her frustration boiled into anger as she realized how careful the king had been just to keep Evangeline away from her. She stalked as far as she dared go on the sturdy branch, her gaze darting from one group of guards to another, but she couldn't see where the carriages went as they were welcomed into the château courtyard.

Emmalee's mind raced as she weighed her options. She could try to take out the guards, but there were so many of them, and they were clearly prepared for her. And if there were others nearby, she'd be risking alerting the others to her presence.

Drawing a deep breath, she mustered up a mixture of courage, rage, and fear—fear for Evangeline more so than herself.

She wanted her friend back.

And there was only one way to do that.

She had to go in.

SHE WAITED UNTIL the dead of night. Two of the moons were nothing but small slivers in the sky, and the third hid behind ominous dark clouds. It left the world around her pitched in darkness.

It was perfect.

Emmalee's hand radiated the coolness of her magic as she lit the field in front of the château on fire. She had been prepared to fight her way in, especially since there seemed to be only one set of iron gates through which to enter.

She'd clearly been spotted because the guards were ready for her as soon as she stepped out from the trees. The fire was probably the biggest indicator. And just as she'd planned, it served as a distraction.

As she made her way forward, she focused most of her attention on deflecting the arrows shot at her from the second- and third-floor balconies as well as along the château wall.

The men on the field outside the château advanced toward her, shields and swords raised. But what could cold metal do against burning flames? Very little, in Emmalee's opinion. And apparently the guards found that out because they screamed and hollered, rolling around on the ground as magic fire licked their skin and armor.

At least she wasn't up close.

Distance made it easier to stomach.

Guards flanked her from behind without her noticing. All her attention had been on the men in front of her. The guards behind herded her toward the château gates, which were closed. She'd be trapped if she didn't get them open.

Emmalee tried to keep her breath steady as she scanned the inside of the gates for a lever that would lift them and let her through. If she could find it, she could use her magic to open it. But it was so dark . . .

The guards kept in close ranks, closing any gap she created when she hurled one or two of them backward across the burning field.

Her dark magic raced through her, waiting to be unleashed onto the guards, but she held back. She had no idea what kind of precautions the king had placed inside to keep her from getting to Evangeline.

Where was that blasted lever?

She had to split her attention between the guards and the gates.

By the time she found what she was looking for, the guards were within a rock's toss from her. She panicked. With a push of both hands, Emmalee flung a large group of the guards backward. With another flick toward the lever, the gates started to lift upward. Men shouted, clearly trying to undo what she'd done, but her magic held strong until there was enough of a gap for her to pass beneath. Then she let the gates close with a crash. For good measure, she wrapped her magic around the men at the lever and sent them flying. Best to keep the gates closed as long as possible.

With a confident grin, she turned to face the guards on the other side of the gates. She lifted a hand, setting the place where they stood on fire. They shouted and retreated.

She turned her focus to the guards spilling out of the château and lining up just as the others had.

Many of the guards marched forward, swords and shields raised. Arrows and bolts continued to fly toward her, but she paid enough attention to flick them away with her magic before they even got close. She did not want to heal from another bolt injury. Two was plenty.

She slowly raised her hands, enjoying the panicked looks on the faces of the men who could no longer see her within a cloud of opaque black mist. She, of course, could see just fine—one of the perks of casting the spell herself. It'd worked perfectly when she'd left the castle in Cyanthia, and it worked perfectly now.

Moving quickly, Emmalee darted forward. As long as the mist held, she might just be able to move amidst them in their chaotic state and get to the front doors unnoticed.

Until the doors slammed shut when she was only a few feet away. Guards started climbing the steps toward the entrance, some tripping when they couldn't see.

The doors remained shut, even as some of the guards tried to open them. That wouldn't do.

Evangeline was inside. That meant she needed the doors open.

With a powerful push from her magic, she blasted the doors. They splintered open, fragmenting from where the lock shattered. The force sent all the nearby guards both inside and outside the château sprawling. She grinned.

The halls echoed with the sounds of her footsteps and the distant shouts of more men. She threw a wall of magic up behind her, preventing any guards from following her inside, at least until she was farther within.

Her heart pounded.

She didn't know where to go.

Emmalee turned a corner, freezing at the sight that met her.

Ten guards stood in two rows at the end of the short hall, shields raised. They waited.

Neither party moved right away.

Forcing a relaxed grin onto her lips—though after the guards outside, it was the last thing she wanted her face to do—Emmalee crossed her arms over her chest.

"If you point me in the direction of my friend, I'll let you go." Some part of her hoped they would take the deal. She wasn't sure what it was, but something about the château gave her a bad feeling.

"We serve the king," one of the men said, and though his voice trembled for a second, he did not. Nor did any of the others.

Emmalee uncrossed her arms, watching each step they took toward her as if they were stalking prey in the forest. Just like the guards outside, they did not break formation, marching.

With a deep breath, Emmalee called upon her magic. Bending the dark mist to her will, Emmalee formed ropes. A few more directions from her mind and the darkness slithered along the walls like vines until it stopped just above the first row of men. For a second, the guards stared at the darkness on the ceiling. The dark magic appeared on the walls as it did under Emmalee's skin—like dark veins.

It was the distraction and pause Emmalee needed. She lowered her hands and clenched them into fists. In the same moment, the ropes leapt off the ceiling, each choosing a victim in the front row. Five nooses tightened around the guards, and as Emmalee tightened her hands, the struggling bodies began to still as each man breathed his last.

When she lifted her chin and glared at the remaining row of guards, it only took a second before they turned and ran. She reached her hand out, sending her magic to wrap around one of the guard's ankles. He fell, slamming into the floor before she yanked him back.

"Tell me . . . where . . . my friend is," she said, gritting her teeth as she held him in place with dark-magic ropes.

"Dungeon. She's in the dungeon," he cried, panic making him pale in the face. "Please!"

Emmalee sent him flying down the hallway after his friends.

Unlike with the guards she'd set on fire outside, there was no magic, no flames or smoke, to spare her the sight of the deaths she'd caused. Her stomach twisted, and she struggled to swallow.

She needed something, anything, to focus on to keep herself from being sick.

When she glanced at the bodies of the five men on the floor, guilt latched on to her mind. Though she tried to push it away soon after it appeared, tiny fragments still clung to her thoughts.

Someone's dad.

Someone's brother.

Someone's son.

But, she countered, stepping over the crippled corpses, she'd given them a way out, and they'd not taken it. That was on them, not her.

It couldn't be on her. She wouldn't let it be—not when Evangeline was counting on her.

The hallways were quite narrow compared to what she had experienced in the Cyanthian castle. It was for this reason Emmalee paused at the end of the hallway to scrawl one of the runes she'd learned in the last few months onto her boots. A silencing rune. As soon as she completed it, her footsteps no longer echoed as a clanging bell would at noon.

Emmalee scouted each hall, peeking around corners and disarming any royal guard she came across.

Thankfully, the château wasn't nearly as large as the Cyanthian castle.

Emmalee traveled down each staircase she came across. If she knew anything about castles, it was that the dungeons were almost always on the lowest floor.

It seemed to Emmalee that the king had focused most of his men on the outside, though she ignored the growing sensation that something wasn't right when, after ten minutes of wandering the halls, a large group of royal guards had not descended upon her.

Emmalee wrapped her cloak tighter around herself as the temperature in the château dropped. Since she had gotten her powers, it had been a rare occasion that she'd been cold. It was strange to have goose bumps rising on her skin and to feel the chill that ran down her spine, making her toes curl in her boots.

But none of it seemed to matter when she descended a final staircase to the dungeon. It was not nearly as long or wide as the one she'd searched previously, and she could tell right away which of the cells were empty and which one held her best friend.

"Evie," Emmalee whispered, checking to make sure the stairs she'd descended were the only entry and exit into the dungeon. They were. "Evie, it's me." Emmalee waited for a response, but in the darkness, Evangeline's form didn't move.

Panic suffocated her, holding her lungs captive.

Glancing around, Emmalee found the ring of keys that would supposedly open the cell doors. Within a matter of seconds, she swung the door open.

"Evie, get up, we have to—" Emmalee realized her mistake as soon as the cell door closed. The keys, which she'd left dangling in the lock, jingled away. "No!" Emmalee shrieked.

Keys in hand, the guard who'd locked it leapt back from the door when Emmalee reached through. She screeched in frustration, pressing her face up against the bars and extending her arm as much as she could. But the guard was out of reach.

Emmalee turned back to the cot on which Evangeline lay. But when she pulled back the thin wool blanket, a blond wig fell at her feet. Sacks of hay lined the cot, and as she bent to pick up the wig, multiple sets of footsteps echoed down the stairs.

They'd tricked her.

She'd been too naïve. Too desperate.

"Welcome to Château Lavfor, Estrada," Butch said, a smug grin plastered on his face as he approached her cell. He stayed several paces back after the guard who'd trapped her warned him about her area of reach. "This dungeon is surrounded wall to wall with magic-dampening metal beneath the stone."

That was why she was cold. Without the protection of her magic, her body felt the true temperature of the castle. It had been a warning—one she'd ignored completely because of her stubborn determination to free Evangeline. And now they were both captured, each one alone.

"Where is she?" Emmalee spat, throwing the wig down onto the brick floor near the front of the cell.

"Back in Cyanthia," Butch said, cocking his head to the side.

"She's not here?" Despite the fury flooding through her, Emmalee couldn't sense the dark magic with which she'd grown so comfortable. She felt empty without it.

"Nope. She happily agreed to work with me in exchange for a bed out of the dungeon and a few other little details. I bet she's curling up with a book right about now, maybe relaxing by the fire. Interesting woman once she starts talking." His voice was too friendly.

"She wouldn't work with you. She's not dim."

"Quite the opposite. Bright light—literally." He laughed at his own joke, but he was the only one.

"Where is she really? If you hurt her, I promise I'll—"

"I'm not kidding. Your Lia helped me come up with this brilliant little plan, whether she meant to or not. And you did too. It is, after all, the same thing you did to me, with a few changes here and there." He nodded toward the cells. "A little less ostentatious, I would say."

Emmalee frowned at the king's mention of Evangeline's middle name, but she didn't correct him. She was too busy trying to stifle the flicker of doubt passing through her at the king's declaration of her friend's betrayal. She had confidence in Evangeline. But she'd been there for over a year. What if she had talked—

No.

Evangeline wouldn't.

"You're a liar and a murderer. I won't believe a word you say," Emmalee muttered, wishing her glare could, in fact, light the king's tunic on fire. How she wished to see him screaming and flailing about as his men had outside the château—as they had on the night her magic had first manifested.

"Whether you believe it or not is of no concern to me." The king waved his hand off to the side. "But you should know that at noon tomorrow, you will receive your trial, and then, should you be found guilty, you'll be executed at dusk."

Emmalee tried not to let her true emotion—fear—cross her face. "And if you're found guilty, *Your Majesty*?" She put as much venom as she could into his title. "What then?"

Butch smiled. "Even if I were put on trial, you'd be hard-pressed to find anything worthy of punishment. I've done my duties as king."

"So, you're above the law, then, are you?" Emmalee challenged, stepping closer to the bars. "Above paying the price for the lives you've broken?"

Instead of responding, Butch nodded to the two guards near the entrance to the dungeon. "I want two down here, two at the top, and three at every hallway intersecting the one above this at all times. No one except for me or one of Marshal Thorne's captains is to speak to her. Understood?"

"Yes, sir," they both responded.

Emmalee glared at the king until he was no longer in sight, having left the dungeon. The anger she'd felt at the moment of the cell door closing returned, and though she called and called, her powers were absent.

The dungeon fell into silence.

Chapter 88

EVANGELINE

Evangeline sat by her window. She was fairly certain the imprint of her rear end would forever mar the cushion, considering she sat there for most of her long days. The first light of dawn crept over the horizon, coloring the world in a swath of gold. The past few weeks had been a blur, marked by Silas's increasingly frequent visits. Since kissing her in the middle of the night, he'd come to see her as often as his duties allowed, sharing meals with her whenever he could.

Each time, though, she noticed the deepening shadows under his eyes, the way his shoulders sagged with weariness. She'd tried to ask him what was going on, but the most she got was a brief mumble about a nightmare.

She was just grateful for his presence most of the time. Besides Benji, none of the other guards bothered to speak with her, leaving her with very few conversation partners. It made her miss Odette. Not so much the cell, but the long conversations and the feeling of not being alone. More than anything, she missed Emmalee.

She'd received another letter from the queen a few weeks earlier, warning her that the king had been planning something and that she'd send word when she learned more. And with the king's silence and lack of summons, Evangeline feared the queen was right. He had to be planning something.

As the sun continued to rise, a servant entered, carrying a breakfast tray. Evangeline turned from the window, offering a faint smile as the young girl put the tray on one of the bedside tables.

"Thank you," Evangeline said, waiting for the younger girl to leave before she crossed the room.

Evangeline carefully checked each tray that entered her room before eating, though she was more subtle about it when Silas was around. She wished there were a way to respond to the queen, to ask questions. But she didn't want to get her in trouble.

Lost in thought, Evangeline almost missed the scrap of parchment tucked beneath the cup, expecting it not to be there.

Her fingers shook when she unfolded the paper. It was another title of a book, more obvious this time than the previous messages.

Winter Bird Migration Patterns in Northern Phildeterre.

Though it took all her patience, Evangeline waited. In the time it took her to finish her breakfast, she memorized the title, reading it over and over again. When she'd finished, she knocked on the door.

"Fancy a trip to the study?" she asked Benji with a warm smile.

"Out of romance books?"

"Unfortunately, but I have a few more I can recommend to your wife." Evangeline closed her door and fell into step with Benji.

He snorted. "She raved about the last series you suggested for days. I'm sure she'll appreciate another recommendation."

Evangeline laughed, the sound echoing through the halls. "The question is, have you started reading them?" She waggled her eyebrows, watching as he blushed.

"No, I mean, not yet. But Nat said we should read one together."

Evangeline nodded. "Oh, I agree. Wholeheartedly."

Benji rolled his eyes as he opened the study door for her. "I'll be out here if you need anything."

He waited outside the room when she entered, leaving the door propped open.

Evangeline glanced over her shoulder, double-checking that Benji wasn't watching. She turned to the shelves of books in front of her.

It didn't take her long to find the book, and when she freed it from the shelf, a folded piece of parchment fell out right away. Evangeline checked the doorway. Still empty.

Bending down, Evangeline kept an eye on the door as she unfolded the parchment as quietly as she could. Every time the paper crinkled, she flinched, freezing in place. But nothing about the doorway changed, and she was finally able to shift her full attention to the paper that lay open in her hand.

A trap has been laid for your friend in Lavfor. The king has departed to go there by the time you're reading this. I write this knowing neither of us can do a thing to stop it. I wanted to let you know, though, because it involves your friend. While you are not there, your name is being used as honey to trap a fly. I'm sorry I cannot bring you better news.

Evangeline's hands trembled as she reread the letter again. Emmalee was in danger. The bracelet around Evangeline's wrist dug into her skin as she folded the parchment and tucked it into the pocket of her trousers. She spun the bracelet around as she stood with her back to the doorway, staring at nothing.

The queen was right: there was nothing Evangeline could do, trapped in the castle with the magic-dampening bracelet on her wrist. She tried to take a few deep breaths, but the thought of Emmalee being lured into a trap sent chills racing through her.

A hand covered Evangeline's mouth, smothering her surprised shriek as something cold and sharp dug into her side.

"For someone the king seems to have an interest in, it was a little too easy to get in here." The man's voice was familiar, and sure enough, when he spun her around and held a long knife to her throat, Evangeline recognized Stoll right away, especially with the burn scars Emmalee had given him.

"Benji!" Evangeline called, noting that the door was closed. How had she not heard him close it? She waited a second before dread seeped into her core. Benji didn't enter.

"Commander Volmar is a little unconscious at the moment. He didn't want to come to play."

Evangeline's heart twisted. "No," she gasped, taking a step back. He pursued, keeping the knife near enough that a single flick would open a carotid artery.

"What do you want?" Evangeline asked, her wide gaze flicking between the knife and the man. She kept her voice low, assuming if she made any more noise, he'd slit her throat.

Stoll was dressed in the royal guard uniform again, unlike when she'd seen him in the king's office, the record hall, and outside her window. The sleeves did a better job of hiding the scars on his arms, but no collar would ever be high enough to cover the wrinkled skin that crawled up the left side of his neck and onto his skull.

"I thought we already covered this. I want your friend to pay for killing my brother and for torturing me," he said, stepping toward her, forcing her to retreat.

"Please, Stoll. I haven't done anything to you." Evangeline shook her head, raising her hands as a pathetic barrier between them.

"You have magic," he said, and the smile on his lips made Evangeline's skin crawl. "Your existence is an insult." He advanced another step, and Evangeline, in a moment of bravery, took several steps back and put a chaise longue between them.

He didn't pursue—at least not right away. With the sick smile he gave her, she wondered how long he planned to toy with her before finishing the job. If she could just keep him talking . . .

"You belong with the worms."

Maybe not that kind of talking though.

"Because I was born this way?" Evangeline asked, her gaze leaving him for only a second to gauge the distance to the door. Her heart raced faster. Too far. She needed to get closer.

"Your kind are scum," he growled. Stoll pointed the knife at her again. "And as soon as I'm done with you, I'll find your friend and every other person like you. You'll all meet the same end by my hand."

Evangeline lifted her chin, but she did not respond. She was closer to the door than he was now, having continued to rotate around the chair. But surely he'd noticed that too. Was she fast enough to make it there before he got to her?

Her gaze must've flitted to the door one too many times, because his smile turned into a snarl. "Don't," he growled.

Before she could lose her advantage of distance, Evangeline sprinted for the door. Relief filled her when she twisted the knob and pulled it open. But before she could go through, Stoll slammed his palm against the door, and her opportunity to escape slipped from her grasp. She froze, her back to him as he pressed in closer to her.

"I said *don't*." His voice was low next to her ear, and Evangeline closed her eyes for a second, begging her nerves to calm down so she could think. "I'm not done yet."

She removed her hand from the knob. She didn't want to turn around—didn't want to see the anger on his face.

"Look at me, little mouse" he said, leaning forward. His rancid breath reached her nose, and she cringed.

Evangeline gasped when he gripped her arm and spun her around, slamming her back against the door.

"Look at me!" Stoll shouted. Still holding her upper arm in one hand, he easily flung her toward the center of the room.

Evangeline landed on her hip but didn't stop to think before she pushed herself back up to her feet. He'd thrown her far enough that she put a table between them without much effort.

"Look at what she did to me! She tortured me for hours! I wish I had that time with you. Oh, the way you'd scream . . ."

"Please, Stoll, just leave," Evangeline said, her voice shaking.

"I don't think I will," Stoll said, and for a second, he paused, tilting his head to the side.

When he returned his knife to its place on his belt, Evangeline took in a small breath of relief, only to let it out as a gasp. Stoll replaced his knife with his sword. "I'm going to do everything in my power to make that woman hurt before I kill her."

Evangeline matched each of his steps with her own. She had no idea how to fight, and even if she had, she had no weapon—nor could she use her magic. The best she could do was stay far from him and his blade.

"You know they're looking for you, right?" Evangeline asked, though she knew full well what his response was going to be.

"Of course I do. But I have a talent for hiding." He moved the sword back and forth while he spoke, as if he were speaking to a casual opponent instead of stalking her to kill her.

Stalking.

Evangeline's chin rose. "It was you in the gardens, wasn't it?" Again, she didn't need him to speak to know that it had been, though he did confirm it.

"I needed to see what your patterns were, when you'd be alone and virtually unguarded."

Alone.

She was always alone. And with Benji hurt or worse, she truly was without help. Who would hear her if she screamed? How close was the nearest servant or guard?

No amount of small talk could save her—could give her enough time to be found—not if no one was looking for her. And if the message in the book was true, Silas had probably departed with the king to go trap Emmalee.

Evangeline's hand brushed against one of the bookshelves behind her, and an idea formed in her mind. Without hesitation this time—she didn't want him guessing her plan again—Evangeline pulled a hardcover book off the shelf and threw it at Stoll. He dodged it, but it gave her enough time to run back to the door and fling it open.

"Help!" Evangeline screamed. "Someone, help!"

She hadn't even taken a step out of the study before Stoll's arm wrapped around her midsection, and he carried her kicking and screaming back into the study.

"Time's up," he said.

Stoll howled when Evangeline swung her heel back, kicking him between the legs. He dropped her. Evangeline landed hard on her hands and knees, and she scrambled away as soon as she was free.

"Don't do this," Evangeline said, jumping to her feet at the same time Stoll straightened.

His eyes were lit with fury, and his face had turned crimson. He moved out of the way of each item she threw at him, from books to the nearest candle.

"Enough!" he hollered.

Evangeline leapt out of the way when he struck down with his sword, sending feathers from an unlucky cushion into the air. She sprinted for the bookshelves nearer to the door. With a book in each hand, Evangeline spun to face Stoll only to scream as a burning fire sprouted from her core. She gasped.

Stoll stood inches away, one hand around the back of Evangeline's neck, the other firmly around the hilt of the sword protruding from Evangeline's chest.

She choked. Dropping the books in her hands, Evangeline tried to scream but couldn't as Stoll freed his blade from her body.

"No!" a different voice shouted from the door, which seemed to be traveling farther and farther from Evangeline.

Stoll stepped back, and Evangeline hit the bookshelf behind her, sliding down it while covering the hole in her chest with her hands. Her warm blood gathered between her fingers, and she moaned as she fought off the darkness surrounding the edges of her vision.

"What have you done?" The second voice, another familiar one, was loud next to her.

Someone slid a hand beneath her, and she cried out as the person shifted her so she rested against a strong chest.

"What should've been done ages ago."

The door slammed shut.

Stoll must've left.

"Evie, hey, hold on. Okay? I'm . . . Oh no . . . I'm going to make this all right. I'm just . . . No, no, no . . ."

The voice was soothing despite the panic slipping out beneath the calm.

Evangeline stared toward the ceiling, her head lolling back. A pair of swirling cerulean eyes met hers.

"S-Silas?" His name was a whisper on her lips. It was getting harder and harder to breathe. Each second, Evangeline's strength lessened until she couldn't keep her hands over the wound.

He was still speaking to her, but it sounded as though he were on the other side of a hill. His words made less and less sense, especially when a buzzing started playing in Evangeline's ear. And then it was all she could hear. The sound lulled her to sleep, dulling the pain in her stomach until she let the darkness embrace her.

Chapter 89

SILAS

S ilas couldn't see straight.

He tugged the hem of her shirt up, lightheadedness flooding through him at the sight of the blood seeping over her soft skin. He'd known he was too late when he saw Commander Volmar collapsed on the floor outside the study.

It was happening.

Just as he'd seen it.

Every. Single. Night. For weeks on end.

Silas could barely draw a straight line. His hands trembled. His breath caught. His heart pounded. Tears formed in his eyes, blurring his vision.

"Hold on, Evangeline," he pleaded, his voice breaking. "Please, just hold on."

He gripped his rune pen tighter and finished the first rune, the familiar tug of his magic filling him as it activated.

It wasn't enough.

He drew another.

And another.

And another.

He poured every ounce of his magic into her, all the while begging her to stay with him. The room spun around him, darkening at the edges as he pushed himself farther than he'd ever gone before. He was on the verge of collapse, his body trembling with exhaustion. The last rune flared to life.

He was spent. He could do no more.

He cradled her gently, brushing her hair out of her face. Bending down, he pressed a kiss to her forehead, his lips trembling. Silas leaned his head back against the bookshelf as the tears he'd been holding back spilled down his cheeks.

He'd been too late.

Too late.

Chapter 90

BUTCH

Butch questioned himself over and over as to why he hadn't given Estrada an immediate trial and execution. A year ago, he would've. But he hated that every time the question arose, he could hear Lia's voice in the back of his mind defending the woman.

There was no way of telling why, but over the past year, it had been harder and harder to deny that he could see why Estrada thought he was responsible for her husband's and daughter's deaths. The words of denial continued to come, but the fervor and sense of innocence behind them had faded—disappeared to the point that, when Estrada had challenged him as to whether he'd stand guilty or not, he'd almost contended that he would be.

Thankfully, though, his pride at apprehending his foe had driven away such feelings as guilt and shame. Estrada was caught—unable to hurt anyone from the cell beneath his feet. And soon enough, when the sun disappeared behind the horizon, she would meet her fate.

Butch sat next to the window, watching the leaves on the trees swaying in a light breeze. He felt light too—lighter, at least, than he had since he'd first heard of Estrada's devastating outburst in Shongbay.

Before long, two of the five captains Silas had sent—Captain Malkim and Captain Herris—were making preparations in what would've been the throne room if Butch's father had not removed the thrones when he'd turned the château into a palace of nightmares.

As the sun started to descend, Butch joined his men in the throne room, watching as the guards set up the cage—also magic dampening—in which Estrada would stand while Butch ran her trial. A cage was not always typical of the trials in Phildeterre, but on rare occasions, usually when the criminal was perceived to be a threat, a cage was used for the safety of those presiding over the trial.

It would not, however, be a typical trial because the council members would not be present. The five captains who had accompanied him, along with a few of their best commanders, would serve to help decide Estrada's innocence or guilt. Butch would be the determining vote in case of a tie, just as he would if his council were there. However, his main purpose in the trial was to ask questions and make sure the trial did not descend into chaos, as it quite possibly could.

The trial started as soon as six guards dragged Estrada into the room. She wore three pairs of magic-dampening cuffs: two on her wrists and one pair around her ankles. The guards at the front had gripped her underneath the arms and dragged her across the floor, saving the time she would've had to shuffle with tiny steps.

There was something satisfying that resonated within Butch when the lock on the cage turned, adding yet another layer of magic protection between him and the woman who would've rejoiced, he was sure, at seeing his head on a spike.

"Let the trial of Emmalee Estrada begin," Butch said, his voice booming in the room, which was half the size of the throne room back in Cyanthia. On either side of him, the captains and their commanders lined up.

"Estrada, you have been charged with multiple accounts of murder, torture, treason, blasphemy against the throne, abduction of a royal family member, and arson, and that's just the start of my list."

"Is it?" Estrada cut in, her voice monotonous. "You could've done us all a favor and at least alphabetized it."

"Do you admit to committing those crimes?" Butch asked, ignoring her banter. The sooner the trial was over, the sooner he would be rid of her.

"Do you admit to yours, Your Majesty?" Estrada asked, a snarl on her lips. "What about all the people you've murdered? Or the lies you've told your people? The villages you've burned to the ground? The—"

"That's enough," Butch said, pleased his voice did not betray him.

"Am I not allowed to use the same excuse?" Estrada asked, her voice ringing throughout the room.

"Excuse?"

"I've done everything for the greater good: seeing you off the throne. You're the criminal, Butch. I'm just one of the only ones who's lived long enough to say it."

Butch swallowed, though he almost choked. All eyes rested on him, each pair belonging to a person waiting to see how he'd react to Estrada's prodding. His tunic felt as though it had caught on fire, and he rolled up his sleeves as he lifted his chin.

"You admit that you've committed the aforementioned crimes?" Butch asked as soon as he'd finished the second sleeve.

Something in Estrada's dark eyes flashed. "Everything I've done has been to get justice for the ways in which you wronged me or to save others from the same terrors." Her voice trembled, though not in meekness, but with power. "You robbed me of everything, *everyone* I cared about. And if this is my last day, let it be known that your king is no better than a common criminal."

"Treason!" Captain Malkim shouted, slamming his hand down on the table in front of him. He turned to all those around him. "You heard it yourself. Blasphemy against the king."

"I agree," Captain Herris added. "I don't need to hear anything else to make my decision. This woman is an enemy to the throne and a threat to all of Phildeterre."

"Call the vote, Your Majesty," Captain Malkim said, his voice filled with more respect as he addressed the king.

The other men sitting around him nodded, and Butch cleared his throat.

"All in favor of declaring Emmalee Estrada guilty of all charges?"

Every single hand rose as they all echoed a resounding "aye."

"Emmalee Estrada, you've been declared guilty of the highest charges, and as a consequence and punishment for your actions, you will be executed by beheading as soon as this trial ends."

The attention of the entire room, which only a second earlier had rested on Butch, fell on Estrada. How would she react to her death sentence? Would she plead? Cry? Scream?

Estrada's resolve remained calm, and with the room as silent as it was, every word she spoke next came in clear, crisp syllables.

"I won't be the last. This country and those with magic have been persecuted long enough. One day, Your Majesty, you will find that those you once thought were closest to you have deserted you on account of your betrayal to your country. I may die, but when that happens, three more will take my place. You could've been different. Could've changed things for the better. But you've resolved to be an enemy to more than half of your people. You're a failure, just like your father and his before him."

"That's enough!" Captain Malkim bellowed. "I won't hear any more of your blasphemy, witch. You speak ill of a good king."

As grateful as Butch was to Silas's captain for stepping in, a part of him resented the young gentleman. In cutting Estrada off for the sake of Butch's honor being preserved, Captain Malkim had, in the king's mind, made him appear feeble and unable to stand up for himself.

Butch rose to his feet. "Send her back to her cell. The trial is over. She's to be executed at dusk." He looked Estrada dead in the eye. "You are condemned to death, and let whatever happens after happen."

Chapter 91

Evangeline's eyes should not have fluttered open. She should not have been breathing. She should not have felt as though she'd gotten a good night's rest.

She'd been run through.

Bleeding.

Dying.

But no longer was that the case.

Gasping, Evangeline startled, sitting straight up. Her hands, which were still covered in her own blood, searched for the hole that was most certainly still in her stomach, to feel the warmth coming from her lifeblood pouring out of her.

It wasn't there. The wound *was not there.*

"How . . . ?" she whispered, pushing herself farther onto the small couch. It was only then she noticed that she was not alone in the study. "Silas? What . . . What happened? How am I . . . Did you . . . Stoll . . ." Evangeline couldn't finish a sentence, couldn't complete a thought as she swung her legs over the edge of the couch and stared at the marshal sitting on the table a foot away from her.

Silas held out a hand to hush her, and her words fell silent. He cupped her face with both hands.

"You're okay," he said, brushing a soft kiss against her lips. "You're okay." His words didn't make sense, and she couldn't tell if the dizziness was from her confusion over what had happened or his soft, desperate kisses.

"Silas, stop."

He did, pulling back far enough to stare into her face.

"Tell me what happened," she said, covering his hands with her own before lowering them to where their knees touched.

"You were attacked. You hit your head when you fell. I moved you to the couch."

"Hit my . . . No," Evangeline said, shaking her head. She shivered as she recalled the feeling of Stoll's blade cutting through her skin, muscles, and who knew what else. "He stabbed me. He . . . He killed me." Evangeline's voice rose in volume. "How am I still . . . alive?" She pulled her hands from his, pulling her shirt down to reveal nothing but a faint pink scar and smooth skin covered in crimson stains.

"Evie, calm down and—"

"Calm down?" Evangeline shrieked, jumping to her feet. "Look at this. This isn't possible," she said, pointing to her chest. "Why am I alive, Silas? What did . . . What did you do?" Her mind raced as she searched his face.

He avoided direct eye contact, glancing to the side and to the door multiple times in just a few seconds.

"I—"

"Magic. It had to be," Evangeline mumbled, her fingers finding the exact spot she'd felt the sword enter her stomach. She let her shirt fall back down, noting how it was ripped and covered in blood. *Her* blood. But as she poked her skin through the hole in the shirt, there was still no wound, nothing but a fresh scar to show that she'd stomped through death's doorway.

"I didn't want you to . . . I couldn't let you die." Silas's voice was soft, and after a few seconds, he finally looked up and met her gaze. "A healing rune. Seven, actually."

"How? You'd have to have . . ." Evangeline stumbled back as realization struck her. "Silas . . . How . . . ?" She gaped at him, her breaths coming in quick succession. She felt lightheaded. "You've been hiding this? All this time in the castle? You . . . You have magic?"

"Keep your voice down," Silas said in a hoarse whisper, raising a finger to his lips as he jumped to his feet. "No one can know." He reached for her, but she stepped back as though he were trying to hurt instead of comfort her. She continued to back away until he stopped pursuing her, shoving his hands into his pockets.

"The king doesn't—"

"No."

Evangeline stood on the opposite side of the room, using the wall to keep herself steady as she tried to process what he'd said. It didn't help that he kept talking.

"It's not the first time I've used a healing rune on you."

"What?" Evangeline's head shot up, and she narrowed her eyes at him.

"In the clearing near Shongbay. That beast had cracked your skull. It was a wonder you were able to stand."

"Beast? What beast?" Evangeline tried to remember, but there were too many things happening in her mind.

"The undead things Estrada brought to life."

Evangeline's eyes widened. "That was you? I mean, I knew you had dragged me away, but I thought someone else had . . . But it was you?"

Silas nodded.

"And those times you disappeared without explanation?" She thought of the time before he'd arrested her, when she thought for sure he was going to kill her, but instead he'd disappeared without a trace.

Sighing, Silas said, "Mind-wiping rune. It'll erase all thoughts for several minutes. I had it on a chain around my neck, but I lost it when I ran into Estrada in the forest. It's . . . What? What's wrong?"

Evangeline was shaking her head, and when she locked eyes with him, her hands vibrated with anger. "Traitor."

"If you'd just give me some time to explain, I—"

"No," Evangeline said, crossing her arms over her chest as confidence—and something warmer—swelled inside her. "You've betrayed your people, and worse yet, you've betrayed the man you claim you're closest to. And I let you . . ." She held back tears. "I thought I could trust you. You traitor!"

"Evangeline—"

"Don't." Evangeline held up her left hand when he took a step toward her. The look on Silas's face made her think he noticed the lack of cuff on her wrist at the same time she did.

He held out both hands, his eyes trained on her raised one, which had begun to glow. "Listen, Evie," he said in a soft voice as he pointed toward the cuff on the table nearest her. "I took it off to make sure the runes would finish working properly, and if you put the bracelet back on, I'll answer any question you ask truthfully. I promise."

Evangeline scoffed. "Seriously?"

"Yes."

"No, I mean do you seriously think I'll believe a word out of your mouth ever again? You may have saved my life, but the way you've chosen to live yours makes you the worst kind of person. You're too much of a coward to stand with those like you, yet you show no hesitation in persecuting them. In *killing* them. You're a traitor, Silas. To me. To the king. And to any person with magic in their veins." Evangeline hated the burn of tears as they formed in her eyes and left fiery trails down her cheeks. "And to think that I . . . I . . ."

She'd kissed him. Over and over and over again. Had dreamt of him. Had longed to spend time with him. Had fallen for him.

What a fool.

She couldn't form the words.

How could she have let herself trust him? Why had it been so easy for him to slip into the normalcy of her imprisoned life? Why was it his face she'd wanted to see every time someone knocked on her door?

Silas opened his mouth to say something, but Evangeline's mind was already playing through how she was going to leave the castle.

"Goodbye, Silas."

"Evangeline, wait! Don't—"

"Sleep." The word echoed through her mind as she extended her hand even more toward Silas. What could only be described as a mist of light left her hand, traveling through the air. Silas stumbled back, trying to get away from it, but the table he'd been sitting on when she'd woken got in his way, and he fell to the floor. Covering his nose and mouth did nothing, and within several seconds, he stopped moving.

Evangeline's hands were trembling as she stuck her head out of the room.

She gasped at the sight of Benji lying on the ground, and she knelt beside him, checking for a pulse. It was faint, but it was there. Tears spilled down her cheeks.

"I'm so sorry, Benji," she whispered, choking on the words. "I'm so, so sorry."

She couldn't stay.

Moving as quickly as she could, Evangeline half considered returning to her room to change her bloody torn tunic, but it would waste the opportunity she'd been given.

With a deep breath, Evangeline continued until she got to the end of the hallway. She could hear voices, and when she peeked around the corner, three guards were walking toward her. Instead of panicking, she called on her magic, asking it to do the same spell it'd done on Silas.

Sleep.

Bodies and metal thudded against stone, and when Evangeline ventured a glance around the edge again, all three guards lay on the floor.

Each time Evangeline heard footsteps, whether it was around a corner or nearing where she stood in the middle of a hallway, she would hide in the nearest alcove and send her magic to take care of the threats. However, between each expense of magic and running through the halls, sweat began to build on her brow.

When she passed the record hall, she paused. By leaving now, she was giving up her best chance at answers about her father. It felt as though she was losing a piece of herself as she took a deep breath and continued.

Her father might've abandoned her.

Emmalee hadn't, and she was in danger.

Evangeline made her choice.

The stairs were nearly within her sight when she stopped dead in her tracks. She had not heard the footsteps coming, had not been prepared to see the queen standing in the middle of the hallway. The shorter woman was the only obstacle preventing Evangeline from escaping down the stairs, but as Evangeline lifted her hand to put the queen to sleep, the woman stopped her.

"Wait," Queen Lenora said, her voice louder than Evangeline would've expected for such a small form. "I'm not going to stop you. I can help." She straightened when Evangeline lowered her hand. "You're trying to leave, aren't you?"

Evangeline nodded. Her magic remained near the surface, ready to be called upon at a moment's notice.

"Follow me, then," she said, spinning on her heels and heading toward the opposite wing.

Several inches taller, Evangeline did not struggle to keep up with the queen, though she did remain several paces back just in case.

"Should I bother asking about your tunic?" the queen asked. She did not bother to look back. "The blood?" she prodded.

"It's mine."

Queen Lenora stopped in her tracks, spinning to face Evangeline, who was struggling to hold back her magic, which perceived the queen's quick spin as a potential threat.

"Yours? But you seem—"

"I'm all right now," Evangeline said, checking over her shoulder to make sure they weren't being followed. "Keep going. I don't know how long I have until they find out I'm gone."

The queen stared a moment longer at the crimson stain over Evangeline's shirt—it was likely on the back too since the sword had gone all the way through—before refocusing on the hallway.

"The safest and fastest way for you to get out is through the stables. Take one of the horses labeled for the guards; they'll be the fastest. You can ride, can't you?"

"I think so," Evangeline said, noting the frown the queen gave her over her shoulder. "I'll figure it out. How do I get to Château Lavfor?"

"You got the message?"

Evangeline nodded. The queen led her into one of the servants' stairways, which was surprisingly empty, although she supposed it made sense since there hadn't been anyone staying on the opposite wing from her.

"Lavfor is up north, but my husband has blocked off all the main roads. It'd be wisest to travel farther west before heading north and then enter Lavfor from above. The château itself will be heavily guarded." Queen Lenora paused near a short wooden door.

"How long will it take to go that way? You said in your message that the king had already left and—"

"It'll take half a day rather than a quarter of a day, but it'll be safer. I doubt you want to end up in the dungeon again."

Evangeline snorted, surprising herself and the queen. "Not on my list of favorite places, no."

"Good. Now through this door is a hallway leading out to the stables. It'll be relatively empty this time of day since most of the servants are out doing their day's work, but you're bound to run into at least one person."

"I'll be fine," Evangeline said, lighting up the dark stairwell with her hand. The queen's eyes widened, and her gaze was trancelike.

"That's incredible," Queen Lenora murmured.

"Thanks." Evangeline dimmed the light. Something about the way the queen had spoken left Evangeline's stomach unsettled. Or maybe that had to do with the rune Silas had said he'd used on her. Either way, it was time to leave. "And thank you for all of your help since they brought me in."

"Your friend opened my eyes. It was the least I could do."

A thought crossed Evangeline's mind. "I had to burn the map and the letter you passed to me to give to Emmalee. If someone found it—"

"I understand. That was wise. But could you do me a favor? Could you tell your friend I had a son? I think . . . I think she'd want to know. At least, she said . . ." The queen's words trailed off, and Evangeline nodded. "Thank you. Now go, and good luck."

Without another word, Evangeline stepped through the door.

Chapter 92

EMMALEE

Emmalee shivered in the cell, her hands and feet shackled to the rough stone walls. The dim torchlight flickered, casting eerie shadows that seemed to mock her lack of magic. She tried to steady her breathing, but the weight of her impending execution pressed down on her with unending force.

They would come for her at dusk, but without a window in the dungeon, she had no way of knowing how soon that would be. It seemed like every minute stretched into eternity.

She closed her eyes, trying to block out the oppressive darkness. Her thoughts wandered to Evangeline. How had she endured months of this torment? How had she managed to stay strong?

As soon as Emmalee had gotten back to the cell and was alone after her trial, every ounce of strength and bit of her brave façade had vanished. She'd dissolved into tears.

Images of Anwell and Hazel filled her mind, and she tried to remember his comforting voice, her daughter's infectious laughter. But she couldn't. They were gone, and soon she would be too.

She thought of Ariella and Faeleen. She was the reason they'd died. If she hadn't reentered their lives, they'd still be alive.

They, too, were gone, sacrificed in the king's relentless pursuit to destroy magic in Phildeterre. Emmalee's heart ached. She wanted to avenge them. All of them.

But she'd failed.

Time and time again, the king had bested her.

She was scared.

Scared of dying, she realized as a distant sound broke through her thoughts. The clinking of metal and heavy footsteps echoed through the empty dungeon.

Her heart raced, and she forced herself to take deep breaths. She would not cry in front of them, and especially not in front of the king.

A group of guards approached her cell, their faces void of any sort of empathy.

"It's dusk, Estrada. Time's up."

Chapter 93

EVANGELINE

At some point between escaping through the castle gates on horseback to the hours Evangeline had spent trying to navigate to Lavfor without a map, she'd gotten turned around. It didn't help that she couldn't just follow the main road without possibly being seen. Any other time, Evangeline wouldn't have been all that frustrated. She was, after all, normally good with directions and not afraid to ask.

But Emmalee's life was in danger, and as far as she knew, people still considered Evangeline to be a wanted criminal.

She had to risk it though. For Emmalee.

It seemed like people didn't so much recognize her as realize she was covered in blood from a wound she no longer had. After assuring several people she was fine, she was grateful each time they finally offered her directions and set her back on track.

The last time she'd asked, the old man had told her she was on the outskirts of Lavfor. He had pointed her in the direction of the château, and unlike most of the others she'd asked, he did not mention the dried blood on her tunic with a look of pure horror.

For that, Evangeline was grateful.

By the time Evangeline rode near enough to the château, she'd already been spotted twice by royal guards. She'd put them to sleep, but after the long day of travel and the lack of food and water, Evangeline could feel the strain her magic was putting on her body. She was grateful she'd chosen to eat her breakfast that morning despite the anxiousness she'd felt to go find the queen's message.

The more she thought about it, the more it felt like that morning had been in some other lifetime. Like she really had died when Stoll had stabbed her. Like Silas hadn't really saved her, and instead it was her ghost who was trying to save Emmalee. As stupid as it was, Evangeline pinched her arm to remind herself how ridiculous that sounded.

Besides, with the guards approaching her, some of whom were also on horseback, she didn't have time to worry over what had happened to her that morning—not until the man who had kissed her senseless and saved her life, not to mention lied to her face on multiple occasions, joined the line of men posted along the gate of the château.

How had he gotten there before her?

Probably took the main roads, because he wasn't a wanted criminal.

She glowered at him.

Silas's voice called out louder than felt natural, though maybe the trees and the walls of the château amplified it in some way. Either way, Evangeline could hear him.

"Don't come any closer." Silas had drawn his sword, along with all the guards who stood beside him.

However, with the horses gaining on her and the only entrance big enough for her and her horse to get through located behind Silas and the guards, she did not stop. She sped up. With white-knuckled hands, she clung to the reins. She'd only ridden a horse a few other times, and she felt as though she might slip off at any moment.

But Evangeline did not stop.

"Close the gate!" Silas bellowed, but he didn't move as Evangeline continued to charge toward him on a galloping horse. "Close the—"

The order came too late.

With one word—*jump*—in her mind, her magic warmed her hands and spread through the horse. As if it could understand her, the horse leapt into the air at the last second, clearing the heads of the men, most of whom jumped out of the way.

Evangeline clung even tighter to the reins, though she did not pull them, even when her body lifted off the horse. When the steed landed on the other side of the guards, she urged it forward as the gate above traveled toward the ground at a rapid speed. Leaning down, she got as low as she could, the two of them barely clearing the gate.

The best part, though, was glancing back over her shoulder to see the look of frustration on the faces of the guards who were trapped on the other side. But one pair of blue eyes held no ounce of anger—just awe.

Silas's voice called out again for the gates to be raised, but Evangeline's gaze found the man in charge of the barrier, and she sent her magic to lull him to sleep as she followed the cobblestones toward an overgrown courtyard.

An overgrown courtyard filled with royal guards standing around a platform. And at the center . . . Emmalee.

Evangeline's presence did not go unnoticed for more than a few seconds, but unlike outside the gate, none of the guards were on horses, and she guided her partner in crime around the men as they raced toward her.

The platform on which Emmalee and two other guards stood was at least a story tall, and as the horse got closer, a crazy plan formed in her head. Wooden beams were attached to the legs of the platform, and before she could hesitate, Evangeline swung one leg over the saddle and vaulted toward the lowest beam.

It hit her like a punch to the gut, but she wrapped her arms around it and, after a few kicks, pulled herself up. Leaping to the next highest beam, Evangeline tried to block out the sound of the men organizing below her. All it would take was one archer—

As if her mind had summoned it, an arrow flew past her left ear and stuck in the wooden beam. Evangeline gasped. When she tried to scan the crowd to see where the archer was, there were too many angry faces staring back at her to tell.

Some of the men were funneling toward the narrow staircase that led to the top of the platform. It was going to be enough of a challenge to take the two guards at the top, let alone the fifteen who were making their way up the stairs.

Separate. The word filled her head, and to her surprise—and the surprise of the men on the stairs—a pulse traveled from her hand to where the stairs were attached to the platform. The beams cracked. With all the weight from the bodies lining it, the staircase started to sway back and forth. There were shouts and cries to move out of the way as the structure collapsed to the side.

Evangeline didn't wait to see if anyone was hurt, or worse. It wasn't something she wanted to see. She didn't want to be the cause of someone else's grief. All she wanted to do was save her friend.

With that thought in mind, Evangeline heaved herself up onto the last beam before rolling onto the top of the platform. She glanced up in time to see the first guard lunge for her, and she scrambled out of the way as he swung his sword down, splitting the wood where she'd just been.

Sleep. Evangeline stuck her hand out, and just as it had worked in the castle, the guard dropped to the platform, snoring. It took her a second glance to realize that he wore a red collar. A captain.

And so did the familiar man holding a sharpened ax blade to Emmalee's throat.

"Not another move," Captain Malkim barked, a glare on his face.

Evangeline held up her hands, stepping away from the edge of the platform for fear the archer who'd shot at her before might try again. Though maybe he had been caught in the commotion with the stairs. She could hope—

"She's been found guilty," the captain said, and Emmalee tried to say something, but they'd gagged her.

"By whom?" Evangeline asked, her voice calm.

"Me. Them." He nodded to the chaos below. "And him."

Evangeline glanced over her shoulder to see who the man was referencing only to make direct eye contact with Butch.

He stood on a balcony which, with the height of the platform, seemed closer than the ground below. He'd clenched his jaw, making the vein along his neck protrude. But while the rest of his tense posture screamed the anger within him without need of words, his eyes told a different story.

Fear.

He was scared—terrified by the looks of it.

Evangeline followed his line of sight . . . all the way back to Emmalee.

She scared him.

And by the smug look on her face, she knew it too.

"Give yourself up, and it'll all—" Captain Malkim collapsed to the platform before Evangeline could fully think the word. As cruel as he was, he appeared quite peaceful in sleep.

Evangeline glanced back toward the king, but he'd disappeared within the castle. Some part of Evangeline was relieved. But whether that was because she had been his prisoner for well over a year or because she did not want to watch Emmalee kill him, she was unsure.

"Good timing," Emmalee said as soon as Evangeline moved the gag so it hung around Emmalee's neck like a dirty scarf.

"Are you all right?" Evangeline asked, ignoring that playful tone in Emmalee's voice. Her mind was already racing, trying to determine a way out of the mess they were in. Down was not an option, but the balcony seemed too far to reach, and there was no telling how many guards were waiting for them on the inside. Their precious king was in there, after all, and they had proven themselves to be nothing if not loyal.

"It figures I come to rescue you and you're the one saving me," Emmalee said.

Evangeline didn't respond, too busy searching the captain's belt for the keys she knew he'd have. All the guards carried the same ring.

Evangeline freed Emmalee's ankles first, which had been bound together by the same two sets of cuffs on her wrists—cuffs Evangeline knew too well.

"What's the plan?" Emmalee asked as the first set around her wrists clattered to the platform next to Captain Malkim.

"I don't know. I didn't really come with a plan. I just knew I needed to get here before . . ." Evangeline's words died off when she glanced at the ax lying on the platform.

"I'm glad you did," Emmalee said, rubbing her newly freed wrists. "How about the balcony?"

"I'm not sure I can make that jump."

"I'll catch you," Emmalee said, but she waited to cross over until Evangeline nodded.

"All right. Don't miss." Evangeline went to twist the cuff on her wrist around in circles, forgetting that it wasn't there. Without the metal piece to fiddle with, she wrung out her hands as she watched Emmalee back to the edge of the platform to get a running start.

Evangeline held her breath. It seemed like minutes—no, *hours*—that her friend was suspended in the air after jumping.

Emmalee caught herself on the edge of the balcony before swinging one foot over and then the other. "Come on," she called, and when Evangeline hesitated, she pointed down to the ground. Some of the guards were charging into the château. "We're running out of time, Evie. You have to trust me."

Before she could count to three, Evangeline sprinted toward the edge. The whole platform shifted just as Evangeline tried to jump. The movement threw her balance off, and instead of jumping, Evangeline flailed through the air. She let out a scream. Falling. She was tumbling down into the pit of wolves ready to tear her to shreds.

It felt as though her arm was being ripped right off when Emmalee caught her. Shrieking and grunting, Emmalee tried to straighten, dragging Evangeline with her. Evangeline watched with wide eyes as her friend pulled her toward the balcony and away from certain death.

The chill of Emmalee's dark magic flooded Evangeline's hand, and the cold left her shivering by the time she got her footing and scrambled over the edge. As soon as Emmalee let go of her hand, Evangeline clutched her arm to her chest, breathing heavily. It throbbed, and she couldn't tell how badly it was injured.

"I told you I'd catch you." Though it sounded like another lighthearted comment, Emmalee's face was carved in stone. "Come on. We need to move."

Evangeline didn't argue. She followed Emmalee as she moved through the hallways. It was strange being in a building that could've fit in the western wing of the Cyanthian castle. Still, the corridors were a labyrinth to navigate.

"He has to be here somewhere," Emmalee muttered under her breath.

"Who?" Evangeline asked, checking behind her as they turned down another hallway.

"Who do you think?" Emmalee asked, her voice as cold as the dark magic flowing down from her hands in waves of mist. "The king. Two birds with one stone and all that." Her mind was clearly distracted, and she didn't seem to notice that Evangeline wasn't behind her until she came back around the corner and stopped.

"Two birds?" Evangeline's voice rose in pitch. "What does that mean?"

Emmalee's face, which had been filled with a look of determination, softened as she took several steps toward Evangeline. Though her arm still hurt, Evangeline hugged Emmalee back when her friend wrapped her arms around her.

"I've been looking for you for ages. Now I finally found you, and what's better, we can put an end to that evil man's tyranny once and for all."

"Em," Evangeline said, choking on the words that first came to her mouth. She didn't want to say them, but they still spilled out. "You can't kill the king."

Taking a step back, Emmalee narrowed her eyes at Evangeline. "Why not? It's what he did. It's what he *does*."

Evangeline shook her head.

It was true—the things the king and Silas had told her about Emmalee. She wasn't the same person, at least not on the surface, not in that moment. Evangeline picked each of her next words carefully.

515

"Lenora had a son," Evangeline said, her voice low, as if she were trying to lure a stray cat from a ledge.

"That's . . ." Emmalee shook her head, though her determined expression wilted a bit. "That's great. But I don't see what—"

"Butch is a father, Em. If you kill him, you're taking that little boy's father away."

Emmalee's face hardened again. "Seems fair."

"To ruin the baby's life? To ruin Lenora's?" Evangeline shook her head. "It's not right, Em."

"You're talking to me about right and wrong?" Emmalee spat, shaking her head as her magic dripped to the floor in graceful waves. "That man murdered my family. He killed Ari and Fae. And others. So many others. Killing him is justice, Evangeline."

"Murder is murder. There is no world in which it is right or justice. What you're talking about is revenge." Evangeline pulled her throbbing arm back toward her chest.

The frustration her friend was trying to hold back spread across her face—first to her lips, which tightened into a thin line, and then to her gaze, which hardened toward Evangeline.

"He told me you'd taken one of his bribes. I didn't believe him." Emmalee's voice was low. "But you did, didn't you? Is that why you're defending him?"

"No!" Evangeline shook her head. "I mean, yes, but no. I told him what he wanted to hear so that he'd free one of the other prisoners and start changing the way magic folk are treated. He's started a law that—"

"I don't care if he's saving orphans and puppies!" Emmalee shrieked. "He killed Anwell. And Hazel, my baby. That man *needs* to die."

How had Evangeline ended up on the side of the man who'd kept her prisoner for over a year? Her mind scrambled for an answer as she took a step back from Emmalee, whose magic was streaming out of her. It snaked around Evangeline's ankles, but besides the cold bite, it paid her no heed.

Instead, it traveled down the hallway in both directions, slipping in and out of the cracks beneath the doorways. Searching.

"Emmalee, you need to leave. You know they won't spare you if they—" Evangeline jumped when Emmalee snapped her attention toward a door near them at the end of the hall. "Em, go. Don't do this."

"Hello, Your Majesty," Emmalee crooned, and before Evangeline could stop her friend, Emmalee ripped the door to a small linen closet off its hinges and hurled it down the hall without ever laying a finger on it.

And there, standing with his broad shoulders rigid and his hand on the hilt of his sword, was Butch.

Chapter 94

BUTCH

From the moment he realized that Lia—or rather Evangeline, as it turned out—would free Estrada from her chains, a river of ice had traveled through Butch's veins.

He'd failed.

Even when he thought he'd won, he'd failed.

So he'd fled exactly as he had as a child hiding from the horrendous things his father was doing to those with magic, only the person he wouldn't have minded seeing experimented on by the sadistic people his father had employed years ago was alive and out for his head.

He'd seen it in her eyes.

And as he'd eavesdropped on Estrada's conversation with her friend—they'd been within feet of his secret hiding place when they'd stopped to fight—it was clear Evangeline had seen Estrada's malicious side as well.

But even with all the time he'd spent with Evangeline, he never would've guessed that she'd try to stop Estrada from hunting him down and tearing his flesh from his bones. Never. Not once had he considered that she might have made a good ally if he had just treated her differently. Not until the door flew off the hinges, revealing his hiding place and a look of horror on Evangeline's face.

"Em, let him go," Evangeline said, clutching one of her arms to her chest. Her tunic was covered in blood, and for a brief moment, Butch remembered what Marshal Thorne had said about Kendrick Stoll attacking her in the record hall. Maybe he'd found her again. But even so, how was she standing if she'd lost enough blood to soak the shirt like that?

"Your Majesty." Estrada lifted a hand.

A freezing mist covered Butch, and he froze, not because of fear, but because of her magic. He couldn't move, couldn't protect his head as she flicked her wrist to the side, tossing him as if he weren't twice her size.

Butch slammed into the wall, his head reeling. Evangeline's shriek filled the air, along with the sound of her pleas toward her friend.

"Emmalee, stop. Killing him won't bring them back. It won't. No matter how much you want it to. Please stop." Evangeline stepped forward, though after hitting his head, it appeared that she'd duplicated herself. Then again, he didn't know all the ins and outs of magic. Maybe she had. He figured, though, that it had more to do with his splitting headache than with Evangeline's magic.

"Don't." Estrada's voice was a growl, but it was not directed at him. "Do not get in my way, Evangeline."

"You're not thinking straight." Evangeline held out both hands, stepping between Butch and Estrada. "If you kill him, you'll be making a mistake."

"The mistake"—Estrada flung her friend to the side, though not nearly as violently as she had him—"would be letting him live."

Once more, a cold chill wrapped around Butch, only this time it slithered into his mouth and nose. He choked, gagging as the magic tightened within him. Clawing at his throat, he wheezed. It suffocated him tighter by the second.

"Stop!" Evangeline screamed. As the world began to fade, a light flashed, and with it came a wave of heat that blew away the cold darkness swallowing Butch from the inside.

He collapsed forward onto his hands and knees, coughing as he inhaled air too quickly for his damaged lungs to handle.

"How did you do that?" Estrada asked, bewilderment mixing with anger in her voice. Her attention rested fully on her friend, which Butch was not going to complain about as he continued to take in the air Estrada had deprived him of.

"You need to *leave*, Em." Evangeline didn't answer her friend's question. "I won't say it again. I don't want to see you hurt or killed, and I know that's what they'll do. Please."

Despite the ringing in his ears, a new sound filled him with hope that he might live to see another day: thundering footsteps.

"This isn't over. Far from it," Estrada said, though Butch was unsure whether the comment had been directed to him or to her friend. Maybe both.

Evangeline backed closer to him, but as soon as Estrada sprinted down the hallway in the opposite direction of the sound of footsteps, Evangeline whirled around and faced him.

The concern that'd been on her face with her friend's threat hanging over his head had disappeared, replaced with an expression he knew all too well: disapproval.

"You're despicable. You told her I was working with you? Why? What did that prove?"

"I'm . . . sorry." His voice cracked as he pushed onto his knees.

"Save it," Evangeline said, glancing over her shoulder. The guards must've been close.

"You stopped her from killing me."

"Not for you. For your wife and son." She shook her head, backing away toward the hallway down which Estrada had escaped. "It'll be too soon if I never see you again."

And without another word, she left down the same hallway as her friend.

When the first guard reached him, Butch accepted help to his feet.

"Which direction did they go?" the captain nearest him asked. He was one of the others Silas had sent. Butch nodded in the right direction. "I'll stay with him. You go," the captain ordered.

The horde of guards stampeded toward where Estrada and Evangeline had left, but Butch knew the two women would be gone before the guards made it down the first hallway.

In less than a few hours, he'd lost all the progress he'd gained in a year. Gone. Both of them. And with it, the lightness he'd felt for those few precious hours.

Chapter 95

BUTCH

Butch stormed through the halls of the Cyanthian castle, his face a mask of rage and frustration. He barely registered the worried looks from the servants and the shaky salutes from the guards. His mind was too busy replaying Estrada's *and* Evangeline's escapes from Lavfor. He'd let them slip through his fingers.

Again.

Lenora must've heard him because she raced out of the family dining room, her eyes wide. "What happened?"

She held Diomedes in her arms, but despite that, Butch strode right past her.

"Butch!" she called, trying to keep up with his long strides. "Tell me what—"

"They're gone!" he shouted, and as he reached his office, he slammed the door in her face.

Inside his office, the rage within erupted. He swept papers off his desk, the contents scattering across the floor. Grabbing a nearby vase, he hurled it against the wall. Books, ink bottles, and maps followed.

If he could do it all over again, he would've killed Estrada on the spot. Next time, if there even was a next time, he vowed he wouldn't hesitate. Next time, he wouldn't be so weak.

Butch's breaths came in heavy labored gasps. His vision was blurred with his fury, tinted red. His muscles trembled from the release of pent-up aggression. He clenched his fists and slammed them down on his desk, shouting as he did so.

The noise drew attention.

He knew it would.

And when the door to his office creaked open and a terrified servant peered in, eyes wide with fear, he straightened.

"Your Majesty, is there anything I can get you?"

Butch struggled to swallow, lifting his chin. "Yes. Clean this up," he ordered, his voice rough from shouting. "And find Marshal Thorne. I will speak to him in the throne room."

With that, he stalked out of his office and past his trembling staff.

Chapter 96

SILAS

Silas strode through the castle corridors, his mind heavy with thoughts of Evangeline. The image of her, hurt and dying. The pain that tore through him at her words, knowing in some ways they were true. And then there was the determination on her face as she'd raced to save her friend.

When he received Butch's summons, he knew it wasn't going to be a pleasant encounter. He'd heard about the king's destroyed office and tried to prepare himself for what was certain to be a tongue-lashing.

He nodded to the guards posted outside the throne room doors, thanking the men as they opened them.

Butch paced back and forth in front of the stairs leading up to the raised dais where his and Lenora's thrones sat. The room felt colder than usual, and Silas wondered how much of that was due to the icy glare his friend shot him as soon as the doors thudded closed.

"Your Majesty," Silas greeted, his voice steady.

Butch stopped his pacing and turned to Silas, his eyes blazing. "How?" He spat the word. "How did she get out?"

"Kendrick Stoll attacked her in the study. He almost killed her. I got there in time to save her, but he escaped. It was too late when I realized she'd gotten the cuff off."

"How?" Butch growled. "You assured me that thing wasn't supposed to be able to come off without the key you hold. How did she get it?"

Silas cleared his throat, shaking his head as he put his hands on his hips. His friend couldn't know.

"I don't know."

"Traitor."

Silas tried to ignore Evangeline's voice echoing in his head. "But she used her magic to put me and any other guard who stood in her way to sleep. One of the lookouts thought he saw her riding away on one of the horses from the stables."

Butch rubbed his temples. "You let her go?" An icy ridge lined his voice.

"No. She escaped."

"You said you saved her when she was attacked."

Silas nodded.

"Why?"

Frowning, Silas crossed his arms over his chest. "She was dying."

"And? She's a criminal, brother! I told you not to get close to her!"

"I know, but—"

"You know that? Really? Because it seems like you forgot that she was a prisoner on numerous occasions. She wasn't *your* friend, Silas. She's Estrada's." Butch raised his voice, jabbing a finger toward Silas. "They both have magic, which makes them enemies of Phildeterre. *Your* enemies. If you hadn't fraternized with her, maybe none of this would've happened and that sorceress's bloody head would be in a basket! Instead, one beautiful woman batted her eyelashes at you, and you instantly forgot what role you play."

Silas choked. No words came to his mind.

Well, no words to say.

Instead, the word "traitor" repeated over and over again until Silas wondered if something in his mind had broken.

He took a deep breath, steeling himself. "Of course, Your Majesty. I sent men after *both* of them, and I'll organize more of Levick's guards to begin thorough searches of the towns nearest to Château Lavfor." Silas stood at attention, his hands clenched into fists at his sides.

Butch didn't seem to care as he climbed the stairs to his throne. When he took his place and finally looked down at Silas, an emotionless mask covered his face.

"I will not be a weak king, Marshal Thorne. Find Estrada. Find Evangeline."

Silas bristled at the king's use of Evangeline's name.

"And put an end to this."

"Yes, Your Majesty."

Wherever Evangeline had gone, Silas hoped it was far enough that he never found her, because his loyalty remained in the same place it had since he'd been a terrified young boy.

With Butch.

With his brother.

Epilogue

LENORA

Lenora's fingers trembled as she dismounted from her horse. She'd traced the path back to the boulder field, back to the place where Estrada had brought her that fateful night. It felt surreal, being there again.

Alone.

It was a risk, she knew, especially with Butch in a foul mood. She could still hear the echo of her husband's angry words ringing in her ears as she tied her horse's reins to a nearby branch.

She'd left the castle without being seen. She needed fresh air, and not just from the gardens. Fresh air not confined by suffocatingly thick castle walls.

Butch's fury had cut her deeply. She hadn't meant to upset him, and it reminded her of all the times her father had lashed out with his tongue.

She felt small.

She needed to be in a place where she could breathe. Think. Feel. If she could've found her way back to that sanctuary where Estrada's tiny house had been, she would've. But since she wasn't sure where the location was, she went to the boulder field.

As she sat on one of the larger rocks, she let out a shuddering breath, wiping away the frustrated tears that had continued to fall since she'd left the stables.

It was strange, but she still found it easier to breathe at the boulder field despite the difficult memories of the night Estrada had used her as bait for her husband.

The pull she felt to the boulder field, to Estrada, couldn't be ignored.

And when Estrada's friend had used magic in front of her, something had clicked.

She'd been drawn to magic.

To Leo first.

Then to Estrada.

The boulder field had once been a very powerful portal to the Dark and therefore must've had some residual magic somewhere deep within it.

It was a dangerous realization, given her husband's war on the very thing that seemed to bring about some sense of freedom in her.

Lenora stood, brushing off her skirt, and took a deep breath. She knew she had to be careful, but after the thrill and relief of helping Estrada's friend, she knew what her role in the castle would be. Even if she did feel guilty about going behind her husband's back, it was for the best.

In the tiny ways she could, she would help those with magic. She would be a force for change within the confines of her beautiful prison.

And to her best ability, she would raise her son to do the same.

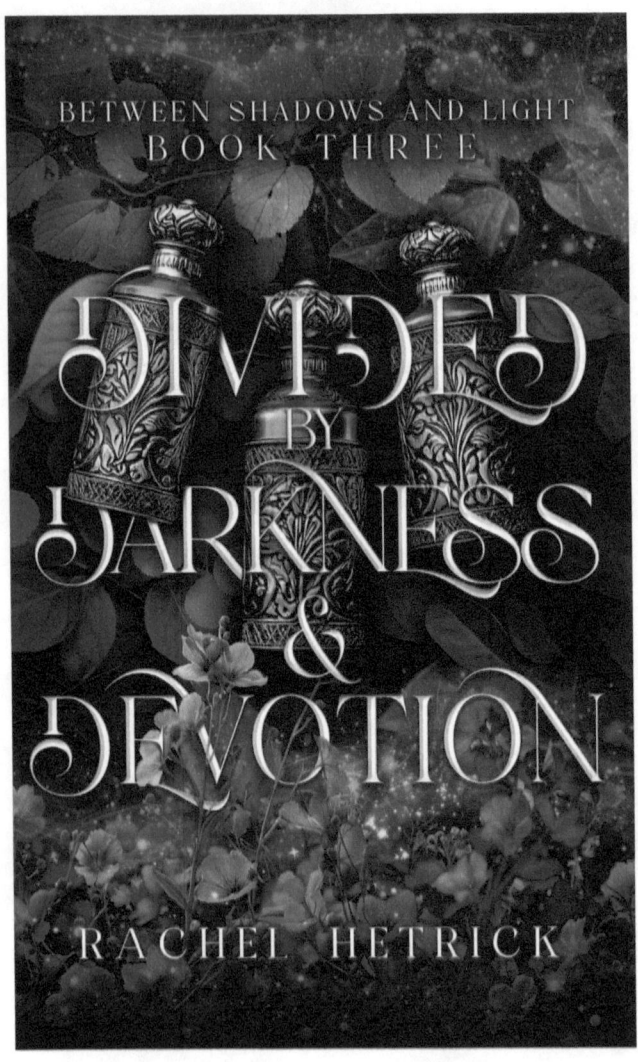

BETWEEN SHADOWS AND LIGHT
BOOK THREE

Divided
BY
Darkness
&
Devotion

RACHEL HETRICK

Keep reading for a sneak preview of BOOK 3 in the

BETWEEN SHADOWS AND LIGHT SERIES

Chapter One

BUTCH

Bones crunched, condensing in an unnatural way. King Butch grimaced but did not cry out when he pulled his hand back from the wall. Of course it would not be as giving as the practice targets in the training rooms on the lower levels of the castle. But the rooms were unavailable. The royal guards were putting a new round of young men through training, and each room was assigned to a different skill.

Unfortunately, that left the king without an outlet. And a broken hand.

And to think, he'd left his wife peacefully asleep in her bed for this.

The walk to the infirmary had become all too familiar—not because he'd needed medical attention, but because the castle apothecary resided in a room nearby.

Since the catastrophic happenings at the château in Lavfor, Butch had struggled to fall asleep almost every night. A sleeping draft had been prescribed by Helena, the royal physician. Butch insisted on walking down to the apothecary and watching him mix up the sleeping draft in front of him.

Estrada wanted him dead. How easy could it be to slip poison into his sleeping draft? No. Butch watched each day as the man ground up the ingredients and mixed them into a thick liquid that coated the tongue in a difficult-to-remove slime.

It was, however, effective.

Almost too effective.

Butch was already beginning to hate how much he'd come to depend on it, trying a few times to sleep without it only to be kept awake by the memories of his failures.

Like last night.

Though it hurt, Butch squeezed his broken hand. The action—or rather the pain from the action—forced his mind to focus on the immediate discomfort instead of the things that could, if he dwelled on them too much, drive him insane.

Helena scurried to the front of the infirmary as soon as Butch walked through the door. It was a long, narrow room with rows of beds on both sides facing opposite each other. At the back of the room farthest from the door were wide arching windows that let in light at some point in the afternoon depending on the time of year.

Though he had been sick and injured enough growing up in the castle, Butch had never once stayed a night in one of the infirmary beds. One of the privileges he'd had growing up was that Helena, or one of the other physicians, would come to him when he skinned a knee, or, once he was older, broke a bone or slipped up and got cut during a dueling session with one of the guards. The worst times, though, were after he'd had a "lesson" from his father.

But the older he'd gotten, the less he'd called upon the physicians and the more he'd met them in the comfort of their place of work.

"What happened, Your Majesty?" Helena asked, leading him to the nearest bed. Most of the cots were unoccupied, but three of them held men, and one held a woman.

"Broken hand," Butch muttered, wincing when Helena moved his pointer finger. The bones, or maybe bone fragments—he was unsure how badly he'd damaged it—scraped together, and the nerves in his hand screamed in pain. Yet the only sound he made was a hissing noise when the fire was too much.

As gentle as she was with her hands, Helena's scolding was less so. "A wall, Butch? Really?"

He shrugged, but his laissez-faire attitude faded away. They'd known each other long enough that he knew he couldn't hide much from her.

But before he could share the tumultuous storm of thoughts constantly swirling at the forefront of his mind, Helena guessed what was happening.

"Does this have something to do with the council? Or maybe Estrada? Or her friend?"

"Don't forget the failing war efforts in the North," Butch joked, though his voice remained flat and monotone.

"So, you took it out on a wall?"

He nodded, watching as she wrapped his hand. It would make his work less convenient to have his hand in a cast, but he'd considered that when punching the wall, hitting it with his nondominant hand instead of the alternative.

He'd still be useful.

Maybe.

Not according to his council.

"Can I tell you a secret?" Helena asked.

Butch raised an eyebrow, but nodded.

"You're the king. The council? They work for you." Helena finished with his hand, patting his shoulder when she'd finished. She'd all but read his mind.

"What about Estrada and Evangeline?"

Helena tilted her head. "I thought her name was Lia." She waved her hand as if to wave away the thought. "Doesn't matter. Are either one causing problems right now?"

Butch frowned, then shook his head. "Not that I've heard."

"Have you ever heard the phrase, 'Don't go looking for trouble, it'll find you itself'?"

"Estrada is a snake waiting to strike. And if I'm not prepared, if the country is not prepared—"

"If you continue to worry like this, Your Majesty, I'm concerned your heart may give out." Though she jested, a somber look covered her face soon after. "I'm serious, Butch. I know you're under a lot of stress and scrutiny right now, but it's only going to make things worse the more you worry about it. Worrying never changed anything."

She spoke wise words, but his attention had drifted to the other people in the infirmary. He didn't know why they were there, yet their simple presence left him with a guilt he'd been bearing since he'd first heard of the damage Estrada had done in her home village. She'd lit many of his royal guards on fire. And there were those who had died the night they'd almost apprehended her. Both times. Then there were the guards she'd tortured for information. And through all of it, he'd been unable to stop her, even when he'd had her on the executioner's stand. One woman had all but ruined the last few years almost single-handedly. And she'd made a fool out of him.

"Your Majesty?" Helena glanced over her shoulder, her brow furrowing in the same direction as him.

"Are we done here?" Butch asked, rising to his feet. "I need to get back to work."

Helena looked at him with disappointment written across her face, but she didn't argue. "If you need me to wrap your hand again, you'll—"

"Come here." Butch nodded, his mind already searching for excuses to say to Silas. It was doubtful his closest friend would believe him if he tried to use a training exercise as an excuse for his broken hand. Silas would see right through him.

Since he'd lost one of his five marshals—who had been murdered by Estrada—Butch had set Silas in charge of reorganizing the men Marshal Levick had been over—at least until Butch could appoint a new marshal.

"I believe August has your sleeping draft ready, if you want to speak with him before you return to your work," Helena said as she walked him to the entrance of the infirmary.

Butch nodded to show he'd heard her before speaking a word of thanks and leaving. He'd pick up his sleeping draft and then go back to his office. That was what his country needed. And it was what his mind needed. A distraction.

BUTCH RUBBED HIS good hand over his face, trying to erase the tiredness off it before Silas entered his office. His efforts were apparently in vain.

"You look like you spent the night hanging upside down from the entrance hall by your toes," Silas said after he shut the door behind him. As was normal, his best friend did not salute since it was just the two of them in the room. However, if any of the other guards were around, Butch knew "Marshal Thorne" would execute every word and action with the highest level of formality.

"Speak for yourself." Butch glowered, looking his friend up and down. "You look like you went a few rounds with a mountain troll and lost." He gestured toward Silas, who raised an eyebrow when his gaze landed on the bandaged hand.

"Wall?" Silas asked.

Butch just grunted in response. He sank into his chair. "It's been a long night," he said.

"I thought you and Lenora went to bed early."

"We did. She's likely still sleeping, if I had any guess. I, on the other hand, didn't sleep at all." Butch rubbed his uninjured hand over his brow before gesturing to the chair across from his desk. Silas sat down, leaning back. "Any news from your men?" Butch asked, ignoring the puzzled look furrowing Silas's brow.

"No one's seen her. Either of them, actually." Silas narrowed his eyes at Butch's wrapped hand. "Is it broken?"

Butch ignored his question. "Levick's men, are they—"

"I have many of them distributed between me and the other marshals. Those under my command are helping with the search for Estrada. Any who weren't reassigned for the time being are on casual duty in and around Cyanthia for when Estrada returns."

Butch nodded. Silas's gaze was still on his injured hand, and sensing that it was likely going to raise more questions the longer it was the object of his friend's focus, Butch shifted it under the desk and out of sight.

"How likely is it that Estrada is still in Phildeterre?" Butch asked, glancing out the window. Most of the horizon was shrouded in trees.

The morning sun tinged everything with a yellow-and-orange hue, almost like the world around him was set ablaze.

Silas adjusted his posture, straightening. "I doubt she'd leave. For one, every border is still controlled and no one can cross without appropriate papers, which she won't have. Plus, her misguided vendetta against you likely will be enough of a reason to stay in the country."

"Wonderful," Butch muttered under his breath. His hand ached below the desk at the very thought of Estrada terrorizing his country just to spite him. "There's been no sign of her at all?"

"None," his friend said, shaking his head. "But I'm sure as soon as she's spotted, we'll hear word."

"And until then, we—"

"Quit taking our frustration out on walls and instead focus on what we can control," Silas said, and before Butch could ask what he meant, his friend lifted his hand to show his bruised knuckles.

Butch couldn't help the small smile that crossed his face. "Agreed."

A knock on the door had both men straightening. Butch cleared his throat before calling to let whoever had interrupted them enter. A young messenger girl curtsied as soon as she stepped foot in the room. Her two braids wobbled when she looked from Silas to Butch.

"A message for you, Your Majesty," she said, handing the sealed envelope in her hand to Silas, who thanked her. He stood and crossed the room to hand it to Butch.

"Thank you," he said, waiting for the girl to leave before opening it. He recognized the seal. His father-in-law had sent him a letter—something he rarely did—and the thought of it had Butch's stomach twisting.

The last time he'd seen Puck, he'd shoved him against a wall and ordered him to leave the castle.

Not his proudest moment.

Or maybe it was.

Kind of a toss-up.

"Well?" Silas asked after several seconds of Butch staring at the letter in his hand. "Are you going to open it? Or do you prefer to stare at it like you've received a death sentence?"

"May as well have," Butch muttered. "It's from Puck."

Silas wrinkled his nose. "Burn it."

"I'm considering it," Butch said, glancing toward his unlit fireplace. "But that would require starting a fire, and . . ." His words trailed off as he slid a letter opener beneath the seal. He unfolded the thick parchment, and his chest tightened before he'd even read the first line. As he scanned the page, deep creases formed over his forehead.

"What?" Silas's voice had lost all its jest. He took half a step forward, then hesitated. "Has something happened?"

Butch didn't respond. Instead, he read the letter again, the uninjured hand at his side tightening into a fist when he'd finished. The urge to punch the wall returned once more, but he settled for slamming the parchment down onto his desk.

"Puck demands I meet with him today." Butch ran his unwrapped hand through his hair. He nodded when Silas asked to see the letter, and he waited until his friend had skimmed it.

"How lucky for us. The gremlin has returned to court," Silas muttered, tossing the parchment back onto the desk with a huff.

"He demanded I meet with him. *Demanded!*" Butch stood and started pacing. "The audacity that man possesses—"

"I wouldn't call him a man," Silas cut in, taking his seat again. He leaned back, clasping his hands behind his head as he stretched his legs out. "More like a leech."

Butch shook his head. "To demand of the king—*his king*—to meet with him. Do we still have my father's pillories in storage?"

Silas snorted. "That'd go over well." He sat forward and nodded toward the letter. "I say meet with him and see what he wants before you go about humiliating a member of your court in front of all of Cyanthia. It wouldn't be the best look for you." Silas smirked. "Even if it would be the highlight of my life."

"I'd rather drink cow urine than meet with him."

"Noted." Silas grinned, watching Butch from where he sat.

Groaning, Butch stopped pacing. "Fine. I'll meet with the beast. But you better look into finding a pillory just in case I feel like putting him in the stocks afterward."

"I'll get right on it." Silas stood, patting Butch on the shoulder as he passed. "Good luck. Don't murder him."

"No promises."

IT TOOK ALL of one second of being in the same room with his father-in-law for Butch to decide he would've drunk an entire gallon of cow urine if it meant not seeing or speaking to Puck again. Scratch that. An entire *tub* of cow urine would be preferable.

He'd pushed open the door to find Puck lounging in one of the chairs, feet propped up on the table. A woman in servant's garb stood behind him, her black hair cascading down her back in waves. Butch didn't recognize her.

"About time you showed up." Puck's lips curled into that insufferable smirk.

"Get your feet off my furniture."

"Is that any way to speak to your beloved father-in-law?" Puck dropped his feet but leaned forward. "*Your Majesty.*"

" 'Beloved' is the last word I'd use to describe you. What do you want?" Butch stood next to the door with his arms crossed. If he got any closer, Butch was concerned he might be tempted to throttle the man.

Puck's smirk widened, his eyes gleaming. "I have a little proposition for you, boy." He leaned back, crossing his legs. The woman behind him remained still, her gaze fixed on a distant point.

"No. Good day." Butch spun, but Puck spoke before he could reach for the door handle.

"You don't want to hear what I learned recently?"

"Not particularly."

"I think you'll find it interesting. Your subjects certainly would." His jeering tone had Butch clenching his jaw hard enough he thought it might snap.

Butch turned back around, his eyes narrowed. "Spit it out. I've got better things to do."

"Do you? Is consorting with magic folk one of those things?" Puck's voice hardened. "I know about the woman, Odette. The one with magic that you released last year."

Butch lifted his chin, forcing his face to remain emotionless even as his heart thudded in his chest. He'd kept it a secret. Only a few people knew because if word got out that he'd pardoned someone who'd been tried and condemned for the use of magic . . .

"What of her?" Butch asked, his voice flat. He put his hands into his pockets, stepping back to lean against the wall next to the door in the hopes that it would appear he wasn't concerned.

"Leave us," Puck ordered the woman, who nodded and curtsied before scurrying out the door Butch held open for her. As soon as she was gone and Butch went back to leaning against the wall, Puck smiled. Or sneered. More so the latter.

Chuckling, Puck pulled a parchment from his pocket. "I have it all here. How you released her, how she's been living freely in your kingdom. Your father would be irate, Butch. And what would the public think if they found out their king was going soft on magic users? In the middle of a war on magic, no less." He slid the parchment across the table, but Butch didn't move from his spot.

The blood in Butch's veins turned to ice. "Where did you get that?"

"I have eyes everywhere, dear boy. Something you should probably keep in mind."

"What do you want?" It came out more as a growl than actual words.

"Simple. I miss my daughter. I want Lenora to come home with me for a few months." Puck waved his hand dismissively.

"And if I refuse?"

Puck shrugged, a cruel smile playing on his lips. "Then the world will know about your little secret. And who knows what other rumors might start circulating? About a weak king, perhaps?"

"You're a snake," Butch said, even as his mind searched for a way out. "You think blackmailing your king is a good idea?"

"You've given me no choice. You've stolen my daughter from me and—"

Butch took three steps from the wall, his blood boiling just beneath the surface as he jabbed a finger in Puck's direction. "Need I remind you, Puck, that you and my father arranged this marriage. I had no say, and neither did my wife. But she is *my wife* now, and you have no control over her anymore."

Rising to his feet, Puck leveled Butch with a glare of his own. "She was my daughter first. And you will let her come home with me."

"I won't put her through that." Butch took another step until he stood across from Puck, only the table between them preventing Butch from ripping his vile father-in-law to shreds.

"Then I'll go to the public, and everyone will know you sympathize with the very people you wage war against. Your people will lose faith in you, magic and nonmagic alike. Your kingdom will fall." Puck leaned forward, bracing his hands on the table. Butch matched his position.

"You're making a mistake, Puck. Threatening me. Threatening my wife . . ."

"I have no interest in debating this further. Tell Lenora she is returning home with me, or I'll ruin you." Puck stood straight, brushing the shoulder of his jacket. "The choice seems pretty clear to me, *Your Majesty.*"

Butch's mind raced. He had no idea how his father-in-law had gotten the information. But in that moment, it didn't matter. He had it, and he was ready to spread it. And it would spread. Like a disease. Like Estrada's fire.

Butch took a deep breath, and his voice dropped to a dangerous whisper. "If anything happens to my wife—"

"You'll what?"

"I'll strip you of every title, every coin, every scrap of power you possess and leave you to rot in the deepest cell of my dungeon until your bones turn to dust."

"Such dramatics." Puck waved his hand dismissively. "Make sure my daughter is ready to leave by tomorrow morning."

Butch's jaw locked like iron, words scraping through gritted teeth. "Get out."

Acknowledgments

Here we are again! After what feels like a never-ending journey, I'm finally able to write another acknowledgments page. Honestly, this book took longer than it should've, but it's finally here!

First and foremost, I want to thank God for the incredible gift of creativity. The stories I write, no matter how challenging or complex, wouldn't be possible without the imagination He's blessed me with. I'm so thankful for His guidance and grace.

To my parents, Marc and Beth—thank you for being my constant source of love and support. You've been my biggest cheerleaders, my sounding boards, and my first readers. Your encouragement means the world to me, and I'm beyond blessed to have you both in my life.

A huge thank you to my sister, Becca, for always being there with a listening ear, a word of encouragement, and a lot of laughter. You are the best, and I'm so thankful for you!

And of course, I can't forget my kitty, Syra, who has kept me company through it all. From yowling outside my office because I'm in the writing zone to cuddling while reading through the proofs, she's been by my side every step of the way.

I want to extend my deepest gratitude to Natalia at Enchanted Ink Publishing. She's been my editor for this book and all of my previous ones, and I can't imagine going through this process without her expertise. Her patience, attention to detail, and unwavering support have made me a better writer with each book. Thank you, Natalia, for everything!

This book wouldn't be what it is without my incredible beta readers. A big thank you to Alicia Gillispie, Ally Adamek, Danielle Waters, Elizabeth Hetrick, Ella Pate, Emily Molinowski, Kristin Schad, Kyla Magar, Marc H. Hetrick, Sarah Orr, Sydney Fowler. You all went above and beyond, and your feedback was invaluable. I'm so grateful for your time, insight, and dedication to helping me bring this story to life.

Special thanks to my mom for proofreading this book not once, but twice! Your attention to detail and perseverance are greatly appreciated.

And lastly but not leastly (yes, I know that's not a word), THANK YOU FRIEND! There is something so magical about sharing the stories that live in my head with others. I hope you enjoyed this book and that it left you excited for what's to come. There's plenty more highs and lows ahead, and I'm thrilled to have you along for the ride.

I hope you enjoyed the book! If you did, **please consider sharing it, writing a review, and telling your neighbor**. One of the best things you can do for an author is to leave a review and a rating!

You are loved and appreciated!

About the Author

Rachel Hetrick has now published seven books (the Infiniti Trilogy, the Fallen Heir Series, and the first two books in the Between Shadows and Light Series), and is excited to release many more. She was born in Colorado, and graduated from the University of Colorado Colorado Springs in 2017 with a Bachelor of Arts degree in English Literature and a Creative Writing minor. Soon after she graduated, she moved to the opposite side of the world and taught English in Asia for a year and a half. However, when the world went nuts at the beginning of 2020, God made it clear that the time had come to pursue her childhood dream of becoming a published author. With the inspiration of many incredible authors on Youtube, Rachel grew as a writer, editor, and now publisher. She has since moved back to Colorado and lives with her Siamese cat, Syra (who kicked Feline Infectious Peritonitis, FIP, in the rear end).

She looks forward to hearing from her readers!

YOU CAN CONNECT WITH RACHEL THROUGH:
WEBSITE: *www.rachelhetrickwrites.com*
INSTAGRAM: *@rachel_hetrick_writes*
TIKTOK: *@rachelhetrickwrites*